SHADOWPLAY

By L.R. Lam

THE MICAH GREY TRILOGY

Pantomime

Shadowplay

Masquerade

THE DRAGON SCALES DUOLOGY

Dragonfall

Emberclaw

THE SEVEN DEVILS DUOLOGY

(with Elizabeth May)

Seven Devils

Seven Mercies

THE PACIFICA SERIES

False Hearts

Shattered Minds

STANDALONE

Goldilocks

SHADOWPLAY

L.R. LAM

HODDERSCAPE

First published in the United States in 2025 by DAW Books
An Imprint of Astra Publishing House

First published in Great Britain in 2025 by Hodderscape
An imprint of Hodder & Stoughton Limited
An Hachette UK company

The authorised representative in the EEA is Hachette Ireland,
8 Castlecourt Centre, Dublin 15, D15 XTP3, Ireland (email: info@hbgi.ie)

1

A CIP catalogue record for this title is available from the British Library

Hardback ISBN 978 1 399 75110 0
Trade Paperback ISBN 978 1 399 75111 7
ebook ISBN 978 1 399 75112 4

Typeset in Warnock Pro

Printed and bound in Great Britain by Clays Ltd, Elcograf S.p.A.

Hodder & Stoughton policy is to use papers that are natural, renewable
and recyclable products and made from wood grown in sustainable forests.
The logging and manufacturing processes are expected to conform
to the environmental regulations of the country of origin.

Hodder & Stoughton Limited
Carmelite House
50 Victoria Embankment
London EC4Y 0DZ

www.hodderscape.co.uk

To my mother, Sally Baxter,
for all she has done for me,
but especially for showing me
the magic of stories.

CONTENT

NOTE ON EDITIONS

Please note: this edition, first released in 2025, is the second volume of the author's preferred texts of the Micah Grey trilogy. The 2014 and 2017 editions of this series are different, so it's recommended that you read the 2025-2026 editions for the smoothest reading experience.

CONTENT NOTES

Violence, domestic violence (mostly off- page and implied), and blood.
A character is alcoholic and several scenes have drunken characters.
There is drugging and some touching and choking without consent,
and mentions of sexual violence and grooming (off- page, implied, in
one character's backstory). There are discussions of surgery without
consent, medical violence, and interphobia. The world is fairly gender
essentialist, with some implied homophobia, xenophobia, misogyny,
and general bigotry. If you have coulrophobia, there are multiple
clowns in the circus. The circus contains animals who are not in ideal
conditions, though there is no overt animal abuse. There is sexual
tension and a couple of soft- focus open- door scenes. Sites like
Story¬graph may have additional content notes added by users.

A REMINDER OF *PANTOMIME*

DRAW BACK THE CURTAIN

Let me remind you of what has happened to Micah Grey, in case it's been some time since you last stepped into Elada. When we last saw Micah, he was on the run from a ruined circus and was about to step onto the magician's stage.

The first time we met him, with a little nudge from me, Anisa—sometimes known as the Phantom Damselfly—he'd stepped through those gates and fallen in love with both the magic and the danger of the circus. He was enchanted by the trapeze act, performed by Aenea and Arik, and he yearned to fly.

Before he ran away, Micah had tried to throw himself into the role of a young, noble lady named Iphigenia Laurus, or Gene: he'd spent time in the Emerald Bowl estates in the country, attended afternoon tea, and debuted into society. He shared a kiss with his friend, Oswin, and even tentatively saw a future with him, though it was unlikely to be a love match. Yet when Gene realized his parents were so afraid of anyone discovering the truth that they were willing to operate on him without his consent, Gene fled. After a few harrowing days on the city streets, he renamed himself Micah Grey and found R.H. Ragona's Circus of Magic.

Micah daringly auditioned on the trapeze and earned a chance to prove himself in the circus. It was not easy. Training with the aerialists Aenea and Arik was grueling. Micah endured hazing and pranks from some of the clowns until Bil Ragona, the ringmaster, and Drystan, the white clown, put a stop to it. Micah performed some of the lowest tasks for the grunts, from scrubbing the loos to looking after the animals.

On his second night in the circus, I revealed myself to Micah, telling him that Chimaera and their magical abilities were returning to the world—and he was one of them. His powers would grow, and I needed his help against a blurred man I saw in visions who wished to destroy them. He didn't want to believe me, of course, and grew frustrated when I could not tell him what little I knew of the future for fear of it not coming to pass. I let him throw his anger at me: eventually, after all, he would discover the truth.

A newspaper article printed with Iphigenia Laurus's face offered a reward for the whereabouts of the runaway noble daughter. The Laurus family hired a private investigator to bring Micah home. He later came face-to-face with this Shadow Elwood on a rare day off with Aenea in the city and managed to evade him. Arik finally retired from the trapeze, and Micah took his place as a performer as the circus left Sicion behind.

R.H. Ragona's Circus of Magic paused for a few weeks in the fishing village of Cowl to practice the pantomime they planned to weave between the acts, so the circus had a chance to stand out in the great capital of Imachara. Micah ended up cast in the role of Princess Iona, with Drystan playing the part of Prince Leander. Micah had discovered that Drystan was another noble runaway, like himself, from the prestigious Hornbeam family.

One of many dangers in the circus was the ringmaster himself. Bil

Ragona had turned more to the bottle. He gambled or spent coin he could not afford on Vestige artefacts rather than ensuring the wage packets were full. He was prone to mercurial moods: he might fire someone one night and give grandiose promises the next. Once in Imachara, his wife, Frit, finally left and took some money from the safe with her. Bil grew worse, and Drystan stepped up to keep the circus going. Micah had been torn between his growing romance with Aenea and his increasing attraction to Drystan.

One night, near the end of the season, Shadow Elwood found Micah. Elwood made a mistake by going to the ringmaster first. Instead of simply detaining Micah until the Shadow returned, Bil lost his temper, especially once Drystan and Aenea came to Micah's aid. Drystan struck Bil with the hidden blade of his own cane, accidentally killing him. Bil had nearly murdered Aenea, but Micah managed to grab my disc, known as an Aleph, from the safe, and it was my turn to help him. He let me step into his body and control his kindled powers. I brought Aenea back from the brink, but in return, Micah could never see or speak to her again, lest she affect what was to pass. Juliet, Tauro, and the shapeshifting Violet, the other three Chimaera of the circus, brought Aenea to the hospital to be treated, and Drystan and Micah left the circus behind them in flames.

The Shadow trailed Micah and Drystan, cornering them in the Copper District on the night of the full moon. Micah remembered the prophecy I'd told him and placed his hands on the Penglass, which responded to his power, releasing a bright light that nearly blinded the Shadow, allowing them to escape.

Drystan and Micah decided to remain together, and the white clown, the pale jester, knew where to go next: the Kymri Theatre, to Jasper Maske, a disgraced stage magician who owed him a life debt. And so that is where we find them, cold and afraid, standing on the threshold, with more adventure, magic, and danger to come.

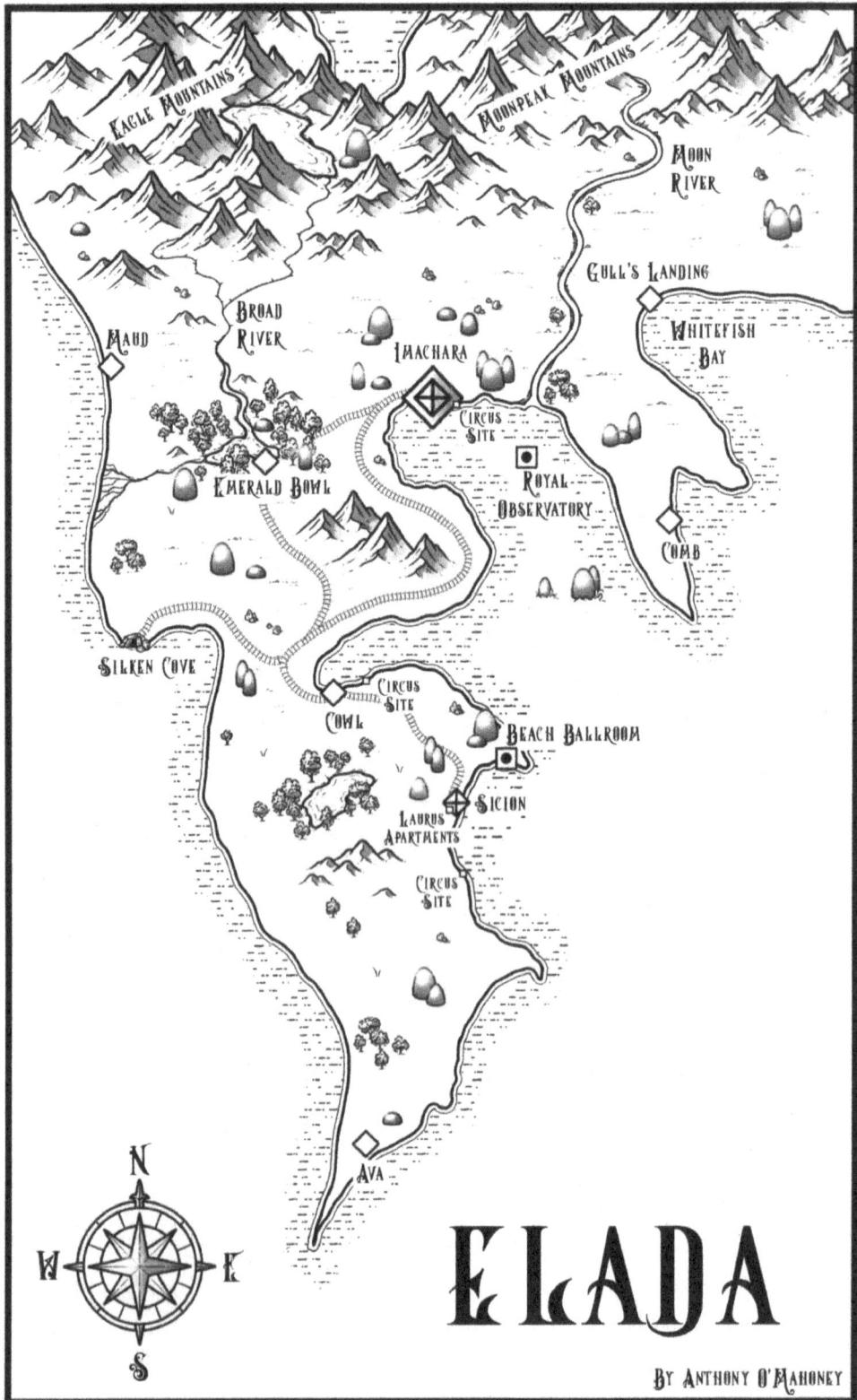

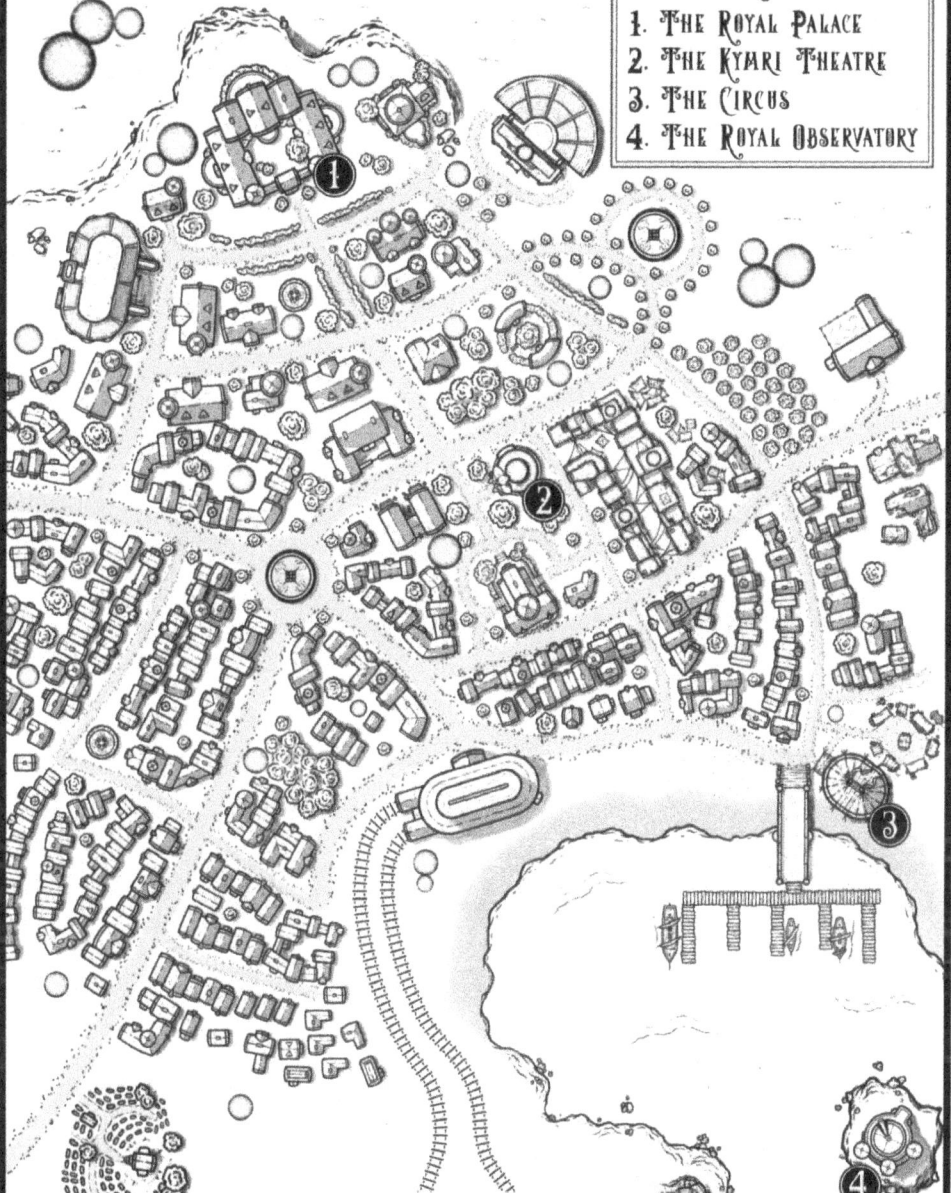

KEY
1. THE ROYAL PALACE
2. THE KYMRI THEATRE
3. THE CIRCUS
4. THE ROYAL OBSERVATORY

THE CITY OF
IMACHARA

BY ANTHONY O'MAHONEY

1

THE SÉANCE

"Countless times, I have drawn closed the black curtains against the daylight, clasped hands with believers and cynics alike, and claimed to commune with the dead. Some believe I actually bring forth ghosts, and others hold tight to their disbelief. But no matter how cynical, there is always the glimmer of fear in their eyes when the supposed supernatural crowds the room with them. When whispers fill their ears and they feel the brush of an unseen hand. Fear of the darkness, and of what they do not understand. Or perhaps it is not fear, but guilt.

Is it ghosts that truly haunt us, or the memory of our own mistakes that we wish we could undo?"

THE UNPUBLISHED MEMOIRS OF JASPER MASKE:

THE MASKE OF MAGIC

Jasper Maske, disgraced stage magician of Imachara, stood aside in the shadowed doorway of the Kymri Theatre.

I stepped inside and followed him down the hallway as Drystan, my companion in crime, closed the door. Loose mosaic tiles slipped beneath my feet, and dust coated everything like a half-remembered dream. I shivered, the motion triggering a stab of pain in my injured left arm. We'd made a hasty sling of torn fabric from my pantomime wedding gown costume. If I didn't move, it didn't hurt too badly.

Was Drystan right to trust this man, with all the secrets that followed us?

Drystan's expression revealed nothing. He wore a coat over his white and pink clown's motley. I slid my less-injured hand into his with the lightest of touches, and he gave me a small, tight smile that didn't reach his eyes. My recently dislocated thumbs were back in their rightful places, but they were still tender. A few hours ago, we'd left R.H. Ragona's Circus of Magic in a flaming ruin behind us. I clung to the numbness of shock, letting it cushion me.

The tall, thin magician pushed open a stained-glass door that depicted a scene of one of the Kymri kings drifting on the river of the afterlife in a boat laden with his possessions.

We entered the cavernous main room of the theatre, though the magician's glass globe did little to illuminate the gloom. More dust dulled the once-burgundy seats, and peeling gilt glinted off the columns to either side of the empty proscenium stage.

"Now, why have an old friend and his companion appeared on my doorstep in the middle of the night, in quite the state of disarray, demanding a séance?" A faint smile curled Jasper Maske's lips. The magician hadn't yet been to bed when we'd knocked, despite the late hour. He was in his late fifties, at a guess, and his brown eyes held the puffy look of a man who didn't sleep much, contrasting against his crisp suit and neat, pomaded hair. He had a sharp widow's peak, and the grey at his temples looked like wings.

"You suspect why," Drystan said.

He took both of us in again, stroking his tidy beard with one hand, his gaze unsettling.

"Very well," the magician said, handing Drystan the glass globe. "Wait here." He navigated his way in the darkness.

The glass globe flickered between us, dyeing Drystan's white hair the orange of a flame and turning his features eerie. The theatre was cold, and I shivered beneath my damp coat. My voice caught before I could speak.

"A séance?" I finally asked. "We need him to harbor us, not spook us."

"It's nothing to do with what the spirits say, not really," Drystan said. "He's been retired from stage magic for fifteen years, but he's as much of a showman as ever. This is more about him evaluating us than some conversation with the dead. He'll make up his mind about us during it, and then he'll let us know if the 'spirits' told him whether or not we can stay."

At the mention of spirits, I bit the inside of my cheek. Drystan stared into the darkness like a haunted man.

I couldn't think about pearls scattered in blood, or the way the ringmaster had thrown Aenea, my fellow aerialist and the girl I'd been courting, across the room like a broken doll. I couldn't think about the impossible power I'd used to escape my bonds, or how the Phantom Damselfly, Anisa, freed from the iron safe and her ancient Vestige metal disc, had taken control of my body to help heal Aenea. There had been a moment when I wasn't sure if she'd give my body back. Juliet, Tauro, and Violet had taken Aenea to the hospital, but I didn't know if she had survived.

If I started thinking about any of it, I'd never be able to stop.

The glass globe illuminated the mosaics on the wall above the darkened lamp sconces. The Holy Couple of the Lord of the Sun and the Lady of the Moon shone overhead. Below them were scenes from the myth of the island of Kymri. The humans that appeared part-animal were Theri Chimaera. The others could be Anthi Chimaera, like me: human in appearance, but with magical powers. Everyone in Elada had thought Chimaera only myths and legends, but the Phantom Damselfly had told me they weren't. Any lingering doubts I had were banished after learning there had been no less than three Anthi Chimaera under my nose in the circus: Juliet, the Leopard Lady, Tauro, the Bull Man, and Violet, a large, violet-black cat I'd watched transform into a woman. Not even the animal trainers had realized what she truly was.

"All is ready," Maske said, returning to the stage.

We entered another, smaller room, the flames sputtering from their candlewicks. A table covered in black lace, topped with a blue crystal ball, was the only furniture aside from a large spirit cabinet in the corner—a sort of portable closet for mediums to use in séances, and an old velvet sofa. A threadbare Arrasian rug lay on the floor, and oil portraits of long-dead monarchs hung on the walls, their expressions disapproving.

"Sit," the magician commanded.

I perched on the hard seat. The Vestige metal base of the crystal ball shone like oil mixed in water, and the ball itself glowed blue as Penglass, the mysterious domes threaded throughout Elada and the other islands of the Archipelago.

"Now, hold hands, if you can," Maske said. I rested my right elbow on the table and clasped the magician's cool, dry palm, his long fingers curling around mine. Drystan put his hand, damp from the rain, into my sling to gently take my other one.

"We call upon you, O spirits," the magician said. "We call upon you through the Veil to answer our questions of the past and the future, and to ask what I should do with these supplicants at my door." His deep voice echoed throughout the room.

I heard nothing. I peeked at Drystan, but his eyes were closed.

Tap.

I held my breath.

Tap, tap.

Tap, tap, tap.

"Spirits," Maske said, "I thank you for joining us this evening and honoring us with your presence and wisdom."

Tap. Tap, tap.

This was how the magician was going to prove that spirits existed from beyond the grave? A few knocks? I frowned, and the magician caught it.

"It seems we have an unbeliever among us tonight," he said.

I fought down a surge of fear. I wouldn't call myself a cynic, with all I'd seen, but that didn't mean I believed *he* was actually communing with the dead.

The table beneath us shook. I nearly snatched my hands away, breaking the circle, injuries or no. The table wobbled and rose several inches off the ground, but the Vestige crystal ball didn't shift, as if it'd been glued down. My heartbeat thundered in my throat.

The table lowered. More raps pattered like raindrops on a tin roof. Whispers rose, the words unintelligible. A woman sobbed in heartbreak and a chill wind ruffled my hair. It reminded me far too much of the Pavillion of Phantoms in the Circus of Magic, where I'd first seen Anisa, that ghost who wasn't a ghost and who now hid, heavy and silent, within a disc in my pocket.

"O spirits," Maske said. "Tell me of my guests. Where have they come from? Are they friends or are they foes?" His brown eyes gazed into the crystal ball, his blown pupils like deep pools of darkness. Shapes flitted in the depths of the blue crystal. Drystan squeezed my hand gently, mindful of my thumb, and I was grateful for the small comfort.

"Tragedy has struck you tonight," Maske said.

It didn't exactly take a psychic to deduce that. I had fresh rope burns around my wrists, after all.

"Your lives have intertwined," he continued. "But shall they strengthen into roots that run deep? It's too soon to say."

Drystan looked toward me, and I glanced away.

"Your future is murky," the magician continued. His voice shifted into a deep, resonating timbre. "But the path forward will soon clear."

The crystal ball on the table brightened until it was so piercing it reminded me of what I'd just done in the Copper District. I'd put my palms on a Penglass dome, and it had responded and allowed me to escape the Shadow that pursued us. I squeezed my eyes shut. When the light cleared and I dared open my eyes, Jasper Maske's face lingered close to my own. Drystan had frozen, mid-blink. The cyan-blue light of the crystal ball cast the magician's face in unearthly shadow. When Maske next spoke, it was in a voice entirely unlike his own, and echoed as though three people spoke at once.

"Take heed, Child of Man and Woman yet Neither. I see a woman in a wine-red dress. Her child is ill, eaten from the inside. I see figures on a stage, playing their parts, the audience applauding as magic surrounds them. Long ago, great feathers flap against the night sky. Another creature, with green, scaled skin, drips red blood onto a white floor. Here, now, Chimaera wait in the wings, and the one who would destroy them is gathering strength. I see a man, checking his pocket watch, counting down the time."

Images switched like slides in a magic lantern in my mind's eye. The back of the woman in the crimson dress, pushing a wheelchair. The slide changed with a *snick*. A woman with great brown wings like an owl, her eyes golden. *Snick*. A green-tinged hand, limp, blood dripping onto the floor, steady as a pocket watch keeping time. *Snick*. A man, his face blurred, and a sense of dread so deep I wanted to scream.

—*Anisa,* I thought, desperately. *Anisa, is this your doing?*

I imagined the Chimaera ghost leaning over me, spreading her transparent dragonfly wings wide.

—*Yes . . . but no. This is your channeling. We'd do well to listen to the spirits, little Kedi, for they are wise,* she whispered in my mind. Was Anisa tricking me to make sure I did what she wanted, or was this something more?

—*I must sleep . . .* she said, and her exhaustion was so strong it almost dragged me down with it. *What I did tonight drained me, and my powers are weakened. These next steps you must take alone. Trust you will know what to do. After this, avoid using your magic. You have grown stronger, but you are untrained, and it is dangerous. When I can, I will help you gain control. Until then, be brave, my child. Be bold. Stay safe.* She faded from my awareness.

Maske's eyes were wide, still gleaming blue with the reflection of the crystal ball. Unseen hands tugged my torn dress and snarled hair. A cold fingertip danced across my cheekbone.

"A magician pulls the strings behind the stage," Maske continued in that eerie, echoing voice, *"and his puppets perform his tricks to regain what he has lost. Chimaera wait in the wings, and the one who would destroy them all gathers strength. You must look through the trees to see the play of shadow and light. The truth of who you are and who others once were shall find you in your dreams and your nightmares."*

I saw Drystan and myself on the stage of the Kymri Theatre, dressed in fine suits and silk cravats. Jasper Maske stood in the wings, his eyes shining with hope. Another figure in a Temnian-style silken dress stood at his side, her face hidden in shadow.

The taps and wailing rose again, and the blue light brightened until I could see nothing but white. A pulse of power, and I fell forward, like a puppeteer had cut my strings, bashing my forehead against the table with a flare of pain.

● ● ● ●

"Micah?" Drystan pulled his hand from mine and Maske's. I felt the current of energy break. "Are you all right?"

My head hurt, and I blinked against my wobbling vision. My injured shoulder throbbed. The grandfather clock ticked in the corner. It felt like the séance had only been a couple of minutes, at most. But unless the clock was wrong, more than a quarter of an hour had passed.

I shook my head, trying to piece together what had just happened.

Be brave. Be bold, Anisa had said.

Maske stared at us, thoughtful as he steepled his fingers together. He wasn't as frightening in the warmer candlelight.

"Apologies, young . . . man." He gave the barest hesitation, and I didn't acknowledge whether he was correct or not. "I do realize my séances can be unsettling for some."

Drystan's half-dried hair stuck up around his head in a platinum and gold corona. "And your verdict? You once offered anything you could provide to me, Maske. A life debt."

He held up his hand. "Yes. Though, judging by what you told me and what the spirits communicated, harboring you risks drawing Policiers to my door." His eyes flicked to my battered face. I swallowed, uneasy at the thought of Drystan and Maske speaking while I'd had my visions.

"How can you be sure Drystan spoke the truth?" I asked.

Maske gave an illusionist's smile. "A magician knows."

Drystan laughed without humor. "Balderdash. You still have your Augur, don't you? Let's see it, then."

Maske lifted his chin at Drystan, and in the tilt of his head, the curl of his lips, I saw something of Drystan's mannerisms as the White Clown. I wondered if Drystan had based his circus persona partly on this magician.

Maske tapped his pocket three times. Out crawled what looked like a small, iridescent beetle, which hummed softer than the far-off buzz of a bumblebee. It lifted its wings, and below them, Vestige metal cogs whirred.

The magician rested the mechanical beetle in his palm. "It's one of my most prized possessions."

I'd heard of Augurs before, of course, but never seen one. They were rare, and the few that remained were mostly with the Constabulary and the courts. While something like glass globes could last hundreds of years without issue, many of the more complicated Vestige artefacts were running low on power. He hadn't used an Augur on us lightly.

"What happens when you lie?" I asked.

"Usually only the wearer hears the alarm, which is handy, but there is another setting." He fiddled with a clasp on the Augur's underbelly. "There. Tell a lie."

"My mother was a giraffe," Drystan said, straight-faced.

The room filled with a rhythmic, high-pitched clicking and whirring. Maske set the Augur on the table, and its wings opened and closed in time. It was not loud enough to drown out conversation, though it was distinctly annoying, and my nerves were already frayed. I grimaced. The clicking faded.

I didn't like that he had used Vestige on us without our knowledge, but I couldn't pretend I wouldn't have done the same.

"Can we trust you?" I asked. The Augur was still activated.

He arched an eyebrow.

I studied the lace of the tablecloth, noting a small burn in the fabric.

"Yes, I believe you can," he said. The Augur was silent. He let that hush hover between us before he reached forward to switch it off.

"Does that mean you'll take us in? You didn't put constraints on that life debt when you made it." Drystan had an edge to his voice. "No strings."

If Maske cast us out on the street, we had nothing. Part of me wanted to grab Drystan's hand and flee all the same. For better or worse, though, the Phantom Damselfly also wanted us to stay. While I didn't entirely trust her, she'd saved me more than once that night, and I was tired of running.

"The spirits told me something," I said, cautiously. Drystan and Maske's faces both turned toward me. "I had a vision of my own."

"You channeled?" Maske asked. "And what did the spirits say to you?" His eyes were strangely hungry as he turned the Augur back on.

Drystan's expression tightened.

I licked my lips, parsing through the words. I had to tell the truth, but that didn't mean I had to share everything I'd seen. "They spoke of the near future. They said: 'A magician pulls the strings behind the stage, and his puppets perform his tricks to regain what he has lost.' I saw Drystan and myself performing in this very theatre. You watched us perform magic, and there was someone next to you, in a silk dress, though I couldn't see her face."

The Augur didn't click.

Maske's mouth fell open, and I sensed Drystan's echoing shock. The magician stood so quickly he knocked his chair over. "Drystan, are you playing some kind of game? Did Taliesin send you? I won't have it—I won't—"

"We came here with no agenda but safety," I cut him off. "I'm only telling you what the spirits showed me because it seemed important."

Maske's eyes flicked to one of the paintings on the wall. The back of my neck prickled, as though I were being watched. Did that painting of King Nicolas Snakewood have holes in the eyes, like in the adventure novels I'd read? My fingernails dug half-moons into the skin of my palm.

The magician came close enough that his nose was inches from mine. Behind the anger and the indignation was that same hope I'd seen in my vision. This had been the right play. I knew it in my bones. Maske's séances might only be tricks, but deep down, he believed in true magic.

"We've lost everything, too," I whispered. "Maybe, together, we can find something new."

Maske's breath caught. He pulled back, his hand going to the collar of his suit. He turned off the Augur. Drystan and I waited, listening to the ticking of the clock.

"I'll ready the loft for you both tonight," he said, finally, and I wanted to sag in relief. "I make no promises long-term, but you can at least stay here for now as I ponder what the spirits said."

Drystan blinked quickly, recovering. "My old room. That'll do nicely." He paused. "Thank you, Jasper."

"You remember I prefer Maske, I'm sure. Taliesin took almost everything from me, but he didn't take my stage name."

"Maske," Drystan corrected himself.

The magician inclined his head before going to the side table and pouring three glasses of whisky. I put my hand over my mouth, fighting the urge to retch. Our circus ringmaster Bil used to stink of the stuff.

Drystan understood and took my glass, knocking back both drinks.

Maske swirled his, staring into its amber depths before taking a careful sip.

"Right, then," he said. "It's closer to dawn than sunset. You must be exhausted." He picked up the glass globe, and we rose to follow him. He led us back through the empty theatre and its dimmed stage. He paused, looking at it with longing. He closed his eyes, and I wondered if he was imagining the place as it'd once been. Clean, shining, and packed to the gills with an anticipatory audience. I caught the same wistfulness as those in the circus. The same desire to spark wonder.

Perhaps the spirits, and Anisa, had told us true: we were exactly where we needed to be.

2

THE SCREAM

"Never are we as honest as at night, alone with our thoughts and night-mares."

ELADAN PROVERB

Rain drummed on the skylight of our new room.

"Apologies for the state of it," Maske said. "I've not had guests in . . . quite some time."

The attic at the top of the Kymri Theatre was musty with dust and disuse, but the roof was sound. Boxes of old wires and rusted springs cluttered one corner. There was a round porthole window of stained glass, but it was too dark to catch its design, with twin beds on either side of the room, desks, and matching wardrobes.

On the way to the loft, Maske had paused to slip into his quarters and returned with a black medic bag. Drystan clutched it against his chest. "It's more than fine," he said.

"Make use of anything in the wardrobes," Maske said. "Sleep as long as you need."

With that, he closed the door behind him. The walls were painted a faded light blue, with darker squares where pictures had hung. It might have been cheery, once.

"Two beds?" I asked. Drystan had said this was his old room. Had he shared it with someone?

"Taliesin's twin grandsons stayed in the loft when both magicians lived here in the Kymri Theatre. I pushed the beds together when I stayed here, though he's moved them back."

"The bedding is fresh," I said, fingering the edge of a coverlet. "Who laid it out?"

We exchanged glances, and I remembered both that feeling of being watched downstairs and the person in my vision. "Are you sure Maske lives here alone?"

His mouth opened. Closed. "I don't know," he whispered.

"What should we do?" I pressed my uninjured forearm against my stomach.

He sighed. "I've reached my limit of worry for tonight, I'm afraid. If someone's indeed here, Maske obviously considers them trustworthy. I expect we'll meet them tomorrow."

"Tomorrow," I echoed. My fear, too, had run out of fuel, replaced by only fatigue.

Drystan set the medic bag on my bed. "Come on. Your wounds need tending to." He'd been punched and thrown around, but beyond that, he didn't have a scratch on him. He'd wiped the ringmaster's blood splatters and most of his clown makeup from his face before we'd fled, but I caught a stain on his pale pink and white clown's motley. Maske had probably spotted it, too, yet he'd still given us a place to stay.

"It's all right. I can do it myself," I said.

"You can barely move your shoulder."

"It's not as bad as I feared." The magic the Phantom Damselfly had funneled through me to save Aenea had helped the wound, alongside the fact that I'd always healed faster than normal. I lifted my elbow to shoulder height, trying not to let my pain show. "See? I'll let you know if I need help. Go to sleep."

He hesitated, but in the end, he shrugged off his coat and threw it across his desk chair. He opened the wardrobe, which was filled with old clothes, then pulled his shirt over his head. I froze. No one else in the circus had much modesty, and I'd seen him change backstage between his clown's motley and Prince Leander's costume plenty of times before, but it felt different here, just the two of us. He took a cloth next to the basin and ewer on his desk and wiped away the worst of the sweat and smoke, the lean muscles of his back moving beneath his skin. Before he could catch me looking, I opened the wardrobe on my side, which was also full of old clothes.

A few minutes later, I glanced over my shoulder. Drystan had changed and crawled beneath the covers and faced the wall, giving me my privacy. His half-dyed hair fell across the pillow.

I let my coat fall to the floor. I couldn't undo the buttons of the ruined dress easily, and so I ripped it and stepped out of the skirts. I wore my drawers, my undershirt, and my Lindean corset to bind my breasts. I glanced over at Drystan again, furtively, but he hadn't moved. I'd never known if Arik had guessed my secret, when we'd shared a cart at the circus. If he had, he'd never let on. Drystan thought of me as a runaway girl, as Frit had. I'd never fully undressed in front of Aenea, either. Maske had mentioned other rooms. I'd probably have to try and nab one if we ended up staying long-term. It'd make this easier.

I eased my way out of the Lindean corset and hid it in the wardrobe. The filthy undershirt joined my other ruined clothes on the floor. A glance at my body showed my injuries, and I fought down a gasp. My chest had been protected from the worst of the blows thanks to my binder, but almost everywhere else was mottled with bruises. I had a long, shallow slash across my lower ribs from the carved ram's head on the ringmaster's cane. I ran my hand along the ridged muscles of my torso. For all my body's strength from being an aerialist, I hadn't been able to free myself from Bil's grasp until I'd been able to reach my magic.

I made quick use of my own basin, wiping myself down with a terrycloth, the movement making my cuts bleed again. In the darkness, the events of the night flooded back: the cheery bells of the circus music, the laughter of the crowd that warred with the weight of the strong hand on my shoulder, and the sickly-sweet smell of chemicals. The taste of the gag in my mouth and the ropes around my wrists. The drunken ringmaster looming over me.

I untied the makeshift sling, changed into drawers from my pack, and pulled on a cotton shirt from the wardrobe that smelled strongly of cedar to ward off moths, trying to stifle grunts of pain.

I opened the medic bag. I sat on the bed and pulled up the shirt to daub the cuts with an unguent. It stung, but the bleeding had already stopped. Carefully, I wrapped a bandage around my ribs, but not my breasts.

I'd escaped Bil's bonds with a spark of magic, but he'd still been too strong. I hadn't been able to reach Anisa's Aleph in the safe. The blows of his cane had rained down hard and fast. Aenea and Drystan had found me. Aenea had thrown herself upon the ringmaster, and in half a moment, he'd struck her hard enough to kill her. Only begging Anisa to help had let me give Aenea a chance at survival, but in return, I'd had to promise never to see or speak to her again.

Drystan had taken up the ringmaster's discarded cane and struck his own killing blow. I'd seen Bil, half-fallen, the blood hovering in mid-air. I'd watched as time became inevitable and he'd fallen to the floor, dead. Anisa wouldn't have saved him, even if I'd asked.

I hadn't.

I closed my eyes against the memories, but they lingered. The feel of Aenea's slack neck beneath my frantic fingers and the slow, weak pulse. The fading rage in the ringmaster's eyes, the way the blood had pooled around his corpse. Violet, the great cat with dark purple fur, prowling through the cart before transforming into a person with a burst of magic. Tauro, the bull man, looming at the door. Juliet, the Leopard Lady, telling me we'd meet again. They'd taken Aenea for treatment, and I hadn't even been able to whisper a last goodbye. My breath hitched in my throat. Was she all right? And if she hadn't made it . . . would I want to know? Or would it be better to always have that hope she'd survived?

My eyes burned. I couldn't cry.

I crawled under the blankets. I felt frozen through. Guilt pulsed through me in waves, tears choking my throat.

I lay in the dark for what felt like hours, my mind spinning, full of regrets. It was close to dawn before my eyelids finally grew heavy.

A shout tore through the air.

I sat straight up in bed, hurting my shoulder and ribs.

Drystan's face contorted as he thrashed against the covers. His mouth opened and he let loose another scream.

"Drystan?" I asked, crossing the room.

He moaned, shaking his head from side to side.

"Hey, hey. Are you all right?"

I crouched over him. He bolted upright and swung his arm, catching me on my injured shoulder. The pain seared through me, my vision tunneling.

I screamed and crumpled to the floor.

My cry broke through his nightmare. He stared straight ahead, not quite awake. He sucked in ragged breaths, coming back to himself.

"Micah?" he whispered, a hand on his jaw. He wiped his ashen face and took me in. His eyes lingered on the bumps beneath my shirt, which had ridden up, and the other between my legs. Even through the pain, I thought: *here it is.* The reality of me was no longer a secret between us. It was both a terror and a relief.

"You hit me." I hissed the breath through my teeth.

"Shit." His eyes skittered back to my face. "Gods, I'm sorry. Didn't mean to."

I panted, trying to breathe through the agony pulsing up my arm.

"Your shoulder?" he asked.

I grunted.

"We should really find a doctor."

"No," I gasped. "No doctors. They . . . they can't know. Too . . . rare. Even if they don't realize I'm from the circus, it'd . . . what I am would trace me right back to who I used to be."

He'd guessed I was Iphigenia Laurus back on that night we'd spent on the pier in Sicion, drinking cheap gin. He blinked once, twice.

"Right," he said, eventually. "Right. Yes."

Drystan helped me from the floor and to my bed. I leaned against him, and his hand rubbed between my shoulder blades. He'd taken it better than I thought he would. He wasn't repulsed, as my mother always said people would be. I hated how pathetically grateful I was for that.

A knock sounded at the door.

Drystan opened it. Maske held the glass globe, his face again half in shadow. He wore a striped nightgown and cap, incongruous with his neat beard.

"I heard noises," he said.

"I had a nightmare." Drystan's voice was flat to hide his embarrassment. "Micah came to check on me, but I accidentally hit his injured arm."

"Let me see," Maske said. "I've some basic medical training."

"I'm fine," I said, even as my eyes stung with pain.

"No, you're not. It's me or a doctor. Make your choice."

"You, then," I gritted out.

Maske set down the globe and came closer.

My torso was hunched, but I took a deep breath and straightened. If he noticed, let him think me a girl. My other secret was safe beneath the covers.

Maske placed his hands gently on my arm, investigating the injury. I moaned, squeezing my eyes shut.

"I've had my share of accidents throughout the years, and I've set a bone or two. I can splint it, and it should heal cleanly enough. But there are no guarantees," he warned.

I hesitated, then nodded.

Maske poured a dose of laudanum onto a spoon. The smell reminded me of when Cyril had broken his arm falling off a Penglass dome. I still felt guilty for that—I should never have put him at risk. I swallowed the medicine, and the honey and herbs chased away none of the bitterness.

Jasper Maske took out two types of bandages from the medic bag and fabric for a new, better arm sling.

He held my upper arm firmly, first wrapping it in cotton before dampening plaster bandages and winding them over the top. Stars of pain shot behind my closed eyelids. The bandages dried into a cast, and the laudanum finally took hold, dulling the pain at the edges. Maske patted me on my uninjured shoulder. My eyelids drooped, but I caught Maske's hesitation. Instead of putting the laudanum back in the medic bag, he tucked it into his pocket. Drystan's eyes narrowed.

"I have a feeling you two are going to make my life decidedly more interesting," Maske said.

"I imagine part of you will like that, old chap," Drystan said, with all the wryness of the white clown. "Considering how interesting your life was when I knew you last."

"I'm no longer that foolhardy man, courting danger so openly," Maske said. "Things have been quiet since you last left, but life is safer that way." In the dimmer light, his eyes were wide and dark, and my skin pricked into gooseflesh.

"I hope neither of you have any more nightmares." He rose.

"Me, too," Drystan replied softly as Maske closed the door behind him once more.

The laudanum made me feel as though I were floating.

"Are you shocked?" I couldn't help but ask into the darkness. "About me?"

He was silent. "Yes, and no. I didn't expect it, necessarily, but I'm not surprised. If that makes sense." He paused. "Did Aenea know?"

"I don't think so," I said. "We never . . . made it that far. I was afraid she might reject me. She might have suspected part of it, as you had. I'm not sure."

He made a thoughtful noise.

"Have you ever met anyone like me?" The medicine was loosening my tongue too much.

"No, Micah. I think you're the most unique person I've ever met."

Despite everything, the edges of my lips tugged upwards.

"Do you really trust Maske?" I asked, my eyelids fluttering shut. "With no reservations?"

"I trust him. But I trust no one without question. Go to bed, Micah."

As sleep took hold and put an end to the worst night of my life until that point, a small corner of my mind wanted to ask: *not even me?*

3

A SCREAM IN THE DARK

"Most Eladans have not travelled beyond the island. A select few may have gone to Girit to visit family, but very few have been to Temnes, Linde, Kymri, or Byssia. Thus, outside of products to buy, the Archipelago must come to them in the form of entertainment—circuses or magic shows, theatre or vaudeville."

**A HISTORY OF ELADA AND ITS FORMER COLONIES,
PROFESSOR CAED CEDAR, ROYAL SNAKEWOOD UNIVERSITY**

The next afternoon, I awoke to a rainbow falling across my face. I hadn't fully caught the stained-glass design: I'd dreamt of dragonflies, and the window showed another in purple, blue, and green glass.

The theatre had two bathrooms with working plumbing, and I took my first proper bath in half a year. My auburn hair had grown out to near my shoulders, but I couldn't tie it back with my injured arm, so I left the waves to air dry around my face. My reflection looked haunted. My cheekbone was bruised from Bil's fist, and the rope burns around my wrists had started fading but hurt. Still, I felt like a new person in my pilfered, cedar-scented clothes, even if I limped down the stairs and every muscle ached.

The Kymri Theatre was full of interesting little details. The skirting boards and moldings were all carved with animals or glyphs, and the walls were painted shades of blue and terracotta. The floors were dotted with colored mosaics.

Eventually, I found the kitchen, a cozy room at the back of the building on the ground floor. The walls were tiled blue and green, the cabinets warm varnished wood inset with blue and yellow glass, and the appliances shining copper. The air smelled of coal smoke and coffee. At the worn kitchen table, Maske glanced up from the newspaper and smiled faintly at me. Drystan had a steaming drink in front of him he hadn't touched. Maske looked as tidy as last night, though the kitchen lights showed more grey in his hair. Drystan had dark circles ringing his eyes. He'd washed off the last of his clown makeup, revealing his familiar, handsome features and the freckles across the bridge of his nose. I only took him in for a second as I focused on the woman seated at the table next to him, and my skin prickled into goosebumps.

She was Temnian, with dark eyes, golden-brown skin, and hair that fell in a dark river to her waist, small sections braided with ceramic beads. She was curvy and wore a green sarong made of Temnian linen secured with a silken scarf.

"Good morning," she said brightly. "I'm Cyan. Mister Maske's assistant." No trace of an accent. She'd been born in Elada or come here when she was quite young, then.

She was, without a doubt, the person I'd seen on stage with Maske in my vision the night before. She'd been the one who watched us from behind the walls and laid out the bedding in the loft.

Drystan finally took a sip of his drink.

"Micah," I said, holding out my right hand, and she shook it firmly. Her palm was warm, and I felt a spark through my skin. Her eyes widened in surprise as I pulled my hand away.

"Coffee?" Maske asked from behind the newspaper.

"Thank you," I said, though without much anticipation. The last time I'd tasted coffee was when I'd spent an afternoon with a spice merchant, Mister Illari, just before I joined the circus. It'd been strong and as bitter as the laudanum I'd taken the night before.

I sat at the table with them and took a sip and found, to my relief, it was far milder than the stuff Mister Illari made. With two lumps of sugar and a huge dollop of cream, it was actually rather nice. Cyan watched me and Drystan closely. I suspected she was as sharp as Maske and would miss nothing.

A scrawny calico cat with a torn ear sauntered into the kitchen and yowled insistently.

"Hey, hey, Ricket," Maske said, getting up and taking a plate of meat scraps from the chiller. He patted the top of the cat's head. "Where have you been hiding?"

"You still have her?" Drystan said, his features slackening in surprise.

"Of course. Can't get rid of the damn thing," Maske said, pitching his voice louder over Ricket's caterwauling, though his tone was fond.

"I know, you've never been fed in your whole life, you poor, pitiful creature," he taunted gently.

"I rescued Ricket when she was a kitten," Drystan explained to me.

The cat scarfed the food, purring like an engine. Maske fetched bread from where it toasted over the stove and Cyan sliced up apples and oranges. I spread a generous smear of butter on the toast and took a bite, stifling a groan. It'd been nearly a day since I'd last eaten properly, and I was starved.

Once Ricket finished her meal, Drystan held out his hand, and she came up to sniff him before headbutting vigorously. Drystan's face broke into the first smile I'd seen since we left the circus as he gathered the cat in his arms.

"Look, she remembers me."

"Wasn't sure she'd forgive you for leaving," Maske said, and I couldn't read his tone.

I took another bite of toast. I realized, if we stayed here, how strange it'd be to live in a building again. To not find granules of sand in each seam of my clothing or in my food, to have stone walls between me and the outside elements instead of the thin wood of a cart or the canvas of a tent. I was no longer surrounded by dozens of people and the constant cries of seagulls. At the same time, the relative quiet was unnerving. It was a domestic scene, except that the magician and his assistant were strangers and we were fugitives wanted for murder.

"How long have you been in Maske's employ, Cyan?" I asked, hoping the question sounded casual.

"A few months," she said. "He's taught me loads already. Says I might even be able to start running séances solo, soon enough."

"So the tapping last night? That was you?"

She gave an enigmatic smile.

"What brought you to the Kymri Theatre?" I asked.

She cut her eyes at me. "You're not being terribly subtle in your questioning, Micah."

"Just curious, is all," I said, trying to look innocent.

"Don't worry, I'm on the run, too," she said. "So your secret's safe with me."

I choked on my coffee and Drystan stiffened. Maske chuckled.

"What do you mean?" I demanded.

"All in good time," Cyan said. "Let's get to know each other a little, first, shall we, before we spill all our secrets?"

Secrets. Always so many secrets, I feared I'd drown in them.

I'd never been good at patience. Maske had mentioned the name Taliesin. I knew he ran the Spectre Shows. Cyril and I had even seen him, once, in Imachara last year. He'd been dressed in a suit, but his two grandsons had performed most of the illusions. My brother and I had tried to recreate some of the card tricks for weeks, but we'd never figured them out. The larger illusions had seemed like proper magic.

A coal popped in the fire, startling me from my thoughts.

Maske had agreed to take us in last night, but, judging by the state of the theatre, he didn't exactly have the means to support us out of charity. I wasn't sure how he managed to keep this place running with only money from séances. He needed a steady stream of ticket sales.

"Drystan mentioned that you're never meant to perform magic again," I said to Maske. "Because of the duel with Taliesin?"

His mouth thinned. "Those were indeed the terms of our arrangement. He accused me of cheating, and I challenged him to a duel to prove I didn't. In addition to being banned from the stage, I wagered something else just as important to me, and I lost that, too. I only barely managed to keep hold of this theatre, and the ability to hold séances, but that was all."

"Could you challenge him to another duel?"

Maske studied me, and I felt both Drystan and Cyan's mirrored stares. Slowly, he shook his head. "Taliesin would never agree to it."

"What would happen if you trained someone else to perform?" An undoubtedly foolhardy idea had sparked in my skull, and I couldn't shake it.

"That was not mentioned explicitly in the arrangement, no," Maske said, slowly. "I suspect it was an accidental loophole on Taliesin's end. I've even taken on a student or two in the past, but none proved suitable enough, so I sent them on their way."

"You haven't taught me any stage magic," Cyan said, indignant.

He looked at her in surprise. "Would you want me to?"

"Of course I would!"

"I heard Taliesin has fallen on hard times," Drystan said. "His twin grandsons perform for him now, but word is they're not as good."

Maske narrowed his eyes at Drystan, but he didn't look surprised.

"If there was some way to disguise us, could you teach us three?" I pounced on his interest. "Challenge Taliesin to a new duel through us, as the spirits showed me, and you could even regain what you lost."

A few expressions flitted across Maske's face. He was considering it, at least.

"What did you lose, exactly?" I pressed.

"The very thing that could help us win, I'm afraid," he said, shaking his head. "Even if I taught you, Taliesin still has it, and I don't. We couldn't hope to win a rematch without it."

His words momentarily stumped me. I knew this whole plan was, in many ways, dangerous. We were fugitives. The Policiers were after us. The Shadow and the Royal Physician who had hired him were likely on our trail. Being so public was not remotely in our current best interests.

At the same time, the Policiers and the Shadow wouldn't expect us to be so bold. I couldn't shake the feeling that this would work, and that this was what we were meant to be doing. I didn't know how, but it was tied into the larger destiny Anisa kept telling me I was tangled up in. Perhaps the spirits had shown me a truth last night.

Now that I'd had a taste of the stage, I wasn't ready to give it up, despite the dangers. I'd only met Maske last night, and even I could tell how much the magician missed performing.

"Train us anyway," I said. "What's the harm?"

"I'm not sure you could be taught—" he started.

Drystan laughed—a short, sharp sound. "Oh, come on, Maske. You taught me plenty, back in the day. I remember it all. And I'm sure you'd find Micah a quick study. He learned the trapeze in a matter of months, rather than years."

"It's a way to make some coin along the way, too," I added. "We'd have to earn our keep."

Maske peered at me, and I could almost hear the cogs in his head turning as he considered our proposal.

"I don't know." He stared at his coffee cup again.

"I know you, Maske," Drystan said. "You'll have been tinkering in your workshop all these years. I bet you'll have dreamed up all sorts of marvelous things."

"We could help bring them to life for you," I added. "The potential reward seems worth the risk, doesn't it?"

Drystan held Ricket in his arms. This was the most alert I'd seen him since the night the circus fell apart. The lure of the stage was a rush.

Maske rubbed his chin.

"Come on," Drystan pushed. "You've hidden away and licked your wounds long enough. Busking street magic will pay more than most other jobs we could get. We can't exactly get up to our old tricks. You still have your Glamours, right? We can use those when we're out of the house, and no one will be any the wiser."

I raised my eyebrows, especially when Maske nodded. What were their old tricks? And how in the world did he have Glamours? The Vestige artefacts that could help change your appearance were rare, skirting on illegal.

"I'm in," Cyan said. "I think I'd make an excellent magician or magician's assistant, myself." She batted her eyelashes. "Come on. Saw me in half. Make me disappear. It'll be a laugh. And Micah's right. We're always keen for more coin."

Maske stood and took our coffee cups to the sink, washing them as he faced the overcast sky through the window. Several orange and red leaves danced on the whistling wind outside. I wished I could read his thoughts.

Drystan met my gaze. This was the direction we needed. A purpose and a goal to focus on instead of everything we'd lost, a way to make ourselves useful enough that Maske would keep sheltering us, and maybe even a step towards whatever bit of fate Anisa kept dangling in front of me.

The old magician paused, pensive. "Well. Neither of you are in any fit physical state to learn anything just yet, anyway. But I'll think on it. We will need to figure out something, money-wise."

I felt a rush of triumph.

Cyan clapped her hands.

"I'm going out for supplies," Maske said. "Cyan, come along with me. I'd appreciate it if, while I am away, neither of you snooped behind closed doors. There are dangerous things in my workshop, and other possessions that are for my eyes alone."

Maske held his gaze with ours, unblinking, and I was reminded of the man from the séance who spoke in three tones at once. What had been a growing sense of comfort around him dissipated, leaving a thick lump of misgiving in my stomach.

Of course, that only made me wonder what else he was hiding.

• • • •

After Maske and Cyan left, I ate another two pieces of toast. My breakfast for the past several months had been porridge and a fried or boiled egg, and fresh bread was novel. My second cup of milky coffee was a mistake, though, for I couldn't sit still.

"Come on," Drystan said. "Let's go to the roof. It has some of the best views of the city." He gave me an echo of his old smile. We trudged up the dusty wooden steps. I paused at a landing, staring down a murky hallway of closed doors. Which one was Maske's workshop?

Drystan laid a hand on my shoulder, silently urging me on. On the landing opposite the door to our loft, we clambered onto the wrought-iron balcony, then the alarmingly delicate metal steps to the flat expanse of the theatre's roof.

Drystan hadn't lied about the view. The theatre was taller than the surrounding tenements, with high enough walls around the edges to give us privacy from any prying eyes. In the parks below, the leaves were turning to fire, the grass dulling. The day was warm, but with a chill on the wind that promised true autumn and rain, tinged with the sharp scent of chimney smoke. The wind whipped our hair as we stared over the vast expanse of Imachara, Elada's capital and former seat of the Empire of the Archipelago.

The grey-tinged clouds cast shadows over the city's swirling streets. Buildings and blue Penglass domes jutted toward the clouds. Some of the tenements below us had laundry hung between the wynds to dry. Flowers were bright spots in the window boxes, a few still clinging to life before winter took them.

I could see the twin spires of the Celestial Cathedral, one made of white marble and topped with gold to represent the Lord of the Sun and the other of dark marble topped with silver alloy to represent the Lady of the Moon. Shorter, rounder Penglass dotted the city like drops of blue ink, their surfaces pristine.

I was grateful that the theatre didn't have a clear view of the beach. How much of the circus had burned? Where were the people I'd spent the last few months with? Juliet, Tauro, and Violet had set off in search of other Chimaera. They'd invited me, but I'd elected to stay with Drystan. But what would become of Bethany, the Bearded Woman, Poussin, the Chicken Man, or Mrs. Lemon, the Four-Legged Woman? There was the strongman, Karg, and the dwarf, Miltin. The dancers. The contortionists. The grunts and barkers. I worried even for the clowns who had hazed me so badly. I hoped they'd all found other work. How many of them hated us for what we'd done to the Circus of Magic?

Drystan lay down on the sun-warmed roof slates, holding a hand to shade his eyes, gazing up at the clouds. Carefully, I joined him.

After a few minutes, I turned on my side. I couldn't stop the hole of grief that opened up, and I bit down on a keening wail. I'd done well to keep the tears back, but they'd finally come, and nothing would stop them.

Glancing over my shoulder, I saw Drystan's shoulders hitch, too. Last night, we'd clung to each other, but there in the light of day, we were each in our own bubbles of misery.

Eventually, the autumn sun dried my tears, though the pain felt no less. I lay on my front, avoiding Drystan's gaze, the sun warming my back.

"So, we're staying," I said when I trusted my voice enough to speak.

His eyes flicked over to me, his skin blotchy from crying. I looked away.

"Yes." His voice was thick. "So it seems."

"What happened during this old duel with Taliesin?" I asked.

"It's his story to tell," Drystan said.

"I can't help but be curious, and I don't think he'll open up to me anytime soon. Can't you share anything?" If I was staying with Jasper Maske, I needed all the information I could get.

He half-smiled, wiping at his face with the back of his hand. "All right. Neither side is blameless in this story. Maske and Taliesin used to be fast friends and partners—together, they truly were the best magicians in Elada, and their performances were legendary. And then, one day, they became bitter enemies."

"Why?"

"Well. Taliesin took credit for one of Maske's illusions. In revenge, the good magician slept with Taliesin's fiancée."

"Ah."

"'Course, it's more complicated than that. Taliesin was by all accounts terrible to Nessa, but even so, I know Maske regrets what he did. He used to be very impulsive, very proud. He's different to how he was back then. They say your personality changes several times over as you age. You at eighteen will not be like you when you're thirty-six."

"I suppose," I sighed, looking up at the clouds. I wondered what I'd be like when I was in my thirties, having lived half my life again. It seemed so far away. I wonder how I'd age as time settled into my features, or when my hair would streak with grey like Maske's.

"What happened next?" I asked.

"Taliesin accused Maske of cheating. You see, you're not ever meant to use Vestige in stage magic. It's considered the mark of a charlatan. Maske, at the height of his wealth, amassed a good collection of artefacts mostly for his own interest. Rumor has it, though, that Maske had a piece of Vestige that helped him create the tricks. He'd dream his illusions up, sure enough, but the artefact would somehow help him engineer it. The end result, though, technically had no Vestige. So, you tell me: is it cheating?"

I shook my head. "I've no idea. Flirting with it, certainly."

Drystan inclined his head. "Aye. And he probably wouldn't be the first or the last to bend the rules a little. It's not like Taliesin was prone to playing fair. Taliesin goaded Maske into offering up his Vestige as part of the wager of the duel. So not only did Maske fail, he also lost something very dear to him. He's still dreaming up all sorts of illusions, I'm sure, but I suspect he can't figure out quite how to make most of them work."

Drystan shifted. "He hasn't told me most of this, mind, but I put it together when I lived with him. He misses performing, desperately, and he hates—he *hates*—that Taliesin has that artefact of his. He clearly has some of his collection, since we've seen the Augur and he's mentioned his Glamours, but he's probably been slowly pawning them off over the years to get by, so I dunno how much he has left."

"If we do manage to learn magic well enough and Maske challenges him to a rematch, would Taliesin put that Vestige back on offer?"

He narrowed his eyes at me. "Why are you so very desperate to perform magic? It'd be a damn sight safer to work at some shop and keep our heads down."

"Would you really be content with that? Living day to day with no audience? The spirits showed me a vision of us performing." I skirted around Anisa and fate. At some point, I'd tell him, but not just yet.

He pillowed his head on his arm. "I won't pretend I'd be happy working in some shop, no. But to answer your earlier question: I have no idea if Taliesin would be foolish enough to wager that bit of Vestige again. Whatever it is, it's clearly something special. And expensive. I suspect this place isn't cheap to keep going, and Maske needs coin more than he lets on."

I couldn't think of anything in the Museum of Mechanical Antiquities that could do something like that, aside from maybe the clockwork woman. I wished I could ask Anisa, but she was dormant.

"What did you do, when you worked with him before?"

He leaned closer, one corner of his mouth quirking. "Who do you think taught me to count cards?"

I blinked. I should have put that together.

"Does he still do it?" It'd likely pay more than séances.

His gaze shuttered. "No." There was another story there, but I wouldn't get it today.

Drystan and I stayed on the roof awhile longer, watching the shifting colors of the sunset. When I started shivering, Drystan led me back inside.

4

HIDING THE TRAIL

"THE DEATH OF A CIRCUS
Correspondence by Arianna Gilbert

"It has been three days since the tragedy of R.H. Ragona's Circus of Magic on the beach of Imachara. Unfortunately for circus lovers, Elada now has one less. Due to fire damage, the untimely demise of the ringmaster, and financial problems with creditors, the circus has gone into liquidation. An auction for assorted circus paraphernalia will be held tomorrow at half past two at Thomson & Farquhar's Auction House.
It is suspected that William Hakan Ragona, 48, was already dead before his cart caught fire.

Two people of interest are wanted for immediate questioning. One is called Micah Grey, 18, a newcomer to the circus, an aerialist and actor. He has red-brown hair and green eyes. The other is Drystan, surname unknown, who was a clown and actor. He is estimated to be in his early twenties, with light blond hair dyed white.

There is a substantial reward for information leading to the capture of these two men. They may be armed and dangerous. Do not approach directly and proceed with extreme caution.

Authorities have high hopes that they will bring these two fugitives to justice before the next Penmoon."

THE DAILY IMACHARAN

The following morning, Maske wordlessly placed his newspaper between us on the table. Sure enough, there was an article about the circus and Bil's death, a brief description of Drystan and me, and an offer of another reward. I grimaced, unable to do more than skim it.

"It's not ideal," Maske said.

Cyan gave a low whistle. "I'll say. I didn't cause near as much trouble when I left my circus."

Drystan and I gaped at her.

"Your . . . circus?" I managed.

"Riley and Batheo's Circus of Curiosities. I was their tarot reader." A shadow flitted over her face, though, and I wanted to know what had made her flee.

Drystan looked as wary as I must have. Cyan asked to borrow Maske's Augur. He huffed, but went to fetch it before handing it over. She switched it on and repeated her words. No clicking. She was telling the truth.

"Why tell us?" I asked.

She shrugged. "I've just learned a lot about you. Fair's fair."

There was perhaps another reason—to reassure us that she wouldn't turn us in. Because even if she was from Bil's rival circus, we now knew she wasn't a normie. She was one of us. Circus folk. Still, part of me found the coincidence suspicious.

Maske was clearly unsurprised by the news. He rose, holding his coffee cup. "Keep your head down. Stay in the theatre for now. When they have no leads, it should blow over." He offered us a surprisingly warm smile that helped chase away the worst of my fear, and he disappeared into his workshop.

I'd already learned Maske kept a nocturnal schedule, and we often heard him tinkering away upstairs. He woke up before me each morning, so I had no idea when he actually slept. I rose before Drystan, so

Maske and I often shared our first cup of coffee alone. We'd either spend it in companionable silence, or we'd chat idly. After that initial séance, I'd found him intimidating, but over those cups of coffee, the feeling gradually lessened.

Once everyone was up, we'd have breakfast together, and then he'd retreat. Sometimes Cyan helped him, and other times she disappeared into the room with the crystal ball to practice or headed into town on errands.

A few evenings a week, Maske and Cyan would travel to houses of the nobility and merchants throughout the city, holding séances. They'd closed visits to the theatre, and Drystan and I didn't dare leave.

While I was impatient to start magician training, Maske gave us space to physically recover. Drystan and I spent much of our time in the loft or on the rooftop, licking our wounds. I slept a lot, with many an afternoon nap, but Drystan didn't fall asleep until close to dawn. A sound outside a window might make us jump. If I heard a siren echoing down the streets, every muscle would stiffen.

While it was a relief to be safe, there was something about being forced to stay inside that left us both on edge. I found myself missing seeing strangers or wishing I could go for a tea with Drystan, at least. Instead, we were hidden away for who knew how long.

Maske had given us some books from the library, so for a lack of anything better to do, I started my studies.

I began with *The Secrets of Magic* by a name I recognized—the Great Grimwood, one of the most famous magicians who had risen to prominence half a century ago. The book looked to be about the same age, and I turned the crumbling pages gingerly. The type was small and difficult to read, but the voice was engaging. The Great Grimwood, whose real name had been Adem Elk, had been born in the fishing village of Whitefish. An incredible inventor, he'd transformed stage magic from sideshow entertainment into a show fit for nobility and royalty.

Drystan paged through a few books, then set them aside. He stared into the distance, often disappearing somewhere I couldn't reach him.

My injuries healed even quicker than before. I took off the sling by the end of the first week, and I no longer needed to nap every few hours.

"What is your favorite sound?" Cyan asked us one lunchtime. Ricket had jumped up on the chair next to her, and she stroked the cat's back.

"Why do you ask?" I still wasn't exactly sure what to make of her.

"I was just thinking how the purr of a contented cat is one of my favorite sounds in the world. There's something so comforting about it, isn't there?"

"I suppose there is," Drystan said, bemused.

"Some of my other favorites are the first birdcall of morning, or the whistle of a kettle. The sound of far-off singing not quite heard." She lapsed into an expectant pause before asking again, "What are yours?"

I considered. "The sound of waves washing along the beach. The rustling of wind through the trees. The steady sound of someone breathing peacefully in their sleep." I avoided looking at Drystan as I said this.

Cyan nodded. "All excellent sounds. Yours, Drystan?"

"The crackle of the fire," he said, and I knew he was thinking of the bonfires at the circus. "The ethereal sound of the chorus in the Celestial Cathedral on Lady's Long Night. It fills you up until there's no other thought left. The crunch of walking on fallen autumn leaves."

"All very good sounds. We should go to the Cathedral at Midwinter. I'd like to hear it."

"Why are you asking?" I narrowed my eyes.

"It's a Temnian thing." She smiled at us widely. "We often ask about favorite scents, sounds, places, and the like, to get to know someone." From our answers, she seemed more at ease around us. I wondered what we'd unintentionally given away.

Maske came into the kitchen as Drystan and I finished putting our plates away. He had a small smear of oil on one cheek.

"What are your favorite sounds?" Cyan asked him.

But Drystan had put his warm hand in mine to lead me up the stairs, so I didn't catch the magician's answer.

• • • •

A few days later, an artist's impression of two certain fugitives appeared in another newspaper article.

"That looks nothing like me," Drystan said, his disgust tinged with relief. "They got my mouth all wrong. And why is your nose so crooked, Micah? Looks like you broke it."

It was true. I wondered if someone from the circus had deliberately described us badly to the artist. If so, I sent them a silent thanks. The sketch luckily didn't resemble a certain printed photograph of Lady Iphigenia Laurus that had appeared in Sicion newspapers a few months earlier, either.

That didn't mean we felt safe.

A week and a half after we arrived, Policiers knocked on the door of the Kymri Theatre. Drystan, Cyan, and I waited with bated breath in the hallway, out of sight, as Maske opened the door. When the officers asked if he'd seen a couple of young men matching our description, he'd said he thought those two would have been found by now, letting disapproval color his words.

The Policiers bristled. The one with the higher voice said: "They will be, sure enough." There was a long pause. I imagined them trying to peer into the gloom of the entryway.

It reminded me of when Policiers had come calling on the spice merchant, Mister Illari, searching for me as the missing noble runaway. Back then, I'd had to worry about being dragged back to my family and forced surgery. Now I had to fear prison, or worse. I clutched Drystan's arm, and he leaned against my uninjured shoulder. Cyan watched us both, but she couldn't hide her own fear as the Policiers lingered, chatting with Maske.

When the officers finally left, we breathed a tentative sigh of relief, but our unease remained. Had any of the neighbors yet realized there were two new residents at the Kymri Theatre? Would anyone make the connection, and what would we do if they did?

The Phantom Damselfly had been utterly silent, even when I picked up the Aleph and turned it over in my hands and thought her name. I had to hope she was still in there, somewhere, and that she'd warn me if the authorities became an actual threat.

A few days later, my feet took me to the door of Maske's workshop when he and Cyan were out on errands. I stared at the doorknob in the shape of a brass fist. I tried to twist it. Locked.

There was a key ring in a drawer in the kitchen. I went back downstairs and examined the keys, ears pricked for anyone coming. One was made of brass, the head an open hand with an eye on its palm. After so long being cooped up and twiddling my recently dislocated thumbs, I was itching to do *something*, anything.

Ricket glared at me accusingly.

"Don't judge me," I told the cat.

Ricket meowed and trotted out of the kitchen, her tail held high.

Her shaming worked. The Policiers at the door had spooked me, but as desperate as I was for more answers, I put the key back in its place.

The next day, Maske was leaving the workshop as I was passing. His head was down, lost in thought. I couldn't help but peek through the open door, but behind him, all I saw were . . . mirrors. Some were normal, others warped as those in a fun house. I caught the barest scents of sawdust, oil, and metal.

Maske glanced up and met my eyes. "I put the mirror maze up years ago as an easy layer of security," he said. "It might be paranoid, but I wouldn't have put it past Taliesin to send a spy in here one of these days. Now, it's more habit than anything."

It was easy enough to imagine that just behind those mirrors would be tables, wood shavings, and woodworking tools. Brass gears, strings, and pulleys, and whatever he was working on. A sardonic smile played on his lips, but his eyes flashed in warning as he bowed his head, as if he guessed my thoughts.

"I remind you no one sees my illusions until they are finished. No one. Do you understand?" His tone was somehow both mild and sharp as steel.

"Yes. Completely," I said, though of course his words only made me wonder all the more what he was hiding.

He headed toward the kitchen, and I found myself falling into step beside him. He put the kettle on the stove. "Tea? We've run out of coffee. I'll have to head to the market."

"Yes, please," I said.

He bundled about the kitchen, taking out mugs and a jug of milk from the chiller.

"We are very grateful for your hospitality," I said, drawing on past etiquette lessons. He was harboring and feeding us even though he obviously didn't have the coin to spare. With luck, though, Drystan and I would take well to his lessons and be earning our own keep soon enough.

He waved a hand, as if it wasn't anything so generous. "It is nice, having this place a bit less quiet," he said. "Once, we always had guests, and of course audiences came through the theatre several times a day."

"It must have been something in its heyday," I said.

His face softened in wistfulness. "It was beyond."

"Can I ask you a bit about the duel?" He seemed in a talkative mood, and I still had so many questions. "How did it go? I keep wondering. Drystan told me that Taliesin accused you of cheating, and I know you lost a Vestige that meant a lot to you, but not much beyond that."

Maske sighed, dropping a lump of sugar into one of the cups. "We'd gone our separate ways, but when he attacked my honor, I felt I had no choice but to challenge him to that duel and put an end to it. I wanted to prove I was better than him. I called upon the Collective of Magic, and they spelled out the terms of the agreement. One performance, with each of us showcasing the best of our acts. The audience and the Collective judged the winner.

"In the months leading up to it, I barely ate. I barely slept. My whole life was magic. I burned with the certainty that I would win." He looked up from the table to the ceiling, seeming older. His magician's façade had cracked.

"But, of course, I lost." He bowed his head. "I lost so much. And here I have remained for the past fifteen years, constantly surrounded by the dusty memories of who and what I used to be."

We sat in silence.

"I'm sure what you have in that workshop is wonderful enough that if you did challenge Taliesin to a rematch, you would win," I chanced.

He half-smiled. "You didn't see what I was once capable of. I'll train you three, as you asked, and we'll see how we go, but I'm afraid my glory days are long behind me. At least I'll give you some skills you can use to help you get by. That might be the best we can hope for. I doubt I'll ever stand on a stage before an audience again."

We hadn't discussed it, but I wondered how long this hospitality would last, even if we did bring in coin, if this duel didn't happen. Six months? A year? It'd be safer to save up for passage to one of the other islands and leave Elada behind entirely. If I left, would Drystan board the ship with me? So many questions I didn't know the answers to.

We drank our tea. He asked about my injuries, and I said I was feeling better. I told him I was enjoying the books he'd chosen for me. We passed a pleasant enough half an hour before he disappeared back into his workshop. I drank a second cup of tea, lingering over it as I realized I'd seen behind the mask of Maske, to the man beneath.

I hoped that Drystan, Cyan, and I could bring some magic back into his life.

● ● ● ●

By the end of the two weeks, Maske decided we'd hidden long enough.

"I'm planning on going into town tomorrow," he said as we had a late breakfast of toast and eggs. "To Twisting the Aces. You could come with me, if you like."

Drystan and I glanced up at him. Even I had heard that was the best magic supply store in Elada.

He smiled thinly. "That certainly got your attention."

"Is it safe to leave?" I asked, even though I was desperate to escape the theatre. I'd never spent half a month cooped up indoors, and Drystan and I were both going stir-crazy.

"I won't say it's riskless, and I'd recommend disguising yourselves with the Glamours, but you can't hide in here forever."

Maske showed us the Vestige on thin chains to wear beneath our clothing. The pendants were like little mirrors that shimmered with rainbows. He asked what eye color and hair color we wanted, or how we'd best like to shift our features. It was fiddly—you had to move through various options one by one. Maske flicked a switch and I watched as Drystan's hair darkened and his eyes turned such a deep brown they were almost black. His features subtly transformed, and he abruptly looked nothing like the young man I knew.

Maske did mine next, and I felt the magic settle over me like a second skin. I looked in the small handheld mirror and shook my head in wonder. My nose was slightly different, and there was a dimple in my chin. Maske had said the fewer changes, the slower it'd run out of power. My eyes were blue instead of hazel. I pulled a strand of my hair away. In the mirror, it looked dark, but to my naked eye, it was its customary auburn.

"How . . . ?"

"You know the truth of yourself," Maske said.

I let my hair fall.

"The illusion only lasts for an hour before it must be manually reset, so you'll have to retire somewhere private where no one can see the pendant," he said. "I used to have more, but I've either sold them or they've run out of power. So be conservative." We were only to use them while we were out and to turn them off as soon as we were home. In a couple of months, when the trail was cold, we might slowly let the Glamour fade.

I switched off the pendant, watching my features reappear in the mirror with relief.

Even with the added security of the Glamour, though, I decided I needed an extra step of protection. In the depths of my pack, I still had the dress I'd taken with me from my wardrobe the night I ran away. It was the plainest one I'd owned, made of brown cotton. It was far nicer than anything I'd worn since, save the aerialist or pantomime costumes. I pulled it on, leaving my chest unbound. The dress was a bit tight across the shoulders, but it fit. After I twisted and pinned my hair, I stared at myself in the mirror, sans Glamour.

I'd worried I'd feel that same sense of wrongness or see that scared version of myself that had run away from my parents' apartments, but strangely enough . . . I didn't. This time, it would be my choice, like when I acted in the pantomime, rather than having feminineness forced upon me. I put the Glamour illusion back on. I amended it just enough to erase the bump at my throat.

I needed a little more. I headed downstairs and knocked on Cyan's door.

"M—Micah?" she asked after she cracked it open, unable to hide her surprise as she looked up at me. I hadn't stood so close to her before and realized she was a good three inches shorter than me.

"Can I borrow some face paints?" I asked, gesturing at my dress. "To help complete the effect."

A line appeared between her eyebrows.

"They're looking for me as a boy, I figure this is safer, at least for now." I pitched my voice a little higher. "Don't you think?"

She stepped aside, letting me into her room. She'd pinned Temnian wax-dyed cotton on the walls, draped so that it looked like the inside of a circus tent, which matched the covers of her bed. Crystals hung on strings caught the gas lamp's glow. From the center of the ceiling she'd hung prayer scrolls—ribbons printed with prayers in Temri script. The trunk in the corner looked similar to the one I'd used in my own cart at the circus.

She went to her vanity and plucked a tin of kohl, another of rouge, and two brushes. "This is all I can spare, I'm afraid."

I unscrewed the tins. They were both half-empty, but I'd only need a little when we were going out.

"Thank you. May I try?" I gestured to her mirror. I only had a small, rust-stained one in the water closet on the uppermost floor. She nodded.

"You've healed quickly," she said as I darkened the edges of my eyes with kohl and my lips with rouge. I tried to subtly change my features with a few tricks I'd learned at the circus. My eyes looked even bigger and rounder, and I'd made the bow of my lips more dramatic. I smeared a little rouge on my cheekbones and surveyed my handiwork. Not bad, though I preferred myself bare-faced and Glamour-less.

Cyan cocked her head. "I honestly can't tell if you are actually a girl or just very good at dressing as one."

"Does it matter?" I countered.

She smiled. "I suppose it doesn't."

"Thanks," I said, both for the cosmetics and her acceptance.

My nerves grew as I climbed the stairs. When I opened the door to the loft, Drystan was sitting on the bed and staring blankly at the stained-glass window. His white and blonde hair was mussed.

Ricket, curled at Drystan's feet, glared at me jealously. The cat followed him from room to room. I wondered if it'd been hard for Drystan to leave her behind. I'd caught him murmuring nonsense words to her or picking her up to rest his cheek against the top of her head, holding her close. Ricket would put up with it briefly before wriggling away, indignant. A few minutes later, she'd be back.

Drystan gave me a double take.

"Do I look too much like Princess Iona or Iphigenia Laurus?" I asked, rubbing my hands together. I was afraid he'd laugh, like it was a joke.

He shook his head, taking me in so slowly I felt my cheeks heat beneath the rouge.

"No, you don't."

"Do I look like Micah Grey?"

One corner of his mouth quirked up. "To me you do."

I didn't know what to say to that.

5

TWISTING THE ACES

"Twisting the Aces is the oldest magic shop in Imachara, and possibly Elada. It began as a small stall in one of the marketplaces, with the old fortuneteller, Fay Larch, selling packs of tarot cards and amulets against the evil eye. She later diversified, selling all manner of magical apparatus.

When attitudes toward magic shifted, her shop likewise morphed. She bought the current premises and sold her wares to the early magicians of her day, from simple cups and balls to props for grand illusion. After her death, her son took over, and his child after him, and Twisting the Aces has continued for all these years, a staple of the stage magic community."

BROCHURE FOR TWISTING THE ACES

The next day, the four of us left the Kymri Theatre and set off for Twisting the Aces. Drystan and I wore our Glamours tucked beneath our shirts, and I felt mine buzzing slightly against the skin of my sternum. I tugged at my skirts self-consciously. Cyan had given me one of her spare coats, which just about fit my taller frame, and a burgundy bonnet and veil. Drystan wore one of Maske's old suits. It was out of style, and he'd had to let out the hem of the trousers. But he'd pomaded his hair, donned a bowler hat and a cravat of Temnian silk, and borrowed a pair of Maske's polished shoes. He cut such a fine figure I'd never have recognized him from that sketch in the newspaper. Fingers crossed, no one else would, either.

It was a half-hour walk to the Brass District, and despite the oversized coat, I was chilly. Autumn had dug in its claws over the last fortnight.

Granite buildings loomed to either side of us. It was good to be outside again after being cooped up for so long. I drank in the sight of unfamiliar faces. Men on a break from factory work in their dirty coveralls, their faces smeared with coal, soot, or grease. Children sold newspapers in the street, crying out the headlines. Harried women with bags of clothes for washing or mending hurried to laundry houses. Here and there, well-dressed men and women in furs picked their way carefully over the muck in the gutter. So many strangers living and working cheek to jowl.

"Here we are," Maske said, nodding to a cracked wooden sign with its name and two ace cards that swung in the wind. Twisting the Aces' door needed a fresh coat of orange paint. The dusty front window display showcased playing and tarot cards dangling from strings, crystal balls, and magic wands lying on paisley shawls.

A bell chimed as we entered. A bored-looking boy with a mop of messy brown hair and a mole near his mouth glanced up at us from the book he was reading.

"Hello, Tam, my boy," Maske said to him. The shop smelled of wood, beeswax polish, and the sharp tang of metal.

I gravitated to large canisters of coins filled with double-headed and double-tailed false marks of bronze, silver, and gold. Haphazard stacks of card decks filled another shelf. There was a colorful riot of silk scarfs, stacks of handcuffs, false gems, and other wares. I itched to run my hands along the rows of pristine and second-hand magic books.

On the left side of the shop was a large, carved Kymri sarcophagus. Stacks of trunks, full-length mirrors, cabinets, and cages. Doves cooed in the corner, and rabbits stared at us implacably as they chewed their food.

I spotted a large tree made of gold, with the leaves from the Twelve

Trees of Nobility carved of jade. A sign next to a necklace draped around the wooden neck and shoulders of a mannequin proclaimed that it'd belonged to the first Byssian queen and was haunted by her spirit. Those two had no price tags.

"This place is just as I remember." Drystan smiled softly.

"I never turn down a trip to the Aces," Cyan said.

"What d'ye want this time, then, Mister Maske?" Tam called.

Maske passed the boy a list. He obviously came here regularly, despite not performing for a decade and a half. The boy scurried about the shop and plucked objects from shelves, muttering under his breath.

"Hey, Mrs. Verre?" Tam called to the back room. "Leave the stock checking and mind the till, will ya, please?"

A tall, slender woman in her late forties came to the front of the shop. Wisps of dark blonde hair beginning to grey fell about her face, and the rest strained against the pins confining it. She wore smeared kohl about her eyes and her lips were painted dark pink. Her dress was a matching hue of muslin trimmed with black ribbon.

"Hello," she said cheerfully.

"I haven't seen you here before, madame," Maske said. "Jasper Maske, at your service."

"Pleased to make your acquaintance. I'm Lily Verre." She held out her hand, and Maske bent over it.

"Charmed, I'm sure," he murmured, before gesturing to us. "These are my associates Celia, Sam, and Amon." Cyan had already been using Celia as a false name, and Drystan and I had chosen ours the night before. I'd liked Sam as it was gender neutral. We gave her cautious nods.

"Are you all magicians?" she asked.

"Enthusiasts," Maske demurred.

She clapped her hands together. "Me as well! It's why I decided to try my hand working here when I saw the 'help wanted' sign. I'm a widow. My late husband—the Couple bless his soul—left me with a tidy income. But I found, without him, I grew so terribly bored. So, I fancied trying my hand at shop keeping! I've only been here a week, but I've met ever such interesting people." She chattered as she wrapped the goods, speaking so quickly I could barely keep up. She had a girlish way about her, her cheeks flushed, and I found her enthusiasm infectious.

Lily Verre rang up the purchases on the brass cash register as Maske flirted with remarkable skill, though she had trouble working the machine and Tam had to walk her through it with growing impatience.

A glass display showcased a blue crystal ball with a Vestige metal base like Maske's. My eyes watered at the price. I squinted. Maybe I was drawn to the dragonfly wings etched into the rainbow sheen of the Vestige metal at its base. Through the glass of the display case, I gazed into its depths.

Images emerged in the crystal. A woman in a red dress, her back turned to me, pushing a carriage down the road, the wind whipping the scarf around her neck.

"Doctor!" I heard her call. The word echoed in three tones at once.

The vision shifted to a crowd of people with signs, shouting and shaking their fists at the Royal Palace. By their signs, I recognized them as Foresters, the growing anti-royalist party. Overlaid on the angry crowd was the face of a man with piercing blue eyes who wore a mask across the lower half of his face.

An audience replaced the crowd, with Drystan on stage next to Cyan. During the séance, Drystan had seemed quietly confident in my vision, but this time he beamed at the audience, his face radiant as he draped a handkerchief over his hand. When he took it away, a white dove flew over the audience.

I heard the flapping of wings and the ticking of a clock. I reached my hand into the pocket of my coat. My fingers curled around Anisa's Aleph, even though I thought I'd left it back at the Kymri Theatre. I blinked, and the Phantom Damselfly looked out at me from the crystal ball, the silver tattoos on her forehead glittering.

—*Be brave, little Kedi,* she whispered. *Be bold.*

Her face transformed into a man with blurred features. I had an impression of wild hair and intense eyes. The lower half of his face was covered by a mask. His hatred seared across my mind. I wanted to scream, but my jaw clamped shut. A blink, and he was gone, leaving only the deep blue of Penglass and a lingering sense of dread.

"Twenty-two silver marks and six bronze," Lily declared, her voice jolting me back to Twisting the Aces. Cyan was looking at me, and I cleared my throat, pretending to look at the other wares.

I let go of the Aleph. When I took my hand off the glass of the display case, my handprint remained. My head throbbed.

Maske tucked the parcels under his arm. "A true pleasure to meet you, Mrs. Verre."

"Oh, call me Lily," she said with a wave of her hand.

Outside Twisting the Aces, the light was so bright I closed my eyes. I heard a ringing in my ears.

I stumbled.

Drystan steadied me. "What's wrong?"

"Dunno, I felt faint all of a sudden," I said. I couldn't tell him what I'd seen in front of Cyan, obviously, but even if we'd been alone, I'm not sure I would have. He'd seen what I'd done to Penglass, and he'd watched Violet transform into a woman. But he hadn't seen the Phantom Damselfly beyond when she'd done her customary performance in the Pavillion of Phantoms. He knew nothing of what she'd told me about Chimaera and how I had some important role to play. I should tell him, but we were still reeling from that night, and I didn't want to worry him until I understood what it meant.

"Do you want to go back?" he asked. The theatre would be safer, but I was too keyed up after what I'd just seen. The thought of lying there in the loft with only my thoughts or old magic books to comfort me was unthinkable.

"No, no, I'm fine. I didn't eat much at breakfast, that's all." It wasn't a lie, but it wasn't the whole truth. When would I ever learn?

"I'm heading back," Maske said. "But you should spend some time outside. Be back by teatime." Maske tipped his hat at us before wandering down the cobbled street in the direction of the Glass District. Was he . . . whistling?

"Old dog," Drystan said, smirking. "He never could resist a pretty face."

"Let's find something to eat, then," Cyan said. "Food always sets me to rights."

Drystan put his arm around my shoulders. I used my weakness as an excuse to lean into him further, comforted by his warmth and the almost spiced scent of his skin. With him dressed in his suit and me in my skirts, I wondered if people around us thought we were courting.

The streets were quieter than they'd been in mid-summer. The clouds promised rain. We came upon one of the smaller market squares. The clock tower in the center was carved into an upright dragon, with the clock face resting between its half-furled wings like a moon. At its base was a puppet show. Cyan went to the food stalls and bought me some almonds roasted in honey. The sugar melted on my tongue. Drystan stole a couple, the almonds disappearing into his mouth faster than sleight of hand. Cyan crunched through her own packet with obvious relish.

We drifted closer to the entertainment. A gaggle of children too young for school sat cross-legged, staring up in delight at the display. The puppets were carved from wood, their clothes cut out from colored paper, their faces well-painted. The show had already begun, but I recognized the political fairy tale "The Prince and the Owlish Man."

A prophecy foretold that the young Prince Mael of Elada would one day break into six pieces. To protect him, his mother and father locked him in a tower. He was not allowed to play. All his possessions were soft and rounded. If he so much as pricked a finger, the greatest surgeon attended him. Prince Mael was watched and guarded by all, and the little boy was thoroughly miserable.

One day, at the window of his tower, he made a wish as the sun set.

When Prince Mael opened his eyes, a young Chimaera perched on his window ledge. He was a youth with the large yellow eyes of an owl. Small feathers tufted his eyebrows. Great wings of banded brown and grey feathers sprouted from his back.

I shivered, remembering the owlish woman from my vision.

"The Lord of the Sun and the Lady of the Moon have heard your prayer," the Chimaera said. "I've come to show you your empire. You shall make friends and foes, you will love and you will hate, but during these ten years, no serious harm shall befall you. In return, you must promise to listen and learn from all those you come across. After a decade, you must return to the castle, your reign, and the fate of your prophecy."

"I swear it."

The owlish man held out his hand. "Then come."

The prince climbed onto his back, and they travelled the world for a decade. He visited many of Elada's cities, towns, and villages. He fell in love with a girl who didn't love him back. He saw how the poor suffered, and how the rich profited from them. He and the owlish man flew across the sea to experience the rest of the Archipelago.

A shark nearly devoured him off the coast of northern Linde. He was kidnapped by bandits in Kymri. He was trapped by a landfall in Byssia. But he always managed to escape lasting harm, often with the aid of his friend with the brown and grey feathers.

Time passed. He grew from a sheltered boy into a wise young man. Eventually, of course, a decade passed.

Upon Prince Mael's return to the Palace, his younger sibling abdicated. Mael ruled as king, marrying a beautiful princess. The owlish man flew away, and King Mael never saw him again.

Many years passed. King Mael did not break, but he did bend. When the colonies threatened war once again, he let them secede and negotiated peace treaties. For that was how the prophecy was fulfilled—the Empire of the Archipelago broke into Elada, Linde, Byssia, Northern Temne, Southern Temne, and Kymri.

The children delighted in the display of monsters, fighting, and a happy ending. They clapped loudly and a man in a dark hood came around the crowd, holding a puppet who asked the children and their parents for coins.

"Huh," I said. "One of those stories that goes a bit over your head as a child, isn't it?"

"Aye," Cyan said. "Total propaganda, but children do sure love things that fly." Her mouth twisted, and with her Temnian background, I was sure she had plenty of opinions about Elada's sanitized fable of King Mael's treatment of the former colonies. The real story wasn't as tidy. The islands' fight for independence hadn't been bloodless. King Mael's treaties had been deeply unfair, causing widespread poverty in the former colonies.

Elada liked to pretend it was still the most powerful country in the Archipelago, but with so many Vestige artefacts running out of power over the years, this was no longer true, and all knew it—especially the other islands. They traded with us, and relations were cordial enough, but they kept hiking up their prices, and while the nobility could afford imported goods, everyone else struggled.

As if to underline our thoughts, in the corner of the square, a man wearing a billboard proclaiming "LEAVES FOR ALL" on the front and back shouted at passersby as he shoved leaflets in their faces.

"Are you tired of being cold and hungry?" he cried. "Are you tired of the Twelve Trees of Nobility taking all the water and sunlight from us? Join the Foresters!"

The man pushed a flyer into our hands. "Make a difference," he whispered, impassioned.

On the flyer, the stylized image of a man was overlaid on the angry, shouting crowd. My breath hitched in my throat. The drawing showed a man with intense eyes, hair in wild curls, the lower half of his face hidden by a mask.

"What's wrong?" Cyan asked.

"Who's this?" I pointed at the man I'd just seen in my vision at Twisting the Aces.

"That's Timur. The leader of the Foresters," Cyan said. "They've got plenty of good ideas, and I agree with the general argument. But I dunno, something about him gives me the creeps."

Drystan made a noise of agreement. "And he's hinted more than a few times that if they can't get power through peaceful protest, they're not above trying more . . . emphatic actions."

What did it mean that I had seen this Timur in a vision? I was about to tuck the poster into my pocket to study later when Drystan plucked it from my hand, crumpled the paper, and threw it into a nearby bin.

6

SPECTRES OF THE PAST

"If the Kymri are predisposed to worship the sun, then the Temnians have more respect for the lunar cycle. During the full moon, or the night the Penglass glows under the stars, there is a huge celebration and feast. Elders dress as the moon and stars and bestow blessings upon those who need them. Special food is prepared that may only be eaten that night— sweet mooncakes and small sips of a drink called Dancing Water made from almonds, fermented honey, and small gold flakes, which is meant to be an elixir for long life. Small amounts of the drug Lerium are also sampled. On this night, men and women are meant to become closer to the Lord and Lady. Their prayers will more likely be heard and their wishes granted."

A HISTORY OF ELADA AND ITS FORMER COLONIES,
PROFESSOR CAED CEDAR, ROYAL SNAKEWOOD UNIVERSITY

We paused in an alleyway long enough for Drystan and I to re-set our Glamours before we wordlessly started back in the direction of the Kymri Theatre. Dark clouds covered the sun, and autumn's chill nipped my cheeks. My mind was spinning after what I'd seen. Was this Timur the man with the blurred face? Did this have anything to do with the Royal Physician who had hired Shadow Elwood?

The wind picked up, blowing fallen leaves down the cobbles. When I realized we were only a few blocks from the Royal Infirmary, my steps slowed.

"Cyan," I said, carefully. "Could you do me an exceedingly large favor?"

She arched an eyebrow. She'd hastily braided her hair after the puppet show, and the wind was already teasing it apart. The sun caught her eyes, bringing out various shades of brown, like jasper. There was a ring of dark blue around the outer edge of her irises.

"Could you go into the infirmary, pretending you're there to visit someone named Aenea Harper?" I paused, swallowing, feeling Drystan's gaze on me. "She was my partner on the trapeze. She was badly injured the night we left and we . . . we don't know if she made it."

She chewed her lower lip. "It'd be risky. The Policiers might be keeping tabs on who visits."

"Possibly. But I can't risk contacting anyone else from the circus to ask, even if I knew where they were and . . . it might be easier, to never know for certain. But now that we're this close . . ." I trailed off. Even with the Glamour, it was too much of a risk.

Cyan fiddled with one of the ceramic beads in her hair. "All right. I'll give it a try."

We turned off, heading towards the nicer part of town, passing the Celestial Cathedral and drawing too close to the Royal Palace. There would be more Policier presence here. Drystan hadn't said a word, but disapproval hung around him like mist.

Cyan stopped at a flower stall and held out her palm in my direction. I dug in my pocket and passed a few coppers, and Cyan chose a cheerful bouquet of daisies, carnations, and baby's breath. We paused outside the Royal Infirmary, which also housed the medical school on the other side of the courtyard. It was an imposing block of granite, severe and unornamented.

"Stay here," Cyan said. She straightened her shoulders and walked up the stairs into the double front doors.

"Take it from a former fool: this is foolish," Drystan said.

"I'm aware. Can you blame me?" I asked.

"No. But whatever you learn, it's risky. If she's survived, you'll want to speak to her. And if she hasn't . . ." Drystan let the unspoken hang between us.

Then it'd rip open all that grief once again, just as I'd started to get through the day without thinking about her so often.

"I won't risk dragging her into my troubles," I said. I didn't add that I couldn't, even if I wanted to. Anisa had made me promise I wouldn't see or speak to Aenea because her story was meant to end that night in the circus. I'd given my word. Having Cyan ask about her on my behalf was already coming perilously close to breaking it.

I watched people pass by as we waited. A girl in the starched uniform of a maid hurried past with overflowing bags of food shopping. A woman struggled to hold the door open. Red skirts peeked from the bottom of her black coat. A man on the street paused to help her. She pushed the wicker chair around, speaking to the child within. He was a small boy, sallow-skinned, and dark-haired. He was long-limbed but unnaturally thin and clutched a blanket about his face as he looked up at his mother.

I see a girl, no, a woman, in a wine-red dress. Her child is ill, eaten from the inside . . .

The words Maske spoke at the séance came back to me, as well as the flash of the vision I'd seen at Twisting the Aces. The woman's light brown hair fell from her bonnet, obscuring her face. She thanked the man and continued into the medical school, her dark red skirts swirling behind her. I wanted to follow, but how would I explain it to Drystan? *Sorry, we need to investigate this woman I saw in a hallucination . . .*

Before I could even consider it, Cyan emerged from the hospital, still holding the bouquet. The tenseness of her shoulders betrayed her anger, and I soon forgot all about the woman in the red dress.

"They wouldn't tell me." She exhaled hard. "Said I'd have to fill out a form and come back later, but someone else went right in while I was there."

"Why?" I asked.

"I'm afraid it might be because I'm Temnian. Most people are fine enough, but then you come across someone . . . she looked at me, and everything about her body language screamed that she thought I didn't belong there."

"I'm sorry," I said, horrified.

She shook her head. "Even I didn't expect it, not really. In the circus, or even the séances, it's not much of an issue. I suppose my exoticism is part of the performance, though." Her words were bitter. She gave a groan of frustration. "I was tempted to kick up a fuss, but I was afraid of drawing attention. I'm sorry, I don't have any answers for you. I wish I did."

The bouquet hung heavy at her side, and she dropped it onto the street. The petals scattered on the cobbles.

"Thank you for trying," I said, my stomach knotted. "And I'm sorry. I didn't understand the risk of what I was asking."

Her mouth twisted. "I know you didn't."

The nobility I'd been raised with were largely Eladan born and bred, with lighter skin and hair. I'd interacted with people from elsewhere in the Archipelago, of course, and the circus had those from all walks of life. Just because I hadn't seen it much firsthand, though, didn't mean that bigotry didn't exist.

A couple of Policiers rounded the corner, and the three of us saw them the same time. Their gaze lingered on Cyan. I felt as though I was being watched. What if the Shadow was patrolling the Infirmary, suspecting I might be tempted to check in on her? I'd knocked him out cold with the light of the Penglass. Even though I hadn't stopped to check, I knew I hadn't killed him. It'd now be personal as well as following the will of his client. Drystan was right. It'd been beyond dangerous to come here.

"Let's not test our luck any further," Drystan said, as if reading my thoughts.

We walked briskly until we turned the corner, not glancing back to see if the Policiers were following. As soon as we could, we picked up the pace, half-running the rest of the way back to the Kymri Theatre. The sky opened, drenching us with rain.

When the three of us stood, dripping in the corridor, I snapped the lock shut behind us with a *clunk*.

Maske was in the kitchen, and we immediately sensed the change in him. His eyes were bright. Part anger, part triumph, part hunger.

He gestured to the half-torn poster on the table. Cyan picked it up, Drystan and I clustering on either side of her.

It was an advertisement for Taliesin's Spectre Shows. There was Taliesin, who was a few years older than Maske, in a top hat and truly impressive grey sideburns. Below him were two younger men in sharp magician's suits and white bowties, gesturing towards a wall of smoke in the center, with images projected onto them.

"I was the one who first showed him how to use a phantasmagoria," Maske said. "Fifteen years of him recycling all my old tricks, all my old knowledge. Those images are even from our old shows. I saw this on the way home and ripped it off the pole. I'd already known about this from all the other Spectre Show posters I'd seen around town over the years. They always showed my tricks with only a few details changed. I finally snuck into the theatre to watch one of the afternoon shows. You're right, Drystan. His grandsons aren't near as good as Taliesin was in his prime. He's even using a variation of my spirit cabinet trick I taught him close to twenty years ago." His lip curled.

"Even with your Vestige artefact," I said, "he really hasn't been able to make anything new, then?"

Maske shot Drystan a look. "I've suspected for years that he wasn't as good as I would have been with what he has in his possession. But I had no way to strike back."

"What artefacts did you lose, if I might ask?" I'd been so curious for weeks.

"Something rare enough that I've never seen its like before or since, and I keep tabs on the black market. But no matter. If I'm correct, and Taliesin hasn't been able to use it . . . then now that I have you three, maybe we *could* actually have a chance at challenging him to a rematch."

My heart lifted. I'd suggested it because of the vision, wanting to learn a new skill and perform, and because Maske clearly also dreamed of performing again. Part of me still wasn't sure if Maske would actually take us up on it all.

"Yes," he said, reading our expressions. "I believe it's past time we begin your training in earnest."

7

MOONS, CLOUDS, SUNS, STARS

"I could list every magic trick in the book, and in intricate, infinite detail describe the reveal behind each one. And you could understand it. But that does not mean you are a magician. It means you know a few tricks. For a trick without context is only a fold of the fingers or a tuck of a prop up a sleeve.

I could teach you how to switch objects. How to pass a cloth over a false bird and bring it away to show a live, cooing dove. A soothsayer might perform the same trick using misdirection to change the sacrifice of a live crow for a dead one covered in maggots. The same trick for different purposes, with very different results.

There is no one way to be a magician any more than there is one way to be human."

THE SECRETS OF MAGIC, THE GREAT GRIMWOOD

re you ready?"

Maske held up a deck of cards.

"Yes," I said. Drystan, Cyan, and I sat at the table where we'd held the séance. It was mid-morning, and the sun streamed through the curtains.

The cards clacked together as Maske bridged them effortlessly. He brought his arms wide, a trail of cards following his hands. They blurred into flashes of red, white, and black. He did it again, and I searched for hidden threads. He shuffled the cards in different ways, tumbling sections over each other; interlacing them and snapping them smartly back into a pack. The cards danced over his fingertips into circles and "S" shapes, each move flowing to the next without hesitation.

With the injuries to my thumbs and shoulder when we first arrived at the Kymri Theatre, I wouldn't have been able to even attempt the tricks Maske was about to teach us now. The bruising around my thumbs was almost gone, and they no longer hurt and only felt stiff. Physically, I'd recovered from the last night in the circus. Mentally, those bruises lingered somewhere deep, and I wasn't sure they'd ever heal.

Maske fanned the cards face down. "Pick a card," he said, flashing us a magician's smile. "Any card."

My fingertips hovered over the deck. The edges of the pack were well-thumbed, the silhouettes of the rampant dragons on the back faded. I chose one.

Maske held it up for us to see.

I'd chosen the ace of stars. Maske shuffled the card back into the deck. He placed the pack upon his outstretched palm. The other hand hovered above the deck, and the top card levitated between his hands.

"Is this your card?" he asked.

Sure enough, it was the ace of stars. "Yes!" I exclaimed, amazed.

His smile warmed, and he returned it to its siblings and fanned the deck again. "Drystan. Pick a card. Any card."

Drystan plucked one free, tilting it towards me and Cyan, making sure Maske couldn't see it. The six of clouds. Back into the pack it went. After more showy shuffles, Maske showed us the deck again, face up.

"And where is your card?"

We searched for the six of clouds, but it was missing. When we shook our heads, Maske opened his mouth and drew out a card. He passed it to Drystan, who took it with no small amount of trepidation, but the six of clouds was quite dry.

We clapped. Maske gave a little bow from his seat, lips quirked. I'd been watching his hands closely, but I still had no idea how he'd done it.

"It seems like real magic," I said.

"So it does. But what you must remember is that stage magic is not only the physical technique of manipulating cards and the like," he said, shuffling with various flourishes. "A deeper instinct is absolutely vital. And that is something that cannot be entirely taught. Knowing how long to pause, what you say and how to say it, your body language, the confidence . . . all of this is what completes the illusion. Take an aspect away, hesitate a beat too long, and the magic is lost."

His demeanor changed. He stood stiff as an automaton, shuffling mechanically. He held up a card—the two of suns—and put it back. By deliberately slowing down and taking away any sense of flair, Maske let me figure out exactly how the trick was done. I met the magician's gaze, and he smiled at my understanding.

"Remember," he continued, "once you learn a trick, you must tell no one. A magician's secrets are everything. If word spreads how a trick is done, then the magic is lost for the audience as well. As much as they might wish to learn the truth behind it, deep down, they'll be disappointed to have confirmation of the trickery. And if any member of the Collective of Magic learns you've been too loose-lipped with how it's all done, then you'll be kicked out or worse. Do you understand?"

Drystan, Cyan, and I nodded solemnly.

"Good. Now, there are a few approaches to magic. Some do claim that the magic they do is supernatural. But it's more honorable to keep the show magical but also tell the audience that it's all a trick that they can't figure out. We start with cards, coins, and other small objects. Sleight of hand, or prestidigitation. This is the foundation of stage magic, and it's the easiest way to begin making your bread and butter. You two come from well-off families—surely you've had a magician at a birthday celebration or something of the sort?"

"Aye," I said. My parents would never have shelled out for a magician, but Anna Yew had one at one of her birthdays a few years ago. Maske and Cyan had guessed that I was from a noble background, like Drystan, though I hadn't shared my surname. Maske knew Drystan was a Hornbeam but assured us he hadn't told Cyan.

"And what sorts of things did these magicians do at these parties?" Maske asked.

"Card tricks, coin tricks, cups, billiard balls, eggs, flowers . . ." I trailed off.

"Exactly. Close-up magic uses everyday objects and does something extraordinary with them. With grand illusion and séances, you can distract with great bursts of light, or darkness, but you cannot do that with something so innocuous. It's all in your fingers." He wriggled his long, thin digits to illustrate. "They want the magic . . . so give it to them."

He walked us through the basics—how to hold the cards, and various ways to shuffle. We did these easy steps for over an hour. Drystan far surpassed me with his fancier flourishes, but that didn't surprise me. He'd shown off when he, Aenea, and I had played cards on the train from Sicion to Cowl. The memory of that stung. I kept dropping my cards. Despite my frustration, though, I was caught up in the challenge of it. When we did something right, Maske made sure to praise us, and that afternoon, he bloomed. I'd seen him smile more in the last half hour of doing magic than the last few weeks. Just as I'd wanted to master the trapeze, I wanted to excel at this, too.

I wanted to take something unassuming and make it astonishing.

● ● ● ●

We broke for a late lunch of sandwiches and lemonade. Afterwards, Cyan went to her room, but Drystan and I tucked ourselves up in the library. It was a small room filled to the brim with books and furnished with overstuffed armchairs. Maske pulled out some volumes and left us to it, retreating to his workshop. Soon enough, we heard a faint banging somewhere above our heads.

"What is he actually doing up there?" I asked.

"Magic, of course," Drystan said, deadpan.

I rolled my eyes.

Ricket wandered in to join us, curling up on Drystan's lap as he picked up *Magick* by Professor Cynbel Acacia. His long fingers curled around the pages as he read, the shadows of his eyelashes falling across his cheeks. Maske's enthusiasm had kindled something in him, and it was a relief to see the Drystan I knew returning.

I was still reading *The Secrets of Magic* by The Great Grimwood. It was interesting, but long.

Ricket eventually moved from Drystan's lap to mine. It'd taken her awhile to warm up to me, but she'd finally decided I was one of her humans.

I stroked her head idly as I read, her purring calming me. I felt lucky that afternoon. The Policiers or the Shadow hadn't caught us yet, despite my ill-considered visit to the Infirmary. We were warm, fed, and learning a new trade. I could only hope that this relative peace would last at least a little longer before real magic and Chimaera inevitably interrupted it. And I wished I knew what'd become of Aenea.

I turned the page. I'd already read the overview of the history of stage magic: priests had often used basic illusions to cement their followers' faith and sway the unbelievers. Vestige artefacts were considered holy and proof of the divine.

The chapter I was reading focused on a period last century when scientists claimed Vestige might be closer to technology than magic. As a result, believers grew more cynical of priests using artefacts in their services. The nobility began to collect the rarer and more valuable pieces in their cabinets of curiosities. Some of the cheaper and more plentiful types found their way to street entertainment, often married to vaudeville or circuses.

R.H. Ragona's Circus of Magic had used a weather machine to begin the nightly performance, and of course, they had Anisa's Aleph in the Pavillion of Phantoms, though Bil had had no idea of her true value. The ringmaster had liked to collect automatons and other smaller Vestige, hoping they'd be good investments. They might have been, eventually, but his lack of immediate coin had proved the bigger problem.

I didn't want to think about the circus.

I glanced up at Drystan, but he'd slumped over in his chair and was fast asleep. I watched him for a bit, smiling to myself, before returning to my book.

Grimwood listed many types of tricks, from sleight of hand to grand illusion. The diagrams explaining the placement of mirrors and the position of fingers confused me at first, yet when I finally understood, I felt a glow of triumph. I took a copper mark from my pocket and tried one of the tricks. The coin dropped from my fingers and clattered across the floorboards, startling Drystan awake.

"Sorry," I said.

"What are you trying to do?" he asked.

I showed him the page. He studied the drawing before setting it aside.

He clasped my hands and walked me through the trick, showing me how to hide the coin between my fingers. His palms were warm, and a blush crept up my neck. Drystan met my eyes. We were inches apart, and everything in me seemed to stop—my breath, my heartbeat, my ability to blink. For a moment, I wondered if I'd paused time again. I felt like we were back beneath the big top, him Prince Leander and me Princess Iona. I remembered how warm his lips had been, the barest scratch of stubble on my chin. The smell of greasepaint and his skin. I craved him as much as a bee does nectar.

Drystan made the smallest sound in the back of his throat. My breath left in a rush, and we glanced away from each other.

Drystan walked the coin along his fingers and made it vanish just as he had when we'd first arrived on Maske's doorstep. His hands were steady.

"There," he said, his voice rough. "You try." We were ignoring what had nearly happened. Even if I didn't know Aenea's fate, my feelings for her hovered between us like an invisible barrier.

I took the coin from him, the metal warmed by our hands. I tried to copy Drystan's movements and made the coin disappear, tucked safely in my palm. Drystan clapped, and my chest filled with pride.

"This hasn't been too sore for your hands?" he asked.

Now he noticed.

"I, um, heal quickly," I said, swallowing.

"I'll say," Drystan shook his head. "I dislocated a shoulder once. I couldn't move it for weeks, and you're already out of your sling."

"How's your book?" I asked.

Drystan let me change the subject. "Clearly riveting, given it sent me straight to sleep. All the salacious bits have been made as uninteresting as possible. Grimwood seems better. I'll read that one when you're finished."

He stood and stretched, the joints in his neck cracking, before scrutinizing the books. He reached up for a volume on the top shelf, and his shirt was short enough to reveal a flash of pale skin again. I stood and ran my hands down the thighs of my trousers.

"Fancy a pot of tea?" I asked, hoping I didn't sound too panicked.

"Please," Drystan said, sprawling back in his armchair and cracking the cover. I glared at the top of his head. He was infuriatingly calm. Or maybe he simply didn't quite feel what I did.

I fled to the kitchen. Somewhere above me in Maske's workshop, a drill whined against metal.

I thumbed through a pile of old newspapers on the table while I waited for the hiss of the kettle. The headlines were the usual doom and gloom—prices would rise on glass due to a temporary shortage of shipments from Kymri. The Foresters had unsuccessfully lobbied Parliament for more seats on the council, so there would likely be more protests. Infected meat had caused sickness in the southern coastal town of Ava. Lord Chokecherry had been caught having an affair with a woman from the lower classes and wanted to leave his wife to marry his mistress. It was causing an absolute scandal.

I hadn't reached out to my brother, not sure how to do so safely. Had he seen the newsletter articles about Drystan and me? If I had gone home with him when I'd seen him on my last night in Sicion, I might have avoided so much trouble. Even though I didn't forgive my parents, I still found myself wondering what they were doing, or how often they thought of their long-gone daughter.

I threw the newspaper with the horrible sketches of Drystan and me into the stove in disgust, watching the edges of the paper curl like the dying leaves of autumn outside.

The kettle gave a piercing cry.

• • • •

That night, I'd hoped to fall asleep as soon as my head hit the pillow, but my mind wouldn't rest. I eventually gave up, taking out the soapstone figurine of the Kedi from the drawer of my bedside table and running a fingertip over its rough face. It was the full moon again, marking a month since we'd left the circus. The Penglass outside glowed its brightest, and I felt its magic calling to me, dancing on the air.

The moonlight through the stained-glass window illuminated the Kedi figurine. I turned on my side, staring at the back of Drystan's head on the other side of the room, wondering if he was asleep or only pretending.

I put the figurine back and took out Anisa's Aleph, trying to read the carved glyphs on it. The metal was warm. I wanted to ask her about Timur, the blurred man, and the vision in Twisting the Aces. But there was nothing. The Aleph might as well have been inert, non-Vestige metal.

There, in the quiet of the middle of the night, my eyes burned with tears, and a sharp pain bloomed in my chest.

I kept thinking of Aenea. The way she looked after we kissed, her lips parted. The feel of her pressed against my side as I rested my chin on her shoulder, her hair tickling my face. The sight of her flying off the trapeze, flipping and catching the bar at just the right moment. The dimple in one cheek as she smiled. All the little facets that made her Aenea. Whether she was alive or not, she was lost to me. I should let her go.

When my tears finally ran dry, I fell asleep with the Aleph in my hand.

● ● ● ●

I walked through a blue fog so thick it suffocated me. I couldn't see, I couldn't hear. I stumbled, my arms out in front of me, desperate to know I was not the only one in this strange and silent world.

Slowly, the vapor lifted and my home of Ven rose from the gloom and the purple-grey of dusk. I flicked my wings in relief, running until I had enough momentum for them to carry me into the air along with a burst of power.

I sang a thanksgiving to the coming night as I flew over the trees and the glowing Venglass. I followed the stream that would lead me home. Soon, I would slip into bed next to my Relean, and he would kiss the back of my neck. The dim light would illuminate his face. His hair was a dark, iridescent green, and his closed eyelids would hide those brilliant irises of blue, with hints of copper and green. He had a little spot of black in the bottom of his right iris. His features might change a little life to life, body to body, but those eyes were always the same.

Our charges would be sleeping in the next room, and all would be as it should be. I had been away too long, visiting the Alder in their misty lands.

But though I flew straight to the Ven, it grew no closer. The bright light faded, until the domes were as dark as death. I hovered in the air as the wind rose. Strange new buildings of stone grew around the Venglass.

I landed on a dome, looking out over this new world I did not recognize. The land was nearly dead, no longer verdant and lush. Humans passed below me and even if they looked up, they did not see me. I was nothing but a spectre among them.

The Chimaera had disappeared. My charges, lost. My Relean, gone. Magic had leached from the ruined world.

"This is a dream," I said on top of the dome. My hands rested against the glass, glowing softly. "I am dreaming. This is not me. I am Micah. I am Micah Grey."

We smiled sadly as we looked out over the world I knew as ours and that Anisa saw only as a ruin of her own.

"Of course this is not your nightmare, little Kedi," she said with our mouth. "It is mine."

• • • •

The weeks slid past. Autumn chilled to early winter, and the streets of Imachara were blanketed with snow. The theatre was always cold, and I often wore Cyan's coat inside, as well as three pairs of socks.

Drystan, Cyan, and I spent so much time shuffling, palming, or hiding cards behind our fingers that blisters, then callouses, formed on our fingertips. Next, we moved onto coins, billiard balls, and flowers from paper cones. We learned how to pick locks and escape from handcuffs. Eventually, I felt as though my fingers were so strong and nimble they had a mind of their own. Next, Maske taught us to place needles in our mouths and draw them out, linked, on a piece of string. My tongue was sore from dozens of minor pinpricks, and I kept fearing I'd accidentally swallow a needle.

He helped the three of us learn how to string the tricks together to create an act that could last half an hour or so. He'd make us do them over and over, watching from the front row of the theatre. At first, we made mistake after mistake. I'd keep tangling up my handkerchiefs, or Drystan would drop a billiard ball. The flowers kept making Cyan sneeze. Maske would watch us with narrowed eyes, considering how someone on the street might see us from every possible angle. He'd point out the smallest flaw, and he expected perfection. While part of me wanted to curse his name, I was also glad he was pushing us so hard. I wanted to impress him.

Once the worst of the cold snap had passed and Maske had decided we'd passed muster, he sent us out into the world to see if we could earn our keep with magic.

8

THE FORESTERS

"We are the roots of society—we give them the soil and the water to help the Twelve Trees of Nobility thrive and receive naught in return but the worms of empty promises. It is time, my brethren, to step into the light and take charge of our own destinies."

PAMPHLET OF THE FORESTER PARTY

"Sir, please, do you have a cigarette I could borrow?" Cyan asked.

Drystan, Cyan, and I stood on a street corner in the Brass District. It was cold, but not frigid. The three of us unrolled an Arrasian rug and propped up a painted, wooden sign proclaiming "Magic and Wonders." The man gave us a mistrustful look, but he patted the pocket of his winter coat and drew out a cigarette. His wife looked on.

"Thank you, sir," Cyan said, a step away from batting her eyelashes at him. It'd taken us a long time to convince someone to take a punt on us, but we might have found our first mark. Cyan was doing the bulk of the crowd work, and Drystan and I were doing the magic tricks.

I rolled up my sleeves. Taking a pack of cards from the pocket of my jacket, I let the man pick it up to see it was a normal deck. I'd decided to dress as a boy today, though the Glamour was still safely tucked beneath my Lindean binder. I felt the pendant humming gently beneath my shirt. When the man passed it back, I tapped the cigarette gently against the top of the cards. Then, I made it seem as though the cigarette passed through the deck before giving it back to him, completely unharmed.

"Fantastic!" the woman exclaimed.

I gave her a small bow. "Thank you, my lady."

Drystan and I next presented her with a bouquet of paper flowers. A small crowd gathered around us. Though we hid it well, we were both nervous that someone would stand at the wrong angle and see how the tricks were done. But the group was appreciative, and soon we heard the clink of coins thrown into our offering box. Cyan turned on the charm, urging more people to come and see some of the most promising young magicians in Elada.

A man in a bowler hat had lingered nearby to watch, holding a bottle of dandelion and burdock cordial. Drystan asked the man for the bottle, which he set on the ground. I licked my lips. This next bit was more complicated.

"Pick a card, any card," Drystan said. I held my breath as he performed the act. He shuffled the deck several times, the man cut it, and then Drystan leaned the deck against the bottle on the ground. People strained to see. Drystan waved his hands over the deck, murmuring a "spell," which was really a list of random words in Temri that Cyan had taught us: "apple, butter knife, shoe."

The chosen card levitated out of the pack. We bowed to scattered applause.

Drystan had performed it perfectly. After hiding away in the theatre, it was a relief to see him joking and acting closer to the fool he'd been in the circus. He wasn't making the audience laugh as overtly as he had as a clown, but he was good at crowd work and knew exactly how to put them at ease. I envied him that.

The man in the bowler hat gave us a nod, threw a few coins into the box with the rest of the crowd, retrieved his drink, and ambled away.

Over the next half hour, we made coins and cards disappear and appear. Cyan did an excellent job luring people in with simple bits of magic. Usually, the coins the people gave us for the tricks ended up clinking into our collection tin. People seemed to be enjoying our show, and I was feeling rather content until the skin of the back of my neck prickled.

I stiffened, nearly ruining the trick. Drystan recovered for me, having a flower appear from behind a lady's ear. She tucked her brown hair behind her ears and dimpled at him.

I peered at every face, but I didn't see those unforgettably-forgettable features or that distinctive wide-brimmed hat anywhere. I tried to relax into the performance, but anxiety tangled in my gut. Anisa's Aleph was up in the loft of the Kymri Theatre. She'd been so silent these last few weeks that she likely wouldn't have been any help at all. Part of me was relieved not to hear her mysterious whispering, but another corner felt abandoned.

A young boy and his father paused, interested, but we apologized and packed up our kit as quickly as we could manage. A few tried to bribe us into explaining how it was done, but we demurred, stating that a sorcerer would surely curse us if we shared our secrets.

I tried to reassure myself. It was our first time out and about since our day visiting Twisting the Aces—of course I was paranoid about being found by the man who likely pursued me. The cold seeped into our bones.

Of course, our luck wobbled again. Two Policiers made a loop around the block. The first time, I'd stiffened, but they'd only looked at us suspiciously. The second time, they confronted us. Cyan edged away.

"Do you have a permit?" one of the Policiers asked Drystan and me. He was tall, with well-groomed muttonchops and a ruddy nose. His partner was shorter and muscled, with a ginger beard. Their pointed hats gleamed under the faint winter sun.

"Did we need one?" I asked, my heart hammering, hoping false ignorance might save us.

"Aye, you do, and surely a pair of buskers know that," Muttonchops said. He seemed more exasperated than angry. "Come into the Constabulary and you can apply for one."

We couldn't go anywhere near the station. Our admittedly bad sketches might be pinned to the wall, or we might somehow give ourselves away. How long had we been performing? The humming of my Glamour around my neck had grown quieter. According to the clock in the square, in about twenty minutes, our illusion would fall.

Drystan and I exchanged a look and bolted.

Drystan sprinted across the cobblestones, leaving behind our props, dodging the ginger-bearded man's grasping hands. I tried to follow, ducking and weaving, but I wasn't so lucky.

Muttonchops grabbed me by the scruff of the neck. I twisted, trying to wriggle out of my coat to free myself, but he held on.

"Ach, come on," Ginger Beard said, picking up our collection tin and rattling the coins inside. "Pay your fine, apply for your permit, and it'll be grand. We can't let you get away with this, or every damn corner will be full of people strumming an instrument or making their little automatons dance."

"Would that be so terrible?" I asked, honestly.

I swore he almost laughed, but I had to remember he was a Policier, and I was still a fugitive. I glanced at the clock on the opposite side of the square. Fifteen minutes.

I was wriggling like a worm, so Ginger Beard sighed and wrenched my hands behind my back, handcuffing me. Drystan would be nearby, but he couldn't help me without winding up in handcuffs, too. He was the one who had killed someone. Cyan was tucked in the opening of an alleyway near our props. She met my eyes and nodded, once. Strangely, the Policiers had paid her no mind, even though she'd clearly been working with us.

The handcuffs were tight, the metal cold. Maske had taught us the basics of how to escape from them, but that didn't mean it was easy to do, especially as I was being frog marched down the cobbled streets.

I had a hairpin up my sleeve, and I slid it into my palm, willing myself not to drop it. The locks in handcuffs were usually a simple, spring-loaded bar with teeth. Ginger Beard was luckily walking at Muttonchop's side, rather than behind. I shimmied the hairpin, inserting it into the serrated metal. It was a long two minutes, but eventually, I pressed the metal hard enough to spring the lock free just as we reached the Constabulary station.

"Sir?" I said, bringing my hands to my front and showing the dangling handcuff. I didn't try to run away. Instead, I smiled at him, trying to be every inch the performer.

Ginger Beard glowered, but Muttonchops laughed, as if despite himself.

"How'd you manage that?" he asked. I'd dropped the hairpin, so there was no evidence.

"Magic, of course," I said, taking the cuff off my remaining wrist and handing them back. "Can I show you another trick?"

"What the—" Ginger Beard started.

"Oh, go on, then," Muttonchops said.

I showed them one of the card tricks Drystan and I had been performing, even if I was acutely aware of time running out. My fingers were stiff from both the cold and the handcuffs, but I willed myself not to drop a card or hesitate. By the end of it, both Policiers were smiling.

I had five minutes of illusion left, at best.

"You're not bad," Muttonchops said.

"Thank you," I said. "I'm still rather new at this, and I really didn't know I needed a permit," I lied through my teeth. Even though it was pricy, we should have paid the coin for it.

He considered me. I looked younger than I was when I dressed as a boy, so he might have thought me fifteen or sixteen instead of eighteen. I widened my eyes, hoping I looked like a doleful puppy who'd been told off.

"Ach, fine. You can get a warning this time. Come in and grab a permit now, and it'll be right as rain." He walked me up the stairs, one hand around my upper arm.

My smile stiffened, and I felt my heartbeat in my throat. "Of course. Is there a loo, though? I'm afraid I rather desperately need a piss."

Ginger Beard sighed. "Aye, there's one inside."

I felt Cyan and Drystan's gaze on my back of my neck as I entered the Constabulary headquarters. Muttonchops pointed me to the toilet and told me to be quick about it.

I practically sprinted towards it. There was no lock, for security reasons, I imagined, so I leaned against the door, fumbling for the Glamour pendant beneath my shirt. I was in the nick of time—the reflection in the scratched mirror showed auburn streaks in my hair, even if my features had stayed disguised. I switched off the Glamour and actually used the loo. I washed my hands, my palms shaking. Moment of truth—if it didn't reset, then a different boy walking out of the bathroom was going to raise many more questions.

I flicked the switch, held it to my chest like a prayer, and nearly wept with relief when I saw my false features laid over my real ones. I tucked the pendant back beneath my shirt, steeled myself, and made my way back to the Constabulary.

I used every coin in the collection tin and my pockets to scrape a permit for a month, and I bought it right under the gaze of the awful posters of Drystan and me on the opposite wall. I had to give my false name, but luckily they didn't ask for more than that.

Muttonchops was smoking a cigarette outside the Constabulary. "I trust I won't see you again, here, yeah, boy?" he asked when I held up my permit.

"You won't, sir!"

He waved me away, and I didn't need to be told twice. I let the smile I'd pasted onto my face drop, and as soon as I turned the corner, I leaned against the wall, my knees nearly giving out from under me.

● ● ● ●

"Lady's nightgown, that was close," Drystan said, finding me a few minutes later. Cyan trailed behind him. Both of them had our knapsacks of supplies on their shoulders, and Cyan clutched the rolled-up rug.

"I caught the end of your act with the Policiers," Cyan said. "Quick thinking."

"Thanks." My mind was racing. "But, extortionate as the permit is, we really can't risk going without one again."

She nodded.

My heart in my throat, we started back towards the Kymri Theatre. It seemed our bad luck was still with us, though, as soon my ears caught the far-off sounds of chanting. Cyan's head turned towards it, too. Drystan took a little longer to pick it up, for his senses weren't as keen as mine.

"Another protest," Cyan said. "Come on, let's try to avoid it."

Too late.

"Equality! Fell the Tree!" I heard, over and over, their voices rising to a fevered pitch. The chanting was charged and angry. A group of people holding signs marched down the street, and before we knew it, we were swept up with them and herded toward Golden Square in front of the Royal Snakewood Palace with no choice but to follow the protest's stream.

The horde blocked traffic. Men and women driving carriages and carts yelled obscenities, adding to the fray. The gates of the Palace were locked, grim guards posted behind the wrought iron. The crush of people made me uncomfortable. We were hemmed in on all sides. Folk kept bumping into me, hard. I grabbed Drystan's hand, afraid of losing him in the crowd. He gripped mine tightly.

The protest finally reached the gates of the Palace. It was a grand, sprawling granite structure in the north of the city. The total grounds were larger than the entire village of Cowl, the place where the circus had practiced before arriving in the capital. Three Penglass domes rose above the roof, integrated into the architecture of the Palace. I wondered if the young Princess Royal was peeking out from one of the many windows.

Drystan's elbow dug into my side. Cyan's arms were wrapped tightly around herself.

I couldn't believe how many people there were. Hundreds, maybe even close to a thousand, all crammed into the square. When I'd seen that poster, and even when I'd read the newspaper articles about the Foresters, I'd thought this a relatively small faction. But there, surrounded by so many people, I realized that anti-monarchy sentiment had grown a lot stronger than I'd realized.

Drystan pointed toward a staircase at the corner of the square. While it was filled with people, it wasn't the same crush, and we'd be able to take the pedestrian bridge over one of the Penglass domes and hopefully escape the crowds.

We pushed our way through the throng. A man stepped on my

toe, and I yelped. Someone's cologne was overwhelming. People were chanting so many slogans simultaneously that I could no longer tell what anyone was saying.

A commotion at the podium in front of the Palace made us pause. A man appeared, and in the push and pull of the throng, he was the picture of calm, holding his arms out. He was tall and blocky, wearing simple, homespun clothes, though they fit him well, and his face was hidden by a plain black mask.

Around me, people murmured his name. Timur. The leader of the Foresters. Anisa had warned me of a blurred man in the circus, and my vision in Twisting the Aces had showed a man with a mask over the lower half of his face. Was this him, then? He was too far away for me to make out his features in any detail.

When I'd asked Drystan about the leader of the Foresters after seeing that poster, he had told me Timur had supposedly worked some mid-level bureaucratic role in the government before he'd grown disillusioned with the whole system. No one knew his true name, and he'd only recently started appearing in public.

"People of Imachara," he said, and his voice carried well enough over the crowd that he must have had a Vestige Projector tied around his throat. The chanting quieted.

"It is time to reclaim our rights," he said. "For too long, we have been the servants of those who have installed themselves above us. Even as prices rise, they grow richer and let us grow poorer. They will never let us rise, no matter how hard we work. It is long past time to bring equality to the entire tree of Eladan society, from the lowest roots to the highest of branches."

People cheered and he smiled at them magnanimously. Something about his manner reminded me of the ringmaster of the circus. He had the air of a showman about him. The air of a liar.

"I don't wish for violence. This change can happen peacefully, with goodwill on both sides. We deserve a government where the people have the right to make the decisions of our country, instead of the monarchy and the nobility who keep secrets from us. Elada is wearing down. As more Vestige artefacts run out of power, we are left weaker and more vulnerable than before. Something has to change. Something has to give. Don't you agree?"

"Aye!" People cried out, stamping their feet.

"We need far more from the former colonies than they want to give. They are bleeding us dry, my brothers and sisters, and I don't blame them for it. We drained them for centuries, after all. But with a new government, free from the taint of the empire and the Snakewoods who kept us all under their blue-blooded thumbs, we can make a true and lasting peace with our neighbors."

He was saying all the right things, but something about his manner put me on edge. He was clearly reveling in the approval of the crowd. If he did ever force a new system of government, of course he'd want to install himself at the top. Was he only another man who wanted more power?

"We must have a united front!" he called. "There are new dangers rising. I hear whispers of creatures with powers that should be impossible. Some say they're as powerful as Chimaera, but these are no fairy tales from myth and legend. Some of their abilities might be more dangerous than Vestige. If that's true, I don't trust the Snakewoods to protect us from them. Do you?"

A chorus of "No!" and "Nay!" surrounded us.

Drystan and Cyan stiffened at my side.

"Nonsense," Cyan said, her voice shaking.

If only she knew, I thought.

Timur's words drove people into a frenzy, despite him saying he was open to peace. A fight broke out nearby. People backed away to give them room. One of the brawlers picked up his discarded sign that read: "LEAVES FOR ALL". He smashed it over the other man's head, and something about the gesture reminded me too much of Drystan swiping a cane with a dagger hidden inside. Red blood streamed down the skin of the other man's forehead. I caught the phantom smell of whisky, ether, and smoke. Half of me was there, in the thick of the crowd, and the rest was locked back in Bil's cart, with ropes around my wrists.

Next to me, Drystan had frozen, pale and clammy, as he watched the man stagger to his feet, wooden splinters in his hair. More joined the fray, swinging fists, feet kicking, elbows striking ribs. I heard the distant wail of sirens. A group of Policiers pushed through the crowd and more sentries emerged from the Palace gates.

The sirens spurred me to tug Drystan, half-dragging him the rest of the way through the crowd and to the staircase, Cyan following close behind. I shouldered my way past people perched on it for a view, Drystan holding onto my waist. We finally reached the top and crossed the narrow bridge; the smaller Penglass domes below had cropped up so close together they looked like a cluster of bubbles.

On the other side, it was blessedly quieter, and we were free.

9

THE PHILOSOPHER & THE FOOL

"Your whole life, you are told by society what is right and what is wrong. What you should do and what you should not. What makes a good citizen and what makes a traitorous one. What happens, then, when you do everything you are not meant to? Break down each and every barrier? Find out how good you are by how evil you can become?

Some say this is how the Alder became great. We might never reach those heights, but what might we unlock within ourselves if we learn how far we can fall?"

THE TYNDALL PHILOSOPHY, ALVIS TYNDALL

Up in the loft, Drystan loosened his cravat. He glanced at me, then away, as I unlaced my boots.

I was shivering badly from the hours outside, the run-in with the Policiers, then the crush of the Forester protest.

I slid into bed, fully clothed, drawing my duvet around myself. I hadn't ended up taking one of the empty bedrooms, but I always dressed in the drafty bathroom downstairs. Drystan was less self-conscious, often lounging on his bed without his shirt after a bath, despite the cold, leaving me studiously avoiding staring at the flat planes of his stomach and chest.

"Let's not tell Maske about the Policiers," Drystan said. "It'll only spook him."

"Sure," I said.

We lapsed into silence. His gaze went distant, and I knew he, too, was disturbed by the afternoon's events.

"You're chewing on a question," he said. "I can feel it. Out with it, but remember, you might have to answer one in return."

I smiled faintly at the reference to our old game. His hair fell over his forehead, and I fought the urge to push it back from his face. His hair was long enough that with his next cut, the last of the white dye would be gone and only the gold would remain. Part of me would miss that reminder of Drystan the White Clown. Freckles dotted his nose and cheeks as though dusted with cinnamon. He went to the furnace in the corner, rekindling the fire.

There was a knock at the door of the loft.

"Come in!" I called.

"Can you open the door?" came Cyan's muffled voice. "My hands are full."

Drystan did, and Cyan came in holding two steaming mugs of coffee. "I thought you two might want these after everything."

"Desperately," I said from my nest of covers.

"It's been quite a day," she said.

"I'll say," Drystan allowed.

She hesitated, her eyes darting between us. She opened her mouth, then seemed to change her mind. I wondered what she'd wanted to discuss: the protest or the run-in with the Policers. I didn't fancy talking about either.

"It's my turn for dinner," she said instead. "Roast chicken and veg."

"Sounds great," I said, falsely cheery. "Thanks for the coffee."

The door clicked shut behind her. Drystan and I stared at each other, at a loss. There was so much to say, but I didn't know where to begin.

I cracked first. "We haven't really talked about that night, have we?"

"We have successfully avoided discussing many things for weeks, yes," Drystan said. I stared at him.

"Do you want to talk about it?"

"No. But we can speak of other things, if you like." The fire blazed merrily in the hearth, already taking the worst of the chill from the air. He hesitated, then sat at the foot of my bed. "I've a question for you, actually. I haven't been sure how to raise it."

"Go for it," I said, though I tensed beneath the covers.

He pressed his lips together. "It's hard to phrase it like I want to. In the theatre, you dress in trousers and look like the boy I thought was a girl in the circus. In the dress, you transform and yet you don't. I have been wondering. How do you feel about it all? Which do you prefer, if you favor a side at all?"

I turned the questions over in my mind.

"I'm fine with being different." It felt freeing to say that aloud. "Overall, I prefer the trousers, and to be seen as a boy, but it doesn't feel wrong to occasionally skip over to the other side, if that makes sense. They're both me."

He nodded. "I see."

"What I don't like is that I never know how people will react if they find out the truth that physically and mentally, I'm between. It's why I haven't told Maske or Cyan."

"Was that why you largely hid it from Aenea, too?"

I kept my grief tightly controlled, but it would break free in countless little ways. I clutched the mug of coffee to warm my fingers and took a sip, letting it heat me from within.

"I was adopted, you see," I said. "A doctor gave me to them for a sum of money."

A faint line appeared between Drystan's eyes.

"It was Doctor Pinecrest," I added.

He sucked in a breath. "The Royal Physician?"

"He wasn't back then, but yes."

"Why?"

"No idea. But me being me, well, it risked all my mother's plans. She was ashamed of me, you see. I was a liability, a drain on those extra finances if I never married. I even had a serious offer before I left."

His eyes went wide. "Who from?"

"Oswin Hawthorne."

"Good family. Nice kid, from what I remember."

"Yes. It might not have been any great romance, exactly, but we were friends and I expect we would have been a good enough team. But my mother . . . she wanted me to have surgery, so his family wouldn't suspect I likely couldn't have children, or risk the secret getting out. I overheard them, one night. They were going to do it whether I wanted it or not. Might not have even told me, first."

He inhaled sharply. I couldn't look at him.

"I'm sorry," he said. "That's . . . I don't even know what to say to that."

"What is there to say?" I balled the fabric of the quilt in my hands. "I couldn't even tell you, in the end, could I? You discovered it."

He was silent for a time. "Do you regret me learning of it?"

"No," I said, glancing up at him and realizing it was true. "And you haven't treated me any differently. I do want you to know I'm grateful for that."

"You're still you." He shrugged as if it was nothing instead of everything. My throat closed.

Drystan chose his next words with care. "Do you think it's as rare as your parents said?"

I strove for a nonchalance I didn't feel. "I was trotted to plenty of doctors during my youth," I continued. "I'm sure there are others. It can't just be me." I swallowed. "I'm not sure that matters as much as what else is different about me."

Drystan's face rippled with trepidation. "What do you mean?"

I licked my lips. "Remember that night on the dock when we drank all that awful gin?"

He laughed. "I mean, vaguely. Because of the gin."

"We spoke about whether Chimaera might be real or not."

"You pushed back on that quite hard, as I recall."

"Because I was afraid of the truth we later both discovered."

"Violet," he whispered. He'd been so in shock, I wasn't entirely sure how much he remembered, but here was my confirmation.

"Violet. Juliet. Tauro. All three of them are Chimaera. And, though I look human, I think I might be one, too. You saw what I did with the Penglass, and how time went . . . strange." I wanted to tell him about the Phantom Damselfly, but something—maybe a lingering enchantment from Anisa herself—stilled my tongue.

He stared into the distance. "It's a lot to take in, but I'm not sure I'm entirely surprised. At university, I read a banned scientific paper looking at birth anomalies over the past century. They seem to be on the rise. Babies born with scaled legs, a tail, webbed toes, that sort of thing. Didn't mention anything about . . . other abilities, though."

"And what happens to these babies?"

"The doctors . . ." he trailed off.

"Operated on them?" I finished, hunching my shoulders.

He winced. "Yes. Barbaric. But I suppose removing a tail is different from—"

"What's between my legs," I said, shortly.

He didn't bat an eyelid. "Well, exactly. If I'd had a tail removed, I don't think I'd miss it all that much. The other, however . . ."

He shocked me into a laugh, dispelling some of the tension. I drank my coffee, then decided to take advantage of his talkative mood. "Your turn. Why did you run away from being a Hornbeam? How'd you find Maske, and why did you leave?"

He didn't answer for so long that I wasn't sure he would.

"Do you realize, Micah," he began, "that despite all you've seen, even recently, you're still remarkably sheltered?"

"I am not," I said, churlish, but deep down, I knew he was right.

He sighed and turned to me, the gas lamp between us playing on the angular planes of his face, the circles under his eyes. Though he hid it well, he suffered. I did, too, but I hadn't killed a man.

As Gene, I would have hugged my friend Anna without a second thought when she was upset. I'd not touched Drystan often, except during the pantomime and that night everything fell apart. How often did boys hug each other, just for comfort? My arms stayed heavy at my sides.

I did not tell him to forget it, that I didn't need to know. Because I did.

We stared at each other, his blue eyes boring into mine.

"Do you want the long version or the short version?" he asked.

"The long one, of course."

He sighed, composing his thoughts.

"I was raised with the best of everything," he began. "And all that sweetness turned me rotten. By the time I went to Royal Snakewood University at sixteen, I was an absolute arsehole."

"University at sixteen?" I asked.

"I was a precocious arsehole. I didn't play well with others. I always wanted to show off my cleverness at every opportunity. I used people, then discarded them when they were no longer interesting to me. I studied philosophy and delighted in debate and annihilating the other students. I had to win, no matter the cost. So, of course, by the time I came across the philosophy of Alvis Tyndall, I was ripe to fall for his bullshit. Have you heard of him?"

I shook my head.

"He's pretty obscure, and the monarchy tried to censor him, which of course made it all the more tantalizing. He believed that you can't truly know where you fall on the scale of light and dark until you try to do your worst. So you can guess where that led. I decided to become a demon."

I swallowed.

He leaned back on his elbows, the light gilding his eyelashes. "When I'd first started at university, I'd been good with money, saving most of my allowance. One night, I headed to a card den, deciding that'd be a good vice to taste. I quickly blew through every copper I had. A few months later, I found myself in a Lerium den, and with the first hit of that drug, I was lost."

I'd heard of Lerium, of course, but no one I knew had tried it. It was made of poppies but also, rumor had it, trace amounts of Vestige metal. It was very addictive, very expensive, and extremely seductive.

"I stole from my family," he said. "First, it was coin. Eventually, I took my mother's jewels." His mouth twisted. "Some of them had been in our families for generations and had sentimental value far beyond their worth. I should have stolen the Vestige instead, in retrospect."

He sighed. "My father was furious. My mother tried to be understanding and find me help. In return, I ended up kissing another boy at an afternoon tea, in full sight of everyone, purely for the scandal of it."

I could easily imagine that. The titters in the conservatory. People whispering behind gloved hands.

"I didn't stop there, of course. I stole sensitive documents from my father's study and made sure they made their way to the press. Didn't even sell the secrets. I left a young woman I didn't care for with child."

"You're a father?" I gasped.

His eyes were shadowed. "She didn't carry to term."

He didn't clarify if that meant she'd miscarried or had an abortion, and I didn't ask.

"But because I didn't do the right thing and offer my hand, her reputation was ruined." He paused. "I knew when I pursued her that I didn't want anything serious, but that didn't stop me. I don't regret many things, but I do regret how I treated her."

My breath caught in my throat. I'd heard some rumors of the wild older Hornbeam boy, but not many specifics.

Drystan fiddled with the edge of his pillowcase. "Eventually, since I wasn't writing my papers or showing up to lectures, and my parents refused to pay for my tuition, that was me kicked out of university."

My skin prickled in unease. "What did you do next?"

He ran a hand along the stubble of his jawline. None of this had been easy for him to share, for all he was doing to keep his body language lax and languid.

"I found the underbelly of Imachara," he said. "And it's dimmer and darker than you could imagine. There were many times when I could have died, and didn't realize how close a line I walked . . ." He trailed off.

"That was where I found Maske," Drystan continued, eyes downcast. "He went by a pseudonym and wore a disguise, for as soon as anyone learned a magician was in their midst, he'd be accused of being a card sharp."

"Which he was." I'd not been sure how to feel about that since I'd learned it. Drystan had taught me the rudiments of card cheating when we took the train from Sicion to Cowl, but that was only for sport. Using the tricks to steal from others was another matter entirely.

Drystan, as usual, guessed my thoughts. "Don't pity those he stole from. They were Lerium merchants or Vestige arms dealers, pimps, or gang lords. They were, as you might imagine, a very dangerous group to steal from."

"And why were you mingling with them?" I asked, already suspecting the answer.

A side of his mouth tweaked. "Because I was one of them."

I wrapped my arms around myself. Drystan wasn't that much older than me, but in that moment, I felt so much younger.

"What did you do?"

"I helped run Lerium for the Antiaris family."

I let out a low breath. Even I had heard of one of the most notorious crime families in Imachara.

"I was . . . involved, if you could call it that, with the drug lord's son, Garrett. I was deep into the maws of Lerium. I kept gambling, trying to get the money back, thinking maybe, if I got enough, I might be able to find my way back into my family's good graces."

He shook his head. "I knew that was futile, but I kept trying all the same." He sighed, settling deeper into the bed and turning towards me. I hung onto his every word.

"After being roundly beaten by Maske at the poker table one night, I suspected he cheated. I've always been pretty good at sensing when people are lying, like when I found you in the circus tent."

"I wasn't very good at telling falsehoods," I agreed.

"I suppose you've had more practice, now."

That bit deep.

"Sorry, Micah," he said, realizing he'd hurt me.

I nodded, not meeting his eyes. "What happened after you found Maske?"

Drystan ran a hand through his hair. "I asked him to teach me."

"And he did," I said, a statement rather than a question.

"Yes, but under the condition that I quit Lerium. He helped me through the sorry weeks as I kicked the habit." Emotions played over Drystan's face, and he shuddered.

"Once I was clean and learned the trick of it, we rarely played at the same table. We did well for ourselves, but one night, Maske took too much, or someone guessed. Maske was . . . he was in a bad state when I found him. If I'd left him there, he would have died."

He exhaled, harsh.

"I brought Maske back to the theatre. He'd helped me, so I helped him. When he was better, we both left the dark parts of Imachara behind. He promised me I could have whatever I needed of him. A life debt. Eventually, I grew restless and realized I had to move on, and I found the circus."

He sat up and gave me a bow from his bed, waving his arms in a flourish. "And that is the bare-bones tale of Drystan Hornbeam."

He had left much of it out, I was sure, but he'd told me the salient points. Even back in the circus, he'd said he'd studied philosophy, and it'd turned him into a fool. Rich noble. University student. Lerium addict. Card sharp. Clown. And now: stage magician's apprentice.

"Thank you," I said. "I know it can't have been easy to share." I couldn't judge him too harshly for what he'd done and the crimes he'd committed. Especially considering he had killed for me.

He shrugged. "I suppose we're even." He rose, grabbing his towel and heading to the washroom for a bath. The rest of the evening passed in our new normality. Dinner with Cyan and Maske. More reading by gas light until our eyes grew heavy.

"Good night, Micah," I thought I heard Drystan say as I drifted to sleep later. "Sweet dreams."

10

THE VANISHING GIRL

"A magician creates magic and mesmerizes the audience. But it is a pantomime, and the audience knows that it's a ruse. It's in the name: a 'magic trick'. They play along as the magician tugs his sleeves to show there is nothing hidden within them, or that the top hat is empty of a rabbit, or eggs, or flowers. Beneath the façade, there is only sleight of hand, wires and contraptions, misdirection at a key moment.

But what the audience does not realize is that it's not always trickery. Or at least, not quite."

THE UNPUBLISHED MEMOIRS OF JASPER MASKE:
THE MASKE OF MAGIC

Three days later, the distant strike of a blacksmith's anvil echoed as the four of us made our way to Twisting the Aces, the wind whipping Cyan's and my skirts into a frenzy. The bell tinkled as we entered the magic shop.

"Hello, my dears," Lily said from behind the counter. "So wonderful to see you again." She had eyes only for Maske.

He greeted her gallantly before rattling off replacement machinery parts and their measurements. I picked out the smaller items we needed from the shelves—candles, invisible wire, magnets to conceal within clothing—setting the wares on the countertop. Cyan and Drystan loitered.

Lily flitted about the shop. "I think the spare cogs are up here," she muttered. Stretching up, she knocked something off the shelf. Out of reflex, I caught it and passed it to her—a square of deep purple glass, set in a frame of lacquered wood of red and blue.

"Oh, thank you, my sweet! I'd been wondering where that was," she said, hanging the glass in the window so that the playing cards dangling from strings shone purple in the light. She resumed her post behind the counter, wrapping the purchases.

My eye fell upon the cabinet with the Vestige artefacts for sale, but I kept my distance from the crystal ball, afraid of more visions.

"When we have our first show, we'll be sure to invite you," Maske said, smiling at her.

She clapped her hands together. "Oh, please do let me know when you perform! And I've heard such good things about your séances, too, you know. I consider myself quite the spiritualist. I went to a séance at Lady Archer's not long ago. She was a frequent customer of my late husband's, and my heart just about hammered out of my chest from the fear of it all, but it was ever so thrilling!"

"Thank you, Lily, that's very kind," Maske said, bowing to her. "Whenever you like, Cyan and I would be happy to hold a séance for you."

"I may take you up on that offer, Jasper."

I swore the man blushed. I noticed he didn't ask her to call him Maske. "Could we arrange for the larger purchases to be delivered?"

"Of course! Is tomorrow all right?"

"Tomorrow will be fine," he assured her.

She bobbed her head. "The Kymri Theatre, right? It's such a lovely building. Is it just as pretty inside?"

"Yes, though I'm afraid it's looking a little worse for wear, these days."

"A lick of paint, a few bouquets, and it'll spruce the place right up, I bet."

"I can hope." Maske nodded to us. "You three run off into town if you like. Lily and I have made arrangements to go for a cup of tea."

"Oh, have you now?" Drystan drawled, amused.

"Indeed." Maske's eyes flashed.

Drystan gave Lily a lavish bow before the three of us stepped out onto the cobbled street.

"She's a good-looking woman but I can't say I see what attracts him. She's exhausting," Drystan said, once free of the shop.

"She's nice!" I protested.

"She's very . . . enthusiastic," Cyan said, diplomatically. "Well, I'm afraid I've plans of my own, too, so I'll see you both back at the Kymri." She gave us a merry wave, and she was off.

"Wonder where she's going," Drystan said, too nonchalantly, once she was out of earshot.

"Me, too."

Drystan and I exchanged a look. We'd been suspicious of her at the start. When she hadn't turned us in, that had lessened. Still— where was she going?

"We're following her, aren't we?" I asked.

"Obviously."

Cyan headed to the Penny Rookeries, the poorer part town. Her plait thumped against her back as she kept up a brisk pace. She swept down a side street and paused in front of a crumbling tenement, clearly waiting for someone.

We'd been trailing her out of curiosity more than anything, but I was suddenly afraid that we were going to find out something we couldn't unlearn.

A few moments later, a man emerged. He was handsome, and about Cyan's age, with a blocky jaw, brown hair and eyes. He was obviously muscled beneath his cheap suit. They walked down the street side by side, close but not touching. He had the loping gait of a sailor.

Drystan and I followed in tense silence. Cyan and the man headed towards the beach. The sight of the sand and sea made my heart ache, reminding me of the crackle of a bonfire, stale candy floss, and cheap beer. On the beaches of Sicion, Cowl, and here in Imachara, I'd found and lost myself all over again.

Cyan and the unknown man sat down on a bench on the pier. Drystan and I went to a seafront pub, but we weren't close enough to overhear the conversation. The longer they talked, the more somber she became, which jarred against her usual cheerfulness. I maybe lipread enough to catch "it's no blessing" along with the shake of her head.

The sailor put his hand to Cyan's cheek. Their lips met, and he brought his other hand to the back of her neck. She rested her arms around his back.

"Well, looks like we were wrong there," I muttered, ashamed and a little embarrassed. "We'd been expecting the worst of her, but she's only snuck off to see her beau."

Cyan pulled away, leaning her head against the man's shoulder.

"Well, at least she's pulled someone rather fine," Drystan said.

"Good for Cyan," I said, laughing in agreement.

We wandered away from the docks and through the winding streets of Imachara. Yet once returned to the Kymri Theatre, my mind clouded over again. Part of me couldn't shake the thought that she was still hiding secrets.

● ● ● ●

Lily Verre delivered our supplies the next day.

"Lily! Come in, come in," Maske said. "Leave the parcels here in the hallway and then you must have a cup of tea. No, no, I insist, just leave them there in the hallway, that's fine."

Lily entered the kitchen, well turned out in a dress of cobalt blue trimmed in black lace. A ridiculous hat festooned with feathers and veils sat perched upon her head, her dark blond curls framing her face. She looked about in wide-eyed wonder.

"This place is a marvel. An utter marvel," she said. "I can't wait to see it when it's bright and cheery."

"Is it as gloomy as that, my dear Lily?" Maske asked.

"A little," she said, crinkling her eyes at him. "It needs a good dusting, that's for sure! I'd be happy to come lend a hand on an afternoon."

Two spots of color appeared on Maske's cheeks. "We'd be grateful, I'm sure."

Ricket stretched and padded her way over to investigate the new intruder. Lily crouched under the table to say hello.

Lily stayed for a cup of tea, chattering away, her mind jumping from topic to topic with a speed I could barely follow. Soon, I gave up and watched in amazement as she kept on. Drystan turned on the charm, telling jokes I recognized from the circus. Lily was an enthusiastic audience, her peal of laughter echoing through the kitchen.

Eventually, she paused to use the facilities. I showed her the way, wary that she might wander somewhere she shouldn't.

"Would you like to see what we've been up to, Lily?" Maske asked when we returned. "We were about to practice a new trick."

She squealed in delight.

Cyan entertained her while Drystan and I set up.

It was dark inside the spirit cabinet. The bonds chafed my wrists. My breath came faster.

"Are you ready?" Maske called from the stage outside the cabinet.

"Almost!" Drystan said. "Are you all right?" he whispered close to my ear.

"I've remembered I don't like being tied up overmuch." Memories of our last night at the circus and the more recent Policier handcuffs made me want to choke.

"Ah." He leaned closer. "Remember. You can escape these bonds at any time. You know exactly how." His lips rested against my forehead, light as a sparrow's wing. He pulled away before I could react, though our shoulders still touched. The dim light fell on the eyelashes resting against the curve of his cheek, the slope of his nose and the curl of his lips.

Inhale. Exhale.

"Ready!" Drystan called.

"On my count," Maske said. "One, two, three!"

In a thrice, we were free from our bonds. Drystan dropped through the trapdoor at the bottom, and I slipped behind the hidden mirrors at the back of the cabinet.

I heard the door open.

"As you can see," Maske said to our audience of Cyan and Lily, "the magicians have disappeared into the ether in the blink of an eye."

The door slammed shut. I counted in my head as Maske continued his patter, describing how magic was all around us and all we had to do was know how to tap into its hidden power. I fought down a smirk.

When I'd counted to twenty, I slipped back into the darkened spirit cabinet, looping my bonds loosely about my neck.

The door opened.

I stepped calmly onto the stage. Cyan clapped.

"Two have freed themselves and one has disappeared. Or has he?" Maske gestured to the empty audience. Drystan emerged onto the balcony, unruffled.

Cyan and Lily jumped up from their seats, clapping enthusiastically.

"Marvelous! Will this be the finale?" Lily asked.

"Oh, no, no, my dear." Maske took Cyan's hand and led her onto the stage. "This is simply practice. She will be the finale."

Cyan cocked her head. "Me?"

"I've designed a trick that shall be magnificent," he said. "It will take a lot of work to get it right, but if we succeed, we will be the talk of the town." On the stage, he always stood straighter, and his voice boomed.

Maske disappeared and brought out a cylinder of fabric held apart by metal hoops, the sleeves fashioned like crude, feathered wings.

"What . . . is that?" I asked. The strange contraption was made out of old, threadbare sheets.

"It's a prototype," he said, defensive. "Now, Sam and Amon, shift the cabinet, will you?"

It took me a moment to remember our false names. We obliged, the wheeled cabinet sliding away from the hidden trapdoor.

"Now, have you watched many pantomimes?" he asked, and I startled as Drystan stiffened beside me.

I starred in one as a girl, I thought. *With Drystan as my true love.* I still had all the lines memorized.

"They are fond of characters coming up through trap doors," Maske continued, oblivious. "They call it a star trap. A star trap can be dangerous. It's very quick," he said. "So, we will have to be careful. And we must trust ourselves and each other to perform."

"Are you sure it's not too dangerous?" I ventured. "We are amateurs, after all."

Maske waved away my fears. "I'll only be showing you the basics for now. But you will master it, and it will be a show to remember. Celia, will you stand over the trapdoor, please?"

Cyan shuffled over, her brow crinkled. Lily watched from the audience, her gaze avid. Maske slid the frame over Cyan's body, forming a decidedly odd dress.

Maske looked her over. "I'll make adjustments to the shape, never fear."

Cyan slid her arms into the winged sleeves. She held them out to her sides, stiffly.

Maske circled her. "I'm not sure what type of wings to make in the end. Feathers? Bat wings? Gossamer won't do—too transparent. No matter, no matter. Plenty of time for that." He moved the fabric from side to side, making notes in a small book. He licked his finger, flipping through pages of intricate diagrams and cramped writing.

Drystan and I watched, transfixed, as Maske continued his lone diatribe. Cyan gave us a helpless look as Maske muttered about necklines and angles. I found myself stifling a grin.

"All right. Put the wings in front of your face like so," he instructed, helping her move her arms. "Now, there're two small hooks at the end of the cuffs. Fasten them together and then take your arms out of the sleeves and stand with them close to your sides."

She must have done so, for he said, "Good". Yet it looked as though the wings were still in front of her face.

"Sam or Amon will be under the stage and will catch you," he said, gesturing at me and Drystan, "and you will be the vanishing girl."

"What about the dress?" I asked.

"I won't ruin the final reveal just yet," he said. "But it shall disappear in a way you'd never expect." He muttered to himself again.

"Can I come out now?" Cyan asked from inside the wire and cloth.

"Certainly, my dear, certainly. Thank you for your help."

Cyan wriggled from under the dress, dusting off her robe. She had several Eladan dresses, but far preferred Temnian tunics.

"Ooh," Lily said. "This is all so magical. And when will this grand performance be? I thought I heard you weren't allowed to perform anymore?"

Some of Maske's vitality wilted, but he drew himself tall again, meeting my gaze. "Soon, my dear. Soon." He lifted his chin, a fire in his eyes. "We've practiced enough that I can see this actually, by a miracle, working. Tomorrow, I aim to re-challenge Pen Taliesin to a duel."

11

GRIDIRON

"The simpler a piece of Vestige, the longer it lasts without needing a charge. There are glass globes that have kept their power for close to a millennium, as far as we can tell, their light never dimming. The more advanced and complicated the Vestige, the more it is at risk of depleting. The weapons went quickly—very few remain functional. But if a country were to discover a new cache of powerful artefacts, or a way to funnel magic back into them, then they would be as powerful as Elada was at the height of its Empire."

A HISTORY OF ELADA AND ITS FORMER COLONIES,
PROFESSOR CAED CEDAR, ROYAL SNAKEWOOD UNIVERSITY

I was in a garden. Other Chimaera strolled along the paths. Most were dragonflies, like me, but several fauns and naiads lounged beneath the trees. The air was thick with the sweet perfume of hundreds of blossoms. Early afternoon lengthened into evening. The small Venglass domes that lined the path glowed in the soft dusk. All was peaceful.

I stretched my arms over my head, content in the moment. Relean walked at my side. His own translucent wings were still, glinting in the light of the Venglass. His dark green hair had lightened with age, his skin was lined, but those eyes were undimmed. Our bodies were several centuries old and beginning to wind down. Soon enough, it would be time to grow new ones.

"I've liked this life," Relean murmured. "Everything seems to have worked out well this time." His voice was as familiar to me as the birds' calls at dawn. The peacock blue and green sheen of his wings glittered. And it was true. There had been no war between factions of Chimaera. The Alder had largely been content to leave us be. The sea had been calm, with no tidal waves, the earth quiet and unshaking.

A faun played music that drifted through the air like the scent of the flowers.

"Sometimes, I cannot lose the feeling that we do not have as much time as we would like," I said. "That there are only so many lives we can live."

Relean drew me close for a kiss. He tasted of honeysuckle, his fingertips as light on my face as rose petals. I looked into those familiar blue and copper eyes before I drew him in for a deeper embrace. Relean was as familiar to me as my own skin. In every life, we found each other.

Above us, the sky blazed. We broke apart, shielding our eyes from the light with our hands. It was as though the sunset returned, lighting the sky with the colors of a forest fire.

It was an Alder ship with furled wings curling over the prow. It landed on the grass, glowing red. I clasped my love's hand in mine.

The door opened, and two Alder emerged. It'd been years since I had seen our creators. They were scarcer in the Ven now, preferring to stay farther up the mountains with their own kind. I always forgot how tall they were, the unnatural thinness of their limbs, the faint blue sheen to their skin. Their large eyes glowed the same cobalt as Venglass.

They inclined their heads at me, and I bowed my head in turn. The rest of the Chimaera had fled at the sight of the craft.

One of the Alder held a small bundle. I fought the urge to sigh even as my heart constricted.

"Your newest charge," one said in Alder, the three-tonal voice echoing in my ears and mind. "Look after this one. It is more important than you know. This is the most powerful one we may have yet created."

"Does that also mean the most dangerous?" Relean asked.

They said nothing more, only walking back to their ship with liquid grace. Within moments, they were gone. But the spell of the garden had broken. The air seemed colder, the scent of the flowers cloying and suffocating.

The child gurgled in my arms. This one had scaled skin and the nubs of horns peeking from its forehead. Relean cupped my face with his hands, reading my anxiety.

"All will be well, my love. All will be well." I drew him into another kiss in the silent garden, the child a barrier between us, before the memory faded to be replaced by another from a few years later I did not wish to remember.

Only fragments remained—like a jigsaw puzzle scattered on the ground, some pieces the blank brown of the backs, and others bright specks of color.

My damselfly body had grown too old, and I'd shed it, though Relean hadn't yet. My new body, made of flesh and bone and nascent wings, was still growing in one of the Ampula tanks. While I waited, I had installed my Aleph in a clockwork woman. I was all cogs, metal, and crystal.

In the middle of the night, I awoke to the sound of my charge screaming.

I ran through the door to the next room, trailing my false fingers against the smooth Venglass walls, and the screaming cut off into a horrible silence.

My charge—my boy, the child entrusted to me—was dead.

I do not remember the sight of his body. That is a puzzle piece with a blank front. The room was empty, but the window had been left ajar. I rushed to it, the Venglass glowing with the coming dawn, but saw no one.

I went to my charge and cradled my hand against his cooling cheek. Already, he had no more substance than a wraith.

I believe I was there for a long while. It is impossible to know. I sent my awareness over the ground, but all was quiet. The night flowers closed, and morning blossoms opened. The Venglass dimmed. The hanging gardens swung in the warm, summer breeze.

Drip, drip, drip. His blood fell to the floor.

Relean burst into the room. But he was too late. Far too late.

"Who did this?"

I shook my head, unable to speak.

"Kashura?" he asked.

Some Alder had turned on Chimaera, deciding their creations were growing too powerful. They called themselves Kashura. And humans were always afraid of those with magic. Even Chimaera themselves had shifting hierarchies.

"Maybe," I said. "It could have been anyone. But he's gone. He's gone, Relean."

The Alder had warned us he was powerful, but he was young enough that his magic had not yet kindled. Now I would never know what he would have become. Relean gathered my false body in his arms, and I clung to him as I sobbed.

Later, I would be reborn into what I didn't realize was my last life, and when that one ended all too soon, I would slumber once again.

I remained asleep for ever so long, my little Kedi.

● ● ● ●

I sat bolt upright in bed, Anisa's memory swirling around me like a ghost until the last of it faded.

Like in that first dream, I had *been* the damselfly. I had seen inside Penglass, or Venglass as she'd called it. I'd seen into the past, to a world long gone. Some details were so clear—the view from the window, the strange possessions in the room. That steady drip, drip, drip of blood onto the floor.

The dragonfly in the stained-glass window glowed bright with the light of the Penmoon. Once more, I wanted to go outside and press my hands against that glass, to drink in the power and let it out again. I balled my hands into fists beneath the covers.

Why had Anisa sent me that memory? She hadn't managed to save that long-ago charge in her care. If she was now protecting me, it wasn't a huge jump to wonder if that meant I was in danger, too.

I shuddered, wrapping my arms around myself. A sob caught in my throat. My eyes burned as my vision blurred. Grief for a young Chimaera boy who'd been dead for centuries, possibly millennia, tore through me.

My gaze fell upon the small, innocuous disc. I wasn't sure if it was my sorrow, or hers. I picked the Aleph up. Another sob threatened to choke me. I was half-tempted to throw the damn thing out of the stained-glass window and be done with Anisa and all these things I couldn't handle. I still didn't believe half the things she told me. I might be Chimaera, but that didn't mean I was anywhere near equipped to save the world as she'd claimed I must.

"Micah?"

I flinched.

Drystan sat up in bed. The open concern on his face undid me again. The Aleph fell from my numb fingers, thumping to the floor.

I sobbed, and not only for the long-dead boy in the dream. I cried for Iphigenia Laurus, for Micah Grey, for the boy Drystan Hornbeam had been and the young man he he'd become. I cried for Aenea, for Frit, and everyone in the circus I'd hurt. I even cried for Maske and for whatever pain in Cyan's past she was clearly trying to hide. Every-where I turned, it felt like there was nothing but fear, heartache, and more loss.

Warm arms wrapped around me. A tear that wasn't mine dropped on the back of my hand. I rested my face against Drystan's neck, his heartbeat against my lips. It was an echo of Anisa and Relean in the dream, but here in the waking world, in the present, nothing between us was muted. This simple touch was what we both needed. Permission to grieve for what we'd taken, and what we'd lost.

When the tears dried, we each returned to our lonely beds. The next morning, neither of us mentioned it and we avoided each other's gaze. Maske had already been guiding and watching us for our street magic shows, but now that he was aiming for a proper duel, we were building that into a grand display, and our practice hours had only grown longer and more complicated. We'd thrown ourselves into it with everything we had.

He'd told us he wanted to weave the act into a story of the greatest magician who was nearly overcome by his hubris.

"Wonder where you got that idea," I teased.

He wrinkled his nose at me. "It's a true mystery."

We soon learned that, while he'd be drawing partly on his own life and what he'd learned from it, the story would be a subtle dig at Taliesin, too.

Maske was more collaborative than I'd expected, allowing us to write some of the dialogue and taking our feedback without defensiveness. When it came to the actual illusions, though, he was king, and he remained mysterious about the finale in particular.

After hours of practice, by late afternoon, I almost wondered if Drystan's embrace, too, had been a dream. I'd volunteered to climb the gridiron. It was a section twenty feet above the stage similar to the aerialist rigging in the big top. It was where we'd attach near-invisible wires for levitation tricks, to throw confetti, manipulate objects, or all sorts of other effects. The wires had grown tangled in practice that morning and I'd agreed to fix them after lunch. Drystan was in the library, Cyan in her room, and Maske was tinkering away in his workshop, as ever.

I held my tongue between my teeth and drew the wires up, winding them into loose spools. It was cramped up there, and the stage below seemed quite far away, even though I'd regularly climbed three times higher in the big top.

After I finished, I headed to the ladder, balancing and placing my feet carefully on the iron. But I had missed a wire, invisible in the dim light.

I tripped.

I hadn't reached for my magic since the night everything fell apart. Anisa had warned me not to, but beyond that, I was also too afraid of what it meant or what I might do. Now, in my fear, my feet kicking through thin air, I let that spark kindle in my chest, and time slowed enough that I managed to grab the railing with one hand, just as I'd once helped Aenea do months ago when she'd fallen from the high wire.

I hung, dangling above the stage. The power thumped through me like a heartbeat.

I sighed, annoyed. I made to pull myself up, but my damp hands slipped. My magic gave me enough time to be surprised and angry at myself and try to twist for a better landing as I fell twenty feet and hit the wooden floorboards with a sickening thump.

For a second, I felt fine before the pain crashed over me in a wave, and I swallowed down a scream.

I'd landed on my side, my hip on fire. At least I hadn't landed on the arm I'd broken when I left the circus. My head rang. I was winded and couldn't cry out for help. I lay sprawled on the stage, trying to sip air into my empty lungs.

Pain warped time even more than my uncontrolled magic. Ricket found me, sniffing my face, her whiskers tickling. She disappeared.

At some point, I heard footsteps. A cool palm rested on my forehead.

"Micah?" Cyan asked. "Are you all right?"

I mumbled something.

"Are you hurt?"

I blinked. It was so bright.

"Dunno," I managed to mutter.

"I'm going to help you up. If something hurts, tell me."

Everything hurts, I wanted to say but simply groaned instead.

She pressed her hands along my spine. "Your back?"

It was hard to narrow in on the pain. "More my side."

Slowly, slowly, she helped me into a sitting position. The ringing in my ears faded, but nausea roiled in my stomach.

"I'm all right, I think," I said, moving my fingers and toes. And I was. Just very, very sore. I rolled over onto my uninjured side, certain I'd have a brilliant bruise.

"You're downplaying it," she accused. "You do that, I've noticed."

Before I could answer, the far door to the theatre opened. Drystan walked in, frowning. "I had the strangest feeling . . ." He trailed off at the sight of me grimacing in pain and Cyan standing over me protectively. "What's happened?"

"I fell." I didn't see the point in lying.

"From the gridiron," Cyan said.

Drystan looked up. "From that height?"

"And nothing's broken?" Cyan asked. She was like a wolf with a bone. She wasn't going to open her jaws and let it go.

She helped me stand. I took a few cautious steps around the stage. "Don't think so," I said. "Just lucky, I guess."

She scoffed. "We've been dancing around things long enough, I think," she said.

I blinked at her as Drystan's brows drew down.

"What do you mean?" I asked, carefully.

"I know you followed me the other day, after we went to Twisting the Aces," she said.

Drystan stiffened. My mouth opened, then closed. I had no idea where this conversation was about to go.

"I don't blame you," she said. "I'd have followed me, too, if I were you."

I coughed. "Right."

Drystan said nothing, his eyes wary.

"All you discovered was a sailor I see from time to time when he's onshore. No great reveal, was it?"

"No," I said, slowly. "It wasn't."

"I'm bringing it up because I want you both to know . . ." She paused, her fingers worrying a bead in her hair. "That I'm not out to get you. I'm simply trying to find my own way. But I do need to come clean about something, and I suspect how you'll take it, at first. But we're running out of time, and I don't know how to do this any other way but honestly."

Drystan drifted closer to me, and I was touched by his protectiveness.

"What are you saying, Cyan?" I couldn't keep the dread from my voice.

"You have a Shadow after you."

"Um," I said, elegantly. We hadn't told Maske about the Shadow, knowing it would have made him less likely to take us in, and I knew Drystan wouldn't have said a thing to Cyan. None of the newspaper articles about the circus's demise had mentioned it, either.

My hip throbbed badly, but this turn of conversation made me wonder if I'd hit my head. "I have no idea what you're talking about." The lie rang false as a broken bell.

"I'd let you get away with that if Shadow Elwood wasn't after me, too."

A tingle spread through my body as she uttered his name. "What?"

I blurted. The panic was crawling through my veins, making my skin itch. I wanted to rewind time and go back to before I'd fallen.

She licked her lips. "The sailor—his name is Oli. We've been seeing each other for a few months. We met at the circus, when I told his fortune. He set sail and only just returned. At my request, he went to Riley & Batheo's to tell my parents I'm all right. They told him a Shadow named Elwood had been sniffing around, and they were afraid I'd gotten myself into more trouble."

"I don't understand," I said. I hurt too much to think straight. I shook my head, but that only made it spin all the more. I staggered to the wing of the stage, bracing myself on a column.

"Micah. Drystan." Her dark eyes bored into mine. "Please. I promise you can trust me. I've caught his trail. I know where he lives. We're all aware that if he finds me, then he finds you, too. It's only a matter of time. We've done well to evade him this long. I'm proposing an alliance. We need to strike first."

I looked at her, somewhat desperately. "How can I even hope to believe that?"

"Because I also suspect why you're able to fall twenty feet and be fine." She paused, bracing herself before squaring her shoulders and meeting my eyes. Some part of me knew what she'd say next as certainly as if Anisa had told me herself. I was about to be hit over the head with another truth.

"I know exactly what you are because I'm like you. Because I also plucked the name Shadow Elwood from Drystan's head."

Drystan recoiled. The ringing in my ears grew louder. Part of me rejected the words entirely. Because accepting them would mean—

Cyan stared at me, her lips parted, but her mouth didn't move as the next three words echoed in my mind. I swore I saw a spark flash in her eyes, blue as Penglass.

—*We are Chimaera.*

12

THE SHAI & THE SHADOW

"Every island in the Archipelago has their stories of monsters in the night that must be guarded against. Some say these spectres, these Shai, these phantoms and ghosts could transform even the most morally upstanding person into something as evil and twisted as the creatures who had corrupted them."

**A HISTORY OF ELADA AND ITS FORMER COLONIES,
PROFESSOR CAED CEDAR, ROYAL SNAKEWOOD UNIVERSITY**

A headache bloomed in my skull, pulsing at my temples. The three of us stood on the stage in a frozen tableau. Her words echoed in my skull.

We are Chimaera.

"Poppycock," Drystan said. He'd heard the words, either in his mind or because Cyan had spoken aloud for his benefit. By the stiffness of his shoulders, I could tell he was terrified.

After all, I'd only recently told him I thought I was a Chimaera. He'd seen magic that night we fled the circus, but not all of it and his memories had been tinged by blood and trauma. Of course he'd think it a trick, another feat of misdirection, certain there was a more logical explanation.

I, meanwhile, felt a certain rightness. Like some part of me knew it was going to fall into place, and all I had to do was follow the motions like an automaton.

"You can't truly be saying that . . . you can read minds," I said, slowly.

She pressed her lips together, pulling her hair over her shoulders and twisting it into a dark rope. "Yes. And I can prove it."

The silence hung between us. She met my gaze, as unblinking as Maske during the séance.

"Close your eyes," she instructed.

I obeyed.

"Think of your fondest memory and hold it close. Remember every detail."

My mind scrabbled in circles. What was my fondest memory?

It came to me. My brother Cyril and me by the fireside one winter's evening in the nursery at our apartments in Sicion. I was four or five, perhaps. Cyril, two years older, seemed so big and grown up by comparison. I was trying to puzzle through an old picture book of his, frustrated that I couldn't decipher the squiggles.

Cyril put down his own adventure book and read me the story, pointing out each word on the page as he did so. It was the tale of *The Prince and the Owlish Man*. The artwork was beautiful, with printed, delicate watercolor paintings swirled with black ink. On some of the pages, the owlish man frightened me, but Cyril's presence made me feel safe. I remembered the crackle of the flames and the smell of furniture polish. I almost sighed with longing. The scene was so real in my mind's eye. I wished I could step back into that time, when my greatest difficulty was not being able to make out a few words on a page.

"You're remembering a boy. He's close to you. A brother? Sandy hair. There's a room with a marble fireplace. A painting of trees in a gilt frame. He's reading to you. *The Prince and the Owlish Man*. You feel warm, safe, and loved."

I opened my eyes. I felt dizzy, and the room wobbled. I slid down the column at the side of the stage until I was seated. "How did you . . . ?" I started.

"I don't know," she said. "One day, I realized I simply could. That the whispers weren't just my own imaginings. I'd respond to something someone hadn't said aloud. I hadn't realized what it'd meant until a man came to the circus for a fortune telling and I heard the word, clear as a bell in his mind: *Chimaera*. I didn't hear it again . . . until I met you."

She twisted towards Drystan. "Do you want me to try with you?" she asked.

"Fuck no." He paused. "Sorry." He looked like he wanted nothing more than to flee, but he was still here. Waiting. Listening.

"I'm not offended."

"Sometimes it doesn't work at all, no matter how hard I try, but other times it comes out of nowhere and I can't stop it. I've noticed it's easier if there's a lot of Vestige around. I try not to intrude. I have learned that people think such terrible things. Things they perhaps do not truly believe or would not do . . ." She trailed off, and I wondered whose thoughts she remembered.

"You can read anyone's mind, at any time?" I asked. She could have learned so much from one careless thought . . .

She shook her head. "It takes a lot of concentration. You're especially hard to read, perhaps because you're Chimaera too."

She flashed him an apologetic look, and Drystan's glower was something to behold. He crossed his arms, as if that'd keep her out of his skull. Something about her expression made me realize she must have known what Drystan had done to Bil, but she was wise enough not to mention it. Not out of pity, but a sympathetic grief.

Could I do it? I concentrated on her. Maybe I caught a flicker of an image—a tear falling down a woman's cheek, a sensation of touching warm . . . fur?—but I couldn't be sure. I blinked, a headache throbbing at my temples. My side hurt something fierce where I'd fallen.

I tried Drystan next. I groped, half-afraid of what I might find. I sensed something, a formless emotion—

He frowned at me. "Why are you squinting at me like that? Are *you* trying to root around in my skull? Don't you dare."

I pulled away. "Sorry. Didn't work, anyway."

He sniffed. "Good."

Cyan bent her head. Silver dust from the Kymri Princess levitation was scattered around the floorboards. Her eyes were downcast, her fingers intertwined. She rubbed her thumb pads together.

"So that's why you were a fortuneteller in the circus?" I asked.

"Nay. I learned to read the tarot long before anything strange happened. But when that man came to have a reading, I had . . . a flash, a vision. My first one. He kept ordering me to tell him what I saw, over and over again. He gripped my upper arms so hard it hurt. He terrified me. But it didn't make any sense. I told him as best I could, he threw some coins on the table and left."

"What did he look like?" I tried to focus on her again, drawing on that spark of magic despite Anisa's warnings, but there was nothing. I felt a surge of disappointment.

"When I try to remember, his face is . . . like the reflection in a puddle when it's raining. That's the best way I can describe it." She shrugged, and I shivered. "I even asked around, after, but no one else in the circus remembered seeing him."

The blurred man.

"What did you see? In that tarot reading?" I pressed.

"Flashes. Monsters. Other Chimaera trapped in glass, I think. There was a young man with bat wings. Two Chimaera, one with wings like owl feathers and the other like a dragonfly. There was a child with a scaled face and horns, and a human-looking child with dark ringlets around the same age. A glow of blue and a pulsing red light, like the sky was on fire." She crossed her arms. "I didn't understand it."

Like Anisa's dreams, though I didn't remember anything about bat or owl wings.

"After that," she continued. "I started hearing or seeing things more often. I learned who in the circus did not like me one bit. Or liked me too much. Sometimes, my dreams come true. And once, a nightmare," she whispered.

"What happened?"

She sat down on the stage, drawing her knees to her and wrapping her arms around them. The dusty seats of the empty audience of the theatre disappeared into the darkness. "The night before I left the circus, I had a horrible dream. A circus accident with the animal trainer, Liam. Someone in the audience would frighten the lion. I told my mother I was going to go warn him. Plead for him to take the night off and not perform that day. My parents . . . they thought it was silly or I was simply stressed. They took me into the city for a day and bought me chocolate limes. I remember the taste." She lapsed into silence.

"But then?" I asked.

"Then the next day . . . it all came true. That evening, it happened just as I'd seen it. Liam was dead, mauled by his own lion. He loved that lion. Called him Pip. They'd shot him, I think. The man and lion lay side by side, their bodies still warm."

Another flash of an image. Cyan, crying, one hand entangled in the lion's tawny fur, the other clutching a handful of the dead man's sleeve. Her parents pulling her away. My headache worsened.

"When my parents realized I had seen a glimpse of what was to pass—" Her words thickened. "They feared I was a Shai."

"A Shai?" I asked.

"A Temnian myth. A demon or a dark spirit who drinks the thoughts out of others' skulls like wine. They're considered evil, and dangerous." Her eyes brimmed with tears. "My parents were afraid of me."

"So you ran away."

She nodded. "I think they regret how they reacted. When Oli went to them, they wanted me to come home. But I'm afraid they'll look at me like they did that night."

My mind was spinning. "Thank you. For trusting us with this."

"I'm relieved you believe me."

"Are you . . . different?" I asked.

She gave a short, sharp laugh. "Beyond reading minds and that one glimpse of the future?"

"Well, yes," I said.

"He means no scales, no feathers, no other physical anomalies," Drystan finally spoke, sounding like the Royal Snakewood University scholar he'd once been.

"No," she said. "The attack, though, it was because there was a little girl in the audience with a lion's tail and ears. Poor Pip must have thought he'd smelled a rival." Her face creased with grief again. "Are there others?"

"There were some in our circus," I said. "A man who seemed part-bull. A leopard lady with canines and pointed ears. And a cyrinx we saw shift into a woman."

She blinked. "We had a cyrinx, too, but I never . . ." She trailed off.

"There are meant to be two types of Chimaera," I said. "The Theri, who are often mixed with animal attributes. And the Anthi, who look human." *Like us*, I thought, unsure if she'd catch it. "Both can have extra abilities."

"How do you know that?" she asked.

"A spice merchant told me, of all people," I said, with a laugh. "He evidently picked up all sorts of things when he travelled for his wares as a younger man."

Cyan shook her head, lost in thought.

"I've told you why I left my circus," she said, eventually meeting my eyes. "I'd like to learn why you left yours."

Drystan stared intently at the stage floorboards as I filled Cyan in on the bare bones of what'd happened the night we left. Bil trapping me in his cart so Shadow Elwood could come collect me. The promise of the reward. How Aenea and Drystan had come to my rescue. I skipped over the Phantom Damselfly and how she'd helped me. It was as if my tongue wouldn't let me talk about Anisa. I spoke around what Drystan did, both for his sake and because I suspected Cyan already knew, and ended with telling her what I'd done to the Penglass to escape the Shadow.

She was shocked into silence for a moment, taking it all in. She inclined her head in thanks.

"I still have some questions of my own," I said, and she gestured for me to continue.

"How often do you fall ill?"

Her brow crinkled. "Hardly ever. Whenever a flu or a cold swept through the circus, I'd never get it. The others used to say I was hearty as an ox." She smiled, but it faded.

"If you touch Penglass, does it do anything? Like glow?"

"I haven't tried. I can give it a go, if you like."

"Might as well. Be careful, though." I sucked in a breath. "This next question is . . . indelicate. Are your parents your birth parents?"

She looked offended. "What in the world—"

I held up my hands, cutting her off. "I ask only because I was given to my parents as a babe by a doctor." I swallowed. "By Doctor Pinecrest."

She stared at me, but there was no recognition at the name.

"He's now the Royal Physician of Elada."

Her eyes widened.

"Do you have any connection to him?" I asked.

She frowned, searching her memory. "Not that I know of."

"He's the one I suspect hired Shadow Elwood to follow me," I said. "He must be using him to keep tabs on—on—Chimaera." It still felt strange, to say the words aloud. How many others were there?

"Well, there is something about my birth parents . . ." She trailed off, licking her lips. "But I don't think it has anything to do with the Royal Physician."

Drystan and I waited.

She gathered herself. "The night I left the circus. After Liam and Pip . . . my mother and I fought. And I heard something she'd never have wanted me to learn."

We said nothing, waiting for her to find the words.

"She said that it served her right, that of course she'd birth a cursed babe after sleeping with a magician."

I blinked, putting it together. Drystan's lips parted.

"Yes," she said. "My parents were good friends with Maske for years. I'm not sure what led to it. I think it might have been just before my parents got together, or maybe it was a dalliance. Doesn't matter, really. I know I don't look half-Eladan. Maske has no idea. I'm not even sure he suspects. I've been too afraid to go looking. But it's why, when I left, this was the first place I thought to come. And it's why, when my parents realized where I'd gone, they let me be."

My head spun. I thought back to Drystan's hints that Maske had been a different man at the height of his power.

"Well."

"Well indeed." She blinked. She started to laugh, the sound echoing through the empty theatre. "It's a strange relief. To share in the secret. To not be so alone with it all."

I agreed, but part of me suspected it wasn't an accident or a mistake that we'd run away from the circus only to end up somewhere with another Chimaera. I very much suspected a certain Phantom Damselfly had known this all along. And at the same time . . . how incredible was it, to realize I was not alone? There had been Juliet and the others, but they had looked visibly different and as soon as I'd learned their truth, I'd had to leave. Yet here was another person who looked human but had extra abilities. A Theri Chimaera.

"So," Cyan said, brisk. "I've laid down the cards, and there's no others up my sleeve. We have a common problem."

"I almost killed the Shadow, the night we left the circus," I said. "He's not going to give up. And if he's after you as well, then you're right. There are too many ways he could follow either of our paths and find the both of us, and we have no idea what will happen if he does."

I met Drystan's eyes, and he gave me an imperceptible nod.

I reached my palm out, and Cyan grasped it and shook it firmly. Her eyes were shining.

"We're in," I said. "Let's catch a Shadow before he catches us."

13

THE DAMSELFLY

"Dreams hold the answers, even if the questions are not yet known."

ELADAN PROVERB

ittle Kedi . . .

I awoke later that night, every nerve of my body on alert.

—*Little Kedi . . .*

Anisa.

I found myself climbing out of bed. I clutched the Aleph, which hummed like an Augur. I shrugged into my coat and stepped into slippers, almost as if I were sleepwalking. I climbed up to the flat roof. Small snowflakes danced along the wind.

The door to the roof opened. I turned, expecting Drystan, but Cyan emerged, wrapped tight in her coat.

"Good evening," I said, some part of me unsurprised.

"A woman whispered to me in a dream . . ." she said. "Told me to come up here."

"I suppose she wants you to meet her," I said.

"Who?"

Instead of answering, I set the Aleph on the ground. Backing away, I hugged my arms around myself as the wavering image of the Phantom Damselfly appeared. She shook her head as though awakening.

—*Little Kedi,* she said, and sighed soundlessly, snow falling through her transparent dragonfly wings. I hadn't spoken to her in over a month, and it was as if I saw her anew. Her features, I knew from her dreams, were closer to Alder proportions—bigger eyes, cheekbones that could cut glass, and a wide, thin mouth. Intricate tattoos traced her hairline, following the long curve of her neck, and disappeared beneath her gossamer dress.

Cyan sucked in a breath. "You can't be real," she exhaled, her eyes wide in wonder.

—*Hello, little bird. I have lived thousands of years. I have seen worlds rise and fall, marvels and horrors you cannot even fathom. You both have lived but a few scant turns of the sun.* She held her hand against Cyan's cheek, though I knew Cyan couldn't feel her touch. *So tell me, then, my child. Which of us is more real?*

Cyan shuddered, taking one step back from the Damselfly.

"Her name is Anisa." I pulled my tongue free from the roof of my mouth. "She's a memory of a Chimaera who lived long ago. She found me in the circus, and she saved my life."

Cyan turned to me. "During the séance on that first night . . . I saw flashes, and thought I heard voices . . ." She trailed off, and I felt her sharp gaze. "I couldn't really follow them. It happened in Twisting the Aces, too, didn't it?"

"Yes. Visions of my own, but I don't know what they mean."

—*You will in time, little Kedi.*

"Can . . . you see the future?" Cyan pressed her lips to stop them from shaking. I'd learned so much about Anisa since I'd first seen her that it was strange, yet also validating, to watch someone else reacting to her as I had.

—*The spirits whisper possibilities. They're written on the wind, in the stars and the sunlight. In dust motes swirling through the air. The world remembers what has happened, and what may yet occur. You need only to look for it. You could learn, if you wanted to.*

Anisa sighed, stretching her wings. She moved closer to us, her feet trailing a light leading back to the disc.

—*I cannot speak long, for I am still resting to recover some of my powers. I am glad you have found each other. There are others who would also hear me. I feel them, flickering like a candle flame, just here.* She tapped her chest. Through her torso, I could see the glow of a distant gas lamp, as if her heart were aflame. *You two are the ones who answered.*

"What do you want of us?" Cyan whispered.

—*I have waited so long. The time is not yet right for the other pieces to fall, and I see little of the pattern.*

"You speak in riddles," Cyan said.

"She usually does," I muttered. "It's quite irritating, really."

I swore the ancient being shot me an annoyed look.—*I speak more plainly than you know. One day, you shall see.*

She turned out and looked over the dark skyline, the yellow windows of far-off buildings like stars.—*The world is so different now.*

The memories came back to me: the verdant fields of green, the blue glass glowing in the sun. "I remember."

Cyan sucked in a breath. "Those dreams I had . . . they were real?"

My head turned towards her. She'd dreamed of the old world, too? I remembered she'd spoken of the vision of the circus and seeing the sky on fire. I shivered.

Anisa swept a transparent hand toward the city.—*Very real. You two now know more about the old world and the old ways than almost anyone else in this new one. I have sent these dreams out into the ether. The Chimaera in my circus may have seen them, but they did not answer my call the way you two did.*

In my dreams, I'd seen an Alder, alive and breathing. No Alder or Chimaera skeletons existed to prove their existence, and only a few Vestige paintings showed them at all.

"It looks like Shadow Elwood is after both of us," I said. "Can you tell us anything about that?"

She closed her eyes, face going blank as she asked the spirits for answers. Whatever they whispered, I didn't hear it. She opened her eyes, blinking serenely at Cyan.—*The Shadow is growing closer. You, my little bird, have already learned where he lives thanks to what you can do. Look inside. The kelpies lead the way. Follow them, you will find enough to make him disappear. There are plenty of other threats, but he will be one fewer, at least.*

"Kelpies?" I echoed, mystified. Cyan's eyes were wide. Snowflakes drifted in the night air, growing thicker.

—*I am running out of time,* Anisa said, her form fading slightly. *You must take care of the Shadow but also mind the woman in the wine-red dress and her child.*

Cyan's brow drew down. "A woman in a red dress?" I guessed she hadn't had that vision. Lines of pain shot from my temples to the top of my skull. The back of my left eye pulsed.

—*She is important. You are both linked to her fate, somehow, though the spirits have not yet shown me why.*

I picked up the Aleph, and Anisa's form grew more distinct before it began to disappear again.

—*I realize you are afraid. You are both Chimaera, and you are my charges*, she said. *I will do my best to protect you. I must rest again. Trust your instincts. Try not to reach for your powers, for it is not safe. I will speak to you again when I am next able.*

She stared at us as she faded from view. Once she was gone, the humming in the Aleph in my hand gradually quieted. I'd been numb as Anisa spoke to us, but the full cold of the winter night gripped me, as though the very core of me was frozen. Cyan shivered just as violently.

"I have done countless séances," she said. "And yet a Chimaera ghost was here, under my very nose, the entire time."

"I know, she's terrifying. Believe me, I know. But she hasn't led me astray yet. She's already given us an angle to approach for the Shadow."

"Breaking into his apartments won't exactly be easy," Cyan pointed out.

"No," I agreed. "But you can read minds, Drystan and I are very good at climbing, and Maske's already taught us to pick locks."

"Opening a set of handcuffs is a bit different." She stared into the distance.

"Let's go to bed," I said. "Nothing more we can do tonight."

We left the rooftop. I paused by the door to the loft.

"How am I supposed to sleep?" Cyan asked me. I could only shake my head at her in response.

She gripped my hand, and her skin was ice-cold.

"Chimaera," she whispered, touching her forehead to mine.

"Chimaera," I echoed back.

And then she was gone.

I entered the loft, clenching my jaw against my chattering teeth. The edges of my vision blurred as I stumbled into the room.

Drystan woke up, staring at me blearily. Ricket was curled at his feet. I looked at my empty bed and I couldn't face it.

"Nightmare?" Drystan asked, voice thick with sleep.

I nodded. Close enough. "I went up to the roof for some fresh air."

"In winter?"

I wrapped my arms around myself. I looked at my empty sheets, then at him. "I'm so cold. Could I . . . could I sleep in your bed?" I didn't know how that boldness had come over me, and I immediately wanted to take the words back, but they floated on the air between us.

The silence lengthened. Just as I was afraid he'd say no, he held up his blanket in a wordless invitation.

Even with that, I hesitated.

"Come on," he said. "No point in you waking up with frostbite."

I licked my lips. In the end, though, it was simple. I set the Aleph down on the side table and eased into bed with Drystan, facing away from him. After a moment, he curled his body around mine. He shivered once at my coldness, but then he relaxed. My fingertips tingled. Gradually, so gradually, I uncoiled as the cover trapped our body heat. Ricket rose and did her endless turning until she finally settled behind Drystan's knees.

Part of me told myself that, despite the invitation, I'd only stay there until I had warmed up and the worst of the fear fled. If we woke up in separate beds, it'd give him the option to pretend it never happened, like him holding me after Anisa's nightmare. Moments later, sleep claimed me, and for the first time in so long, I felt safe.

● ● ● ●

When I awoke, my mouth felt fuzzy, and my eyes were bleary.

I faced the center of the loft, daylight streaming through the dragonfly-stained glass.

I realized where I was, and I was abruptly wide awake.

Drystan was still curled against my back, his breath warm against my neck. His arm lay around my torso, his hand on my chest. My unbound chest. My entire body prickled, my face burning.

My mind whirled as I wondered what I should do.

I should slip from the covers and go back to my bed like I'd planned. But I was so warm, so very comfortable. Drystan's arms cocooned me, and sleep lured me back with its siren call.

Drystan yawned and stretched, pressing against me again. Ricket meowed softly in indignation at the bottom of the bed. My muscles stiffened, even as I hoped he wouldn't pull away.

"Good morning," he said, eventually, into the back of my neck.

"Morning," I said. Carefully, so carefully, I turned around to face him. His eyes were soft with sleep, his hair a mess of golden waves.

"This is a very small bed for two people," he said.

"Sorry, it must have been uncomfortable, and I didn't mean to intrude—" I started sitting up, but his hand gently but firmly pressed me down.

"Relax, Micah. I invited you." He blinked in surprise. "You know, I think this is the first night I've slept practically all the way through since—"

Since the ringmaster.

"I'm glad," I whispered. His eyes searched my face. He was so close that I felt the soft exhale of his breath. I studied him right back, drinking in every freckle, the way his eyelashes lightened to blonde at the tips, and all the many shades of blue in his eyes.

"What are we—?" I started.

He silenced me with a finger to my lips. The words died in my throat. He took his finger away, and my lips tingled. Without a thought, we shifted. He rested a hand on my cheek and, finally, his lips pressed to mine.

It was far from the first time I'd kissed Drystan. Our lips had touched dozens of times in the pantomime at the circus. But this was the first without hundreds of eyes on us. The first without pretense.

A small sound escaped his throat as he pulled me closer to him. I was too desperate to care about morning breath. My hands twined about his neck and tangled in his hair. Our bodies fit against each other, a thin layer of clothing all that separated us. I could feel his every muscle. I shivered as he ran his fingertips up and down my side, before his palm lay flat against the small of my back and pulled me even closer to him. I felt a tightening of my nipples and a stirring between my legs.

Embarrassed, I broke the kiss and shifted my hips back from his. Drystan's pale lips were pink, his pupils wide and dark. He was heart-wrenchingly beautiful. What would he want with me?

"What is it?" he asked, his voice husky. My stomach tightened with desire.

"But I'm—"

"Micah," he breathed, and I was not sure if he was answering or interrupting me. He pulled me back to him, and I pushed away my fear.

He sensed my hesitance and my nerves at doing anything more. I concentrated entirely on Drystan—the sight, smell, touch, and taste of him. I did not kiss him as a man or as a woman. I simply kissed him, and he kissed me.

14

THE NEW WAGER

"Sometimes I can't quite believe the anger I am capable of. These many years later, I still despise Taliesin. I blame him for everything. For throwing my life away, for costing me my family and my livelihood. That anger was what drove me to darkness. I stole and I cheated and I lied and I liked it. One day, I will get him back for hurting me. For now, I'll nurse the hatred."

JASPER MASKE'S PERSONAL DIARY

There he is," Cyan said, pointing. "Do you see?"

The following afternoon after morning stage magic practice, Drystan, Cyan, and I were deep in the Brass District, tenements and Penglass looming over us. I wore my suit, since I'd not fancied the dress that morning. Sure enough, on the corner up ahead, I caught sight of a distinctive hat.

Shadow Elwood.

Cyan had found him as if she were following a deer trail. We followed the hat as its wearer moved and bobbed through the throng of people. Part of me wanted to run the other way. Anisa had said he hadn't discovered our whereabouts yet, but it felt beyond foolish to go looking for him. He was a professional. Surely, he'd realize he was being tailed?

We hung back, following Cyan's lead as we twined through cobbled streets. Sometimes, Cyan would drag us into an alleyway for a moment or two, then bring us back out.

"He's a naturally suspicious fellow, which makes sense given his line of work," Cyan said, keeping her voice low. "But he doesn't know we're following him. I can sense that much."

We did have an advantage. Drystan's jaw set. I wasn't entirely sure he believed she had extra abilities rather than clever mentalist tricks. We still hadn't mentioned the topic of real magic when we were on our own in the loft. Granted, we were increasingly spending time doing . . . other things up there.

If Maske or Cyan sensed the change between Drystan and me, they hadn't commented on it. We were taking it slow, whatever this was between us. I was equally amazed and terrified.

The Shadow walked with purpose, head up, back straight, hands deep in his pockets. A balloon vendor obscured our vision, and we impatiently pushed around her and barely caught him turning a corner. Our boots thumped along the cobblestones.

"This is where Shadow Elwood lives," Cyan breathed. "Third floor, suite G."

He stopped in front of a tenement. We jumbled to a halt. The back of Cyan's hand brushed mine, her skin warm. With bated breath, we watched as the Shadow slid a key from his pocket into the lock and made his way inside.

"You plucked that from his mind?" Drystan asked.

She shook her head. "No. He's hard to read, overall. Sometimes I can't get anything at all."

"If he had something like an Eclipse, would that shield him?" I asked. Anisa had found him blocked before, too.

"Maybe. They're pretty dear, though."

"The Royal Physician owns the Museum of Mechanical Antiquities."

She gave a low whistle. "That'll do it. But no, I got the information from flirting with the porter and peeking into his mind. See him, there? Rather handsome, don't you think?"

"His face is a bit too square for my tastes," Drystan said, deadpan.

She laughed. "Aha! I knew it!"

She gave us a significant look that we pretended not to see. We shared a room, so I suspect she assumed we'd been together a while, rather than it being a more recent change.

"So we know where he lives," I said, my heartbeat too fast. "Now we have to figure out how to break in."

"Break in?" Drystan echoed. He, after all, hadn't been privy to the conversation with Anisa on the roof.

"He'll have files in there on all his clients," I said. "There'll be something in there we can use as ammunition. I'll bet he's crooked on some level. If we can get him thrown in jail, he can't come after us again."

"And if he's not crooked?"

"He will be," I said, firmly. "And even if he's not, there might be more information on the Royal Physician, if he is a client. That'll be something."

"You're still proposing breaking and entering," Drystan said.

I shot him a look. Bold of a former criminal to chastise me for a little crime. "Do you have a better idea?"

He narrowed his eyes at me.

"Well, we can't do it just now in broad daylight, anyway," Cyan said. "We'll need to surveil him properly, each of us taking shifts. Get a sense of when he's home and when he's out. Let's get back for now. We can start tomorrow."

She set off in the direction of the Kymri Theatre, her long plait swaying like a pendulum. Drystan and I followed her.

Once the Kymri Theatre doors closed behind us, I wanted nothing more than to start planning our attack on the Shadow, but Maske met us in the hallway, his eyes blazing.

"Keep your Glamours on and come into the parlor, if you please," he said, voice low. "Pen Taliesin and a representative from the Collective of Magic are here. They've responded to my challenge."

• • • •

Maske sat at the séance table in the parlor, every muscle tense, pointedly staring at the younger man and not his age-old rival. He'd made a pot of coffee, but none of them had touched the steaming cups or wee cakes Cyan had made yesterday in front of them. Drystan, Cyan, and I were perched on the settee in the corner, balancing our cups precariously in our laps.

Maske, though in his late fifties, was full of such endless energy that he never struck me as particularly middle-aged. Taliesin may have won the old feud between them, but he'd lost against time. Deep lines engraved his face, and his back was humped underneath a rich mink coat. Golden rings bedecked his long, gnarled fingers, and he had a bad tremor. The whites of his eyes had aged to the yellow of old parchment. He looked like he was held together with string and matchsticks and a strong wind could blow him away.

The other man next to Taliesin, by contrast, was all straight lines and calm stillness in his smart suit and an expertly folded green cravat held in place by an emerald pin. His sideburns and waxed moustache were of the latest style, and he had the long fingers of a magician.

"Good evening," the coiffed man said. "I am Christopher Aspall, the representative of the Collective of Magic of Elada. I am the solicitor of the organization, and a retired performer myself." A thin leather briefcase leaned against his shin.

"I am here," Aspall continued, "to respond to Jasper Maske's challenge, issued to the Collective of Magic and Pen Taliesin seven days previous, and to respond to Taliesin's claim that you are already violating the terms of your agreement signed by both parties on the fifth of Lylal, 10846."

Maske's eyes snapped to Aspall's face. "I have not violated the contract."

"Horse piss," Taliesin spat. Most of his teeth were gone, the rest ruined gravestones in his mouth. "You've hired these pups and you're teaching them magic."

"You know full well no performances have been held at the Kymri Theatre in these many years."

"But you're planning on it." Taliesin pointed a shaking hand at Maske. The teeth, the shaking, the unnatural brightness in his yellowing eyes: Taliesin was truly one of the Delerious—a Lerium addict. He gestured at us. "You think I'm not well aware they've been busking on the street?"

"Per our agreement, *I* would not be performing magic on-stage."

Taliesin sputtered. "It is your magic they'll perform, and your magic cannot go on the bloody stage."

"If you recall, the wording did not ban me from teaching magic and allowing others to perform, even in this very building," Maske said, mildly. "I studied the phrasing very carefully. What a pity you didn't catch it."

Taliesin's scowl deepened as Aspall cleared his throat. He brought out a folder from the leather briefcase, opening it to reveal the original contract between Maske and Taliesin. He made a great show of reading it over silently before he spoke. Showmen. They never lose their taste for the dramatic.

"While I have come here at Taliesin's behest, I am impartial." He gave the last word the slightest emphasis. "I am here to represent the Collective of Magic's best interests. And, after much careful study of the syntax of the agreement, the Collective's official pronouncement is that . . ." He paused again for effect. We leaned forward in our seats. ". . . that Jasper Maske is *not* violating the terms of this contract as long as the performers are not doing the exact same tricks that were well-known when these two magicians were in business together as Spectre and Maske, and as long as Maske does not directly take the stage."

Taliesin gave a wordless cry of rage. Aspall's nose wrinkled. He wasn't as impartial as he pretended to be. Everything about Taliesin was twisted, and I'd rarely felt such instant distaste for someone. I would bet that if souls were visible, his was as warped as they come. He couldn't have been like this when he performed with Maske, or they'd never have worked together. Had the drugs transformed Taliesin so completely?

A small thought trickled through my mind, despite my best intentions: I wondered what Drystan would have looked like now, had he not given up Lerium. Cyan's head turned towards me, and I hoped she hadn't caught that.

"I thank you, Solicitor Aspall, for your ruling on the agreement," Maske said, a small smile playing around his lips. "And what does the Collective of Magic say of my challenge? Fifteen years has been long enough, and Taliesin, after all, no longer properly performs himself, either. I've a few years left in me, yet. I'd like to make the most of them."

Taliesin's lips pulled back from his teeth.

"I proposed a rematch," Maske said, holding his head high. "In three months' time. Between my magicians and Pen Taliesin's boys. I'll clarify my terms. If I win, then I have permission to perform again in the Kymri Theatre, or on any stage I like, and I also receive the Vestige artefacts I lost in the previous arrangement."

I went cold. He'd trained us for street magic, and we'd begun putting together a longer stage-show, but we hadn't even practiced it from beginning to end yet. Was he right to put this much faith in us?

Taliesin hissed in a breath, but his eyes lit with the lure of the gamble. "And if you lose?" he asked, aiming for nonchalance.

Maske paused, then squared his shoulders. "If we lose, then I will continue to not perform magic, and Taliesin can gain possession of the Kymri Theatre."

The silence in the room was almost another presence. He'd risk our home? I sensed Drystan's shock, but Cyan's expression was implacable. She'd known.

Taliesin grinned, a fearsome sight in his ruined face. "You think whelps who have just started to learn magic have any hope of beating my boys, who've been performing since they were practically in nappies?"

"I do," Maske said, with quiet confidence. "I have every faith in their capabilities, and my own." I was touched, though still not entirely sure the trust was not misplaced.

The two magicians stared at each other, and the hatred between them was so thick you could slice it with a butterknife.

"All right," Taliesin said, his eyes narrowing. "I like it. Lord and Lady, why don't we go ahead and make this real interesting: if you win, you can have the deed to the Spectre Theatre. If I do, I get the rest of your Vestige collection."

"I'd accept that," Maske said, without hesitation.

My eyes were wide as I watched them.

Taliesin's lip curled. "Need to consult my lawyer, like, but if he gives me the go-ahead, we'll make it all official."

Maske's eyes flashed, and in that moment, I saw the man who had once been a card sharp. He'd goaded the older magician into a bluff where he couldn't fold.

Taliesin leaned back, folding his shaking hands over his concave stomach.

"Well," Aspall said, somewhat taken aback by the turn of events, "if you are both in agreement, then we shall meet at the Collective of Magic's headquarters on Thistle Street in another week's time at 10 o'clock. But the three-month clock starts now. In the meantime, I will discuss this with the Collective and ensure that this meets with their approval. The thought of two magician rivals emerging from the shadows to the limelight again will no doubt please them immensely. I know that many, like myself, were great admirers of the Spectre and Maske shows as children." He coughed, and the brief glimpse of the man beneath the solicitor's façade disappeared. "You have until the meeting to change your minds. Once you put the ink to paper, it is done."

Taliesin coughed wetly. "I expect much the same result as last time, young Aspall. Merely proving the point once again."

Taliesin heaved himself to his feet, and the rest of us rose, too, as politeness dictated. Taliesin's tremor had grown visibly worse. He threw a cool look in our direction. I forced myself to meet his stare.

"Hope these whelps don't embarrass you as much as I think they will, old boy," he said.

Maske's hands tightened to fists, the knuckles whitening. "You may find that the last fifteen years have treated us very differently."

Taliesin looked about at the faded glory of the Kymri Theatre. He arranged his fur coat, the gold rings on his fingers glinting. "That they have. I'll enjoy redecorating this place once it's mine. Two theatres for Spectre's Shadows in a few months. I'll start a proper empire, eh? Well, must be off. Jasper." He inclined his head. I half expected to hear it creak like an unoiled door.

"Pen."

Maske stayed poised for flight until we heard the front door close, and then he collapsed back into his chair.

"We're doing it," I said. "We're really doing it."

Drystan perched next to Maske, taking his hand in the first sign of affection I had seen between them.

Maske grinned, bringing up Drystan's hand and shaking it in victory. "Oh, Taliesin has no choice in it now, really. I knew the Collective would jump at the chance. They've been salivating for more publicity. Magic shows have fallen out of favor recently, compared to some of the bigger vaudeville or circus acts. He can't turn it down without losing face. This is exactly what I'd hoped for."

"But you've risked the Kymri Theatre," Drystan said.

Maske's smile wilted, ever-so-slightly. "Yes, if I lose, then I'm well and truly done, and we're all in a pickle. But to be honest, I'm afraid I'll lose this place within the year. I still owe money to the bank for it, and the repairs to bring this place properly up to snuff are eye-watering. The séances only bring in so much and I'm almost out of Vestige, anyway. Winning this duel is absolutely vital."

I wrapped my arms around myself, feeling vaguely sick.

He grimaced at our silence. "Taliesin is right: his boys have been doing magic for years. He'll also have a better understanding of what the audience wants and the current fashion. I'm a decade and a half out of date. The last illusion is proving so tricky. Gods, maybe this was a mistake." He blanched, his earlier bravado wilting before our eyes.

"But if you win . . ." Drystan pointed out, trying to pull Maske out of the spiral before it took firmer hold. "Then you get it all back, and more."

"And you will win," I added, encouragingly. "You're the Maske of Magic! You taught him everything he knows. And look at him, he's such an addict he's a Delerious ruin of a man, now. We can beat him and his grandsons, no problem.

"We have three months," I said. "A lot can change in a season. I've learned that well enough."

I wasn't anywhere as confident as I pretended to be. We were outcasts from the circus and absolutely novice magicians. We hadn't even mastered the levitation illusion yet.

"Teach us everything," Cyan added. "Hold nothing back. We'll do you proud."

Maske nodded. "You're right. Apologies for my momentary lapse. Of course we'll win. And then I'll be able to perform again . . ." He faltered. His next words were whispered in awe: "I'll be able to perform again."

"Yes," I said. "Then you'll regain your title as the greatest magician in Elada."

Cyan held out her hand, and Maske put his over hers. Drystan and I added ours. The four of us stood in a small circle, our hands clasped in a promise.

He looked at the three of us, his eyes beetle-bright.

"Well, then," he said. "We'd best get back to practice, then, shouldn't we?"

15

DUST MOTES

"With each life, they learn more and become the truer essence of them-selves. With each passing generation, our children are growing into what we hoped they would be. Of course, there is always the threat that they will learn too much."

TRANSLATED FRAGMENT OF ALDER SCRIPT

The next day, we threw open every window of the Kymri Theatre, despite the layer of snow on the ground and the bite in the wind. Even though the final performance would be at the Royal Hippodrome, the place was well overdue for a clear-out and we didn't want to practice somewhere so dust-covered. So, after hours each day preparing for the duel, we spent hours more polishing up the Kymri.

The work warmed us. We swept dust from the stage, and then sanded, stained, and varnished the planks until it shone. We scrubbed the aged velvet of the seats, mending the tears. We cleaned the mosaics and glued the loose tiles back into place. We washed the stained-glass windows. I climbed to the roof and made it possible for light to shine through the grimy skylights again.

Cyan's sailor Oli also arrived to lend his muscles in the cleanup and to offer his services as a stagehand. He was on shore leave over the winter, so it worked well, even if Drystan and I were anxious about having another stranger in our midst. But Cyan assured us he was trustworthy, and soon enough, I saw why she liked him. He was steady, even, and though he was a man of few words, he was thoughtful. I mentioned off-hand once that I liked pistachios, and he brought back a packet when he next went to the market, just for me. To help us out and to save money, he ended up moving into the theatre until his ship was due to set sail.

Lily Verre, true to her earlier promise, came to our aid as well. She and Maske had been stepping out regularly. While Oli easily did the work of two men, Lily instead dusted vaguely and brought bouquets of roses "to freshen the air," even though no members of the public would enter the Kymri Theatre for months, at best. The roses did make the old theatre look that much cheerier, though, and they did smell nice.

I wasn't about to scrub down the theatre in a dress, so I wore male clothing. Neither Oli nor Lily commented on it. We made sure to go by our false names and keep the Glamours on, even if Maske fretted about using them so often. I was Sam, Drystan was Amon, and Cyan was Celia. Oli had messed up the latter once or twice, but Lily thankfully didn't seem to notice.

We were so busy that the three of us had made little progress on the issue of Shadow Elwood. We did make sure one of us watched the apartment building as often as possible, noting the Shadow's comings and goings and trying to find a good time to attempt a break-in. We needed to act sooner rather than later, but we couldn't pretend it wasn't daunting.

At the end of the week, decades of grease and grime no longer coated every surface. We discovered the original pinkish beige of the walls before coating them with a fresh lick of buttercream yellow.

When the paint dried, we surveyed our handiwork. Lily had gone home, and Oli was out drinking with some of his mates. My back ached from the dull, repetitive motion of scrubbing, and my palms were somehow both wrinkled and chapped from filthy soap suds.

In that moment, though, none of that mattered. The Kymri Theatre sparkled. I could imagine audience members filling the seats. The rustle of skirts, the waving of fans, and the crinkle of paper as men and women consulted their programs. Before, the dusty seats only seemed like they could be filled with ghosts. Now, it was a place ready for magic and wonder.

"Tomorrow is the meeting with Aspall and Taliesin," Maske said, breaking the silence of the theatre. "Once it's signed, that's that. Are you in?"

"Absolutely," Cyan said.

"Yes," Drystan said, and I added an "aye."

Maske inhaled deeply, then let it out. "Then we'll see this through to the end."

With that, he twisted the controls, and the chandelier of gas lights above us shimmered to life, bathing the empty theatre in a warm yellow glow to match the walls. I breathed in the smell of the varnish, lemon-soaped water, and roses.

It wasn't a circus ring, but it was our new stage.

● ● ● ●

To celebrate, Maske invited Lily Verre for tea. Of course, he himself didn't do any of the cooking, locked up as he was in his workshop until she arrived, but the rest of us chipped in. Lily came armed with two bottles of wine. She wore a russet dress, and the light caught some of the silvers hiding in the dark golden hair tumbling from its chiffon.

We gave her a tour of the Kymri Theatre.

"You worked your magic on this place, right enough," Lily said.

"Thank you, my dear Mrs. Verre," Maske said. It was kind of her. There were still cracks in the plaster, and some of the seats in the theatre were damaged or missing, but it looked a good sight better than it had before.

We sat in the kitchen rather than the formal parlor.

Oli had helped by doing all the shopping and chopping everything. Cyan had made a few Temnian dishes. She'd kneaded dough for something called mooncakes, the smell of yeast filling the air, and marinated chicken and vegetables in a thick, spicy sauce before cooking them on a skillet. She also made rice, a fluffy grain I'd only tried a time or two before.

I'd been helping with the meals and wanted to show off my rudimentary cooking skills, so I'd made little savory tarts filled with leeks, cheese, and bacon. Drystan made an old circus favorite for another dessert—peanut brittle. It'd be an extremely disparate meal, but it was ours.

For a time, the only sounds were the clink of cutlery and the splash of wine into glasses, and then Maske and Lily carried the conversation through the meal. Oli ate with a single-minded determination. I was too hungry to do much but follow his lead and put one spoonful of food after another into my mouth.

"It's a shame about those Forester protests, isn't it?" Lily fluttered. "Frightful, really. Not that I'm completely unsympathetic to their cause, mind, but the protests are truly getting out of hand, aren't they?"

"Out of hand?" Oli asked. He had a distinctive Whitefish accent, a small fishing village to the north of the peninsula. He'd been practically born on the water, he'd said, so of course he'd been called to the sea.

"Well, there were those fights outside the Palace the other week," she said. "Now there's been vandalism of the one of the estates in the Emerald Bowl."

"What happened?" I asked.

"They cut down all the trees around it and painted 'LEAVES TO ROOTS' across the windows," Lily said. "That's a bit much."

"Ach, the paint will wash off." Drystan waved his hand. "No real harm done, but they get their message across."

"Exactly," Oli said. He was clearly sympathetic to their cause.

"Which family?" I asked.

"The Ash-Oaks, I believe," Drystan said. Of course, he knew why I was curious. "Don't think they were even home at the time."

That family was staunch royalists. Lord Ash-Oak was an adviser to the Royal Steward and very active against the Foresters.

"Still, the Steward will be calling out for their blood, I'm sure," Drystan continued. "He'll want to nip this in the bud."

"If they find and arrest this Timur fellow, that'll kill the movement's momentum," Maske said.

"No one's been able to catch him, though, have they?" Cyan asked.

"He seems a slippery sucker, true enough. No one knows who he is or where he's based," Oli said. "Not even those heavily involved in the movement."

I felt a . . . knocking on my mind, like someone was asking to enter. Cyan's brows furrowed.

—*One of Oli's friends is a Forester*, she said, her lips unmoving. *Keeps trying to get him to go along, and he went to a meeting but didn't like it much.*

I reeled in shock, setting down the wine glass with a clatter.

—*Sorry. I wasn't sure if this would actually work. But it did!*

I tried to *push* her from my mind, and she was gone. I clutched the coffee cup until my heartbeat returned to normal. Drystan gave me a curious look.

Maske's words broke through. ". . . they may wish to overturn the monarchy and plenty of people are sympathetic, but these antics make them look like petulant children full of theatrics. What happened to petitions and due process?"

"Petitions were ignored." Drystan swirled the wine in his glass.

"Oh, my word, I think I regret bringing up the topic," Lily said. "That's enough politics for an evening, don't you think? Hold on, I brought a fizzy wine. Drain whatever you're drinking."

She brought a bottle over to the table and passed it to Oli. I gulped down the last of my wine.

"We're here to celebrate the theatre looking sparkling and the eve of the magician duel becoming official. Come on, everyone give me your glasses."

Oli freed the cork with a *pop*.

She filled our glasses generously before holding up her own. "A toast, to the Maske of Magic and his . . ." she paused, squinting at us. "Taliesin calls his boys the Spectre's Shadows since they do shadow plays as part of their act. How about . . ." She paused, glancing up as she considered. "Maske's Marionettes! Everyone loves a bit of alliteration. Oh, I can see the posters now."

Maske considered. "I like it. Do you?" He had two high spots of color in his cheeks from the wine.

"Sure," Drystan said. "It's got a certain ring to it," I agreed.

"Excellent!" Lily said, holding up the glass again so enthusiastically the wine splashed over the side. "Oops. To the Maske of Magic and his Marionettes!"

Our glasses clinked. I drank deeply. Drystan met my eye and smiled, holding his glass a little higher in a second, wordless toast, though to what, I wasn't sure. I echoed the gesture, my stomach fizzing with more than wine.

• • • •

It was such a simple thing, in the end, to sign a piece of paper.

We went to the headquarters of the Collective of Magic. It was a large townhouse in the Gilt District, and we were led into a grand office on the ground floor. The head of the Collective of Magic himself, Professor David Delvin, presided over the proceedings. He was a wizened old man and wore loose robes over his suit, as if he were really a wizard. The wrinkles on his face showed he'd spent most of his life smiling. Maske and Taliesin both treated him with reverence.

I'd decided to switch the skirts for a suit, both to better match Taliesin's boys and because, when we'd been surprised by Taliesin in the parlor, I'd been dressed as one. Our Glamours were safely beneath our clothing. Cyan tucked her hands into the sleeves of her tunic. She could've worn an Eladan dress, but it'd been a deliberate choice to arrive proudly Temnian. Taliesin eyed her warily, and it didn't surprise me much that he'd be leery of outsiders, even as he stole details from her culture for his shows.

For the first time, we faced our direct competition. Sind and Jac Taliesin were of average height, with solemn faces, tawny eyes, and brown hair pomaded into perfection. They were so alike I couldn't tell them apart. Their new, crisp clothing contrasted sharply with ours. Their magician's assistant was evidently Taliesin's grand-niece. Flora was a pretty young woman, with hair that shade between light brown and dark blonde, and bright green eyes. The three Taliesins stared at us, haughty and confident.

Aspall read the new terms aloud. A duel in three months' time, in early spring. If Maske won, he'd receive the deed to the Spectre Theatre and the mysterious Vestige artefact, and be able to perform again. If Taliesin won, Maske's personal performance ban was upheld, Taliesin kept the artefact, and Taliesin received the Kymri Theatre. The agreement was long and peppered with legal jargon.

Briefly, I wished my brother Cyril were here to double-check the contract. He would have noticed any sneaky turn of phrase in a second and made sure the agreement was as fair to our side as possible.

Homesickness echoed through me. Once, I lived in a place such as this room: rich woods and fabrics, and a warm fire in every grate.

"Do all parties verbally agree to the terms?" Aspall asked when he finished.

"Aye," Taliesin said.

"Aye," Maske echoed.

"Then all that is left is to put ink to paper."

Taliesin added his blotted scrawl to the bottom of the creamy paper, which contrasted sharply with Maske's tidy signature. Sind, Jac, and Flora signed next, and then Drystan, Cyan, and I put our false names down. I tried to hide my smirk at the fact that, technically, it wasn't legally binding for us. Cyan signed in Temri script.

Aspall folded the contract, and Professor David Delvin pressed his seal into the hot wax.

"Congratulations, all," he said, his voice strong. "I'm excited to be there in the audience. I've some excellent plans for the final venue, and the Collective is here to assist with publicity." The Collective, in return for its support and management, would take a fifty percent commission on ticket prices. Steep.

He shook our hands individually, meeting everyone's eyes with a smile. His palm was warm and dry.

And then it was done, and there was no going back. Over the next three months, we had to find the Shadow before he became a problem, continue to avoid Policier detection, and learn to perform well enough to help Maske win—otherwise, we'd all lose what was left of our new life.

16

THE WOMAN & THE CHILD

"The sun comes up, the sun comes down.
At night the moon goes round and round.
Chimaera creep and sneak and peek.
They'll gobble you up then pick their teeth!"

ELADAN CHILDREN'S NURSERY RHYME

Two weeks later, I stumbled down the stairs for coffee, and Lily and Maske were seated at the breakfast table. I was a bit taken aback—I'd really come to enjoy Maske's and my routine of drinking a cup of coffee together before the others woke up. Lily wore a robe, and her hair was in disarray, while even Maske's perfect hair was mussed. They looked guilty as children who'd been caught with their hands in the biscuit tin.

"I—I—" I sputtered, and then, though I wasn't proud of it, I ran away.

As I scurried back to the loft, Cyan poked her head out of the door of her room.

I opened my mouth, but she said, "I know."

"Does Lily care for him?" I asked. I didn't want him hurt.

"If you think she's talkative, then you haven't heard her mind. So much noise I can't pick out a thread, but sometimes I catch emotions. And she absolutely glows when she's around him."

"Good."

"It's your watch on Elwood's apartments today," she reminded me.

"I'll go out soon. First, I desperately need to tell Drystan what's happened." I grinned at her and her laughter followed me up the stairs.

● ● ● ●

When we were on Shadow duty, we usually ended up sitting in the window of a tearoom across the street, nursing a pot of tea as long as we could. That morning, I was decked out in my dress, but I hadn't bothered with the Glamour, relying instead only on cosmetics. Maske was getting nervous at us using the Vestige pendants too often. They could last another decade, or they could go dead tomorrow—there was no real way of knowing. There had been no articles about Drystan and me since the initial ones, and I was confident that between the gender switch, the paint, and those terrible sketches, I was safe enough.

I'd tried to pin up my hair, but Cyan had just cut it for me and it was too short to stay up properly, and curls kept escaping. I doodled on scraps of paper, glancing up every minute or so. I'd started a few letters to my brother but ripped them up or burned them instead of sending them. The act of writing to him was still helpful, but Cyril hadn't heard from me in months, and he must be worried sick.

We'd fallen into a routine since we'd signed the contract for the new wager. While Maske was keeping us busy with lessons, practice, and busking, we had managed to keep an eye on the Shadow. Cyan had even asked Oli to lurk for us a few times, which I hadn't liked, but she hadn't told him details and we were too desperate to turn down the extra eyes.

I saw no sign of the Shadow, not that I'd expected to. We'd learned that Elwood rarely left the house before noon. He'd gone out and returned late on the first night of the week's end the last fortnight, so that seemed the best time to strike. We'd had Maske teach us more about picking locks under the guise of magician's tricks.

We'd had a few fierce debates over who would do the actual breaking and entering and who would stand guard. Drystan and I had pointed out that we were trained acrobats, and Cyan had rolled her eyes and dropped to a perfect handstand right in front of us, her skirts sliding up and giving us a glimpse of petticoats, pantaloons, and shiny, low-heeled city boots. She'd grown up in the circus, after all. In the end, though, she'd agreed she would be best placed to keep watch, considering she could warn me in my mind if the Shadow returned unexpectedly. She still wasn't happy about it.

I was about to pack up and head back to the Kymri Theatre when I caught sight of a tall woman pushing a child in a wheelchair. I froze. She wore the same red dress I'd last seen outside the medical school when Cyan had tried to look in on Aenea for me. Her hood was pulled up against the chill, obscuring her face, but this time I had a better view of the child bundled up in blankets.

He was maybe ten and painfully thin, and what little I could see of his skin was pallid yellow. They passed right by the tearoom window. I watched her hooded form retreat for a moment before I threw the coins on the table for the tea and slipped out behind her, abandoning my post.

I shoved my hat on my head and put on my gloves as I trailed her. It was bitterly cold, and my cheeks stung. Something about the woman in the red dress's posture was defensive, her shoulders hunched, her head shifting back and forth. I kept out of sight as best I could, but as she turned a corner, I had an overwhelming rush of dizziness. It hit me like a blow, and I bent over, bile burning my throat. I didn't throw up my tea, but it was a near thing. My body tingled and I broke out in a cold sweat. The spark in my chest was back, even though I hadn't reached for it, and it felt as though the magic were trying to escape my skin. I fell to my hands and knees, careless of the people watching me. The thin layer of snow soaked through my skirts. My vision doubled. The snow around me was shifting and swirling.

I scrabbled at the magic in my chest, trying to draw it back in. Anisa hadn't taught me anything yet, and I didn't know what I was doing. I was working only on instinct and a frantic hope.

With a last wrench, I managed to pull the power back into myself. It faded, and I sucked in breaths, whimpering in the back of my throat.

"Are you all right?" someone asked.

I glanced up, blearily, to see a flower girl, a basket of half-frozen blooms over one arm, holding out her hand. She was a few years younger than me, and her hair was hidden in a thick woolen hat. She had a beauty mark by her mouth and a smudge of soot to the left of her button nose.

"Fine, fine, thank you," I said, but I took the proffered arm. I rose to my feet, unsteadily. The young woman wasn't looking at me, but down at the snow.

It'd shifted, looking like frozen sea waves that radiated from where I'd fallen. Her mouth fell half-open in surprise. I wrenched my hand away.

"Please don't tell anyone," I said to the flower girl, digging in my pockets and giving her what few coins I could spare in the hopes it'd buy her silence.

I stumbled away, and thankfully, she didn't follow.

Of course, I'd lost the woman in the red dress and her child, but it didn't take a Shadow to suspect where she'd gone. The Royal Infirmary and the Snakewood Medical University were just across the square. I was weak and shaky, like I'd gone too long without eating, but I also felt like I was on the cusp of discovering . . . something.

I went to the medical school and chanced climbing the steps and walking into the main foyer. I attracted some odd looks with my wet skirts. I arrived in time to see a doctor in a grey suit with a carefully groomed moustache and sideburns gesture to the woman in the dress to follow him down the hallway. Her hood was down, and she wasn't facing me. She pushed the child's wheelchair for her, and then they were gone.

I stood, looking at the empty space where they'd been, feeling suddenly lost.

"Can I help you?" someone asked to my right. A medical student, judging by his dark robes. The young man was about my age. He was stoutly built and a little shorter than me, with brownish curly hair, brown eyes, and round cheeks. He wore a bulky, woolen coat, and was studying me curiously.

"Oh," I said with a false laugh. "I think I've gone and walked into the wrong building. This isn't the Infirmary at all, is it?"

His eyes crinkled as he smiled. "Afraid not. I'll walk you over, if you like. I'm on my lunch break."

"Ah, that's kind of you," I said, my heart hammering.

We left the front doors of the medical school and crossed the square towards the Royal Infirmary. When the woman had disappeared, I'd thought I'd lost the thread, but my bones buzzed with the strange sense that I was back on a path unfurling in front of me like a carpet.

"Are you injured?" he asked, eyes catching on my sodden skirts.

"Oh, no," I said, waving a hand. "I just took a tumble in the snow, but I'm fine." *Aside from the whole not being able to control the ancient magic a Chimaera ghost said I'd use to save the world,* I added in my head.

I cleared my throat. "A friend of mine came here for treatment a few months ago. She'd been very hurt in an . . . accident. I haven't had a chance to find out whether or not she made it."

"How long ago?" he asked, his eyes softening in compassion.

"Beginning of autumn. I've been away, you see. I've also been avoiding it, because . . ." I trailed off.

He nodded. "I understand. Because then you'd have to face the loss, if it is indeed one."

"Exactly, yes."

We reached the Infirmary.

"Would you . . . come in with me?" I asked. "My friend tried to check for me a few months ago, but they wouldn't tell her anything. You're a medical student, so maybe you'd have better luck . . . ?" I trailed off, resisting the urge to wring my hands.

"Sure, I'll do my best. I know some of the receptionists can be a bit tetchy."

"Thank you," I said, grateful not to be facing it alone, even if it was with a stranger at my side.

The Infirmary smelled of antiseptic. The waiting room was about half full. A few people were obviously ill and injured, clad in casts and bandages. A man coughed wetly into a handkerchief. Another woman was heavily pregnant, her husband holding her hand.

The medical student and I went up to the registration desk. The nurse, a man in his thirties, stared at us, stone-faced.

"Hello," the medical student said, cheerfully. "I'm a fourth-year student. My friend here is wanting to check in on the outcome of a patient who was treated here a few months ago."

"And, as a medical student, you are well aware I can't give out patient information to whomever simply walks in and asks for it," the nurse said, eyes flicking to me. "Do you have identification that proves you're next of kin?"

I shook my head, mutely.

"Sir, please, it's simply learning whether the patient was discharged or not. That's all," the medical student said. "My friend here has been worried for months, you see, and I said I'd try to put her at ease or at least give her the answer, so she knows whether or not to grieve."

This student was so warm his charm could melt butter. Still, the nurse was chilly.

"Come on, just a yes or no answer."

He sighed, then relented. "All right, fine. Patient name?"

The student looked at me.

"Aenea Harper," I said, stepping closer to the counter. "Came in the first night of autumn."

With a sigh, he rose to head to the back room where the files were presumably kept.

"Lord and Lady," I said. "I feel like I'm going to be sick."

"Well, there's plenty of bed pans and bins in a hospital. Want me to fetch you one?" The medical student quirked one corner of his mouth.

I laughed weakly.

"I'm crossing my fingers you get good news," he said, demonstrating.

"You're wasting your lunch break on a stranger," I said.

He shrugged. "It's no bother. I've plenty of time to grab a sausage roll from the bakery across the way."

"What's your name?" I asked.

He held out a hand. "Kai Molleson, at your service."

I shook it. "I'm—I'm Anna Yew," I said. I didn't want to give him my false name, but using the one of my friend from Sicion made me miss her with a pang.

"Pleased to meet you, Anna."

The nurse came back, and my fear spiked. I must have looked at him with such naked hope and fear that maybe I melted him a little, too. I held my breath.

"Aenea Harper was successfully discharged a week after she was admitted. She was expected to make a full recovery."

I let out my breath slowly, taking that in. Every muscle in my body tingled in relief.

"Do you have any idea where she went?" I asked.

He gave me a withering look. "She didn't leave an address, but even if she had, I obviously wouldn't be able to share that information."

My knees quivered. Kai's hand hovered at my elbow.

"Right. Thank you," I managed through blurred tears. "Thank you."

The nurse glanced over my shoulder. A short queue had formed.

I stepped out of the way, and Kai and I left the Infirmary. The sun was brighter, reflecting off the snow. My eyes stung and watered.

"I dunno if I would have found that out if you hadn't been there. I'm in your debt," I said.

Kai smiled. "Not a problem, Anna." He patted his stomach. "I am quite hungry now, though." For a moment, I thought he'd invite me along with him, but he realized I clearly needed to be alone.

"It was lovely to meet you, and I'm glad your friend is all right," he said, instead. "Perhaps we'll meet again one day."

"Perhaps we will." I smiled at him. He was kind, his face honest, and I sensed he was someone who could be a friend. Part of me wanted to invite him to the magic duel. But Aenea's name had appeared in the papers. Slight as the danger was, I couldn't risk him putting together who I really was.

Kai gave a last wave and disappeared, leaving me to take the long, cold walk back to the Kymri Theatre alone with the emotions that swirled through me like snowflakes on the wind. Aenea had made it.

She was alive.

17

THE SPECTRE SHOWS

"A magic lantern is a machine that can project images on glass plates using a light source. While it is sometimes assumed to be Vestige, most magic lanterns use concave mirrors and there is no usage of artefacts at all. Many of the slides are hand-painted in incredible detail. While many magic lanterns might show lovely images, they can also be used in the type of horror theatre known as phantasmagoria (or fantasmagoria), which is frequently used by stage magicians. The lanterns project sometimes terrifying images onto canvases of smoke that touch on the subject of death or the afterlife and remind us that the end comes for us all."

THE SECRETS OF MAGIC, THE GREAT GRIMWOOD

That week's end, Drystan, Cyan and I headed to the Spectre Theatre to watch the twins perform in the Spectre Shows. Maske had gone before he'd officially decided to challenge his old rival, but he thought we should scope out the competition as well.

The three of us arrived just before the show began. A burly, bald man with a curling tattoo of a bear on his neck stood near the door as a security guard, and he narrowed his eyes at us as we passed. We bought our tickets and chose seats near the back. The large Spectre Theatre was only half-filled, which gave us hope, but I was itching with nerves, both for the show, and what Drystan, Cyan, and I would be doing afterwards.

We'd delayed as long as we could. That night, we were finally going to break into Shadow Elwood's apartments.

I glanced at Drystan out of the corner of my eye. I'd been acting withdrawn since going to the Infirmary. When he finally asked what was wrong, I'd told him Aenea had survived. Since then, a little schism had appeared between us. We still slept in our pushed-together beds, but we hadn't even kissed in a few days. Perhaps we pretended it was because we were so busy preparing for our heist, but we both knew it was more than that.

The light dimmed and music from a gramophone played with a pop and a hiss. My gut dipped with the same excitement I'd felt when I'd first watched the circus, but it was tinged with nerves. The curtains pulled back and one of the twins entered the stage dressed in a sharp black suit. I couldn't tell if it was Sind or Jac. He was soon followed by the other. They gave matching bows and launched into their tricks, aided by their cousin, Flora, who wore a beautiful blue gown with plenty of beading and fringe. Her curly blonde-brown hair was in a tight bun and her lips were painted bright red.

As the show progressed, dread twined through me. Maske had told us that the Spectre Shows were stale compared to Taliesin Spectre's heyday, but that didn't mean his grandsons weren't talented.

They started with small tricks—scarves appearing from sleeves, opening a closed palm to reveal a live butterfly fluttering away— before rolling out a spirit cabinet and having their assistant disappear. I breathed a small sigh of relief that she didn't appear at the back of the audience as we had in our practice sessions, but having her drop down to the stage on a rope from the gridiron above was possibly even more dramatic.

Their patter was witty, weaving in commentary from the recent Forester protests to the upcoming Midwinter festivities of the Night of the Dead and Lady's Long Night.

They continued to 'abuse' their poor assistant, putting her into a box with only her head and feet sticking out before sawing her in half and then in quarters. They levitated her, then she disappeared in a shower of sparks. I could guess how a fair number of the tricks were done, but others eluded me.

The Taliesin brothers chose volunteers from the audience and performed mentalist tricks. They guessed how many siblings the strangers had, what objects would be in their pockets, the name of an uncle that had died. I was impressed until Cyan whispered in my ear that they were planted actors.

After a brief intermission, where we disappeared to the rest room to re-set our Glamours, the brothers raised a phantasmagoria, telling a story through images projected from a magic lantern onto a shifting canvas of smoke. Skeletons and hooded figures trailed along the undulating background. The Night of the Dead had come early.

"Once, the Reaper came to the world himself to collect the dead," one twin said.

A hooded figure with a scythe emerged onto the vapor.

"He would take those who died one by one in his robe to the River of the Dead, where the good would cross to the twilight lands by gentle waters."

A slide flicked, and men and women swam down a great, swirling river that undulated on the shifting smoke.

"Both the good and the wicked would sink into the dark currents below before returning to the land of the living. As they passed through the Reaper's robes, they forgot all they were and all they'd ever been. Each new life was a blank slate, a chance to begin again, as it is for us now."

The brother changed the slide, showing a lone figure. "A woman decided to trick Death. She sought the help of a Chimaera wizard, who gave her a spell so that she would remember who she was when she passed through the River of the Dead."

The wizard in a pointed hat and robes gathered a great ball of energy, which moved toward an older woman bent with age.

Another slide. Death held his cloak open, and the woman moved into his embrace.

"When she crossed through, she remembered all those many lives. And she knew if she returned to another, she would forget it all again. She decided instead to stay within the waters."

The woman's silhouette was suspended in the middle of the phantasmagoria, the currents rippling around her.

"This upset the balance. Because of Death's error, the Lord of the Sun and the Lady of the Moon forbid him from collecting souls personally. Now, of course, we must find our own way to the river, without Death there at our side to comfort us."

The smoke swirled into darkness and the gas lamps brightened. Flora, as the magician's assistant, stood on the stage. She wore a white wig. The other brother stood in a dark robe. The "old" woman shimmered with the light of her "spell". She ran at the hooded figure. Death held his arms open to her and when they met, they both disappeared in a puff of smoke.

Applause deafened my ears as the curtains closed on the empty stage. They opened again to show the two Taliesin twins, their assistant between them. They lifted their joined hands and bowed before the curtains fell.

As we rose to leave the theatre, Cyan bit her lip. I knew what she was thinking without using any powers: our acts were good, but I couldn't say for certain whether the twins' work might be flashier.

"We have to beat them," I muttered as we shuffled down the aisle to the theatre exit. We were about to leave when the bald man with the bear tattoo from the door blocked our path, crossing disturbingly muscular arms over a wide chest. A moment later, Flora flitted to his side.

"I thought I recognized you three," she said. Her lipstick had smeared slightly, and she wore a coat over her costume. "Sind and Jac have asked to speak with you."

I was more than half-tempted to ignore that request, but Drystan cocked his head, one side of his mouth quirking. "Well, then. Lead the way," he said.

Another of Flora's curls escaped her bun as she took us backstage. She knocked on the dressing room door. After a wait long enough to border on rude, we were allowed to enter.

The Taliesin brothers lounged in their chairs, bowties loosened and white shirtsleeves rolled up to their elbows. They regarded us coolly, neither bothering to rise. I glanced at Cyan. I caught the barest flash of blue in her narrowed eyes, and she took a step back.

—*Which is which?* I thought at her.

—*Sind on the left and Jac on the right. Sind's mind has your expected level of disdain but Jac is imagining me undressed. Think we'd violate the terms of the arrangement if I throttled the prick?*

—*Only if they discover the body.*

"So," Sind drawled. "Enjoy the show?"

"It was illuminating," Drystan said, and Sind's attempt at dryness had nothing on him. He was a desert. "Put any worries about beating you to rest, I must say."

"That so?" Sind's voice hardened.

Jac opened a box and pulled out a pipe. It was long and thin, almost delicate, dark enough it might have been made from ebony. Drystan stiffened as Jac unfolded a paper packet and put something dark and sticky in it. The unmistakable sickly scent of it reached me.

Lerium. I'd smelled it whenever I'd walked past a den.

Jac lit the flame and took a deep inhale before passing it to Sind. Flora sighed, rolled her eyes in disapproval, and left us to it. The door snicked shut behind her. The blue-black smoke curled through the room.

"Want any?" Sind held the pipe in our direction magnanimously. Drystan's hands balled into fists, his nostrils flaring. His pupils had expanded, and I could read the naked *want* on his face at the scent of the drug.

"Come on," Sind pressed. "Let's put the competition aside for a moment for a good time. It's our old men who can't get over the past. Practically desperate to whip 'em out on the table and measure 'em again, aren't they?" The drug had already taken hold. His smile was vague.

"No, thanks," I said through gritted teeth.

"Aw, look at them, turning down our hospitality," Sind said, passing the pipe to his brother. "Must be allergic to a good time, I'm afraid, Jac."

Jac's eyes lingered on Cyan's curves. "Shame."

I *desperately* wanted to punch him.

Drystan leaned forward with quiet, controlled rage. "Go ahead and let that Lerium rot your brain. It'll make it all the easier to take you both down a peg or two in a few months. We're plenty happy to oblige."

"What we have cooking makes your parlor tricks look like entertainment for a child's birthday," I blustered. "Magic lanterns and smoke, is that really the best you can do?"

The twins took in my ill-fitting suit and a face that looked young for a boy.

Sind sucked in another lungful of Lerium. "You don't have a chance of winning," he said, blowing out the smoke. "We were practically born on this stage. We've been doing sleight-of-hand since we could walk."

Cyan scoffed. "And with all those years, this is where you're at? You do realize it's obvious to everyone in the audience that your heart's not in it," she said, and her voice rang with a certainty as if she were reading their fortune. Their stage presence had been perfectly fine, but she'd found a weak spot, and she was pressing it. "You only do this because your grandfather makes you, not for any love of this type of performance. I bet he made you quit anything else you preferred. A sport, perhaps, or . . . a musical instrument." She made a show of pausing, then pointed at Jac. "Trumpet, I'll guess."

"How did you—?" he sputtered.

"Your mentalist tricks were weak, you know," Cyan said, her smile widening. "I'm ever so much better."

The brothers rose, and the three of us stared them down.

"Believe me," Drystan added. "You've absolutely no idea who you're tangling with." His face was perfectly calm, but his expression was eerily similar to the one he'd worn just before striking Bil with the cane. Foreboding ran its fingers down my spine, and in that moment, Drystan seemed a stranger.

Sind leaned closer. "Get out of here before we bloody that pretty face of yours so badly you'll still be wearing the bruises by the time we finally face off onstage."

Drystan batted his eyelashes. "Oh, you think I'm pretty, do you?"

Sind swung his fist. Drystan dodged it easily and jabbed him in the throat hard enough to make Sind sputter and drop back. Jac yelled and raised his arm, but Drystan ducked and kicked the boy's ankle out from under him. The twins were magicians, not brawlers like their man at the door, and they were no match for Drystan and his tumbler's reflexes. Within moments, the twins were both on the ground, gasping, as Cyan and I looked on in amazement. I'd barely even had time to ball my hands into fists.

"We'll see you in a few months," Drystan said, so sweetly. "And I expect the result of the wager will be much the same as tonight."

Flora came back into the room, drawn by the ruckus, the bald man behind her. Without missing a beat, he grabbed Drystan and I by the scruff of the necks. Cyan swore at him in Temri, demanding he let us go as he practically dragged us back through the foyer. The collar threatened to cut off my breathing, and I was perilously close to grabbing that spark in my chest and using it to make him pay.

The man threw us out onto the cobbles outside, and I half-skidded along the frozen pavement.

"See you at the duel," Sind and Jac said, brave once again behind their mountain of a man. "Now we'll really enjoy taking you and your old man for everything you've got."

The doors of the theatre closed. Painfully, Drystan and I got to our feet. Cyan's face was tight.

I grimaced. "We shouldn't have provoked them so much."

"Felt good though, didn't it?" Drystan brushed himself off. "Could have gone worse, I'd say, but let's hope our next errand goes a little better."

18

NIGHT ERRANDS

"There is always the chance that darkness can conquer the light. The sun and the moon may illuminate the sky with their love, but the darkness of the universe is wide and deep. Death may find a way to snuff the stars one by one and to wrap the sun and the moon in its sable embrace."

FROM THE APHELION

The shadows of the Shadow dressed all in black.

We'd returned to the Kymri Theatre long enough to change. Maske was out with Lily again, and Oli was drinking with some of his sailor friends. I changed into the dark shirt, leaving off my Lindean binder for comfort. Drystan and I tied dark rags around our faces, and we shrugged on empty packs. We wouldn't be bothering with Glamours tonight.

"A moment," Drystan told me. "I'll meet you downstairs."

Cyan waited for us in the entrance way. She wore an Eladan dress and coat. Beneath her bonnet, her hair was plaited into a crown framing her face.

I checked the clock in the hall, fighting the urge to tap my foot impatiently. Drystan finally appeared, a little out of breath. He smiled in the dim light of the hallway, holding something up in triumph. "I knew the old rascal wouldn't ever sell this bit of kit."

It was a wand-like device made of Alder metal, the end pointed like an insect's antennae.

"That's an Eclipse," I breathed.

He did a few fancy flourishes as if it were a simple magician's wand instead of something incredibly valuable.

"Stop it, they're delicate!" Cyan made to grab it, but he held it out of her reach. "I can't believe you broke into his workshop and his Vestige collection." Her eyes were wide. She clearly hadn't realized Maske had an Eclipse, either.

"Don't worry, he'll never find out. I'll put it right where I found it as soon as we're back, promise."

"He'll never forgive you if he finds out," Cyan said. I felt similarly conflicted.

Drystan's smile faltered. "I know, it's not my finest moment. Admit it, though, we need this. The Shadow's bound to be a paranoid fellow. Having an Eclipse means, even if he has a Banshee, we can get inside."

A Banshee was a piece of Vestige that the very rich tended to use as a sophisticated alarm. Cyan crossed her arms, but I sensed part of her was kicking herself for not thinking to check what else Maske might have lying around. We already knew about the Augur and the Glamours, and she was aware that we needed all the help we could get. If the Shadow's client was the man who owned the Museum of Mechanical Antiquities, he could very well have a loan of a Banshee if he was paranoid enough, which I guessed he was. What's more, Anisa had already suspected Elwood had an Eclipse of his own, which was why she'd struggled to read him at the circus. I had her Aleph in my pocket, hoping she'd have enough magic to help us if we ended up needing her, but I wasn't counting on it.

"Why, exactly, does Maske have such illegal Vestige kit?" I asked. Drystan gave me a look.

I sighed. "Yes, yes, I know. Former card sharp and criminal. But why does he *still* have it? This alone could probably pay for many of the Kymri Theatre's repairs." It reminded me, perhaps a bit unfairly, of Bil. He, after all, had hoarded artefacts that might have been better exchanged for coin to help run the circus.

"Not easy to sell, even on the black market, without it being traced back to you. Also, if you had one, would you let it go? Dead useful." Drystan waggled the Eclipse before tucking it into his inner coat pocket and patting his breast for safekeeping. "Come on. Let's go."

We set off into town, barely speaking and keeping to the darkest part of the streets until we arrived outside Shadow Elwood's apartments. It was close to ten at night, which was when Elwood had set off to go to a nearby pub, the Golden Goose, during the last two weeks. We waited, tense and silent. Part of me hoped we wouldn't see him leave, so we had an excuse to turn around, go home, and try again later after more preparation. Or never.

A cab passed, the horses' hooves echoing on the cobbles.

Of course, at ten on the dot, the front door to the building opened, and Shadow Elwood stepped out, hands in his coat pockets. He'd swapped his wide-brimmed hat for a new top hat. He took out his pocket watch and glanced down at it.

I see a man, checking his pocket watch, counting down the time . . .

I exhaled slowly as the Shadow set off without a backward glance. No more excuses.

"Lord and Lady, I hope we don't regret this," I muttered.

"Chin up, positive attitude, please," Drystan said. "Cyan," he said, inclining his head at her. "Kindly be our eyes and ears."

She rubbed her gloved hands together, stamping her feet in the cold. "Get in, get out. Don't linger. And once you're in, turn off the Eclipse, or I might not be able to reach you, Micah."

"Got it." I exhaled. "Let's go, then."

Cyan leaned against a streetlamp. If anyone asked why she was loitering, she planned to say she was waiting for a sweetheart to meet her and take her dancing after he finished a late shift at one of the nearby public houses. Part of me worried—after all, I'd been raised to believe a girl on her own at night was never safe. Also, any passing Policiers might assume she was a moonshade and try to run her off. But Cyan was not as easy prey as I'd been when I'd first run away, especially with both her Chimaera powers and the little knife in her pocket.

I took a steadying breath as Drystan and I rounded the side of the tenement building. There was a drainpipe we'd established would be our way to Elwood's window on the third floor. I took the lead. I climbed confidently. The empty pack flapped against my shoulder blades. Within a few minutes, we were perched on his windowsill, breathing hard, staring at each other in the gloom.

Up here, the plan seemed, if possible, even more ill-considered. I wished Drystan and I had been more in sync, that we'd moved beyond the unspoken awkwardness we'd felt since I found out Aenea had survived. Half of me wanted to tell Drystan that it was too dangerous, and we should climb right back down. Yet the three of us knew the Shadow wasn't going to give up, and the Royal Physician's pockets were deep enough that it was only a matter of time before he found us. Beyond that, I was also desperate to see what answers might be on the other side of the glass.

Drystan switched on the Eclipse. Its end glowed green, pulsating like a heartbeat. Energy prickled along my skin. Nausea rose up in me. I swallowed, and the feeling soon passed.

I took out a lock pick roll and jimmied the window open. It was a simple catch, but then again, Shadow Elwood probably didn't expect anyone to break in this high up, especially if he had a Banshee.

Drystan took off his muddy boots, wedging them into the corner of the windowsill, and I did the same. Drystan crept inside, every muscle poised for flight. He made a slow circuit of the room, prowling like a hunting cat, the Eclipse doubling as a quivering torchlight.

I slunk in behind him, leaving the window open a crack. Drystan switched off the Eclipse, and we paused, half-fearing the shriek of a Banshee. But all was silent. I rubbed my hands against my arms as I took in the Shadow's apartments.

Elwood was messy. This was worrying. Perhaps he was simply untidy, but more likely, he'd done this on purpose so that if anyone came snooping, he'd know from one askew fold of cloth.

Despite the disarray, the trappings of his wealth were obvious. Crystal decanters for brandy on the kitchen island. A rich Arrasian rug beneath our feet. Working as a Shadow, especially one hired by the Royal Physician, seemed a lucrative line of work. There was no fire in the grate, though, and the apartment was cold.

I gravitated toward the desk in the corner of the room. No photographs of loved ones. Nothing to reveal much of anything about him at all.

"Where the hell are his files?" Drystan asked when he opened the drawers to find them empty.

I went into the bedroom. My gaze fell on the antique tapestry in the corner that wouldn't have been out of place in the public wing of the Palace. It depicted three kelpies—smooth horses the color of green glass, rising from the ocean, water weeds in their black manes. Dark storm clouds lurked on the horizon. The kelpies' eyes showed the whites in fear, as though something in the water pursued it. I felt an instant revulsion towards it. I put my hand in my pocket, and the Aleph grew warm in my palm.

"In here!" I called over to Drystan. He came in, and I pulled back the tapestry.

Sure enough, we found a small alcove and a filing cabinet.

"Nice one, Micah," Drystan said, and I glowed. It was advice from a long-dead Chimaera rather than my own innate cleverness, but her tip had saved us precious time.

We got to work.

Elwood's filing system was neat as a pin, in contrast to the messy flat. All his clients had their own folder, labeled by name and date. Sure enough, there was a file marked "Laurus, Iphigenia." I drew it out with shaking hands.

In it was a page of information on me. Birthplace: unknown. Birthdate: unknown. The stark, black words stared at me accusingly. Had my parents simply chosen a birthdate for me? I wasn't sure why that cut me deep as it did, but it sure stung all the same.

I read on, rubbing the back of my hand against my nose. The file stated the schools I had attended and the names of my private tutors. My last recorded height and weight was in there, along with my hair, eye color, and blood type. I tucked it away in my bag, deciding I'd read the file in full later.

There were so many folders, and we didn't exactly know what to search for. My gaze lingered on a file titled "Chokecherry, Malinda," remembering that name from the headlines of one of the newspapers I'd flipped through the other week. Lady Chokecherry. I took it out. Turned out Shadow Elwood had been hired by Lord Chokecherry to spy on his wife to see if she was cheating on him. Sniffing out adultery: a Shadow's bread and butter. The file was cursory; the sum marked "unpaid". But next to her file was "Chokecherry, Alfred." Here

was our first piece of ammunition: the Shadow had been double dipping. I held my tongue between my teeth and set both files aside.

There was a file on Drystan, but no other Hornbeams. Drystan
plucked it free and scanned through it, a line between his brows.

"Well, it's fairly thorough," he said, unhappily. "Though he hasn't
linked me to Maske, it seems, which is lucky. Otherwise, he probably
would have already found us through me." He set it aside as we kept
looking.

Lady Hawthorne had hired Elwood to see if her husband was visiting other ladies while she stayed at the Emerald Bowl. He had been,
at least as of three years ago. I put that folder away with a sigh, wondering if Oswin knew.

The very last folder in the filing cabinet held the other file we'd
been searching for: Zhu, Cyan.

I opened the file. Sure enough, someone had hired Elwood to find
her, but the client name was blank. The details of her background
were scarce. Two years older than me, born in Elada, as she'd told us.
Her mother was a contortionist and tarot reader, and the father who
had raised her was a juggler and fire eater.

The observations section was also blank, like mine. There was no
secret dossier list of other Chimaera, as far as I could see. I was disappointed. I'd been hoping for more.

Drystan had found a lacquered box on the top of the filing cabinet.
He opened it and froze. I looked down. It was filled with vials of a black
substance, a little syringe, and a long tie for the arm. I recognized the
smell from the twins after the Spectre Shows. My heart jumped.

"Guess the Shadow dabbles in Lerium, too."

Drystan unstopped the vial and took a sniff.

"Drystan!" I hissed.

He rolled his eyes. "You have to inject it or smoke it to feel anything." His condescending tone grated. "Though this . . . this isn't Lerium. Or not like I've ever seen it."

"It's not?" I crept closer.

He took out a vial, holding it to the light, and I could see that it wasn't black, but green. He gave a low whistle, turning it back and forth. "Smells like Lerium, though. I'm not sure what it is, exactly. Must be new."

I was unnerved by the hunger on his face, an echo to his expression when he'd stared at the Taliesin twins' pipe.

I crept back to the window. Cyan stood just out of the light of the streetlamp, her hands deep in her pockets, her breath misting in the air. I glanced at the clock. We'd already been close to half an hour.

"We should go," I said. "Let's grab as many files as we can. We've already got some proof, but I bet there's more. Let's take those vials, too."

—*He's coming back!* Cyan's thoughts were like a bird batting at a cage. *Shadow Elwood! He's coming back, with a woman. Get out. Now!*

I put my hand in my pocket.—*Have we missed anything?* I sent Anisa.

A flutter, like she was turning over in her sleep, then nothing.

We stuffed our packs as full of files as we could, crumpling some in our haste. I tucked the lacquered box into the top of my pack, buckling it closed. Drystan tugged the tapestry back into place.

We were about to sneak into the lounge when we heard the front door open. Had they raced up the stairs? Drystan and I exchanged a panicked look as we heard Shadow Elwood cough and stumble into the lounge.

Quickly, Drystan and I slid under the bed. It was dusty, with spare socks and a few books. Drystan and I lay pressed against each other, the bedsprings scant inches above our heads. We heard Elwood stomp into the apartment. He must never have made it to the Golden Goose if he was back so soon. He'd spent hours there when we'd tailed him.

Indeed, he wasn't alone.

"I hereby invite you into my home, Leda," the Shadow said, confirming he did indeed have a Banshee. His invitation must have allowed her to enter without setting it off.

Leda laughed, low in her throat. I heard her tottering about the lounge, as drunk as he was. I couldn't see her, so I imagined a woman the Shadow's age or a little younger. He'd gone from sober, or near enough, to absolutely sozzled in less than an hour. I could hear them kissing—sloppy, sucking sounds. Drystan's gaze met mine, wide in the darkness beneath the bed.

"I really hope they don't decide to fuck in here," he whispered, his voice little more than a breath in my ear. I clamped my hand over my mouth. All the nerves and fear of breaking into a stranger's house threatened to burst from me. I buried my face in Drystan's shirt, silent laughs racking my body. He shook as well, gripping me tight. I thought of how perplexed the Shadow would be if he stumbled into his bedroom and discovered two hysterical boys beneath his bed, and that started me all over again. Tears gathered in my eyes and my face must have been tomato-red from the effort of keeping quiet.

When our amusement finally ebbed, the fear returned, stronger than before. The only solace was that, if he found us, the Shadow would need us alive to collect his reward. I could smell the lemon soap Drystan used to wash and the spicy scent of his skin. His stubble scratched against my forehead. As the Shadow and his lady embraced in the next room, I clung to Drystan more tightly, the recent awkwardness between us forgotten in our dismay as the Shadow and his lady friend came into the bedroom.

"Oh, Leda," Elwood said. Leda tripped and left her shoe by the bed, a little satin dance slipper, decorated with crystal beading.

Please, please don't let her bend down to pick it up. My nose tickled with dust. I pinched my nose shut to stop the sneeze. The other satin shoe joined the first as Elwood threw Leda onto the bed.

"My sweet summer rose . . ." he murmured, and I made a face at Drystan. He bit his lip against his grin. The Shadow and Leda were making all manner of noises on the bed, and the springs sagged alarmingly in the middle. How long would we be trapped here, and what other sounds would we have to endure?

Articles of clothing continued littering the floor of the bedroom. Leda's dress, a pale, watered green silk decorated with pink roses, slid off the bed. Her corset fell next, followed by Elwood's coat and waistcoat flung across the room.

"It's absolutely freezing in here, my love," Leda said, her voice low and sultry.

"I'll soon warm you," he said.

"The cold from outside is in my bones." I heard the rasp of her hands rubbing her skin.

"Come on, then, my dove."

Elwood and Leda's naked feet came into view. A ropey scar twined about Elwood's hairy ankle. He led her into the washroom, turning on the tap for the bath, but he paused before joining her.

"A moment, my sweet."

He left the washroom door open as his feet grew closer to us. He paused by his trousers, which were right by the bed. He reached down and I saw his hand, a scant few inches from my face. He rummaged in the pockets and found a lambskin prophylactic. We were as quiet as could be, but his hands and feet stilled. He went about the room, opening the wardrobe door and rifling behind his clothing. The Shadow came back toward the bed. He began to crouch. Drystan and I tensed, ready to fight if we had to, my body thrumming with nerves. I let that spark catch in my chest, even though Anisa warned me against using it. I remembered the churned, frozen snow and the flower girl's shock at what I'd done.

"Sweetling," Leda called. "The water is warm."

Shadow Elwood paused. Drystan and I held our breath.

He laughed ruefully. "Coming, darling." He padded to the washroom. As soon as the door closed, Drystan and I were out from under the bed, covered in dust.

We darted through the lounge and opened the window, hoping the running bath would cover the sound. He turned on the Eclipse long enough for us to climb back onto the frigid windowsill, stuffing our feet into our boots. Drystan turned off the Eclipse. I felt a surge of energy above me as the Banshee switched back on and immediately began screeching. I panicked, but I distantly heard Shadow Elwood cursing about the damned thing, and realized he thought it was malfunctioning because of Leda rather than actual intruders.

It was a tense climb down the drainpipe. The alarm was so loud it echoed against the stone buildings. The sounds might bring someone to the windows out of curiosity and annoyance, and we could only hope our dark clothing blended in well enough with the stone.

I exhaled in relief when my boots were back on the cobblestones. The street was empty and deserted but for Cyan. The three of us headed back to the Kymri Theatre, stuffed to the gills with secrets.

19

SHADOW CAPTURE

"Could a mermaid love an angel?"

TRANSLATED FRAGMENT OF ALDER SCRIPT

The next afternoon, Drystan and Cyan were practicing one of our grander-scale illusions: "The Sleeping Kymri Princess". Maske, Oli, and I were in the audience. I held two cymbals at the ready.

"I learned of this magic from the great wizards of the golden Kymri plains," Drystan said, pitching his voice so it carried to the back of the empty theatre. "I read about a ritual under the full Penmoon where they performed a spell that might allow me to harness the powers of the ether of the stars." He held his arms apart. His palms were coated in silver glitter. He sprinkled some over Cyan, who was resplendent in full green Kymri robes stitched with golden symbols, a brass circlet resting upon her head. She sparkled in the light of the glass globes and lanterns scattered about. Drystan's stage presence was already miles better than the Taliesin twin grandsons.

He laid his hand against Cyan's forehead, bidding her to close her eyes. When he took his hand away, he left a smudge of silver. He held his hands wide, muttering an incantation.

Cyan collapsed backwards, her nickel and copper bangles clinking. As her head and torso fell, her legs raised until she levitated off the floor, her body level with Drystan's waist. Her unbound hair brushed the stage. Drystan moved his arms, which was my cue to crash the cymbals. Cyan rose higher, until she was level with Drystan's chest. Drystan grabbed a hoop hidden behind him. He passed the ring around Cyan's "sleeping" body, to prove that no secret wires held her aloft.

"Through the ether, the Princess of Kymri is now light as a feather," Drystan intoned.

The moment was magnificent, and I set down the cymbals to clap, but before my hands could even touch, the screech of metal echoed through the dusty theatre. The hidden ledge Cyan lay on tilted madly from the harness attached to Drystan's waist. Cyan cried out as she crashed to the floor.

Maske and Oli ran onto the stage. Cyan sat up, indignant, her circlet askew on her forehead. Maske disentangled Drystan from the equipment.

"What went wrong?" Drystan asked.

Maske studied the metal framework. "My figures must have been slightly off. The ledge should have supported her. Are you hurt, Cyan?"

"Just a sore bum." My bruise from falling off the gridiron had faded, but I winced in sympathy. Now that I knew she was safe, I tried and failed to stifle my mirth.

"It's not funny." Cyan scowled in my direction as Oli helped her up. She rubbed her hip.

"It's a little funny," I said.

One side of her mouth quirked. "Fine. Only a little," she said, straightening her circlet.

"Apologies again. I'm entirely at fault." Maske sighed. "I think that's enough practice for today. I'm going out. Spend the afternoon in the library if you like."

"Where are you going?" I asked. His suit was especially immaculate today. "Twisting the Aces?"

"Initially. I'm meeting Lily Verre again."

"Ooh," Cyan teased, singsong.

Spots of color bloomed on his cheeks. "I trust you'll entertain yourselves well enough while I'm away," he said, stiffly, straightening his suit jacket. He walked off as dignified as he could be with the three of us giggling behind him.

Drystan brushed himself off, only covering himself in more glitter. "Ugh, remind me not to let Maske make me use this stuff for practice again. It gets absolutely everywhere."

I wanted to tease him and tell him he looked pretty as a pixie, but the words died on my tongue. We were dancing around the distance between us, pretending nothing was wrong after I'd learned Aenea had lived. "Right, it's good timing, anyway," I said, brisk. "We've business with the Shadow to finish."

We'd gone through all the files we'd stolen and found a tidy pile of proof that the Shadow was crooked. Beyond double dipping, he'd stolen secrets and done a bit of blackmail. In short: he'd been quite naughty. All we had to do was hand it all over and hope the Constabulary and the Crown took it from there. The vials, however, remained a mystery. We investigated them, holding them up to the light, smelling the liquid again.

In a gap in the velvet, something glimmered. "Hold on," I said. "What's this?"

Drystan picked up the top velvet layer of the box with the drug vials. Underneath was a blue oval of Penglass set in a Vestige metal frame.

Cyan leaned toward it, her eyes wide. "Lord and Lady. I think it's a Mirror of Moirai."

"What's that?" I asked.

"Maske always wanted to get his hands on one of these," she said. "Very rare, but I'm not sure exactly what it does beyond that. Said it could be used for communicating with anyone else who had a mirror."

Drystan switched it on. Alder script emerged on the screen, as well as the outline of a hand.

He fiddled with the controls. I almost felt as if I could puzzle out the strange Alder script, but then the words eluded me. At one point, something that looked like a stylized map appeared on the screen with a few glowing, moving dots.

Cyan frowned at it before her forehead smoothed. "Look. It's Elada," she said. She made the area that was now Imachara larger. Over the centuries, it had somehow mirrored the layout of the capital, and we could see its tangled streets as if we were birds flying over-head. "Gods," Cyan said. "I'd love to give this to Maske, but how in the world would we explain how we got our hands on it?"

"Let's not mess with it too much," I said. If the Shadow was using it to communicate with this client, we wouldn't want to accidentally link to the Royal Physician.

We wrapped it up carefully and put it back in the bottom of the box beneath the vials, but it made me uneasy. I realized that if we sold it at some point, we'd have enough to help Maske with more repairs, or to book passage out of Elada if we really needed it. Elwood would also be livid to discover we'd stolen something so obviously valuable.

At midnight, we set out on our quest to turn in the Shadow.

The Constabulary never fully closed, but the headquarters itself functioned on a skeleton crew at night. There was the risk of being spotted. We could mail the proof, but what if it somehow went missing? Drystan and I had Glamoured ourselves beyond recognition and even added the illusion of a Policier officer's uniform over our normal clothes. We'd loosely based our faces off the Policiers who had handcuffed me the first time we'd busked, and quickly realized a ginger beard did not suit me any more than muttonchops favored Drystan.

Cyan would keep watch and come to our aid if needed. We'd try to find a quiet moment, pop the envelope through the letter box, and flee.

The city was dark and glittering with frost. Up ahead, the sky was clear, though the gas lamps made it difficult to see the stars. I couldn't wait for this to be over and to return to the Kymri Theatre knowing we'd done our best to solve the issue of the Shadow, once and for all.

We'd almost made it to the Constabulary before it went completely pear-shaped.

Cyan's inhaled breath was our only warning before something cold, hard, and metallic pressed into the small of my back. Drystan and Cyan whirled. I felt the Shadow's breath on my neck. I held my palms up. We were three against one, but we also didn't have a gun. I had a little dagger in my boot, but no hope of reaching it.

"Impersonating an officer with the help of a Glamour," the Shadow said. "Imagine what they'd do to you if they found that out."

"Shadow Elwood," I said, my heart hammering. I reached for that spark in my chest, but while it'd sometimes appear without me wanting it, now that I was desperate, the power slithered out of reach. Anisa's Aleph was back at the loft, and she was still dormant. This part of the city was dead quiet. No one was around, and all the windows were shuttered and dark at this hour. No help was coming.

—*Keep him talking*, Cyan said in my mind. *I'm going to try something, but I have no idea if it'll work.*

"How'd you find us?" I asked.

"I don't know how you little shits got into my apartments," Shadow Elwood said, "and I don't much care. But you were beyond stupid. You not only stole the thing that could help me track you down, but you went and touched it."

The Mirror of Moirai. I kicked myself. I'd no idea if we touched it, he could use it to trace us.

"Now. You're going to hand over everything. My files. I'd like that box and what's inside, too. In return, I'll quit your case, and we leave it at that. How's that sound?" He pressed the gun harder into my kidney for emphasis, and I stifled a grunt of pain.

Drystan bared his teeth, his fingers balling into fists. He was sizing up the Shadow, looking for an opening or an angle, but he also wasn't about to risk me getting hurt.

"Pass," I said.

He chuckled. "There are a few other options. I could make you burn the files in Drystan's pack there, then walk you down to the Constabulary and turn you in for impersonation alongside being a fugitive on the run from the law."

A line appeared between Cyan's brows. I was reaching desperately for my magic, wishing I better knew the rules or how to control it.

"Do you really think we believe you'd leave us alone?" I said. "You'd probably shoot us in the middle of the night anyway and leave our bodies in some back alley."

The Shadow tutted. "The messier choice is I pull the trigger right here, take what you have off your corpses, then head back to wherever you're hiding in the Glass District and grab my files." My heart lifted to learn that while he'd narrowed down our location, the mirror wasn't exact—he wasn't aware we were in the Kymri Theatre specifically. How had he found us tonight, then? A combination of the mirror and bad luck on our part?

—*Just a little more . . .* Cyan said. She stared at Shadow Elwood with such intensity I half-expected him to burst into flames. I kept groping for my magic.

"I'll have you know I'm a crack shot," he said close to my ear. I realized he'd likely killed before to protect his name and reputation, and he wouldn't hesitate to do it again.

"*Let him go*," Cyan said, her voice echoing in my ears and my mind. Cyan's eyes blazed blue, and with her burst of power, I felt the Glamour illusion fall from my face and clothes. I had no idea how she'd done that as I finally, finally managed to grab hold of my unreliable power.

I broke free of his grasp and used my magic to send the gun skittering across the cobbles. Shadow Elwood staggered back, moving stiffly, as if he wasn't in full control of his body.

Drystan leapt into action, jabbing the Shadow just as he had hit Sind after the Spectre Shows before kicking the Shadow's knee hard enough to make him fall. Elwood bared his teeth and grabbed at Drystan, his fingernails scraping against his woolen coat. Drystan punched the Shadow in the jaw, and the sound of his fist hitting flesh was beyond satisfying.

My magic was roiling within me and risking escape. The streetlamps flickered as I staggered after the gun and picked it up. The Vestige metal derringer sparked in my hands, and I almost dropped it. It felt as if I was drawing the magic from the Vestige into myself.

I walked towards the Shadow, raising the gun. Elwood's gaze was challenging, as if he suspected I wasn't strong enough to pull the trigger. But I didn't need to—my magic had other plans. It slithered like a rope around his throat. His breath caught. I saw the fear there, finally, and I tightened the lasso. The magic desperately wanted to break free, to do more, to *hurt* him more than he'd ever hurt me.

"*Sleep*," Cyan said in Alder, the word echoing. I somehow understood her. "*Sleep*."

The Shadow's head lolled forward, but his lips were turning blue. The power was growing in me, and all I knew was I loved the feeling of it.

"Micah," Cyan said, in warning, but I barely heard her. There was a push on my mind, more insistent. —*Micah, stop.*

A hand pressed between my shoulder blades. "Micah," Drystan said in my ear.

The magic snapped back from the invisible rope, and every gas lamp on the street extinguished, leaving us in darkness.

I dropped the gun and fell to my hands and knees and emptied the contents of my stomach. I could barely see, barely hear. Drystan's hand between my shoulder blades grounded me.

Eventually, the ringing faded, and I came back to myself. Drystan stared at the unconscious form of the Shadow, then Cyan, before his eyes fell on me. He couldn't hide his fear, and I was abruptly ashamed.

What had come over me? What had Cyan done? With a word, she'd sent a man unconscious. What had I almost done?

"Quick," Drystan said. "Let's finish this."

He hauled the Shadow to his feet, his head lolling. I came up at his other side. I was afraid to do any more magic, but I was more terrified of being discovered, so I carefully pulled the Glamour illusion back over my face. The magic lay in a film on my skin, and I wanted to inhale it into me, as if it'd refill what I'd lost.

The street had been empty, but a few men, collars up against the cold, rounded the corner. With the absence of lights, they could barely see us in the gloom.

We were only a block away from the Constabulary Headquarters, but it was difficult work to half-carry, half-drag him. A few others were out and about. Drystan made sure to loudly admonish his friend Karl for getting himself absolutely legless again. The people on the street gave us a wide berth and carried on.

The Constabulary Headquarters came into view. It was a blocky, two-story building with a blue gas lamp illuminating the thin pillars and stone steps in front of it. The windows inside were lit, but no one was leaving or entering.

"Come on," Cyan said. She peered at our faces and nodded, confirming mine and Drystan's illusions were holding. She drifted back, letting Drystan and I take it from there.

We dragged Shadow Elwood to one of the stone pillars. I reached into his pockets and used his own handcuffs to secure him in place. Drystan took the packet of incriminating evidence from his bag, slipping it into the Shadow's coat pocket and making sure the white of the envelope was clearly visible.

That done, we darted back across the street and into a nearby alleyway. Cyan narrowed her eyes, and her eyes flashed blue again. A moment later, the front door of the Constabulary opened just in time for Shadow Elwood to groan.

The officer's head turned towards the slumped figure at the pillar. He called inside, and another two officers came out. One of them picked up the envelope, reading the "For the Constabulary: one crooked Shadow" scrawled on the front. One of the Policiers turned his head, searching the streets, and Cyan, Drystan, and I backed deeper into the alleyway shadows. Sure enough, though, they took him inside. We'd done all we could.

The three of us trotted down the other side of the alley and then sprinted through the frosted city back to the Kymri Theatre. Once we were back inside, we stared at each other, wide-eyed, in the dim light of the hallway.

I was reeling with what had happened on the street: my magic, Cyan's abilities, and Shadow Elwood revealing how far he'd been willing to go.

"I have no idea how that worked," Cyan said. "Why did dropping the Glamour help?" She looked exhausted, practically swaying on her feet.

I shook my head at her. "Less interference, maybe. Or you drew on the Vestige somehow?" I wanted to sleep for days. "Have you done that before? Made people listen to you?"

"Once, maybe. Not often." She stared down at her shaking palms, as if they frightened her, before looking up at us with a grin. "It was pretty wicked, though, wasn't it?"

"It was," I said, trying to hide my fear and not sure I succeeded. Elwood might have known we were in the Glass District, but that hopefully meant the Royal Physician didn't realize we were at the Kymri Theatre. Part of me wanted to smash that Mirror of Moirai, just in case. Still, we were definitely safer than before.

"We did it, though," Drystan said, echoing my relief. "We captured the Shadow."

20

THE BLUE LIGHT

"The strange, unearthly light,
On the full Penmoon night.
The blue glow on your skin,
You and I are here again."

THE BLUE LIGHT, BY MICAH GREY

A couple of days later, Maske showed us one of the automata he was selling—a mermaid, her skin a luminous brown, her hair cropped close to her skull, and eyes dark as coal. Her neck had delicate gills, and small fins sprouted on the backs of her forearms and along her spine. The mermaid's tail was an emerald green, and she wore a heavy necklace of shells and stone that did not quite cover her breasts.

"She's lovely," I said.

"If I switch that lever, she's able to swim underwater, but I think she's very low on power," Maske said. "I can't risk using any more before selling her. Not even to see her swim one last time." He stroked the mermaid's face with the back of a fingernail before wrapping her carefully in cloth and sliding her into the case.

"Another woman I've abandoned, eh?" He said it with a cracked smile. After Maske returned from the auctioneer's, he retired to bed early, not even coming down for dinner.

The next morning, Maske was in much better spirits when Drystan and I entered the kitchen. The magician was drafting a revision of the winged woman trick at the table, drawing the delicate cogs of the machinery onto the checked paper.

"How goes your illusion?" I asked, trying to peer at his sketch. He slid a blank piece of paper over it.

"All in good time, Micah," he said. "All in good time." He smiled at me, but I sensed some frustration beneath.

As Cyan and Drystan reached for mugs, I opened the books Maske had left on the table for that day's lessons.

"Séances?" I asked as Drystan passed me a steaming cup of coffee. I smiled at him gratefully. Ricket trotted into the kitchen, demanding food, and Drystan obliged.

"We've gotten a very interesting invitation this morning." Maske placed the creamy sheet of paper on top of the books with a flourish.

Cyan's eyebrows rose even before she opened the envelope, so I suspected she already had an inkling of its contents.

The three of us bent close together to read it:

Mr. Jasper Maske and his Marionettes:

You are cordially invited to provide dinner stage magic entertainment, with a séance to follow, at the residence of Lord and Lady Elmbark on the 21st of Dalan, the Night of the Dead. Kindly provide your response by week's end.

Cordially yours,
Mr. Edgar Nautica, Head Butler of the Elmbark Residence

"The Elmbarks are a prestigious family, aren't they?" Cyan asked. Her eyes were bright with excitement, but Drystan's jaw muscles tightened. Dread spread through me as the full implications set in. I'd once dined at the Elmbark residence with my parents and Cyril after going to the opera in Imachara.

"Indeed they are," Maske said.

"Who else will be there?" Drystan asked, his voice terse. Drystan's family were friendly with the Elmbarks, and he'd probably been to their estate in the Emerald Bowl countless times. He was the same age as their oldest son, Harry. The younger brother, Thomas, was Cyril's age.

"I asked the messenger but he wasn't entirely sure. He did say, though, that it'll be some of the most powerful names in Elada." Maske's lips curled in triumph.

"Oh, did he now?" Cyan clapped her hands, delighted. Drystan and I, by contrast, clutched the edges of the table.

"I'm not sure it'd be wise for Drystan and me to go," I said, catching the way Drystan's jaw ticked.

"But you must!" Maske said. "The séance and the evening entertainment must be the talk of the town."

"We are still fugitives on the run from noble backgrounds," I pointed out. "What if there's someone there who might recognize us?"

"What is your family name?" Maske asked. "You've never told us."

I paused. "I was once Lady Iphigenia Laurus of Sicion," I said, heavily. I didn't see the need to keep it secret any longer. Cyan had probably already gleaned it from my skull at one point or another.

Maske's eyebrows flickered in surprise, though I wasn't sure if that was from hearing the name or the gender of the title. "Well, that's a noble family, to be sure, but they're based in Sicion and not exactly the inner ring of the Twelve Trees, no?"

"That's true enough," I admitted.

"You are both from Sicion, so it's unlikely you'd brush shoulders with someone you know," he continued. "You'll wear Glamours, of course. It's no more dangerous than going on stage in front of many more people in a few months. This is good practice to see how your disguises—and performances—hold up under scrutiny."

The magician had a point.

Maske leaned forward. "They're offering us fifty gold marks. That's enough to do some repairs, take a leave from busking while we prepare for the duel, and buy the rest of the materials we need for the finale."

"Fifty gold marks?" Cyan said, faintly, and I echoed that surprise.

It was a pile of money, to be sure, but panic buzzed around me like an irritating fly. Maske leaned forward. "What's more, they invited *us*. Not Taliesin." He grinned, his teeth white and sharp.

Cyan twisted the end of her braid around her fingers, looking thoughtful. She met my gaze. She had been doing séances with Maske since the beginning, but now I understood what a blinder of a game she'd truly been playing.

Maske had his Vestige crystal ball, and numerous other artefacts we could spirit away in our pockets. The Elmbark residence would have a cabinet of curiosities, and when we'd fought the Shadow, we'd felt like we'd drawn on some of the power in the Glamour and Elwood's gun to enhance our own. She'd told me reading minds was easier if there was a lot of Vestige around. All Cyan needed to do was ask someone to picture the dead person they wished to speak to and pluck details from their mind to tell them exactly what they wanted. According to the Great Grimwood and the Collective of Magic, though, that would be cheating.

Cyan's gaze sharpened, and I wondered if some of my misgivings had slipped through whatever made me harder for her to read. After what had happened with Shadow Elwood, wasn't she herself nervous to conduct a séance and reach for her powers? Anisa had warned us not to, after all. By the way she toyed with one of the braids in her hair, I guessed yes, but it wasn't as if she could tell Maske her hesitations, either.

—*It'll be fine*, she sent me. *The rich simply want an evening of entertainment, and they'll get it. I'll be careful. Might not even need to use my extra abilities much at all.*

It felt like she was trying to reassure herself as much as me.

"The Night of the Dead is in a week and a half," Maske said, bringing me back to the kitchen. "It'll be busy, practicing for this on top of the preparations for the duel. We'll pause the street magic, but again, with that coin, we aren't as reliant on busking."

The Night of the Dead was the night before the Lady's Long Night, the longest night of winter. The Lady's Long Night represented the hope of a turning point—that brighter days and spring would return. Yet the night before that celebration, some said the currents of the River of the Dead could flow back through the world and the spirits could wash back onshore. It was a perfect night for a séance.

"I want you two learning more about this aspect of performance. The atmosphere of a séance must be just so," Maske said. "Dark enough so that if one of us needs to sneak about, we'll be able to, but not so dark that nothing can be seen. Props are useful, especially in superstitious households. I've kept a record of almost every house I've been to, writing down the names, appearances, and dispositions of each member. Many of my clients are a repeat business, so I tailor my approach, but the Elmbarks are new, which makes things more difficult. I'll teach you several variants, but only practice, time, and intuition will help you discover which approach is best."

He was warming up to his lecture. "A séance is very different from stage illusion. In a magic show, most of the audience doesn't believe you're really doing anything supernatural, even if you pretend you are. But with a séance, it's different. Some are complete cynics, others are unsure either way, and others believe or desperately *want* to believe."

He squeezed his eyes shut and opened them again. "You'll have both enemies and allies at the same table. They are also active participants. It's not one volunteer called up from the audience. Each person in turn may be asked to divulge something personal. Each will have loved and lost."

He paused. "I view séances differently from my magic performances, though over the last fifteen years, they've not exactly warred for my attention. While I am deceiving people at a séance, sometimes I feel as though I help them. Grown men have wept like broken-hearted babes at my table when they think they have made contact with a long-dead loved one. They've felt like they've been able to say goodbye. Sometimes, fanciful as it sounds, I do believe the spirits work through me."

"As do I," Cyan added. In her case, though, it might well be true.

Their words hung in the air between us.

"You showed an aptitude for it that first night, Micah," Maske said. "Do you want to be involved in the séance?"

I snuck a glance at Drystan. "I'd rather do the dinner stage magic if there's a choice in the matter."

"Same," Drystan echoed. While I knew he had no compunctions around potentially conning people with his card sharp past, he had his clear preference, and I wanted him at my side.

Maske nodded. "That is what I was thinking. You and Drystan will take the first part of the evening, and Cyan and I'll take the second, but we'll need your help with some of the séance effects. So read up," Maske said, tapping the books. "We'll start practicing in earnest tomorrow."

He rubbed his face with his hands. He'd cut down on séances in recent weeks and spent every spare hour either in his workshop or instructing us on magic tricks. He was patient overall, rarely snapping, even when we kept making the same silly mistakes time and again, but it was obvious he was exhausted and stressed about our chances of winning.

I crept upstairs and tucked myself into bed to study, but couldn't concentrate. A night of magic and séance was exciting, but daunting.

Setting the book aside, I held the disc that contained Anisa. She'd gone quiet again, and neither Cyan nor I had had any more dreams or visions. Standard Vestige couldn't recharge, but Anisa was unlike other ancient artefacts. What if, no matter how sophisticated she was, she simply couldn't recover her power? If she were awake, I knew she wouldn't approve of us doing this séance, but we weren't exactly in a position to refuse, no matter the risks.

Eventually, my eyes grew heavy.

What felt like moments later, Drystan and Cyan's tread on the stairs woke me up. The stained-glass window was dark. It was evening. I slid the disc under my pillow.

"Come in," I said before they knocked.

They entered, Drystan closing the door behind him. "You slept straight through dinner," he said. "I tried to wake you, but you were dead to the world."

I shook my head, still feeling bleary. "I suppose I was tired."

Cyan took in the beds pushed together with an arched eyebrow, but didn't otherwise comment.

"The paper came late today," Drystan said. "But look." He placed it on my lap.

The front-page headline read: "CROOKED SHADOW BEHIND BARS".

The article said an anonymous tip-off had informed Policiers that the eminent Shadow Kameron Elwood had been found tied up and delivered like a gift to the Constabulary. On his person had been a packet that showed he'd fabricated evidence in many of his cases or else had a conflict of interest by hiring both sides of a case. His apartments had been searched, with more evidence seized. Policiers had already discovered that one innocent man had been falsely imprisoned for ten years, in no small part due to Shadow Elwood's compromised testimony at the trial.

"Ten years," I breathed. We'd done this mostly for ourselves, but I was glad we might have helped others with our actions, too.

"I know. Elwood was a—" Cyan called him something unbearably rude in Temri.

I kept reading. Shadow Elwood said he'd be mounting an appeal, which made me nervous.

I looked up when I finished reading. "What if the Royal Physician pays for his legal fees?"

Drystan sucked his teeth. "Shadow Elwood truly cooked his name and reputation by messing with all these other cases with high-profile nobles. I'd be surprised if the Royal Physician wanted to part with any more coin. I think he'll wash his hands of him."

"He might hire someone else," Cyan pointed out.

"At least they'd likely be starting from next to nothing. I'd still call this a win," Drystan announced, his eyes glowing with triumph.

I tried to echo his smile, wishing I felt as certain. "We made a good team, didn't we?" I said.

"We did," Cyan agreed.

Drystan gave a nod. Looked like he'd finally laid down his last suspicions of Cyan. We hadn't decided what to do about the mysterious vials and the mirror we'd found at Elwood's yet. I'd hidden them in the loft.

"Do you want any dinner?" she asked. "There's some stew in the pot."

"Maybe later," I said. I had no appetite.

She rose and stretched. "Right, then, I'm heading to bed nice and early. Feel desperate to get my first night's proper sleep in weeks."

"Night," I called to her retreating back.

"Night," Drystan echoed.

The sound of the door closing echoed through the loft. Drystan and I stared at each other in the dimness. It was still early in the evening, and after my nap, I was wide awake.

"Let's go outside," I said, impulsively. "No Glamours, just as we are."

Drystan shifted, unsure.

"Shadow Elwood is sorted, and if the Policiers haven't found us by now, I don't think they'll pick up our trail." The guilt would always be with us, but we couldn't let it rule us completely.

He relented, his eyes lighting up. "Yes. Let's."

I was full of nervous energy as we put on our jackets and shoved our feet into our boots. We tiptoed down the stairs and slipped out of the front door, not wanting to disturb Maske, Oli, or Cyan. Snow lay thick upon the ground. The world was dark, the brightest stars shining down on us like pinpricks of light through black cloth. The air was fresh and crisp.

"Where shall we go?" Drystan asked.

"I dunno. Anywhere we like." I threw out my arms towards the hidden sliver of the moon and let out a laugh. As I'd suspected, no one was on the streets when they could be tucked up safe and warm in bed.

Drystan and I ambled through the streets. He was in fine spirits, his eyes bright and his cheeks pink with the cold. He threw his arm around my shoulders. The windows of tenements and the gas lamps shone sodium yellow. The sky clouded over, and a few snowflakes began to fall like petals.

The domes were glowing softly in the moonlight. Drystan considered one as we passed.

"Have you—" he began, then stopped.

"What?"

"Silly, really. But I was wondering if you'd tried touching Penglass since . . . that night."

Whatever I'd been expecting him to say, it wasn't that. He so rarely brought up the circus, and especially not what happened at the end.

"No," I said, apprehensive, but his words woke my own curiosity. I'd asked Cyan to touch one in front of me once, but it hadn't reacted to her at all. Whatever I was able to do, it wasn't something innate to all Chimaera. The mystery of the Penglass had only deepened.

"I could try," I said. It felt dangerous, and I knew Anisa wouldn't want me to. But she wasn't here, and she hadn't even woken enough to admonish me for using my powers the night we caught the Shadow. Part of me wondered if she'd ever rouse from her hibernation again.

We found a Penglass dome only a little taller than us hidden inside an alley next to a shop with boarded windows.

Drystan stared at the glass in apprehension.

"Stand here," I instructed, "so anyone walking by won't see."

He complied. I took a deep breath, my bare palms hovering above the surface. Excitement coursed through my veins right alongside fear. Had it really been months since I had last done this? Would the glass be like it was the night with Cyril, or like the night in the Copper District? The moon was such a crescent that the glass's power should be at its weakest.

"Keep your eyes shut until I tell you whether it's safe," I warned.

He did, and I closed my eyes to near-slits.

I pressed my palms to the cold glass. Beneath my hands, the dark cobalt began to glow. The light reflected off the snow until it seemed as though we stood on diamonds. I took my hands away, widening my eyes. It was safe, and my powers felt steady. The imprint of my hands remained, glowing as softly as the night I'd gone climbing with Cyril.

"You can look," I said.

Drystan crept closer, the blue light illuminating the planes of his face. His eyes were wide with wonder, his lips parted.

Drystan reached out to touch the glass, but it remained dark under his fingertip, just as it had with my brother. I drew a few swirls like the winter wind, illuminating the snow a little more. The ice crystals glittered.

It was easier to look at the Penglass than him. "Things between us have been . . . different." I finally broached the subject. "We were distracted by the Shadow, but also . . ."

"Aenea," he finished. He swallowed. "You chose her first, after all, and I know how much losing her hurt you." He met my eyes, his irises as blue as the glass. "I wouldn't stand in your way, if she's who you want."

"You're not my second choice, Drystan," I said, the magic in my veins making me braver. "I suspect she'll be at Nickleby's vaudeville show, but I haven't gone to see her. What Aenea and I had . . . it was lovely. It was sweet, and it was kind. But equally, I'd never quite been free enough to tell her the truth. Something always held me back."

I licked my lips, and his eyes tracked the movement.

"But with you . . . I felt like even from the beginning, you saw straight through me. There's never any pretending. You've seen the good, but also the ugly. The dangerous. And you haven't turned away. Aenea isn't in the story of my future," I said, echoing Anisa's words. "But you are."

He took a step closer. It felt like we were standing on top of a

Penglass dome higher than any building in the city, and one wrong step could send us tumbling.

"Why would I turn away? You've seen me far darker than you could ever be. I've told you who I used to be, what I used to do, and you didn't flinch. Maybe Alvis Tyndall was right in that the darkness can make the light shine brighter. This, right here, what you can do, what you are . . . it's beautiful." He came close and wrapped me in his arms. "You're beautiful, Micah."

My breath hitched in my throat.

Our lips met. I pushed him against the glowing glass, the stubble of his chin scratching mine. I rested a hand on the Penglass, the cool blue light bathing us as we kissed, careless of who might see.

21

HIDDEN MESSAGES

"Sometimes, I wish séances were real. That I could reach through the Veil and speak to those I have wronged. I'd apologize to my wife, Beatrice. I'd apologize to Nessa, who I briefly stole from Taliesin simply because I could, rather than out of any real affection. She deserved better than that from me. There are so many men and women I've wronged. So many I've reduced to ghosts and shades of themselves. They surround me, but I can never let them know I regret what I have cost both the living and the dead."

JASPER MASKE'S PERSONAL DIARY

Four pairs of hands met in a ring about the séance table. Maske had invited Lily to one of our practice sessions, and Oli, Cyan's beau and our newest lodger at the Kymri, also joined. Cyan sat where Maske had the first night we'd come to the Kymri Theatre. Drystan and I, meanwhile, were hiding beneath a tablecloth, as we would at the Elmbarks' in the room where the séance would be held.

I peeked through a gap in the tablecloth. The curtains of the parlor were drawn and the flame from only one candle flickered, casting long shadows along the walls. The Vestige crystal ball rested on the table before Cyan. Alder script had been drawn on the dark tablecloth in chalk. Tonight, the séance was hers, not Maske's.

We'd studied nonstop over the last five days, and here was our first test.

"We welcome you to our sacred circle, Jasper Maske," Cyan intoned. Her face was covered with black gauze, as if she were a bride of Death himself. She was wasp-waisted in a corset and a black Eladan-style dress. Only her hands were bare, decorated in swirling designs of silver glitter, her nails painted black as night.

"This evening, we call the spirits to peek their heads up from the currents of the River of the Dead, to whisper the words they wish they could have told us in life. I've experienced such heartache and grief that I've learned I can pull back the Veil and pass along the messages of the dead. Jasper Maske, we shall start with you. Close your eyes and imagine someone who has passed that you wish to speak with. For we have all known, loved, and lost."

Maske concentrated. I knew Cyan had considered choosing Lily, but found her mind too loud, and she had very clear boundaries about not reading Oli, which I understood. Part of me was desperately curious about what spirit the magician would request.

Cyan's brow crinkled as she spied on Maske's mind. On cue, Drystan and I tapped the floorboards, and Cyan triggered the shaking mechanism beneath the table. That was an addition we could bring with us and install to make almost any table at the Elmbarks' suit our purposes. Lily's eyes flew open in obvious delight. Oli's jaw clenched and his shoulders stiffened. He wasn't a cynic—he had gone to Cyan to have his fortune read, after all—but I suspected that had been more of an excuse to talk to the girl who had caught his eye at the circus.

"Someone comes to me through the mists of the otherworld . . ." Cyan shuddered, her head falling forward. My chest hummed.

Whispers in Alder echoed in the room. "She hears us, too. She hears us, too. *She hears us, too.*"

Cyan's head rose, her veiled face turning towards me, and my spine turned to ice as a cold wind whipped through the room and time slowed down. Lily was mid-blink. Oli's nostrils were flared in fear. Maske stared ahead, unblinking. Even Drystan was frozen next to me beneath the table, his features cast in shadow.

Cyan's black gauze faded to mist, drifting away from her face. Her eyes glowed the bright blue of Penglass, and the crystal ball on the table blazed the same hue. She spoke in Alder, her voice echoing in three tones at once. She tilted her head towards the ceiling, and the last word ended in a scream.

I heard a sob. It was mine.

Cyan broke her hold with Maske, her free hand raising in my direction. I found myself moving as if in slow motion, pushing past the tablecloth and coming to her side. Fear thrummed through me as her fingertips rested on my forehead, deathly cold, and I jerked with the force of the vision.

● ● ● ●

I was once again in the body of the damselfly woman. Cyan and I were side by side. I knew it was her, though her body was different. A severe widow's peak topped her heart-shaped face. Her lips were small and thin, her hair a cap of feathers banded brown and grey. Her tawny yellow eyes blinked at me. She was thin and bird-boned, her skin a dark olive.

And then there were the wings.

They rose behind her, impossibly large, all faun, chestnut, and charcoal. She flapped them, buffeting me with a gust of air.

I looked down at my own shimmering limbs. My wings rose behind me, as insubstantial as a wish in comparison.

We stood at the edge of a cliff made of white stone. Venglass sprawled down to the crescent of a bay. Ships with purple and red sails drifted on the water. The air was too warm and humid, close as a lover's touch.

Between the Venglass, tall tropical trees reached toward the clear sky. The wind carried the scent of hyacinth, dark, loamy soil, sea salt, and an unfamiliar spice. I guessed that we were in Linde—Linde as it was when Alder and Chimaera lived side by side with humans.

"Matla," my mouth said in a voice that was not my own. Cyan, I tried to say. Are you there? *But my mouth would not form the words. I was only a passenger in this body. As she spoke, my sense of self as Micah Grey faded further.*

"Why are we here?" Anisa asked. We'd travelled half the world through one of the portals.

"We must stop a death here tonight, at all costs," Matla said.

"Who?"

Matla, the owlish woman with Cyan hiding behind her eyes, shook her head. "The Kashura are planning to kill another Chimaera."

The phantom memory of my previously murdered ward filled my nose with the iron tang of blood. We had another ward, and they were safe at home with Relean.

"Come," Matla said, spreading her wings. "We haven't much time."

She dove off the edge of the white cliffs. I flew after her, my damselfly wings cutting through the thick, warm air as though it were water. The part of me that had never flown dimly marveled at it.

As we glided toward the Venglass Domes of Sila, I wished Matla had told me more before we'd left. I had nothing to protect myself but the small dagger in its sheath at my hip and an Acha in the pocket of my robe.

A few inhabitants of Sila glanced up at us as we passed overhead. The Chimaera here were more aquatic than those from the mountains of the Ven, their skin silvered with fish scales, moist like a salamander's, or rough as the beaded texture of lizards.

Paths lined with colored stones wound through the cobalt Venglass. The scent of sizzling meats from an open market permeated the air, along with the sounds of goats bleating and humans laughing and haggling.

The jovial atmosphere of the market warred with the absolute dread and fear Matla emanated as she darted through the air, bringing us over the town and into the dark tangle of jungle. We landed on the branch of a breadfruit tree, tucking our wings tight against our backs as we climbed down the trunk.

We pushed our way through the undergrowth, not speaking, spurred on by an undeniable sense of urgency. My hand never strayed far from the dagger's hilt at my hip.

We came to a small Venglass dome, incongruous in the middle of the jungle. There were no nearby growths. Matla glanced over her shoulder at me, blinking owlishly. She held a finger to her lips and set her hand on the glass and it lit. She drew the glyph for opening, and the glass melted away, revealing an entrance large enough to admit us.

Underneath Anisa, the part of me that was still Micah Grey desperately tried to memorize that glyph, but it slipped away like a dream.

Matla entered, drawing her long, thin Acha. It cast a light that only the two of us could see, and broadcast a subtle illusion, so that someone glancing down the hallway might not see us at first. The part of me that was Micah recognized it as an Eclipse, though it was doing something I'd not seen anyone use it for, exactly. Matla held her curved scimitar in her other hand. I drew my own weapon. It was dark, but Matla could see in the gloom, so I followed the whisper of her footsteps.

We went deeper and deeper into the earth. It was hard for two Chimaera who preferred wide, open skies. I wondered why Matla had asked me and not a stronger fighter or someone higher in the ranks of the Chimaera. Far off, we heard agonized cries, as if something or someone was being tortured. My wings shook.

We entered a room. Two male Alder loomed over a creature strapped to a table. Engrossed as they were in their grim task, they had not yet seen us.

Matla crouched into a fighting stance, holding up the Acha. In her *other hand, she brandished her curved sword, and the light caught the bright green poison at the tip. My blood ran cold. I wondered where she had found Vitriol, the only poison that could kill an Alder. Or a Chimaera.*

She launched herself into the room, giving an avian shriek.

The Alder turned from their charge on the table, surgical instruments in their hands. Matla swiped one of the Alder through with her scimitar, and they dropped, their wounds smoking. The other whirled, skittering back from the table. They fought, the Alder barely holding back Matla's furious attack. Matla shrieked like a hunting owl.

"Get the boy!" she cried at me. "The boy must be saved!"

I broke from my paralysis, moving to untie the bonds holding the Chimaera on the table.

He had the flat face of a snake and reptilian eyes. His body glistened dark green in the light, and his eyes were the brilliant emerald of a cat. He was hairless and naked, and two jet black horns sprouted from his forehead. Matla had brought me here to save the spitting image of the charge I had lost.

The child panted in pain. Red blood stained his skin from where they'd cut him. It looked as though they had planned to implant something into his torso. It rested on the table next to the surgical instruments, the Vestige metal speckled with intricate blue and black designs. Cuts on the child's head were sewn closed.

I untied the child's bonds, keeping an eye on the fight between Matla and the other Alder. I stepped over the corpse of the first one. I knew what group these two belonged to.

The Kashura Alder made a mad swipe and grazed Matla's wing. She screamed in pain and rage. Feathers fell.

Leaving the child, I took my little knife, darting in from behind. The Alder twisted, but I managed to leave a long gash along his ribs. Matla recovered and stabbed him in the arm, grimacing in triumph.

Yet our makers were a strong and strange folk. Even faced with his death, the Alder's eyes blazed with disgust, his lips curled in hatred. With a move too swift to follow, he grabbed the weapon from Matla's hand and plunged it into her stomach.

I cried out as though I were the one impaled. I launched myself at him, stabbing my little knife into his throat, hitting his jugular. Blood spurted and he dropped the weapon. I grabbed it, letting my knife fall to the floor. Wasting no time, I pushed it into his chest with all my strength.

"You're too late," he whispered to us in his three-toned voice. "All has already been set in motion. The creature is strong enough. All Chimaera must fall."

I ignored the dying Alder, bending over Matla. She sucked in wet, sticky gasps.

Tears streamed down my face as I ripped off a strip of my shirt and held it to the smoking wound in her stomach. We both knew it was too late. Vitriol could slay Alder, and it could kill us even more easily. Underneath Anisa's consciousness, the me that was Micah railed against the walls of her mind like a moth caught in a lampshade, desperate to know if Cyan was all right.

"Save the boy," Matla whispered. "His name is Ahti. Raise him with your other charge. We need them both. Raise them to be good, and kind, or he will lose control and all is lost."

I heard a great shuddering gasp from the table. The horned Chimaera boy jerked and went still. I was not sure whether he was unconscious or dead.

Matla groaned in pain. "He must be good, or all is lost. All is lost." She coughed against the burbling in her throat. I clutched her hand.

"I'm sorry," I said, over and over. "I'm so sorry."

"Not your fault," she managed. "It is mine."

I rested my hand on Matla's cheek as her life slipped away and the room deep within the Venglass dissolved around us.

● ● ● ●

I was thrown from the Phantom Damselfly's ancient life and back into my own.

Lily had her hands clasped over her mouth. I must have appeared to them as if from nowhere.

Cyan fell from her chair and lay jerking on the floor, clutching her stomach. She was choking out more words in Alder.

Maske went to her, peering at her expanded pupils. He turned her on her side so she wouldn't choke on her own tongue. Oli hovered in anxiety as Drystan stumbled out from beneath the table, pale and wide-eyed. Maske ran to get his medic bag as Oli cradled Cyan in his arms.

I swayed, the edges of my vision darkening.

"Micah," Drystan said, snapping his fingers in front of my face.

"Come back to me," Oli kept saying, his voice low and urgent. I had the sense he'd seen her like this before. When?

"You're all right, Cyan," I said, my tongue loosening. "It wasn't real. Only a memory. A very old memory." I meant to send that to her as thoughts, but Drystan, Lily, and Oli's faces told me I'd spoken aloud.

Well. Nothing for it. I steeled myself. "Matla?" I asked her.

Cyan's eyes rolled toward me.

"Are you Cyan or are you Matla?" I pressed.

"I don't know," she said, in Alder, but I could somehow understand it. At least it didn't echo in three tones, and I could only hope Lily and the others didn't realize which language she was speaking.

"I don't know," she finally repeated in Eladan.

Lily was wringing her hands. "My father sometimes had fits," she said. "I used to tell him facts about himself, to help bring him back from memory lapses. It might help?"

I didn't have any better ideas. "Cyan. You are Cyan," I said, more firmly than I felt. "You were born in Elada. You are Temnian. You were raised among circus folk, and you told fortunes. You love Oli, your sailor who is right here at your side. You live in the Kymri Theatre. You see more than most."

"Cyan," Oli echoed, and bent down to kiss her forehead. "I'm here. I'm right here." He stroked her hair, letting his touch ground her.

She inhaled. "Yes. Cyan. I am Cyan." She muttered to herself in Temri, and her fluent outpouring of that tongue reassured me. Matla was gone, dead thousands of years.

Maske returned with the medic bag. Cyan was still pale, her hair matted with sweat against her forehead.

"She should go to a doctor," Lily said.

"No," Cyan said, faintly. "I'm all right. I just need to rest. I'm sorry. It's been a long time since I've had a fit like that."

"I think it's time I head home. I don't want to be in the way," Lily said, gathering her bag. She hesitated. "I hope you feel better soon."

"Thank you," Cyan managed, and Lily fled.

"You've overstressed yourself," Maske said, his face creased as he studied Cyan. "Perhaps I put too much pressure on you. We've been working such long hours."

"No," she said. "It's nothing to do with that. Don't blame yourself for this."

Oli helped Cyan stand, one arm around her shoulder and the other rubbing her lower back. She met my eyes, and I nodded. I'd watched her die in another's body. That tied us together in a way that couldn't be broken.

She left the room. Beneath Maske's concern, I sensed his anxiety over whether we'd be able to do the séance at the Elmbarks' in a couple of days' time. This practice one hadn't exactly gone to plan.

"Get some sleep," he said to us before he followed Cyan and Oli.

As soon as Drystan and I were alone in the parlor, I started shivering so violently my teeth chattered.

"Micah?" he asked.

I didn't answer. I could sense the phantom wings against my back and when I glanced down at the skin of my arms, I half-expected to see them shimmer with iridescence.

"What do you need? What can I do?" His hands gripped my shoulders, holding me up.

I tried to answer him, but my tongue was like a dead slug in my mouth. My eyelids fluttered as I sensed an outpouring of dread above us.

"Cyan," I moaned, and tried to make my way to the door. My legs failed, and Drystan hauled me to my feet and half-dragged, half-carried me to the stairs.

Oli met us partway up. "Help," he said, his voice tight with fear.

The bath was still running. Cyan lay slumped on the floor against the tub, fully clothed but for her boots and one sock, her eyes closed.

Drystan turned off the water while I checked her pulse and color.

"She's not well," I said, alarmed by the whites of her eyes when I pulled back the lids. "I think we do need to take her to a doctor."

Oli dashed from the room to fetch Maske.

"Cyan," Drystan said, slapping her cheek gently. "Come on, Cyan."

She opened her eyes as Oli returned with Maske, but they didn't focus.

"I've called for a carriage," Maske said. "It should be here soon."

Cyan stretched her arms out towards the magician. "Papa," she moaned piteously, and my heart went out to her. She spoke the truth to him, and he didn't even recognize it.

Oli picked up Cyan gently, and he carried her downstairs, Maske hovering behind them. Distantly, I heard the front door of the Kymri Theatre open and close. I hoped Cyan would be all right, but I wasn't doing so well myself.

"I'm so cold . . ." I said, my teeth chattering.

Drystan rubbed his hands against mine, but I only shook all the harder. He turned the tap on again, the water steaming. He stripped me down to my undergarments, his hands chafing my arms, palms, legs, and feet. I was touched and embarrassed in equal measure.

Without ceremony, he placed me into the tub. I gasped with shock at the heat, even as I welcomed it. My fingers and toes burned as if they were recovering from frostbite. I sagged against the edge.

"Micah, what's happening?" Drystan asked, stroking my hair back from my face.

"I dunno," I managed.

He perched on the edge of the tub. "It's something Chimaera, isn't it?"

"You'll think me weird. Weirder."

"Try me."

It was time. "We had a vision of the past, long ago. In the time of the Chimaera. It's not the first one I've had, but it was the strongest." I told him the bare bones of what I'd seen. The Alder in the garden. Anisa's first murdered charge. Matla, the Kashura, and the Chimaera boy Ahti. My explanation was garbled, and I jumped around, but he listened to everything as my limbs loosened in the heat. Drystan stayed at my side, gently scraping my scalp with his fingertips until I wanted to purr like Ricket.

"The Damselfly," he said. "I usually avoided the Pavilion of Phantoms. I always found her frightening."

"I don't know if I trust her, or if I should, but she saved our lives the night we left the circus, and she was the one who told me of the kelpie that helped us in the Shadow's apartments." I paused. "I'm sorry I didn't tell you sooner. I tried, but it was almost as if she stopped me. Perhaps she did."

"Why doesn't she now?"

I shrugged. "Either she's too deep in slumber or . . . she's decided it's time you knew."

Drystan's face rippled in unease, and I understood. Neither option was comforting.

When the water started to cool, he helped me out of the tub. We paused. His eyes were on my face, but I was all too aware he sensed my body so close to his, the undergarments wet and transparent.

His arms slid around me, even though I was slippery and dripping. I clutched him close, comforted by his solid presence. When I pulled away, I could see the outline of his muscles and the pink blush of his nipples through his damp, white shirt.

With a burst of bravery I didn't know I had, I pulled his shirt off, gasping at the feel of his skin on mine, only my Lindean corset separating us. After everything that had happened, I was desperate to be back in this body, to feel alive and present.

My lips worked their way to the soft skin of his neck. For a moment, I feared he'd pull away, but his breath caught. We were frightened, me by what I had seen and Drystan by what he'd watched me go through. We staggered back to the loft, kissing as much as we could on the way.

He pushed me onto the bed, and we touched each other hungrily, going further than we had before, though not quite all the way. As I ran my fingertips over his skin, I felt the last tatters of Micah Grey come back to me, and I let the ghost of that old world fade away.

22

CONFRONTING THE CHIMAERA

"No matter how much we've searched, we have found no archaeological evidence of either Alder or Chimaera remains. No bones. No definitive cremated ash. No graveyards. No mummies in ice or desert. Only Vestige. It is no small wonder that many believe the Chimaera never existed at all. Sometimes, in a darker mood, I wonder that, myself."

PROFESSOR CAED CEDAR'S UNPUBLISHED NOTES

Cyan returned from the doctor a few hours later. Drystan and I went downstairs to find her leaning against Oli, pale as milk. He helped her straight to bed.

"How is she?" I asked Maske.

"Faint, but the doctor said she should recover within a day or two." He held up a hand. "Come. I believe it's time you told me what's going on under my roof."

He led us to the library. I curled against the seat cushions, weak as a newborn kitten. Drystan leaned against the back of the chair as Maske folded his fingers in front of his face, his eyes unreadable.

"On the carriage ride back, she told me to close my eyes and imagine my favorite memory," Maske said.

I felt the blood drain from my face, though part of me was curious as to what he might have pictured.

"She proceeded to tell me off because I was instead thinking about what I'd been doing in my workshop that afternoon. And she was able to explain my work perfectly, in far too much detail, even though I trust that she wouldn't have gone in there without my permission."

He shot a glance at Drystan, who gave no reaction. Drystan wasn't going to admit he'd broken in before we went to Shadow Elwood's apartments, and Maske wasn't quite going to accuse him. I'd asked Drystan what he'd seen in the workshop. He'd said that wood shavings littered the floor. Saws, dowels, clamps, and nails were all carefully in their place. In the far corner, one of Maske's inventions had been covered in cloth, but there'd been enough of a gap that Drystan had seen something gleam bronze in the low light. He hadn't snooped more than he'd had to, but Maske would still have considered it a betrayal.

I sucked in a breath, caught in the middle.

Maske leaned back, relenting. "Is it true, then? That Cyan has . . . some sort of prescience?" he asked, but he didn't seem as surprised as I'd have imagined.

"You should ask her," I said.

"I shall. I met a woman once," Maske said. "A mentalist who seemed as if she could truly read my mind. You already know that magicians tend to phrase questions a certain way, giving hints and picking up on body language. She was so good at guessing and so specific, I couldn't believe it. Perhaps they had an advanced signaling system I simply didn't catch, but the person she brought up from the audience seemed just as astonished, and I don't think he was a plant. Part of me wanted to believe that it was . . . real magic." He laughed, half in wonder, half in self-deprecation. A gleam came into his eyes, and I knew he was wondering if there was a way to use this to our advantage in the séance.

My eyes narrowed. "Cyan nearly died tonight, Maske. Do keep that in mind."

His chest puffed in indignation, but he abruptly deflated. "You're right, you're right." He rubbed his face with his hands.

He stared at me. "Is there anything else I should know about? How you yourself spoke to spirits, perhaps?"

I swallowed. "They spoke to me, and I listened. I dunno much more than that. There's much about the world we don't understand, isn't there?" I had no idea how to even begin to tell him everything. It wasn't that I didn't trust he'd believe me; it was more that I was afraid his head might spin like a top. "Speak to Cyan first, and if she shares, then so will I. How does that sound?"

He considered me, rubbing his whiskered chin. "I'll take that, for now." He glanced at the grandfather clock in the corner. "You should head to bed."

He left us, his footsteps heavy in the foyer. Drystan stared into the banked coals of the fire, looking almost as tired as I felt. His hair fell onto his forehead. Feeling bold, I reached out to brush it back.

Neither of us spoke, each lost in our thoughts. When we went to bed, I stared at the ceiling until Drystan's breathing finally evened next to me in sleep. I was afraid of what I might see if I closed my eyes.

I felt a flare from the Aleph. I almost went down on my own, but I paused and stared down at Drystan before shaking him awake.

"Anisa is calling us. If you want to meet her properly."

He nodded. I took the Aleph from the bedside table drawer. I wasn't sure if he'd be able to see and speak to her as Cyan and I did, but I didn't want to hide anything from him anymore.

We crept down to one of the many empty rooms of the theatre. Cyan waited for us, wrapped in a robe, her hair tied up in cloth to protect the braiding and beads. Dark circles bruised the skin beneath her eyes.

"You saw it all, didn't you?" Cyan asked me.

"I did."

"It was all real," she said as Drystan watched silently. "Wasn't it?"

"An echo, yes," I said. "Like an old recording on a gramophone."

She put her head in her hands. "I don't want this. I don't want any of this."

"Neither do I." I drew the Aleph from my pocket. I pressed the button and set the disc down, and the tower of smoke swirled in the middle of the room.

The fumes cleared and Anisa materialized, her wings flickering to life.

—*Little Kedi*, she greeted me, before turning to Cyan. *I'm sorry, one who was Matla.*

Cyan flinched and backed away until she reached the wall. "I'm not Matla."

—*You were, for a time, little bird*, she said. *You saw what she saw. Felt what she felt. Died within her.*

Drystan's breath caught, and Anisa turned her attention to him.
—*I'm strong enough that you can hear me now, can't you, pale jester?* Seemed she'd given Drystan a nickname, too, though I wasn't sure I liked it.

"Yes," he whispered. "I can hear you."

I took a shaking breath. "Why did you show us the vision?"

—*Some of this, I would not choose to share, but the past sometimes demands that it be known. Almost all of us are gone now. So many Alephs have been lost over the centuries, never to be found.* Her expression turned mournful, and I knew she was thinking of Relean, the love she hadn't seen since the old world broke.

—*You are involved in what's to come. You will be influential, in your own way. Even you, pale jester, despite the fact you are not Chimaera.*

My breath caught. Something in Drystan's eyes dimmed.

"There must be others better placed to help," I said. I thought of Juliet, Tauro, and Violet. The cyrinx had the power to change her shape and to heal. I'd inconsistently slowed time and moved objects with my mind, but I couldn't control it.

—*None I would trust.* She held her arms out to us. *You are young. Your hearts have not hardened to the realities of the world. Your dreams have not yet fallen through your fingertips. You still know hope, and that can make all the difference.*

"We're not children," I snapped. "People have nearly died because of me. Cyan has seen horrible things in people's minds. You're aware of what Drystan did to protect me. Don't pretend we're innocent."

The ghost of a smile played about the phantom's lips. —*To me, you are but children, and you would be if you were wrinkled as your elders. I have lived a hundred lives, and seen things you could never imagine.*

"Please." The word tore from my mouth, ragged as a shard of glass. "Enough. What, then, are we meant to do?"

She paused, as if listening to the spirits. Whatever they whispered, I couldn't hear it. —*The blurred man has not yet properly begun his plan, but he will soon. And I can only hope that you fare better than Matla and I did, all those years ago. It is why I called to you.*

"Called to us?" I asked, dread settling in me like a stone.

—*Surely you guessed why you went down to the beach the night you found the circus, little Kedi?*

The air left my lungs. "Because . . . I've always loved the ocean," I said, faltering.

—*It was soft as a whisper, but you felt my call. I thought you would come to me, that first night, but you visited me the next.*

I shook my head.

"And me?" Cyan asked.

—*Oh, little bird, I sensed you from afar as your powers grew. Who, after all, do you think sent you the dream of the lion tamer?*

She clapped her hands over her ears. "No."

I darted forward, clutching the Aleph with shaking hands. "Stop sending us dreams and visions without warning. Stop speaking in riddles. Or we won't help you."

—*Oh, but you will, little Kedi.* She smiled beatifically. *You will.*

I pressed the button, and Anisa disappeared. Drystan watched us both, standing apart, his arms wrapped tight around his chest. I went to Cyan. She folded into my arms, and I held her, my fellow Chimaera, as she tried to process to the feeling of dying in another's body.

"I'm sorry," I said to them both, as Anisa had said to Matla, even if none of this was any of our fault. "I'm so sorry."

23

THE NIGHT OF THE DEAD

"On the Night of the Dead, the dead come out to play.
On the cold, dark wind of winter, they come to stay.
They whisper to remind us before the light of day:
You will join us, for death cannot be held at bay."

ELADAN CHILDREN'S RHYME

Cyan and I spoke to Maske in the parlor a few days after she'd returned from the doctor.

I watched as Cyan told Maske that she had the ability to
read minds. His expression slackened in wonder, then curiosity. He
asked question after question, and Cyan answered them, though I noticed she downplayed the true extent of what she could do. He next
rounded on me, and I did the same, mostly focusing on things he
would have already noticed, like my ability to heal quicker than normal. I left out my other powers and we didn't call ourselves Chimaera.
Of Anisa, we said nothing. We asked Maske not to mention it to Oli,
though we revealed Drystan knew it all.

"It's a curious irony, isn't it?" Maske said when we'd finished. "Two under my roof with the very abilities that would allow us to win, but if performing stage magic tricks that include Vestige is cheating, this would be, too. Still, what a temptation."

"We don't need it to win," I agreed. "Your inventions on their own will do the job well enough."

He couldn't hide his own flicker of doubt. "You've been using your abilities in the séances though, haven't you?" he asked Cyan.

She grimaced. "I have, now and then. I don't mind cheating there, and it resulted in more coin, didn't it?"

"That it did," he agreed. "But what of the Elmbarks? Is it safe, considering what happened in the practice . . . ?"

Cyan's lips thinned. "I've been wondering that, too. But I think I can do it without drawing on my powers much. I'll be careful. Combined with Drystan and Micah's more practical effects, we should be fine. We can't exactly risk pulling out of it, either, can we?"

"That we can't," Maske agreed, and he couldn't hide his obvious relief. He shook his head, an amazed smile on his lips. "It's rather extraordinary, though, isn't it?"

Cyan and I returned the smile, relieved that he wasn't afraid.

"It is," I agreed.

Anisa kept her visions away from us, or so we thought, but all Vestige suddenly seemed to contain echoes of the past. I was afraid to look into Maske's crystal ball, and whenever we went to Twisting the Aces, I avoided the whispers emanating from the display cabinet. Even the Glamour felt uncomfortable next to my skin. Cyan and I didn't discuss either what had happened with our powers when we fought Elwood or the vision again. It reminded us too painfully that even if we had both been circus folk, we were now even further from being normal. We had no idea what Anisa actually planned for us, so we used stage magic to distract ourselves from the real kind.

Blissful routine followed, and we sank into it gratefully. Mornings

were for magic lessons, early afternoons for constructing the appara-
tuses and costumes, and late afternoons were for séance work. Oli
toiled away as our stagehand in return for room and board.

In the library one evening, a book caught my eye: a tome on ancient magic and artefacts by Professor Mikael Primrose. His wife had
been the one to write that etiquette book that had plagued me during
my old life as Iphigenia Laurus. I pored over the dense text before
bed. Professor Primrose held many postulations on Penglass—that it
was created from the same substance as Alder ships, which I could
now confirm from my vision of Anisa in the garden. He thought that
the Alder had left and taken the Chimaera with them, and that humans alone chose to stay—or were left behind. Soon after, smoke
scorched the sky and most of the world drowned beneath the waves.

The Alder were largely an enigma. Why had the Kashura turned
against Chimaera, and had they been right to fear them? I considered
asking Anisa, but I feared she'd either be vague or ask something of
me in return.

I dreamed of that ancient Lindean jungle that night, but I don't
think the Phantom Damselfly sent it. I prowled through the jungle on
all fours, content that nothing could hunt me.

I woke up next to Drystan on the dawn of the Night of the Dead,
wondering what the next evening would hold, and wishing I could
take some of that predator's strength with me.

• • • •

The carriage cut through the thick purple-grey of Imacharan dusk.
Maske, Cyan, Drystan, and I huddled beneath the blankets, but our
breath misted in the air as the driver took us through the winding
cobbled streets to the nicest part of town. The crescent moon had
thickened in the last week and a half.

Cyan wore her black Eladan dress with a Temnian silk sash. In her bag was the lace veil for the séance and silver paint for her face. In addition to our Glamours, my eyes and Drystan's were lined with kohl and we'd pre-emptively spent some of our earnings on new suits with Temnian silk cravats. We both looked rather dashing, if I did say so myself. We'd learned that subtle exoticism tended to go down well with the nobility, so we were leaning into it, ever-so-slightly. I tried to shove my unruly nerves back into place.

We pulled up to the Amber Dragon building on a rich street of the Gilt District of Imachara well-lit by gas lamps. The turrets of the building was topped with oxidized copper and dragon statues. The Elmbarks had a three-story townhouse.

Maske met our eyes. "We've practiced for every eventuality. Remember your roles, and let's make sure the Elmbarks have an unforgettable Night of the Dead."

Cyan's eyes glittered. Drystan gripped my hand, hard, then let go.

The teeth of the cold wind nipped at our fingers and ears once we exited the carriage. I pulled my collar up against the stinging snow. The doorman opened the grand door for us.

Our shoes clacked along the granite floor of the entryway. Every detail telegraphed wealth. Marble columns, gilded frames, emerald silk wallpaper. Maske and the butler shook hands, and I knew Maske would have slipped a coin into his palm as payment for continuing our ruse if he noticed anything amiss.

We went up a flight of marble stairs and entered the grand, main room where we'd hold the séance. The walls were draped in black velvet. A large Arrasian rug hid most of the parquet flooring. White wax candles illuminated the carved fauns and fairies of the wooden columns to either side of the grand room. This was where they'd hold dances and other parties. There was little furniture save the séance table and chairs in the center of the room and another table at the corner of the room for drinks and, after dinner when it was time for the séance, mine and Drystan's future hiding place.

Guests trickled in over the course of the next half hour, but we hit our first snag of the evening when none other than my mother and brother walked into the room.

My breath caught and my heart beat so fast, I practically felt it hitting my sternum. Why were they here in the capital instead of in Sicion? Perhaps they'd come up to find Cyril quarters for university when he began in the spring. But how had they wrangled an invitation to an event like this?

Drystan followed my gaze and stiffened, and Cyan must have gleaned enough from my expression and thoughts that her eyes went wide. Maske didn't notice our distress as he spoke to Lady Elmbark. I held my breath until my mother and Cyril's eyes swept the room and landed on me, yet I saw only blank curiosity. I supposed I shouldn't be surprised. My brother hadn't recognized me when we'd first crossed paths on the streets of Sicion, even without a Glamour.

—*Are you all right?* Cyan risked sending me.

—*I don't know,* I said. *I honestly don't.* I wanted to turn tail and run, but I couldn't risk drawing attention to myself.

Mother's lips were curled. She must've felt like the cat with the cream, being among people from the inner ring of nobility. But her face was thinner, the lines about her mouth and eyes deeper, her skin flushed beneath the makeup. Her hair was a different shade of brown; she'd dyed it to cover the grey. I couldn't believe how much she had changed. My brother, in contrast, was the very portrait of good health. He was taller, his face somehow more mature, as if he had settled into his features. His fair hair curled over his ears.

The Lord and Lady Elmbark were both dressed in somber grey with matching necklaces of bird bones and feathers. Lady Elmbark wore preserved bat wings in her hair. I'd heard the Elmbarks were fascinated by the macabre and behaved as if they already had one foot in the grave. A tall man with a trimmed brown moustache and short beard and a finely tailored brown suit stood next to them, a bright feather boutonnière on his suit coat as if to deliberately clash with their solemn apparel. He wore a small, derisive smile, as if he knew the punchline to some amusing jest that none of the rest of us could hear. I noticed my mother kept glancing at him nervously and giving him a wide berth. While the man was vaguely familiar, a few other faces registered more clearly: Lord Wesley Cinnabari, with his swoop of dark hair and neatly groomed beard, Lady Rowan, her red tresses in an elaborate braid that fell to her waist, and Lady Ashvale, whose crown of grey curls was threaded with what I suspected were real diamonds. These were some of the families closest to the Snakewood Throne. How *had* my mother gotten herself and my brother invited to this, and why hadn't Father come? Perhaps a legal case had kept him in Sicion. This wouldn't have been his type of thing, in any case.

Soon, the Elmbarks led their guests to the dining room.

—*If you overhear anything potentially useful for the séance, send it my way, please,* Cyan whispered in my mind, and I sent back a wordless affirmative. Drystan and I waited in the corner of the séance room until everyone settled into their first course and were ready for the entertainment.

"They won't recognize you," Drystan whispered in reassurance. "No more than they know me. Remember: beyond our disguises, we're the hired help. Not that important beyond what we can do for them. Think of this as only a night of more misdirection."

I nodded, his words bolstering me as we entered the dining room.

A gramophone played eerie, appropriate music. The tablecloth was black. Flickering candles in silver candelabras were the only sources of light. Unfortunately, we were stationed right by the gramophone, so it was difficult to catch any conversation over the haunting music and clinking of cutlery.

Once the guests were on their second course, Drystan and I entertained them with close-up magic. Drystan took the lead with a story about a young jack who fell in love with a queen despite the jealous king, cutting the deck and drawing up the relevant card at the right moment in the story. I found myself smiling as I watched his long fingers and the curve of his lips. The jack disguised himself as the queen's jester and they ran away together. None of the nobility suspected that the magician in front of them had once been one of their own.

Next, Drystan and I went around the table and made coins appear from behind ears. I stayed on the side of the table furthest from my family and produced falling blossoms for the Lady Rowan, who blushed like a maid. Guests chose cards and Drystan levitated and threw them onto the ceiling, where they stayed for the rest of the meal.

By the end of his entertainment, people had stopped eating and were watching Drystan in particular awe. He'd gone for the full flourishes to draw attention away from me. Lady Rowan was wearing one of my paper flowers tucked behind her ear. My mother hadn't eaten much but she'd drunk plenty. She and Cyril had enjoyed the magic, at least, and they'd barely spared me a second glance.

The man in the brown suit clapped just as hard as the rest of them, but his eyes narrowed, as though he was trying to figure out the method behind the tricks. A cynic, then. I noticed he still wore his white gloves. When Drystan and I gave a last flourish and left the guests to finish their dessert and returned to the main room, my stomach rumbled.

"You did brilliantly," I said to Drystan, and he swept me his best bow.

"Thank you, thank you. I know, I'm incredible." His smile faded. "Are you all right?"

"I'm grand," I said, brushing off his concern. "Maske, Cyan—need any help setting up for the séance?"

"Nay," Cyan said. "I think we're all set."

Drystan and I re-set our Glamours and changed into dark clothing and tucked black stocking masks with holes cut out for the eyes in our back pockets. I rummaged in my pack and quickly ate some cheese, nuts, and dried fruit, passing some to Drystan.

Cyan's eyes grew unfocused. "They're coming through."

Drystan and I took our place beneath the other table and pulled on our masks. We put our eyes to careful gaps in the tablecloth as the guests trickled back inside. I felt like we were mice behind the walls eavesdropping on the big cats of Imachara.

Cyril chatted with Thomas Elmbark about starting their studies at the Royal Snakewood University later in the spring, but their conversation had the forced politeness of childhood friends who realized they no longer had much in common.

My mother's profile was turned toward the only window not covered by dark velvet curtains. I remembered that when we were young, during a summer at the Emerald Bowl, she'd told Cyril and me to count the stars outside our window until we fell asleep. I closed my eyes against a sudden pang of complicated homesickness. If I'd taken a different fork in the road, I might be one of these guests waiting for the séance to begin. I'd sit at that round table, my legs crossed demurely, healed from surgery. Maybe Oswin and I would have even been wed by now. I far preferred my place hidden beneath the table.

Before the séance began, Lord and Lady Elmbark wheeled out their cabinet of curiosities for a Vestige demonstration. To me, it always seemed a bit foolhardy to blithely show guests one's most valuable possessions, but I was curious to see what was in their collection.

The butler first unfurled a tapestry. It was made of fabric that didn't decay like wool or cotton and depicted centaurs and winged beings. I even spied a damselfly woman. As the butler rolled it back up, I caught sight of another figure hiding behind the damselfly—a creature with green skin and horns. Before I could blink, the tapestry was back in its canister, and I was left with more questions without answers.

Next, the butler pulled out a small hand harp. He ran his fingertips along the strings. They made the sounds like a dampened finger dancing along wine glasses. The tones lingered in the air before fading. The guests gave muted applause. My lower back began to cramp, but I wasn't about to shift position and risk missing anything.

Next, he brought forth a glass globe. A flower similar to a rose was suspended within, though its blossom was more bell-shaped. Its petals were a brilliant turquoise that darkened to blue-black at the tips. The now-extinct flower was preserved at the height of its beauty for all eternity.

The next item was an oval mirror framed with shimmering Vestige metal. But when someone looked into it, they saw not their reflection, but a beach with turquoise waves lapping across white sand. It reminded me of the Mirror of Moirai we'd stolen from Shadow Elwood.

Lastly, the butler showcased the Elmbarks' unsurprisingly impressive automaton collection. Practically all noble families had them. Even my mother had convinced my father to let her buy one—a little sleeping mechanical baby poking out from a spiral shell, like a hermit crab. Among the Elmbarks' figurines, I recognized the mermaid with the emerald-green fin and close-cropped hair that Maske had sold. Maske's smile remained fixed upon his face, but his eyes didn't leave the figurine that had so recently been his.

The demonstration ended, and our séance would soon begin. My nerves heightened. The curtain fell over the window, the lamps extinguished, and the guests were left in complete darkness.

Drystan and I slipped from our hiding places and helped with the last bits, our footsteps muffled by the carpet, before slipping back beneath the table. The lights brightened but stayed dim enough to cast everyone half in shadow. Cyan sat at the head of the round table nearer my vantage point, the black veil across her face, emanating an air of knowing mystery. Nervously, the guests took their seats around the table as the winter wind shrieked against the windows, rattling the glass.

"Good evening, fair lords and ladies," Cyan said, speaking with a light Temnian accent. "You may call me the Widow. I welcome you here on the Night of the Dead, when the barrier between worlds grows thinnest."

She lifted the dark veil from her face, revealing silver swirls painted across her forehead, a crescent moon and stars in the center. With a start, I realized she'd changed her markings. She looked like a Chimaera ghost. She looked like Anisa.

"Please join hands so we may find you the answers you seek from beyond the grave. Death stole all of those I've ever loved too soon. In return, the Reaper saw fit to let me peek beyond the Veil and share what I know. To let others have the solace I can never find."

A rustle as everyone complied. I held my eye to the gap in the tablecloth.

"Please remove your gloves, esteemed sir," Cyan said to someone. "The skin-to-skin contact of the living strengthens the bond to the other side."

"If you insist, fair Widow." The man in the brown suit said, faintly amused, as he complied. A small gold ring on his left pinkie finger glinted in the light. But his right hand . . .

I'd seen a clockwork woman's head at the Museum of Mechanical

Antiquities last year with Aenea. This hand could have nearly been its match. Clockwork gears and pistons shone a dull brass, and the hand was covered with a substance that could be mistaken for skin save for the fact it was transparent. He stretched his fingers, and his hand moved as fluidly as a real one. A sardonic smile played on his lips as Cyan couldn't hide her shock. Some around the table were surprised, but others had clearly seen it before. My mother looked at it in fear.

Who *was* he?

Cyan struggled to recover.

—*What can you glean about him?* I thought in her direction.

—*Not a thing, which is strange. This house is full of Vestige, and I can hear the others as clear as a bell.* She frowned.

The man with the clockwork hand studied Cyan with interest.

—*Careful. You've been silent too long*, I nudged her.

"Servants, if you'd be so kind as to dim the lights," she said.

The room darkened. A few moments later, the crystal ball in front of Cyan glowed blue, illuminating her from below and just catching the faces of the other guests suspended in darkness.

Cyan cleared her throat, and she gathered back her air of mystique as she met the attendees' eyes one by one. "Lady Ashvale," she said. "Will you please share the name of a beloved you have lost?"

"Robbie," Lady Ashvale said after a pause, her voice small. "Robbie Ashvale. My son."

"Close your eyes, please, my Lady Ashvale," Cyan instructed. "Think of young Robbie. Remember what he looked like, or the sound of his voice. Everything about him. I know that a mother's heart never forgets."

Lady Ashvale gave a small sob, but she bowed her head. Cyan closed her eyes.

"Robbie Ashvale," she said, her voice strong. "I call upon you. Your mother is here. Come back, if only for a time." She paused, waiting for me to grab my props from the bag.

"Robbie, are you here?" she asked. "If so, please give us a sign."

I rang the bell, and everyone at the table jumped except for the man in the brown suit, Maske, and Lady Rowan.

"Robbie?" Lady Ashvale said, the word rising in heartbreaking hope.

I rang the bell again and Drystan tapped his fists against the walls, like footsteps.

"Robbie, will you share your story with me?" Cyan asked.

Another ringing bell.

Cyan tilted her head back. I felt a pulse of power through the room. Cyan's voice deepened, echoing. "I see Robbie. He is seven—the age he was when he was taken from you. He remembers drowning, that it was so cold. He remembers you trying to wake him. He was standing right next to you, but you didn't see him."

Lady Ashvale's shoulders shook. My fingertips went cold.

—*Cyan?* I sent.

She was drawing on her abilities too strongly, or perhaps the spirits really were speaking through her, and she couldn't stop it. Beside me, Drystan sucked in a breath.

"Age beyond the Veil has no meaning," Cyan continued, her voice still echoing. "Now he is a young boy of ten, the age he would be this night. He's sprouting like a weed." She smiled fondly. "I see him as a youth of fifteen, the dark hair falling into his blue eyes. Now he is a grown man, so very handsome and forever in his prime. He misses you. He loves you. But I promise you, he is happy. And he says he will soon travel down the River and join the world of the living again. His spirit is leaving us now and heading back beyond the Veil, but he wants me to tell you one last time: he loves you, and he always will. In this life, and the next, and the one beyond that."

Cyan opened her eyes, and I caught a flash of cobalt blue behind the lace. I shuddered. This was too much, and I wasn't even sure if she was entirely in control of her powers. Was she taking images of a grieving mother's son and weaving them into a web of pretty lies, or was the spirit of Robbie truly speaking through her?

Lady Ashvale's eyes were wet. Normally, in noble gatherings, such a display of emotion would be beyond unseemly, but not within the circle of the séance. It was obvious that these were words Lady Ashvale had been desperate to hear. She was imagining her son, grown and happy before journeying to another life.

"Thank you," she whispered.

"You're most welcome," Cyan said.

—*Bring it back, Cyan*, I warned her. *Whatever you're doing, bring it back.*

I groped towards her with my power, and it was as if she clasped my hands. The taste of magic on the air dampened.

The séance guests were hushed, almost reverent.

"Who else has lost?" Cyan asked. She was shaken, breathing heavier and trying not to show it. Maske's eyes were sharp, but he wasn't displeased at how the séance had gone so far. Lady Elmbark's mouth was half-open in shock, and Lord Elmbark seemed beyond delighted.

"I . . . I am not sure if I have," my mother said, her voice quivering. My breath caught in my throat. She'd always been deeply superstitious, so I'd not expected her to speak. Her cheeks were hollowed in the dim light of the candles.

Cyan nodded. "Yes. I know of whom you speak."

—*What do you want me to say?* Cyan asked me. I sensed none of her other magic.

I took a shuddering breath. After a moment, Cyan echoed my words to my mother.

"The one who you miss is lost but not gone. Your child has not passed into the flow of the River, but is currently dreaming, and so the spirits can sense . . . her presence." I'd hesitated on which way to refer to myself, but settled on 'she,' at least for tonight.

"Where is my daughter?" my mother whispered, and part of me winced. *Son*, I wanted to say. *Or child. But not daughter.*

"The spirits are not sure. But they do say . . . that your child is safe."

"Will I . . . ever see her again?" There was such stark hope in my mother's voice that I doubled over, my eyes stinging with tears, despite everything. Drystan's hand rested between my shoulder blades, rubbing his palm in small circles.

Cyan sensed I was overcome, and her next words were her own. "Your child follows a new path, and she has transformed. It may lead her back to you, or somewhere new. But she is among friends who cherish her deeply, my lady. I can promise you that."

My mother bowed her head. A few other guests asked for a message from the dead, but I barely listened. Cyan kept the messages short and to the point. I reached for Drystan. His arms gripped me tight. I should despise my mother, and part of me hated her still for what she'd almost done. At every turn, she'd tried to make me someone I was not. And yet I ached as if my entire body was a bruise.

The man with the clockwork hand did not ask for a message from the dead, I noticed. Drystan let me go and added the sound effects as needed, letting me recover. Eventually, my tears dried into stiff tracks on my cheeks. Cyan plucked details from the guests' minds, painting a picture of life after death: a world much like ours, but softer around the edges, like a dream.

At the end of the séance, she asked the spirits to return to the spirit world through the crystal ball, which glowed blue before darkening. This last trick needed both Drystan and me. Cyan jimmied the hidden pedal beneath the table, making it first shake and then levitate. The séance members gasped.

"Keep the faith," Cyan called. "Do not break the circle. The spirits will not harm you." The lights extinguished.

Now or never.

While it was pitch black, I crept out from my hiding place to Cyril and slipped a note I'd hastily scribbled into the pocket of his jacket. Risky, but I had to see him again. I scurried back.

The lights brightened.

Many eyes were wet. The table had the hushed reverence of a church service. As the guests left, most took a moment to thank Cyan, holding her hand and sliding extra coins into her palm. She thanked them with a grave incline of her head. The man with the clockwork hand said it'd been a marvelous performance.

"It was no performance, sir," she said, her tone flinty. "It was the work of the spirits."

"Of course, please excuse my poor turn of phrase." He gave her a shallow bow. Cyan's nostril's flared in annoyance.

Lord and Lady Elmbark took Maske and Cyan into the other room to settle payment.

"Let's go," Drystan whispered, but I shook my head. We were meant to stagger our leaving.

"Stick to the plan," I said. He hesitated but nodded. He left the table and grabbed the props before slipping down the servants' staircase. The butler's earlier bribe would have kept it abandoned. Drystan would go first and wait for us in the carriage.

The man with the clockwork hand came back into the room, pulling his gloves back on slowly. "I'll be a moment," he said over his shoulder. "I wish to ruminate on what I just saw, if you'll allow me."

"You're never any trouble, Doctor," Lady Elmbark demurred, and a shiver ran down my spine.

Shock hit me like a punch. I hadn't caught his title before now. I realized why he'd looked vaguely familiar: he was the doctor the woman in the red dress and the child in the wheelchair had visited at the medical school. The jaws of foreboding opened around me.

The doctor finished tugging on his gloves.

"I know you're under there. You can come out now, if you wish," he said.

The jaws snapped shut.

"I won't tattle. I simply wish to say a quick hello and congratulate you on a job well done."

He waited, clearly not going anywhere.

Resigned, I took a breath and crawled out, too curious for my own damn good.

"Hello there," he said, squinting at me. "I assume you're there somewhere under that mask."

Resigned, I took it off. I was confident in the Glamour, but then I felt something like . . . a *twist*. My illusion sparked and fell. His eyes flashed with satisfaction, and I realized my error too late.

"You've proven rather difficult to find, Iphigenia Laurus."

Some part of me had suspected this since the moment I'd seen the clockwork hand that he now held out for me to shake.

"Allow me to introduce myself. My name is Doctor Samuel Pinecrest."

The Royal Physician of Imachara.

24

AN IMPORTANT INVITATION

"The Royal Physician of Imachara is one of the most esteemed positions in the country. The doctor, when in residence, attends to the royal family for all of their health requirements. Often, Royal Physicians have known more about the royals than even their closest advisers and have therefore become unofficial consultants in turn."

A HISTORY OF ELADA AND ITS FORMER COLONIES,
PROFESSOR CAED CEDAR, ROYAL SNAKEWOOD UNIVERSITY

I stumbled backward, my eyes darting to the door. The Royal Physician splayed his false hand. "Wait."

"What do you want?"

"I think we have much to discuss, don't we?" He let his arm fall to his side. He was pitching his voice warm and friendly, but it was still clipped and too articulated. Every one of my muscles tightened in distrust.

"How do you feel about pretending you never saw me and have no idea who I am, and I go on my merry way?" I hid behind the sarcasm, but the quiver in my words gave me away.

He laughed.

"I'm not out to get you, Iphigenia."

"That's not my name."

"No, it isn't any longer, is it? All right then. Micah Grey." He smirked at my flinch. How many of my secrets had this man collected?

"You had me followed," I said.

"Quite cruel, what you did to Shadow Elwood," he said, conversationally. "Though I suppose if he had behaved a bit better, you wouldn't have been able to sew him up so neatly. No matter. He'd already proved his use."

"What the fuck do you want?"

"Now, that's not very ladylike," he said, a glint in his eye.

"I ran away from being a lady."

"That you did." He paused. "It must have been difficult, seeing your mother here tonight."

My nostrils flared with anger at his cool politeness. "She's not my mother, though, is she? Not my birth mother, anyway."

He raised his eyebrow. "You think you have it all figured out, do you?"

"I've put together enough to know better than to trust you."

He rubbed the back of his neck with his false hand. "I understand why you don't, but I mean you no harm, Micah. Truly. You were my charge. I kept meaning to check up on you properly when I returned from abroad, but my new post took up so much of my time. When I found out you ran away, I felt responsible. I hired the Shadow simply to make sure you were well."

"That's a mound of elephant shit," I said.

He narrowed his eyes at me. My rudeness was getting to him. Good.

The murmur of voices through the walls grew louder.

"We need to speak more, privately," Doctor Pinecrest said, his voice low and urgent.

My mouth tightened. "No, we don't. You need to leave me alone."

"It's about your health," he said.

"I'm perfectly healthy." I raised my chin. "There's nothing wrong with me."

"I'm not talking about your physical differences. Come see me in two nights' time. Ruby Street. Number 12G. It's the top window to the left of the ivy trellis, if you don't fancy coming in the front door." His mouth quirked.

"What a pretty trap. No, thank you." I was acting far braver than I felt. I worried my knees would collapse.

"It's not a trap. I promise. I don't give a damn what happened at the circus, and I've no interest in turning you over to the authorities." The doctor grabbed my arm and drew me closer. His clockwork hand was cold through my sleeve. He had dark eyes and his skin was permanently tanned from countless days in the sunnier islands to the south. "I'll leave the window by the trellis unlocked," he whispered. "You have to come."

"Why?"

He let go of me and adjusted his gloves, slowly and deliberately, before sauntering towards the door. At the threshold, he paused.

"Because if my suspicions are correct, your newly awakened powers might be making you very ill. Cyan's seem more stable, from what I witnessed, though she's plenty powerful. Yours, I highly suspect, are not. If you ignore the issue or can't find a way to control your magic, it'll only grow worse. Ruby Street. 12G. Two nights' time. Let's say eleven o'clock, if that's not too late?" He smiled tightly at me. "I think, soon enough, you'll see that you need my help, whether you like it or not."

He gave me a short, formal bow in an echo to the one he'd given Cyan. "Good night, Micah Grey."

I stared after him, a rushing roar in my ears. My skin had gone cold and clammy. That spark in my chest spread throughout my body, and the glass globes in the room and the crystal ball on the séance table flickered.

Maske and Cyan walked back into the room to see me prove the Royal Physician's point rather dramatically by fainting into a boneless heap on the floor.

• • • •

I dipped in and out of consciousness as they took me back to the Kymri Theatre.

"No doctors," I kept muttering. "No doctors. Especially not him."

Up in the loft, Drystan removed my coat and shoes and tucked me into bed. I stared at the ceiling. I'd never been so much as troubled by a cold, and now I'd fainted several times and been plagued by headaches. I felt weak as a kitten.

Cyan bustled into the loft. Some of the markings on her forehead had smeared.

"What happened?" she demanded.

"Did you have any idea who the man with the clockwork hand was?" I asked them.

"I'm sure the other guests must have said his name," Drystan said, a line appearing between his eyes. "But it's like I can't remember."

Cyan stilled, putting it together.

"It was Doctor Pinecrest, Royal Physician of Imachara," I said.

"Fuck," Drystan said.

"Yeah, that was about my reaction."

"What does he want with us?" Cyan demanded.

"He claims he means us no harm. He says my powers are going to become increasingly uncontrolled and will make me sick." I licked my lips. "He said your powers are steadier."

She froze as she realized that he'd known exactly what she'd been doing during that séance.

"He says I should visit him, the night after Lady's Long Night. Gave me his address."

"You can't go," Drystan said.

"I'm not sure I have a choice." There had been the near-miss on the street with the snow, and the night we'd captured Shadow Elwood. Cyan had felt my magic flare, I suspected, but I wasn't sure if Drystan or Maske fully realized what was going on in that room. If I hadn't fainted at the Elmbarks, would my powers have snapped? What if I'd hurt someone?

"He's aware of where we live and who we are," I said. "I don't think he'll simply leave us alone now."

"Do you want us to come with you?" Drystan asked.

I nodded. "Not into his actual apartments, maybe, but if you were nearby, it'd be reassuring."

"Of course," he said.

"We're in this together," Cyan said. "And if he tries anything, I swear I'll find a way to break into his mind and turn it to mush." She almost bared her teeth. But beneath her bravado, I sensed both relief and disappointment that he hadn't invited her.

Another wave of vertigo made me dizzy. I lay my head on the pillow, willing the room to stop spinning.

"Get some rest," Cyan said. "Hopefully it's like how I felt after our shared vision, and you'll be better in the morning."

—*Anisa will hopefully be able to teach me control better, like she promised*, I added to Cyan, privately.

She met my eyes. —*Maybe she'll be able to help me tame my powers, too. Not sure I trust her any more than the Royal Physician, but if I had to take my pick of the two, I'd go for the Chimaera ghost, I suppose.*

I agreed.

"Good night, both," she said aloud, closing the door behind her.

Drystan slipped under the covers. I rested my head on his chest and wrapped my arm around his waist, my knee resting on his thighs.

"It'll be all right, Micah," he said. "We stopped the Shadow. We'll figure out this next problem, too."

As the strong, steady beating of his heart lulled me to sleep, I wished I could believe him.

25

LADY'S LONG NIGHT

"Once there was a prince who was very cruel. The King and Queen lived in fear of him. Though nearly grown, he was prone to tantrums and violence. One day, he went hunting in the woods and came upon a white hind. He was struck by her beauty, but he raised his bow.

As the hind looked at him, the wooden bow in his hands sprouted branches that twined around his arms, pinning him in place. He wept and begged to be let go, but she left him there. A day and a night later, she finally returned, this time in the shape of a beautiful nymph. She let him go, but she'd seen the evil in his heart and said if he continued on this path towards darkness, any piece of wood would act the same as the bow, and eventually, one would pierce his heart.

The prince returned to the castle and ordered all wood to be burned, with only stone and metal to be used within the grounds. Fire would burn with peat or coal. Priceless decorations were destroyed or sent to distant corners of his land.

Years later, the prince, now a king, married a timid princess. He, of course, was unkind to her. One day the Queen went into the woods to weep. The hind found her, once again transformed into a nymph, and gave her a wooden wand, bidding her to leave it beneath their bed that night.

The next morning, the Queen awoke to find the wand had grown into a tree, the branches woven into the stone pillars of the bed heavy with brilliant blossoms. The trunk grew from the King's chest, and his eyes were open and blank. He would never hurt anyone else again. The Queen ruled in his stead for the next thirty years, and was far fairer a monarch than he would ever have been."

"THE CRUEL PRINCE AND THE HIND," HESTIA'S FABLES

The low gong of the doorbell echoed through the Kymri Theatre.

"I'll get it!" I cried, trotting down the stairs. I dampened my enthusiasm long enough to check through the peephole that it was indeed who I'd been expecting.

I opened the door and threw myself into my brother's arms. He'd found my note.

When I finally pulled away, I took his coat and hung it up. He was in the same suit he'd worn to the séance, but he wore a dark blue shirt with it, which was fitting for the Lady's Long Night. I was using the holiday as an excuse not to think about Doctor Pinecrest and the appointment I was meant to have with him the following night.

Maske brought us some coffee, and he, Drystan, and Cyan gave me and my brother privacy.

Cyril took in the clean but shabby room. The curtains were mothnibbled. The cracks in the plaster still hadn't been fixed. He focused on me, next. I wasn't wearing the Glamour, of course. I'd donned light brown trousers and my trusty boots. I wore a woman's blouse, a grey, unbuttoned waistcoat, and my chest was unbound. I'd only cut my hair once since I'd chopped it off before running away in spring, and it grazed the top of my shoulders. My face was bare of paint, but I'd borrowed a pair of Cyan's earrings. He was seeing me at my most comfortable and at home in my skin.

I gave him a heavily edited version of the truth, skipping over the darker moments and leaving out most of the magical business. He filled me in next, and I suspected he also redacted certain details. The main thing I learned was confirmation that mother's health was growing worse, and that father was considering sending her to Fir Tree, a "ladies' spa," which was in truth a treatment center for women.

I tried to tamp down on my guilt, but of course, my brother caught it.

"Your running away may have been the catalyst, but it's not your fault," he stressed. "Mother and Father haven't been getting along for some time now. It's a good idea to treat her issues before she grows worse."

"At least she's getting a choice," I said, darkly. Cyril didn't try to defend her, nor did he try to convince me to come home. I also didn't ask why he was here instead of with them on Lady's Long Night.

"How's Oswin?" I asked.

"He's good." He paused. "Engaged to Tara Cypress. They'll marry when he finishes university, I expect."

I'd thought Oswin must have found someone else by now, but it was strange to have it confirmed. "He actually got into university?" I asked, keeping my voice light. "Can't believe he passed his exams."

"It was a near thing."

We spoke of this and that until our cups ran empty. I brought him to the kitchen for a top up. Ricket yowled at Cyril, but after a sniff of his outstretched hand, she gave him a headbutt of approval.

"You've already met them, after a fashion," I said. "But I'd like to formally introduce you to Jasper Maske, Cyan, and Drystan." I resisted the urge to shuffle my feet like a child.

"Pleased to make your acquaintance, Lord Laurus," Maske said, shaking hands.

"Please, call me Cyril."

Cyan gave my brother an approving look from the top of his head to his toes.

—*Hey!* I thought at her as he bent over to kiss the back of her hand. *You have your sailor.* Oli was out that night with some friends.

—*I still have eyes,* she sent back, dimpling at my brother. "Lovely to meet you. Micah's spoken of you so fondly."

"I must say you're, uh, not as frightening today," Cyril said, a little sheepishly.

She laughed, gathering her hair over her shoulder. "I'm not that frightening, promise."

I shot an exasperated look at Drystan at their flirting. He only smirked in response.

Maske poured more coffee into our cracked cups. I stirred my customary sugar and milk into it, but Cyril kept his black. He looked about with unabashed curiosity.

"Oh," he said. "I brought you some gifts." He went back to the hallway to fetch them, and Maske thought it'd be a fine idea for us all to open our gifts before heading to the Cathedral, instead of the usual tradition of opening them right before bed. I took the stairs up to the loft two at a time and came down with my wrapped parcels, excited to share them.

Cyril brought little sweets for Maske, Cyan, and Drystan as well as me, which was thoughtful of him. He also gave me a stash of coins, which I protested but was secretly grateful for. He promised that the next time he came up from Sicion, he'd bring me my old Ephram Finnes novels.

Maske gave me one of his pocket watches and Drystan a fine suit and handkerchief to wear on the stage. Cyan gave me a preserved dragonfly cocoon from Temne. It was dyed bright blue and lined with gilt paint. I thanked her, knowing no one else, save maybe Drystan, would understand the full reference. She gave Drystan a massive box of caramelized nuts dipped in sesame, which she knew he particularly liked. He opened it, ate a few, then passed the box around.

I gave Cyan a pot of gold eye paint I'd seen her linger over at a marketplace, and she hugged it to her chest, thanking me. Drystan, Cyan, and I had pooled our coins to give Maske—well, a mask. It was made of black velvet embroidered with six-pointed stars, the thin crescent of a moon curling over an eye.

The Collective of Magic had recently decided that Maske and

Taliesin were allowed to go on stage long enough to briefly introduce our acts. He was absolutely delighted and said he'd wear it for that, and, if we won the duel, all his performances after that. The three of us glowed in satisfaction.

Drystan and I exchanged gifts last. He had been the most difficult person to find a present for. In the end, I gave him a small flute that sounded a bit like an owl's call, for he used to sometimes borrow Sayid's instruments and play at the circus fireside. I'd bought him the nicest one I could afford, with little vines carved into the wood and colored with green enamel. His face lit up when he opened the case, and I flushed with pleasure and relief that he liked it.

When I opened his present, I felt as though I had offered him a lowly trinket. He'd given me a necklace that was somehow neither masculine nor feminine, but just right for me. It was made of thin rectangles strung together, long enough that I could hide it underneath my clothing. Each had an Alder word engraved on it. He told me they were meant to say "luck," "faith," "fortune," and . . . "love."

I blinked fast against the tears that marred my vision. Drystan stood behind me and put the necklace on, his fingertips grazing the skin on the back of my neck. We finished our drinks, and the cold metal warmed against my skin.

All five of us went to the Celestial Cathedral as dusk fell, the Penglass domes glowing subtly beneath the crescent moon. I steeled myself against their wordless call. I'd tried to remember the glyph I had seen in the vision with Anisa and Matla, but though I could recall the general shape, the rest eluded me. Cyan hadn't remembered it either. Perhaps that was for the best.

On the long promenade that led down to the Snakewood Palace, floats draped with white fabric fluttered in the winter wind along with scattered snowflakes, flute music echoing down the streets. We bustled through the crowds until we found a good view. Men and women dressed as Chimaera—angels, dragonkind, mermaids, and others—waved as the floats moved down the boulevard. They wore all white, as though frosted, the faint blue light of Penglass settling on them like a shawl.

There had been Forester protests and rising tensions throughout the capital, but that night, at least, any animosity faded away as all were mesmerized by the slow waving of the false Chimaera.

After the parade finished, we went to the Celestial Cathedral. Its spires of white and dark marble rose towards the night sky. I'd never considered myself particularly religious, despite my mother dragging my brother and me to church every holy day, but there was something about sitting on a pew under a high, vaulted ceiling, surrounded by ornate statues and stained glass, that made me feel peaceful. I'd always liked that hushed silence, like holding a breath.

When the service began, the High Priest trundled onto the alter, awkward in his heavy white and gold vestments. He led the people in prayer, and I mumbled the verses with the rest of the congregation. I lifted my eyes to the darkened windows, wondering if the Lord and Lady truly heard our prayers.

The priest finished his sermon and relinquished the stage to the choir. Two dozen men and women in dark blue robes embroidered with stars lifted their faces, their voices reverberating throughout the cathedral. Drystan's hand found its way into mine. They sang of love of the night and the day, and how the darkness made the stars and moon shine that much brighter.

When the last note faded, the silence was absolute.

Service ended. Outside, the snow swirled around us. People's faces were contemplative after the service, their noses pink with cold. Some murmured amongst themselves, but most were quiet. I looked back at the Celestial Cathedral, light glowing through the stained-glass windows. The snow danced upon the wind, the flurries thickening until we could barely see.

"I should head back," my brother said, his teeth chattering. I envied that he'd be returning to a room with a roaring fire, while we returned to the cold, drafty theatre. "Thank you for inviting me along."

"It was our pleasure," Cyan said, and Drystan shook his hand.

"Luck be with you on the Lady's Long Night," I said the traditional words, and threw my arms out for a last hug.

"And Luck of the Lady to you, Micah," he said, bending down to kiss me on the cheek. My brother hunched his shoulders and disappeared into the snow.

26

THE DOCTOR'S APPOINTMENT

"I remain frustrated that I was unable to continue my observation of Iphigenia Laurus due to her sudden disappearance. Beyond the physical differences, there was the puzzle of her slow, steady heartbeat, the high oxygenation of her blood, the apparent immunity to illness—all combined, it was something I have never seen in the history of my medical practice, and even all these months later, I find myself wondering what else I might have been able to learn from further observation and tests."

UNPUBLISHED NOTES OF DOCTOR BIRCH

The next day I couldn't focus at all on magic practice. Maske told me off multiple times for dropping things or for missing my cues. My only thoughts were for the night and the looming visit with the Royal Physician. Maske, too, was wound tight. Now that the séance was completed, there was nothing to distract him from the upcoming duel.

Maske had grown thinner over the last couple of months. The only breaks he took were to go to Lily or when she came to call on him at the Kymri Theatre. Even then, he kept these visits brief, and I was convinced that, half the time, he was sleeping in his workshop instead of his bed. While he'd fixed the Kymri Princess levitation trick easily enough, he was obsessed with the final illusion, and I suspected it wasn't proving so simple.

When he finally dismissed us, I went up on the roof to watch the sun set. Cyan soon joined me.

"I hope you've stayed out of my head," I said, without turning around.

"It doesn't take my powers to guess that you're nervous," she said.

To prove her point, Drystan arrived a moment later.

They sat on either side of me. The sunset was a brilliant orange and red, the golden clouds streaked across the side like brush strokes. It was beautiful. I was far too keyed up to enjoy it.

"Tonight, I'm going to put some other Vestige in my pockets," Cyan said. "It might help me discover as much as I can through you, if you'll let me." She swallowed. "I want to know how much he's learned about me and what he's up to."

I nodded. "You have my permission."

"Dunno how long I'll be able to keep it up, or even if I'll be able to do it," she said. "I've never tried to actually eavesdrop through some-one else's eyes before."

Drystan's expression flickered with something like jealousy.

"If it doesn't work, I'll tell you both everything." I dragged out a long sigh. "I wish I hadn't poked out from beneath that table. It was like sticking my head up from a parapet."

"He already knew you were there. Maybe he is telling the truth, and he only wants to help," Cyan said, though she looked beyond skeptical.

"How have you been feeling?" Drystan asked me.

"Absolutely fine," I said, and it was the truth. "Maybe it's all a trick."

"It almost certainly is," Drystan said.

Cyan's eyes shadowed. "Are you going to take Anisa's Aleph? She might be able to glean more from him."

I'd been asking myself the same question. "Dunno. Don't exactly want to risk her falling into Pinecrest's hands, but she also might prove useful if things go south. Maybe you should take her, though."

"Mm. Could be a good compromise."

"I called her out for a few minutes this morning," I said. "She said I should go, but she has no idea if he's the blurred man or not."

"So we're all going into this blind as a bluff man," Drystan said. "Excellent."

We watched the sun fade over Imachara.

"Are you all right?" Drystan asked me in the loft later that evening. We changed into the same dark clothing we'd worn to break into Shadow Elwood's apartments.

"Not particularly, no."

He wrapped me in a hug, and I sank into it gratefully. He rested his forehead against mine.

"I'm fine," I said, our noses touching. "I think."

"I've been naughty again," he said, pulling back.

I looked at him in puzzlement until he pulled the Augur out of his pocket. "I liberated Maske of one of his Vestige objects again, but I figured you'd want to know if Pinecrest is telling the truth. Be careful with it, of course. It's already on the setting where only you will hear the alarm."

I was touched. "Thank you," I said, slipping it into my pocket.

"Well," I said. "Let's see what the bastard has to say, then, eh?"

• • • •

The three of us stepped out into the night. The sky was clear, the thickening crescent moon just bathing the streets in a silver glow.

We made our way to Ruby Street, keeping to the darkest shadows or scaling the roofs. It felt good to have Drystan and Cyan at my side.

Finally, we reached Ruby Street, which wasn't far from the Constabulary Headquarters. Statues of griffins stood guard at the front doors of Doctor Pinecrest's tenement building. Sure enough, I spotted the ivy trellis. The lit window at the top left was propped open. A silhouette appeared, waiting. I took a deep breath.

"We'll be right here," Drystan said. "If anything happens, think at Cyan, and we'll be up there faster than you can say 'vivisection'."

I managed a weak laugh. Chewing my lip, I glanced up at the window again.

Some of the ivy grew so thick that it was difficult to find good holds. I had already lost some of my aerialist calluses and muscles, but long years of climbing meant I made short work of it. At the window, I glanced down.

I could make out the glint of Drystan's eyes from the shadows, only because I knew he was there and my eyesight was keen. I felt Cyan, as if she perched in a corner of my mind like an owlish woman.

—*Here goes*, I thought, and opened the window to slip inside.

At least I entered the right window. Doctor Pinecrest was decked out in a pressed grey suit and white gloves. I swallowed as I closed the window behind me, leaving it propped open in case I needed to make a hasty escape.

Doctor Pinecrest smiled pleasantly. "Welcome, Micah. Thank you for coming. Please, sit." He gestured to a chair.

I crossed the room and perched on it gingerly. A large anatomical chart of a human being with arms and legs outstretched, expertly rendered, hung on one wall. A cupboard that looked a little like our spirit cabinet dominated another. On the top of it was a glass case with a gilded human skull—or almost human. The canines were pointed, reminding me uncomfortably of Juliet the Leopard Lady from the circus.

Doctor Pinecrest noticed my stare. "Ah. My cabinet of curiosities, housing some of my most prized artefacts from my Vestige collection." He paused, as though he expected me to ask what was in it. Of course, I was desperate to know what a man who owned the Museum of Mechanical Antiquities would choose to keep in the privacy of his own home, but I wasn't about to rise to the bait.

"I thought you'd live in the Palace, being the Royal Physician and all," I said instead.

"I do, most of the time, but I keep my old quarters. I thought you'd rather meet here."

He was right. Annoyingly. "Well. Here I am, as you asked."

"Still not particularly one for pleasantries, are you?"

"I'm not here for pleasantries. I'm here for answers."

Pinecrest smiled again, as if he found my insolence amusing. "Of course. Would you like some tea?"

"No." I paused. "Thank you."

His smile grew. He briefly disappeared into the kitchen and brought out a full tea service, setting it on the low table between us. I gaped at the rare Vestige set, made of a dark material that wouldn't burn a hand but would keep the liquid warm almost indefinitely. He could have boiled the water last week and it'd be ready for tea.

Pinecrest poured for both of us, even though I'd declined, the steam rising between us. My chest tightened.

"Milk or sugar?" he asked.

"Milk and two sugars," I relented.

He passed the tea to me, and I stared at it dubiously. When was it cool enough to drink? And could I trust he hadn't put something in it?

"You're not my child, you know," he said, taking a sip of the tea. I startled.

"That, uh, never actually crossed my mind," I said, honestly. "I figured you . . . dunno. Grew me in a vat. Stole me from some orphanage for experiments. Or I'm secretly a royal."

"No, no, and no. I found you, or rather, you were gifted to me."

"What?"

"It was a warm spring evening. I heard the crying from my laboratory. I opened the door and there you were. A little pink thing squalling at the top of your lungs." He took another sip of his tea as my heartbeat pulsed in my throat.

The doctor shook his head ruefully. "I wasn't sure what to do at first. I had no experience with children, you see. But, eventually, I picked you up and you quieted. I glanced around the street, but no one was there. So, I took you in. I unwrapped you, examined you to make sure you were healthy, and what I found gave me a bit of a shock."

I looked away from him, crossing my legs.

"You seemed healthy enough, but I didn't know exactly what to do with you." His gaze was rueful. "I thought I was doing the right thing, giving you to a family like the Lauruses. They were struggling to conceive another child. I knew they wouldn't turn down an offer to move up another ring of nobility."

He dripped sincerity, so much so that I was immediately mistrustful.

—*Can you read anything from him?* I sent, carefully, out into the street.

Cyan's response was immediate.—*Not a jot.*

The Augur in my pocket was dead silent.

"You left me with strangers for nearly eighteen years and never called on me," I said. "And there was no ulterior motive for it at all?"

"You were a child; I found you a home. I thought little more of it all for years."

The truth, maybe, but not the whole truth.

"So what changed?"

He merely smiled in a way I didn't like one bit.

"Did you invite my family to the Elmbark séance?" I asked.

He cocked his head. "They were already acquainted with each other from the Emerald Bowl, I believe."

My adopted parents were closer with the Elms than the Elmbarks. I should have put together who he was as soon as I'd seen how nervous my mother was around him.

"Are you aware of why I ran away from home?"

"Not specifically, no."

"They were going to operate on me." I let the pause draw out. "To make me more . . . marriageable."

His mouth dropped open. "They wouldn't dare. I would never have allowed that."

"Oh, they definitely dared." I exhaled in frustration. "I don't like doctors. Too many have decided they know what's best for me without giving me any say in it."

"The others had no notion what they were dealing with." He made a dismissive gesture.

"And you do." I made it a statement rather than a question, gripping the sides of the armchair so hard I feared ripping the leather.

He paused. "I learned of other abandoned children, some with physical anomalies, some without, that later demonstrated . . . unusual abilities. Things that have not been recorded in history since the time of the Alder and the Chimaera."

My mouth was dry. I dared a sip of my tea, and it nearly scalded my tongue. It was some sort of herbal, floral blend. It was not the usual type of thing I drank, but it was nice.

"Telekinesis," he said. "Regeneration. Telepathy. A few have been born with atypical anomalies. Scales, a lion's tail, webbed feet."

I wanted to ask him about the woman in the red dress and her child, but how could I bring it up without mentioning visions?

"I don't have any scales," I said. "Though I've my other differences."

"Your physical sex is unlikely to be related to these abilities. You simply have two extremely rare conditions. I noticed things about you even during the few days I had you as a babe, in retrospect. I gave you an immunity shot, and within hours, the needle mark was gone. And you always started crying precisely half a minute before someone knocked at the door."

The surface of the tea in my cup quivered.

"Whatever you are, Micah Grey, it's extraordinary."

I had no idea what to say to that.

Pinecrest cleared his throat. "One of the reasons I brought you here tonight was to make sure you are healthy. On the sexual development side, there can be difficulties with which I am familiar, but that is not my main concern. I didn't mean to alarm you, but there is a high risk of complications with some of the children I have studied. A few have died unexpectedly without even suspecting they were ill."

My ears started ringing, and outside on the street, I was sure Cyan gasped.

"Died?" I echoed.

"I'd like to examine you, with your permission."

"I'd really prefer you didn't," I said, as evenly as I could. "I hardly feel as though I'm dying."

"The illness came on very quickly, and within days or weeks, they were gone. I've asked you here tonight, alone, but I will ask Cyan to come another time, too, if she'll have me. You should both be examined." He stared at me so knowingly, I suspected he knew she had heard the words.

I set my teacup down.

"Any dizzy spells? Or fainting?"

I paused.

"Do you feel odd around Vestige? Strange voices in your head? Or visions?"

I froze.

"Let me make sure you're healthy, at least." There was a soft plea in his tone. A crack in his careful persona.

"Fine," I agreed through clenched teeth. His expression eased.

Doctor Pinecrest went into another room and returned with a medic bag. He took out a stethoscope and asked me to unbutton my overshirt. I did, my hands shaking. To some of the doctors I'd seen over the years, I'd been nothing more to them than a freak on display. An object to be studied.

Pinecrest took off his white gloves and left long enough to wash his hands. His touch, both human and Vestige, was gentle and firm, yet I flinched when he moved the Lindean corset to take my pulse. It both reminded me of the cold, antiseptic smell of the doctor's offices and of the night Bil had checked if I was female.

I expected him to ask me to undress, but he didn't. Perhaps he knew I would bolt at that. Instead, he asked me to describe the intricacies of my anatomy, and I blushed to the roots of my hair.

He pressed my abdomen, asking if there was any pain or tenderness. There wasn't. He asked about menstruation and I answered truthfully—that I had but so far only twice, three months apart. Doctor Pinecrest took no notes, but I was sure he memorized every word I said.

He examined the color of my nails and the veins underneath the skin of my wrist. The false skin of his clockwork hand even had tiny wrinkles and folds around the knuckles.

"How did you lose it?" The question was out of my mouth before I could stop myself.

He released my arm, holding the clockwork hand aloft, the dull brass glinting beneath the translucent muscle. Hidden deep within the brass-like mechanisms, I caught tiny flashes of blue crystal.

"Something ate it," he said.

I blinked. I don't know what I'd been expecting, but it wasn't that. "What?"

He tidied away his medical supplies. "I was on a dig at night in a

South Temnian jungle, hoping to recover a Vestige artefact. It might have been furred or scaled. Or both. Whatever the beast was, it attacked me." He pushed up the hem of his shirt, and I gaped at the four deep scars that scored his ribs. Claw marks. He tugged his shirt down. "I managed to stab it with the knife in my belt, and it fled. It only had a snack as opposed to a meal, I suppose. Between blood loss and the infection that followed, I nearly died."

"I'm sorry," I said, because I felt I should.

He shrugged. "Ancient history, now. I'd stuck my nose where it hadn't belonged. And I did find that Vestige, though, so I consider the cost worth it." There was that cat-like grin again. He didn't elaborate.

"Where did you get your . . . new hand?" I asked, almost mesmerized by the slow flexing of his false fingers.

"I already had it in my collection."

"At the Mechanical Museum last summer, I saw the clockwork woman's head. The night I ran away, I'd heard my parents talking about the surgery. They mentioned you, though I had no idea you were the Royal Physician until I read your name on that plaque."

The clockwork woman had been beautiful, resting in her glass display case, levers attached to pressure points at the base of her neck, which, when pulled, caused her to show different emotions. My eyes clouded with the memory of Aenea's face beneath the glass globes as I'd leaned in to kiss her that afternoon last summer.

"Ah, yes, I remember her well," Pinecrest said, bringing me back. "A lovely specimen. I put her in the museum so others could admire her, too." He rubbed his beard with his false hand. "Well, young Micah, I have good news. Physically, you appear to be in perfect health, and I don't see any of the markers of the illness some my other subjects have shown."

I sank back into my chair in quasi-relief.

"But if you have any physical problems—a fever, a cough, flu, anything of that nature—you must come see me as quickly as possible. For you are, without a doubt, someone with these extra abilities."

"A Chimaera, then?"

He gave a slow incline of his head. "Or something very like those myths, yes."

"How can you be sure?"

"I can tell by your color and musculature, and how slowly your heart beats."

"I was in a circus for months. Maybe I'm especially healthy."

"Hm." He pressed his hands together. "And how are you mentally?"

"What, are you asking if I'm mad?"

"It wouldn't be surprising if you were dealing with anxiety or depressive episodes, both after what you endured in the circus and from experiencing things you can't explain. Vestige passing along messages, hearing the odd phrase that could be someone's thoughts. A dream that turned out to be prescient. Moving an object with your mind, if only a fraction of an inch."

I heard the barest whisper in my mind from Anisa's Aleph, safely tucked in Cyan's pocket:—*Careful . . .*

"No," I said. "Nothing like that." The Augur clicked, but only I could hear it.

Doctor Pinecrest stared at me, eyes unreadable.

—*Can you hear me, Micah?* he asked.

It took everything in me to not respond, but I hesitated too long, and my poker face wasn't as good as Drystan's.

"Are you quite sure?" Pinecrest asked aloud. "If you have, it's important that I know."

—*I think you can hear me, Micah Grey.*

I kept my face blankly attentive, though my palms dampened with sweat. Was he a Chimaera as well, or did his Vestige limb give him powers he shouldn't possess?

"Why is it so important?" I managed.

A corner of his mouth quirked. "Vestige is something we do not fully understand, and we never will, unless the Alder come back to explain it to us. I have one of the largest collections in the Archipelago and most of it is still a mystery to me, despite the experts that have studied it. My hand, for instance," he said, holding it up again. "I am not sure how many of these . . . clockwork bodies were crafted. I assume the Alder created them, like they did the Chimaera, but for what purpose? Were they guards, or experiments? I'd give a lot, maybe even my other hand, to learn the answers to those questions."

I knew some of the them, thanks to my visions from Anisa. The clockwork bodies were temporary forms for Chimaera who had Alephs and could live several lives. Anisa had been a guard, caring for certain charges. But I'd give him nothing.

"Some Vestige, however," he continued, "can be dangerous. I've heard stories of a Vestige gun that turned on its owner, and a toy that strangled the child who played with it. It's rare, but more prone in those who have an existing sensitivity to Vestige. Which is why, if you have heard these echoes, I must know."

He waited.

"There's nothing," I whispered. "I haven't experienced any of that."

The clicking of the Augur he couldn't hear gradually faded.

"Well," he said finally, "that is most promising."

"I think I shall be going now. It's late." My head swam with all I'd learned, and all the doctor insinuated.

He held up a false finger. "Another thing before you go, if you please. One last question."

"Yes?" I asked, not without a little trepidation.

"Do you want to go back to your old life?"

I stared at him.

"I could speak to your family. Have them guarantee not to operate."

I didn't even need time to consider it. "No."

"I see." He smiled blandly, as if it didn't matter to him. "Your new life as a magician is treating you well, then?"

"Yes," I said, sure I sounded tetchy. "Very well."

"I've heard about the duel between Taliesin and Maske."

"You and the entire city. A rematch between Spectre's Shadows and Maske's Marionettes," I said with a wry smile.

"I was thinking of attending," he said, strangely hesitant.

"You're welcome to, of course. It'll be a good show, and we certainly aim to win." The words and my accompanying smile were forced.

"Wonderful. I'll be there." He walked me to the window. Down below, I knew Drystan and Cyan would be waiting anxiously nearby.

"Remember, if anything strange happens to you, come to me immediately. I have a medicine that can help: physically, mentally, and psychologically. And . . ." He hesitated. "I would feel terrible if something happened to you. I've only ever wanted you to be healthy and safe. I hope you can believe that."

I pressed my lips together.

"I hope you reconcile with your parents one day, if that's not too forward to say. I remember how much they wanted you."

The memory of my mother's hopeful, heartbroken face at the séance came back to me. I banished that ghost. "Good evening, Royal Physician Samuel Pinecrest."

"Good evening, Micah Grey."

—*Until we meet again.*

His words twined through my mind. A promise.

Or a threat.

27

THE NIGHT THE WORLD
NEARLY ENDED

"Why did the Alder leave, or what happened to them? Did Chimaera ever actually exist? Will they ever return, as some of the old myths claim? These are questions that have haunted historians for centuries, including myself, and will likely haunt us for several more."

A HISTORY OF ELADA AND ITS FORMER COLONIES,
PROFESSOR CAED CEDAR, ROYAL SNAKEWOOD UNIVERSITY

I ran into Drystan's arms when I reached his and Cyan's hiding place beneath the trees. So many conflicting emotions swirled through me, I wasn't sure whether to sob, or scream, or laugh. I couldn't shake the feeling that Pinecrest was toying with me like Anisa was, and dangling answers just out of reach.

We headed back to the Kymri Theatre in silence, and I was grateful for it.

The stairs leading to the loft felt so steep. Exhaustion tugged at me.

I told Cyan and Drystan everything, leaving nothing out. Drystan's jaw worked, and Cyan grew paler when I shared the doctor wanted to see her.

"I won't do it," she said. "I don't want to be anywhere near him."

Drystan rubbed his hand over his face. "I wish he'd never found you, Micah."

"Me, too," I said. "But he's known about us for a while. I wonder how many others he's keeping tabs on."

"Let's go to bed," Cyan said. "Nothing more we can do tonight, and we've another long day of practice tomorrow."

Drystan groaned. "Like every other day. It's relentless."

"We have to win," Cyan said. "We have to win for Maske and for ourselves." She squeezed my hand before she left.

Drystan and I changed and slid into bed. I pressed my feet into the backs of his knees, and he exclaimed at how cold they were. I laughed, unrepentant, snuggling closer.

He fell asleep quickly. He hadn't had any nightmares since we'd pushed our beds together. Sometimes he went quiet and looked haunted, but more often than not, he was again much closer to the white clown I remembered.

I envied his easy slumber.

In the middle of the night, I heard a knocking at my mind. I crept back up to the roof and pressed Anisa's Aleph. Snowflakes drifted from the sky, and the Penglass of Imachara glowed under the light of the full moon as Anisa swirled into view.

—*I believe I'm strong enough to begin training you*, she said. *I think we can both agree that it's time.*

"Yes. Teach me," I said. "So far, I've managed to bring my magic back, but I'm afraid of what might happen if I can't control it."

"You should be."

She stepped towards me, but I panicked and backed away.

"I said teach me, not possess me," I said.

—*Very well*, she said. *Relax.*

Reluctantly, I acquiesced. She instructed me on how to breathe, how to clear my mind. She helped me draw up my magic, then did . . . something to send it away again, without entering my body.

She placed her transparent hand against my chest. "When you feel that spark, imagine you are swallowing a star to extinguish it."

I tried. The spark came easily enough, but it began to burn. She reached into me, so quickly I could barely blink, and snuffed it out like a candle.

My wonder chased away some of my misgivings. How had she done that?

"How did you make that look so easy?"

—*When you live and breathe magic for centuries, it is easier.*

"But I don't understand the rules," I complained.

—*Not even the spirits know all its rules. Only magic contained within Vestige means it functions reliably. You can gain a measure of control, with practice, but magic sings to its own tune and you can only affect it so much. The sooner you realize it, the better. It is foolish, dangerous hubris to believe magic can ever be fully tamed.*

I shivered.

—*Your powers are still much weaker than they might become. Practice clearing your mind in the morning and the evenings. We can keep doing this together until you're able to do it on your own. It's like a muscle. It will grow stronger. But if you can't control your emotions with me, then you will not be able to do it alone. I will not be able to step in and help.* She stepped further away from me, our lessons over for tonight.

"Why can you recharge if you rest, whereas other Vestige can't?" I asked. It'd been bothering me.

—*I am different to most Vestige, as you've already gathered,* she said. *I was once a being of flesh and bone, after all, and my Aleph is one of the most advanced artefacts the Alder ever created. But my power is not infinite. It can only recover so much, and I cannot recharge to full strength. I must be careful not to overexert myself.*

I turned that over in my mind. It seemed truthful, but it was always difficult to know with the Phantom Damselfly.

"What about this sickness Pinecrest mentioned?" I asked next. "Is there any truth to it?"

Her lips tightened. —*It has been a long time since Chimaera have been in the world, and I am not entirely sure why people like you or our little bird have returned. The abilities seem dampened compared to when Chimaera were numerous. The one who was Matla is strong, but only when around what you call Vestige. If you and she went somewhere where there were no artefacts, she would not be able to hear a single stray thought. Vestige amplifies her latent abilities, and yours.*

Cyan had already discovered some of that herself, but Anisa's words frightened me just as much as Pinecrest's had. "Is Vestige dangerous?"

—*Anything sufficiently powerful that you do not understand can be dangerous.*

I wanted to ask: *are you dangerous?* But I feared I already knew the answer to that.

"Do you think Pinecrest is a threat?"

—*We should tread carefully with him. He smiles like a snake hiding fangs.*

"I found it more cat-like." I sighed. "I'm never going to be safe, am I? There's always something or someone after me. I can't even trust myself or my evidently enigmatic powers. I want to know *something.* Clouds above, Anisa, I want some actual answers."

—*You have been patient. I can show you something else, if you truly want more answers, or to see what I am so afraid of happening again.*

She reached out her transparent hand and rested it on my cheek. I could feel nothing, but I found the gesture oddly comforting. I took in a shaky breath. Could I really take any more impossibility this evening?

"Show me," I whispered.

She leaned forward and, as she kissed me on the forehead, the vision rose around us.

• • • •

My wings flickered behind me. I was in Penglass—or Venglass, as Anisa called it—but half of it was dark, as though partly submerged in a cave. It was cold, and the furniture looked wrong to me, as if it were an older fashion than what I was used to. Late sunlight filtered through a wall of blue glass. My two wards, Dev and Ahti, played together in the corner. Ahti laughed as he raised his toys with his mind to balance on the tops of his horns. Dev, the Kedi, levitated glass globes that circled them both, like planets around a star. Both of their brows were furrowed with concentration.

"Food!" Relean called from the next room. The toys and globes fell to the floor.

"Turn off the lights, please," I told them, and after a quick burst of power from Ahti, the lights in the globes winked out.

We ate. Soft music played and I relaxed. I had been tense since we came into hiding from the Kashura. The world had fallen apart out there in the cities. Here, we could pretend all was safe for the children, if only temporarily.

The Kashura were turning the world upside-down looking for Ahti. They wanted him for some purpose that I knew must be thwarted.

In less than a week, we would be gone. A few of us were making plans to head for another world beyond the Veil where we could hide, at least for a time. The idea of the journey frightened me. I had lived all of my lives here. But it could be a new beginning, and somewhere where we could be safe.

The low thrum of an engine rose outside. I paused mid-chew. It could be the ones Matla had worked with, coming to drop supplies, but they had visited only two days ago.

All of us froze in fear. The music echoed through the kitchen and down the hallway. We heard the sound of a glyph being drawn at the door, and I hung my head in defeat. How had they found us?

It happened in moments.

Their thundering footsteps drowned out the music. They wore armor, faces obscured by visors. They slapped cuffs over our wrists and dragged us out of our brief sanctuary. The children cried. My hands went numb. As they marched us down the hallway toward the craft, I heard the last notes of the music before it faded.

How quickly the world could change. A generation ago, the Alder would never have dared do something like this, even the ones loyal to the old ways. They would never have hunted Chimaera, no matter how powerful.

All it takes is one leader to spark the flame, and it all burns.

If the Kashura Alder had their way, there would be no more Chimaera, and this would be my last life. My last time with Relean. My last time caring for my charges. I had been loyal to the Alder, almost to a fault. And for that devotion? All the history and knowledge I learned as a curator of this world—it had all turned into dust.

"This shall pass," Relean said to me. "We will persevere. The world will make itself as it needs to be."

I wished I could believe that.

Our footsteps shuffled as we were escorted into the craft. I did not let myself cry. I did not want Dev and Ahti to see my fear.

That would come soon enough.

••••

The vision shifted. Weeks had passed. I was in a Venglass cell. Outside, the world burned. The sky roiled orange, red, purple, and grey. Smoke rose toward a bruised sky. Flames licked and devoured all in their path. Dev slept in the cot in the corner. They had taken Ahti and Relean, but that morning, they'd thrown Relean back in the cell with me. He wouldn't tell me what the Alder had asked or done to him, but I was grateful to have him at my side once again.

"I think this is truly the end. I hid our Alephs in a safe place before they took us," Relean said, his voice low and urgent. "Remember: There is a chance that we'll be together again. I don't want this to be the end."

Relean had seen what was coming. I had put too much faith that the Alder sympathetic to their creations would protect us. When it came down to it, they, too, had abandoned both humans and Chimaera to die. The Alder had left us all behind.

"I wish we'd been able to stop it." My words were thick.

"I wish we had done more," Relean said.

Dev slept. Outside, comets fell to earth, blooming into roses of fire. It wouldn't be long.

I drew Relean's face close for a kiss, clinging to him. We drew our wings around us as a pitiful, translucent shield.

Something large hit the prison. The walls and floor shook. The smell of smoke filled the air. Alarms sounded. Dev woke up, crying. I held out my arm, and he came to me as we waited for the end.

We began to cough as the smoke thickened. The searing heat made us fall to our knees. There was no escape. Not while wearing this body. I fell to the floor and, as another blast detonated, I felt myself leave my physical self behind and my last life in the old world came to an end.

• • • •

I shuddered as I came back to myself, rubbing my hands against my arms. I knew how Cyan had felt after our shared vision. Now I'd learned what it was like to die. I'd felt Anisa's heart stop and her limbs burn away to nothing. My throat felt raw from ancient smoke.

"What happened after that?" I asked.

—*My memories end there. And the worst part was knowing it was my ward, my child, my little Ahti, who had ended the world.*

I reeled, the revelation hitting me like a punch to the gut. "What do you mean?"

She touched my forehead again, drawing me into another vision. This one was like the first she had shared with me—more of a waking dream than a memory.

• • • •

This time I was myself and stood next to Anisa. The sea boiled and more fire rained from the sky. All was eerily quiet. A red Alder glass ship flew through the air, racing for the stars. But a piece of debris collided, and the ship floundered before exploding, burning wreckage raining down on the scorched earth.

Anisa spoke aloud. "Ahti could control the elements with telekinetic energy. When I found him in the jungle, the Kashura and their human allies were trying to isolate his power. They succeeded in dampening his abilities, but only temporarily."

Anisa turned to me, her eyes wide and dark. I could almost smell the smoke from the dying flames. "He had it in him to save the world or destroy it. They were trying to direct his power, somehow, hoping to kill the Chimaera one by one. When he realized what they were doing, he fought back against the Kashura the only way he knew how. But his powers were too great for him or the Kashura to control, and the world paid the price.

"Every Chimaera indeed vanished, disintegrated into nothing. The seas continued to rise, everything burned, and so many died..." She trailed off. "So much destruction for nothing. And it all could have been avoided."

"How?"

"Dev." She looked back out at the patches of fire, the tendrils of cruel, dark smoke. "My little Kedi. Dev had his own powers, but the greatest was that he could almost... absorb or negate the effects of Ahti's magic. They were two sides of a coin, two ends of a balanced scale. If Dev and Ahti had been in the same room, there at the end, fate might have taken a very different fork in the path."

I reeled from this.

"I had been close to dormant for millennia. It was only when I sensed you that I managed to fully awaken, to stretch out my senses and discover what I could do in this form." She looked down at her body. In the vision, she seemed alive. Real. "It does more than even I suspected. It did not feel like an accident that I found you. And you remind me so much of Dev, my little Kedi."

My body thrummed with foreboding. "Mister Illari told me the myth, but what does the term mean to you?"

"It is largely as he said. It is a word that ancient humans gave to those who did not identify as solely male or solely female, whether physically or mentally."

"And they were worshipped?"

"Some, just as several men and women were." She contemplated me. "I've known male, female, eunuch, and Kedi Chimaera. The Theri were as varied as could be. I myself have lived as a man, now and again, though I usually chose to be a woman. I have been an artificial being of clockwork and I have been flesh and bone. The power of life simply exists. To many, what body it inhabits is largely irrelevant."

I looked away from her, unsure what to say. The sea raged beneath us, and a fierce wind whipped our hair.

"Do you miss Relean, Ahti, and Dev?" I asked.

"Every second of every day. But hope is often all that has sustained me through the centuries. There's a chance that Relean's Aleph survived, even if I haven't found it. But my main goal is to ensure that this"—she swept her hands out over the wreckage—"does not happen again. For someone as powerful as Ahti could appear again. Perhaps one already has, and the blurred man is looking for them. And this time, that Chimaera could end the world for good. But if you . . . if you are like Dev and I can help you control your magic . . . then perhaps we stand a chance."

The fires darkened to glowing jewels scattered across the land as the sea frothed, white and angry.

● ● ● ●

Cyan shook me awake. I was lying on the rooftop of the Kymri Theatre. I could tell I had been up there long enough that a normal person would have frozen.

But I was not normal.

She ushered me back into my room. Drystan, deeply asleep, didn't move.

—*Thanks for finding me,* I thought at Cyan. *You should go back to bed.*

She strode to the door, the hem of her robe whispering along the floorboards. She paused, turning back to me. Wisps of her dark hair had escaped the long braid down her back.

—*Sometimes she speaks to me alone, too, you know.*

The door closed behind her, leaving me in the dark. I curled around Drystan, huddling into his warmth, wanting nothing more to do with ghosts and memories of the night the world nearly ended.

28

SCIENCE, MAGIC & STORY

"A good magician's performance tells a story. Each act should build on the next, becoming ever more engaging to fill the audience with wonder. It's a bud that unfurls into a flower, meant to woo the audience."

THE UNPUBLISHED MEMOIRS OF JASPER MASKE:
THE MASKE OF MAGIC

Time slipped past, days blurring into weeks, drawing us ever closer to the night of the duel. In the early mornings, Anisa and I practiced calling forth and extinguishing my magic, hoping it'd be enough to keep my unruly powers in check, so I never had to go back to Doctor Pinecrest.

Maske and his marionettes shut ourselves off from the world, practicing stage magic from after breakfast to long past dusk. We'd grown confident enough that it was proving fun. We'd improvise or try out different approaches. We were adding a new illusion that involved something Maske called a Pepper's ghost, and it involved crafting choreography that worked with the angles of mirrors. I was to be the ghost, and Drystan would try to vanquish me.

When we tired, Drystan would provide some clownish antics to amuse us, the laughter giving us the energy to practice that bit longer. He taught Cyan some of his tumbler's tricks, which she was able to pick up quickly thanks to her previous circus training.

In the evenings, we'd sometimes play cards around the kitchen table, betting with buttons. Maske, the old card sharp, put even Drystan to shame, always winning unless he decided to deliberately lose. He taught Cyan and me a few of his techniques, not that I expected to ever properly put them to use.

As the snow melted outside the windows, snippets of news found their way to us, through newspapers or visits from Lily when she dropped off supplies from Twisting the Aces. She usually stayed for at least a cup of tea, telling us of the latest antics of the Foresters, gossip from the magic store, or generally trying to bolster our spirits. She always brought flowers and berated us for staying indoors so much. Sometimes, she spent the night, but she'd often disappear by breakfast, leaving only her bouquet of roses behind.

● ● ● ●

Finally, and yet all too soon, it was the week before the grand rematch. The city was plastered with lithographic posters advertising the duel. The design mimicked old posters from when Maske and Taliesin worked together. Back then, they had stood side by side, wielding magic against little devils and smiling serenely at passersby.

The upper half of this poster showed Maske and Taliesin glaring at each other in a battle of wills. Maske looked younger and more handsome than he was in reality. They'd put Taliesin in a head wrap bedecked with jewels and shown him as he would look if the drugs had not ravaged him. Below Maske, Drystan and I wore our magician's suits, our features and hair color matching our Glamour illusions, and Cyan in her Temnian dress. We were drawn as if Maske were the puppeteer controlling his marionettes, black lines from our joints leading up to his outstretched hands. Our open palms held blue fire.

Taliesin's boys had legs that turned into smoke, as though they were spectres, and they held red fire. Small imps with forked tails perched on their shoulders, whispering into their ears. Flora was behind them, in a white dress, her arms outstretched.

It all certainly painted a picture.

Tickets at the Royal Hippodrome had already sold out. The Palace had offered to lend several Vestige projectors and radios so that people gathered in parks and public places would be able to see the duel even if they couldn't afford the tickets. This was a great honor, though I wondered if it was also an attempt to placate the rising ire of the people. Forester protests continued apace, and there were almost as many posters with Timur's face about the city as the ones advertising our duel.

Two days before the re-match, we invited Lily to be our test audience for the full performance. Oli was busy behind the scenes as our lone stagehand. My nerves fluttered. This would be the first time anyone would see the entire thing. Lily was so excited she could hardly sit still. She wore a dress of watered green silk and cream lace for the occasion.

The lights dimmed. We went through our various tricks with practiced ease. When I closed my eyes, I dreamed of cards, flowers, and the flapping white wings of doves. It was better than dreams of a long-dead damselfly's past. Though Drystan and I were both doing stage magic, Drystan was the true star of the show. The story we'd woven through the performance centered around him, a younger version of Maske desperate to be one of the greatest magicians of our time.

As we neared the finale, Drystan sat in a chair, his head in his hands. Behind him rose a tall gauze curtain that looked a little like an artist's canvas. Drystan stood and twirled, waving his arms and muttering incantations. The gauze fluttered and then pulled away, revealing Maske's final illusion.

An automaton in a flowing dress with wide sleeves stood on a podium. Her face was made of smooth brass, her false glass eyes fixed on a far-off destination. It was the first time I'd seen her properly. She wasn't Vestige, of course, but made by Maske himself. A shiver passed through me all the same as her head moved mechanically to survey the empty theatre. It looked like a primitive echo of the clockwork woman's head.

The automaton took a shaking step forward, and Drystan reached his arms out towards her.

"My creation is more beautiful than I could ever have imagined," he said. "If only she could be transformed from metal to flesh and bone." He paused, his eyes lingering on the props of magic books stacked to one side of the stage. "I wonder . . ."

He circled the automaton. Her head moved jerkily, following him. I tried to shove down my unease and focus on the illusion. Our whole show was a perfect fusion of science, magic, and story. If we could pull it off, I knew the audience would love it.

"Be careful," I warned. "Those who meddle with magic often regret it."

I'd learned that too well.

Drystan arranged more props around the stage—beakers and a magic wand. The beakers of liquid bubbled, sending swathes of purple and blue fog onto the floorboards. The automaton raised her hands above her head to cover her face, but midway through, we heard a screech, and she stopped. Her head slumped forward.

Drystan paused. Cyan, who was beneath the stage so she could rise through the star trap once the automaton dropped, clambered onto the stage and glanced towards me and Oli. We shrugged.

Maske fiddled with the gears on the automaton's back.

"I don't understand . . ." he muttered. "She worked fine just this morning."

We all stood frozen as if in a tableau vivant. Maske lowered his head, resting it on the shoulder of his creation.

And he broke.

It was disconcerting to see him cry so openly, even if I understood why. The duel was the day after tomorrow. If his final act was broken, then our chances of winning were infinitesimal. This finale could be incredible, but only if it worked.

Gently, Maske gathered his stiff automaton in his arms and carried her away to his workshop.

The rest of us stood in silence. Lily cleared her throat self-consciously.

"Maybe I should go speak to him. Oh, and it was so wonderful before it went wrong. Poor Jasper . . ." She trailed off.

"You're probably the only one who could comfort him right now," Drystan said. Lily lifted her skirts and bustled away. Oli came over and wrapped an arm around Cyan. She leaned her head against him. I wanted to do the same with Drystan, but my arms stayed heavy at my sides.

I heard low laughter in my head. I frowned at Cyan. Her wide eyes met mine. It wasn't her.

It was Anisa.

I took the stairs two or three at a time, crossing the loft and grabbing the Aleph. I pressed the button and waited for her to appear as Cyan and Drystan followed me into the attic.

"What do you want, Anisa?" I asked.

She only stared at me with her infuriating, mysterious smile.

"Were you laughing at Maske?"

—*I laughed not at him, but the situation. The magician does not know how to repair what he has created.* She shook her head. *But that illusion is the very one he needs to win.*

"Why do you care about our little duel?"

Her smile widened, as if she found me amusing. —*It is important to you, and so it is important to the spirits. They showed us the stage, and we must take our steps upon it.*

She took a few steps, pacing as she had in the Pavillion of Phantoms.—*I also find the magician intriguing. He is a man who has lived many lives in such a short amount of time. He pursued a life of false magic, and it consumed him. He then used those same tricks to steal money rather than entertain. The pale jester found him, and they helped each other, but the magician stagnated. It is only now, with you, him, and then the little bird, that he blooms once again.*

I sunk my head into my hands. "And now it's ruined."

—*Not necessarily.*

I looked up at her. "What do you mean?"

—*I can fix it,* she said.

My breath caught in my throat. I gazed at this strange incorporeal echo from a time long gone. "Will you?" I asked carefully.

—*That depends on you.*

I tried to read her expression, but in the dim light of the loft, she was more transparent than she was by moonlight.

"Why?"

—*Because to do so, I would need your body again.* She blinked once, owlishly serene.

Drystan hissed in a breath.

Everything within me screamed that this was a terrible idea. But we had to win this duel. Maske needed this. *We* needed this. I wanted to stay in the safe haven of the Kymri Theatre, where I could dress as a girl or a boy and nobody cared. I'd grown to care for Maske and

Cyan. Drystan thrived as a magician. I'd run away from one home. I'd lost the circus. I didn't want to lose this place, too.

I closed my eyes. "All right. I'll do it."

—*I thought you might, little Kedi,* she said.

I opened my eyes. She held her hands out, beckoning me, and I stepped into her embrace. Her image flickered and settled along my skin before disappearing. She reached down with my hands to pick the Aleph up from the floor, sliding it into my pocket. As on the night the circus ended, I was a passenger in my own body. Anisa had control.

Drystan peered at me. "Are you all right, Micah?"

My lips curled into a smile. "Never better." My hand reached for his and my body drew him in for a kiss.

I could feel everything. His lips. The stubble of his chin. He didn't respond, but neither did he pull away. His body was stiff. I railed in my mind, trying to regain control of my body. Drystan moved away, his expression darkening.

—*What are you doing?* I screamed in the confines my mind.

"I could almost feel it," she said with my mouth, sadly.

"Do what you're aiming to do, Damselfly, then give Micah back his body."

"Of course, pale jester." She smiled at Drystan with my lips and carried on down the corridor, him following. Cyan went to find the magician.

My body opened the door to Maske's workshop, where the mirror maze met us. Anisa walked through it, unerringly finding the path. In the reflections, my face was serene and eerily empty.

My body pushed open a last mirror and entered the workshop. I smelled grease, sawdust, and the acrid tang of metal, reminding me of the circus.

The automaton rested on the table in the middle of the room. The large dress for the illusion hung nearby on a wooden mannequin, an even cruder echo of a real person. Maske wasn't there. I sensed he was in his room with Lily.

Anisa moved my body to the automaton. The panel over her abdomen had been removed. Inside was a mass of cogs and wires.

"Anisa," Drystan warned.

"Let me concentrate, pale jester," she said. "Unless you don't want my help?"

He went silent, crossing his arms.

My hands reached into the depths of the chassis, moving, detaching, and reattaching. I felt her hold the tip of my tongue between my teeth. After perhaps ten minutes, she took my hands away. I'd no idea what she'd done, but the interior of the automaton looked . . . tidier. Complete. Anisa fitted the plate back on the abdomen and screwed it back into place.

The door of the workshop opened. Maske emerged from the maze moments later, with Cyan tiptoeing behind him. No sign of Lily or Oli.

"I told you *never* to enter my workshop," Maske said, voice tight, nostrils flaring. "Get out, all of you. Get out." His voice quivered with emotion.

My face folded into a smile. "Not just yet. Apologies for entering without an express invitation, but it was necessary. I fixed your trinket for you, magician."

He looked at me, perturbed by the change in my voice and the way I spoke.

"Micah?" Maske asked, uncertainly.

"Turn it on, then, magician," my mouth said. "See what happens."

He reached shaking hands to pull the automaton into a standing position. He pressed the button at her back.

The automaton "awoke". Swinging her head back and forth, she continued to lift her arm into position, her crude fingers making the motion that would fasten the sleeves of the dress together, had she been wearing it. She drew her arms down to her sides and froze. At this point of the illusion on stage, she'd be lowered through the star trap.

Maske pressed the button again, and she went through all the movements once more—twisting her head to follow where Drystan would circle her, raising her arms, and lowering them again. The movements were smoother than even before she'd broken.

His anger at us entering his workshop vanished in an instant. Maske's face twitched, as if he had so many emotions swirling through him that his face could not decide which to register.

"I don't understand," he said. "How did you fix it?"

Cyan stepped forward. "We thank you, but I think you've over-stayed your welcome, damselfly."

"Cyan?" Maske's voice faltered. "What is going on? Micah?"

"That's not Micah," Cyan said.

A low laugh escaped my throat. Deep, sultry, and completely un-like my own. Drystan flinched.

My body set Anisa's Aleph on the floor and pressed the button. She held my arms out. Swirls of blue light danced over my skin and then, with a sickening lurch, Anisa's projection emerged from my body until the Chimaera ghost stood at my side. Once I could, I wrapped my arms around myself.

Maske took in the silver markings that Cyan had copied for the Elmbark séance and the large dragonfly wings. The magician reached down and picked up the Aleph, slack-jawed with awe.

"Her name is Anisa," I said, my voice hoarse. "She first spoke to me in the Pavillion of Phantoms in the circus, and I took her with me when we left. At the séance, the first night we came here, she spoke to me again. She sent Cyan and I the vision during that practice séance. She's sent us dreams." My mouth was dry.

Cyan looked at Maske anxiously.

"This . . ." he began, then faltered. "The Vestige I lost to Taliesin . . . it was one of you."

Anisa's transparent head whipped towards Maske. —*What do you mean?* she sent, and Maske and Drystan flinched at the sound of her voice in their heads.

"I won a strange metal disc in a card game as a young man," he said, turning the disc over in his hands. "There was a ghost inside who sometimes helped me with the mechanics of my illusions."

—*What did this ghost look like?* Anisa's eyes blazed so brightly that I took a step away from her.

"A man, with wings like yours." His voice was soft with wonder.

—*What was his name?*

He shook his head. "He never told me."

—*His eyes, were they banded with blue, green, and copper? With a little dot of darkness, like the wing of a monarch butterfly, just here?* She pointed to the bottom of her right iris.

"Ye-es," he said, drawing the syllable out and blinking fast. "You— you knew him?"

Anisa's eyes closed, and Cyan's mouth opened as she put it together.

—*Relean,* Anisa breathed, her tattooed forehead rippling with that same hopeful heartbreak she had whenever she thought of the love she'd lost.

Had he survived the centuries, too?

"If we win the duel, Maske gets that Aleph back," I said, slowly.

A soft smile played about Anisa's lips. Her eyes shone. She walked over to Maske, leaving a trail of light from the hem of her dress and back to the Aleph. She rested a phantom hand against the older man's face.

—*I am glad that my Relean helped you. But, even if you win, he is not yours to keep, magician. Deep down, I think you know this already.*

"Yes," he said. His eyes landed on his bronze creation. "How can I thank you, for fixing her?"

—*You have already given me more than enough, for you have given me hope that Relean has survived, and that soon enough, we will be reunited.* Her eyes shone with transparent tears.

Maske closed his eyes, then opened them. "Can you see the future, damselfly?" His expression was stark with hope.

—*Sometimes.*

He leaned his head against her phantom hand. "Will . . . will we be the champions of this re-match?"

—*The spirits have not shown me the outcome of your duel, but I will say this.* She looked over her shoulder at Cyan. *Whether or not you are the victor, you have already won more than you could ever imagine.*

Cyan barely suppressed a flinch.

"What do you mean?" Maske asked.

—*I expect you shall see find out soon enough, magician.*

She gave him a kiss on the cheek, which he wouldn't feel, and disappeared back into her Vestige metal disc. We stood in a semi-circle around it, shocked into silence.

I hesitated, then finally picked up the Aleph and put it back in my pocket.

They all stared at me. I bit my lip.

"Lord and Lady." Maske exhaled. "Magic and wonders. Another dragonfly beneath my roof this entire time. I can't believe it."

We lapsed into silence again. Maske glanced at the clock in the corner of his workshop. "Look at the time. I suggest we retire early. We've all had quite the evening, and tomorrow's the last day to practice." Maske ran a reverent fingertip down the automaton's face. "Whatever her motivations, I am most grateful to this Anisa. Thanks to her, we have a chance."

As Drystan and I went back to the loft, panic clawed at the edges of my mind.

All that happened finally hit me like the blow of a hammer. A doctor telling me I might be dying. Anisa and her unshaking belief that I was somehow supposed to save the world. The damselfly taking control of my body only to learn that the love of her many lives might also have survived the years.

I didn't lose consciousness, but everything went fuzzy. Strong arms encircled me.

Drystan lay next to me, telling me to breathe. I sucked air into my lungs, swallowing down the fear. I clutched him, my head on his chest, until his heartbeat gradually brought me back to myself.

Drystan and I stared at each other, drowning in words unspoken. His mouth twisted, and he rose long enough to undress for bed. My eyes lingered on the muscles of his back in the low light as he reached to pluck his sleeping shirt from the washing line.

He slid back next to me, but this time, our bodies didn't touch. I'd rarely been the one to initiate affection, and without a doubt, I was always the one who stopped things before they grew too heated.

I licked my lips and moved closer to him, sliding my arms around his waist and resting my cheek on his shoulder. He sighed, some of the tension leaving his muscles.

"I'm sorry," I said.

"For what?" His tone wasn't harsh, but clearly implied that there were various things I could be apologizing for.

"About what Anisa did earlier."

"That was her. Not you." He turned his head away, and I couldn't tell what he was thinking. "There's all these extraordinary things happening around me, but I . . . I'm not Chimaera. I feel useless."

"You're not. You're by far the better stage magician than me. You were invaluable when we went to Elwood's apartments. You've been here every step of the way."

His breath caught. "Every time I see her . . . it's like my brain can't process it. I'm already forgetting the sound of her voice, already doubting it was real."

I'd told him about Anisa's role in the past. How she'd raised her charges, and how the world had nearly ended. The only thing I hadn't told him was everything about Ahti and Dev—because to speak it aloud would make it feel true, and I didn't want to believe it.

"Do you trust her?" he asked.

"I don't know. She's so . . . so not quite human . . . but I don't think she's lying. I do think she wants to find her family and help make sure that Chimaera and magic come back into the world."

"But . . . should they come back, if some of them are strong enough to do that much damage?" he asked, hesitantly.

I said nothing. The thought had crossed my mind too, after all.

He shook his head. "It's like something from a fairy tale. One of the darker ones, used to frighten children into behaving."

"Perhaps." I paused. "I can't imagine what it must have been like, for Anisa to realize after so many centuries that she might be reunited with someone she'd loved in a dozen lifetimes. I've felt how much she loved him, and how much she misses him, even all these years later." Drystan's arms were around me, his hands gently stroking my back.

"I can imagine a little," he said.

My breath caught. He put a fingertip beneath my chin and tilted my head up until our lips finally met. He smelled of soap and skin. I took off his shirt and threw it to the floor. I ran my fingertips over the lines of his muscles. He had a small scar by his collarbone, and a little constellation of moles along his ribcage. I pressed my fingertips against them, memorizing each detail. He tangled his fingers in my hair, dipping his head to nuzzle my neck. I gasped.

He took off my shirt, and it joined his on the floor. His fingers paused on the laces of my Lindean corset. I bit my lip and nodded. I knew, once we began, this time we would see this through to the end.

He undid the laces, one by one.

29

THE SPECTRE'S SHADOWS

"Tonight is the night Elada has been waiting for: the duel between Taliesin Spectre and the Spectre's Shadows and Jasper Maske and his Marionettes. The future of these magicians' lives hangs in the balance. Who will win and who will fail? Place your bets here today! Are you feeling lucky?"

SIGN OUTSIDE SUNBEAM BETTING COMPANY

We arrived at the Royal Hippodrome late in the morning the day of the duel, our nerves jangling like a badly strung guitar. We'd opted not to practice at the Hippodrome itself for fear that someone would spy on us. Instead, we had measured the stage to the closest inch so we could practice back at the Kymri.

Professor David Delvin, the head of the Collective of Magic, decided who would perform first by a coin toss. Taliesin and his kin won, so they'd go before us. I wasn't sure how to feel about this—we'd know what we were up against. Yet, if they did well, it wouldn't be particularly good for our morale, and it'd be much harder to wow the audience and get them on our side.

We prepared as much as we could. Oli took our cloth-wrapped props into one of the storerooms backstage and locked them up. I'd been edgy before circus shows, but it paled in comparison to this, even though I had no risk of falling sixty feet. We changed into our costumes and reset our Glamours. I had brought Anisa's Aleph with me, just in case, though I hoped I wouldn't need her for anything.

An hour before the show, Taliesin, Sind, Jac, Flora, and the bald guard from the Spectre Theatre came to find us. Maske stood straight, his eyes flinty as he gazed at his rival. He wore a new cravat, and his hair was perfectly pomaded.

"Jasper, old sport," Taliesin wheezed, grinning to show the ruin of his mouth. His eyes were bright with Lerium. The twins were impeccably dressed in their magician's kit, their faces showing only smug derision. Cyan narrowed her eyes at whatever thoughts were in their heads. Flora's face was stony, and the guard seemed to be there mostly to be intimidating, which was working.

"Taliesin," Maske replied. "Tonight, we finally set things to rights."

The old man gave a phlegmy laugh. "The scales were already balanced fifteen years ago, Jasper."

Maske smirked, buffing his nails on his shirt. "You unfairly weighted the scale in your favor. Let's not have a repeat performance of that tonight, shall we?"

Taliesin leered. "You're one to be tetchy about the rules, card sharp."

"I never cheated at stage magic, and you well know it."

Taliesin pulled his lips back from his Lerium-stained teeth.

I stepped between them. "We'll soon find out who wins. Fair and square."

Taliesin spat derisively as he and his shadows left. We watched them go.

"Are they planning to cheat, Cyan?" Maske asked. "Can you tell?"

"The twins and Flora aren't, surprisingly enough," Cyan said. "Couldn't get a read on the guard. Taliesin is so off his face on Lerium,

I can't tell. I'm surprised he could even focus his eyes, much less speak."

"Let's hope that means the codger's too addled to try anything." Drystan's mouth twisted.

"Don't put anything past him," Maske warned. "But it's long past time to beat that bastard once and for all." His eyes blazed, and in that moment, I saw the man who had been capable of counting cards in front of hardened criminals.

"We'll beat him," I said, more confidently than I felt.

We had to.

• • • •

The head of the Collective of Magic, Professor David Delvin, and the solicitor, Christopher Aspall, showed us to our private box in the theatre to watch the first half of the performance. Our feet sank into the lush carpet, and the chairs were upholstered in an expensive red velvet.

I tried not to gape as I saw who was in the other private boxes. Directly across from us was none other than the Princess Royal herself. Nicolette Snakewood wore a tiara perched in her dark curls, and a red and gold dress. Her cheeks were pink with excitement as she craned her head towards the empty stage. She'd grow up to be one of the most powerful people in the world, but she was still excited for a little magic.

Sure enough, Doctor Pinecrest was at her side. His eyes met mine across the theatre, and he inclined his head. I reluctantly echoed the movement.

—*Break a leg, Micah Grey*, he sent me. I pretended not to hear.

The other boxes housed prominent nobility and some of the biggest merchants and property owners in Elada. People occupied every seat, waving fans and perusing the programs. I spotted Lily Verre in a good seat near the front, Tam from Twisting the Aces next to her. My palms grew damp. There were so many people, and many more would be out in the parks, bundled against the cold, watching us on the blank sides of buildings thanks to Vestige projectors. There would be so many to see if we failed.

The lights dimmed in the body of the theatre, then brightened again.

Taliesin bustled onto the stage in a velvet tuxedo, but all the cosmetics and fine clothing couldn't hide his tremors. He held out his hand and gave a shaking bow to the audience.

"Tonight," he said, his voice carrying well thanks to the acoustics of the Hippodrome, "I present to you the Spectre's Shadows. I have taught my grandsons everything I know, and you will see and agree, without a doubt, that they are the greatest young magicians in Elada. Their magic is so powerful, even Death himself balks at their prowess."

He smirked at the audience, gave a last nod at Maske, and stepped to the wings.

The twins, resplendent in their suits, strode onto the stage from opposite sides, bowing low. In unison, they waved to the scattered applause. They launched straight into it, proceeding to pretend to try and kill each other in increasingly creative ways.

Sind first took out a pistol and Jac held up his hands in surrender before twisting and grabbing one from his own pocket. They circled each other, calling out insults.

Sind fired and Jac flew back, but when he stood, only colored confetti fell from the "bullet wound" and he bowed to muted applause. Jac next threw a dagger that apparently went through Sind without causing injury. It stuck fast to a wooden post behind him, quivering.

The performance was very like the Spectre Show we'd seen, yet on a larger scale. Gone was the demonstration of small-scale magic. All was grand illusion, meant to impress and be seen from the farthest seat in the theatre.

They caused each other to explode and disappear in a cloud of smoke, only to reappear on the other side of the stage without a hair out of place. The audience gasped with shock and amazement. Several people clutched the hollows of their throats as they watched.

In the Collective of Magic's theatre box, the magicians' faces were impassive as they judged the illusions before them. I wondered if Cyan could pluck out what they were thinking but also wasn't sure I wanted to know.

The twins next brought out the magic lantern for their phantasmagoria. Death appeared again on a shifting curtain of smoke. The magicians bowed before it. Death wove his hands and little figures appeared in the fumes. Chimaera with the wings of bats and angels flew overhead, and below, people with forked fishtails and fins on their backs swam through the currents of the River of the Dead. Beings with the legs of fauns or horses or the large horns of antelope, deer, or bulls staggered toward their fate.

"You have escaped me, for your magic is mighty," a disembodied voice I recognized as Taliesin's boomed through the theatre. A projection of Death's hooded head undulated on the shifting smoke. "You are the only ones I will ever bow to. In return, I will grant you more power." Death bowed to the first twin, and then the other, before disappearing.

The next few illusions showcased the twins reveling in their new abilities. Coins fell from their pockets to scatter on the floor, rolling and spinning.

They levitated themselves, and I narrowed my eyes. From this distance, I could see a few of the wires, though perhaps that was only because of my good eyesight. Hopefully, the Collective would catch that error as well. But would that be enough? All of their other illusions so far had been expertly performed.

I bit my lip so hard I feared drawing blood. Every illusion was a calculated message: nobody could defeat them. Not even Death.

—*Micah*, Cyan said to me, as though she sensed the trend of my thoughts. *If I wanted to, I could make them stumble. I could distract them so easily.*

I knew she didn't offer that lightly. Oh, it was tempting. So tempting. If the Taliesins had a mind reader in their midst, they wouldn't hesitate at all to use that power to win. It was one thing to tap her abilities for a séance, but to deliberately meddle with their show would go against every tenet of the Collective of Magic.

I shook my head minutely. —*If we did that, we'd be no better than Taliesin was all those years ago. Our act is good on its own merits.*

—*I thought you'd say that*, she sent, but I felt her relief, too. *Maske was tempted, but deep down, he wants to win this fairly, too.*

—*We can beat them*, I said. *We can.*

—*I hope you're right.* With a resigned sigh, she turned her attention back to the performance.

The twins stepped into two spirit cabinets, locking themselves inside. There was a large bang and a blast of light. The doors swung open to reveal the empty back of the cabinet.

Another flash of light and a crash of cymbals, and the twins appeared again. But another set of twins were there as well, flanked to either side. I squinted at the stage. It must have been something to do with mirrors similar to a Pepper's ghost, but I couldn't see the angles. The four twins coalesced into a single person, who bowed low before turning on his heel and disappearing into a wisp of smoke.

I sank lower into my seat as applause filled the theatre to the rafters, fighting the urge to cry. Maybe I'd been too hasty to warn Cyan against meddling.

How could we hope to win against this?

30

MASKE'S MARIONETTES

"A shadow play is an old form of storytelling. The puppets are often made out of flat, wooden figures with cut-out detailing, and the joints are articulated. The figures are held up between a source of light and a screen. People may also use their bodies' shadows, as in the well-known example of making a dog's head with a hand. This type of theatre is found in all islands of the Archipelago but is most popular in Southern Temne. As you can imagine, there is much potential for it in stage magic."

THE SECRETS OF MAGIC, THE GREAT GRIMWOOD

The show paused for intermission. Out in the foyer, the audience mingled in the gigantic cavern of marble and gilt, sipping drinks and discussing the Spectre twins as a dance troupe undulated on a smaller stage.

Taliesin's workers cleared the props away, and the three of us and Oli labored to move our gimmicks into their proper places. In actuality, we should have had another stagehand or two, but Maske didn't want to hire anyone he didn't trust, and it's not like we could have afforded it, anyway.

We stepped back once everything was ready, panting with effort. It was almost time. We reset our Glamour illusions five minutes before the hour was up. By the next time we had to do this, we'd be finished with our routine.

Maske cleared his throat. "No matter the outcome, I want to

thank you. Without you, I'd still be moldering in that theatre. If I lose this time, I'll know I gave it my all and had the best help possible." He sniffed. "But Lord and Lady above, I really want us to win."

He drew us into a hug. I squeezed all three of them as tightly as I could.

We broke from the embrace.

Christopher Aspall came to find us. "The show will begin in five minutes. I wanted to tell you personally." He clasped hands with Maske. "It will be a privilege to see your illusions on stage once again."

"Thank you kindly, Mr. Aspall," Maske said. "No matter the outcome, we aim to put on quite the show." Maske reached into his pocket and took out the moon and six-pointed stars mask we'd given him on Lady's Long Night. He put it on, tying it securely.

Drystan, Cyan, and I took our places, and, for the first time in fifteen years, the Maske of Magic went out long enough to introduce us.

"My beautiful, wonderful people of Elada," he said. "I thank you most humbly for coming to view our spectacle this evening. What follows, I hope, will delight and astound you. This performance has been a labor of love, created with care by all of us. I may call them my marionettes, but they are the ones who have lifted me up these last few months. This is the story about the dangers of letting the hard edges of pride cut away your softness. And a reminder that, even after a time in the shade, you can always step back out into the light. Thank you."

My throat closed at his words. He stepped aside, the curtains drew back, the glass globes brightened, and the stage was ours.

●   ●   ●   ●

There, in the Royal Hippodrome, Maske's semi-autobiographical tale came to life. Drystan played the young man studying to be a scientist who stumbled upon a book of magic. He performed a brief, furious flurry of legerdemain, with scarves pulled from sleeves and a dove flying from beneath his coattails as it had in my vision at Twisting the Aces. The audience laughed at his unabashed surprise and delight at this new magic. I was set up as Drystan's friend and fellow magician, similar but not meant to be Taliesin. My character also read from the book, despite being warier of its dangers.

As the two young magicians learned more, the tricks grew increasingly elaborate. We set out to impress a lady, played by Cyan, of course, and we flirted with her through our tricks. Drystan gave Cyan a bouquet of flowers from thin air, which she turned into a shower of glitter. I tried to keep up, but I was deliberately less elegant at the tricks. I was playing second fiddle, and my character resented it.

We'd adapted the Kymri Princess trick to better fit the story, and Drystan next levitated Cyan above his head, with me scurrying up to the gridiron to help manipulate wires, and she tilted her head down for a kiss.

That bit I didn't like so much, but I knew they'd only be thinking about how to move their bodies to slide into the next part of the story. They were friends, now, but nothing more than that.

When Drystan lowered Cyan, he gave her another kiss on the cheek and a small jewel remained where his lips had rested. Cyan planted the jewel into a pot where a tree grew from it and bore tiny apples before the audience's very eyes. She cut one in half and gave him back the jewel from the core to more applause. The Jeweled Arbor was one of my favorite tricks—another perfect blend of science, magic, and story to enchant the audience.

While they'd grown the tree, I'd prepared for my main illusion. First, I came back onto the stage in an oversized coat and warned Drystan about the dangers of becoming addicted to magic. To prove the point, I did a series of quick changes, a curtain in front of a cabinet closing for only a second to reveal me in a totally different outfit. This section provided a last bit of levity before the tone shifted, and it was also where I played with gender. The coat dropped to reveal the bulky Kymri princess dress, then a sleeker dress beneath it. A man's tunic that was in fashion about two hundred years ago. And, then, finally, I was back in my magician's suit. Next, it was my character's turn to delight in his own nascent powers, and I did things like swallow a sword and breathe fire—tricks I'd learned back in the circus.

Drystan became more powerful. His illusions grew darker. My character tried to warn him to turn away, to resist corruption of arcane arts. Drystan and I disappeared into the spirit cabinet, as we'd practiced. In the dark, we were close enough to touch, and we snuck a quick kiss before we disappeared behind the mirrors. Cyan opened the spirit cabinet doors, and a white dove flew out of the empty interior to shock and delight the audience. Drystan appeared in the back of the theatre instead, striding down the alleyway between seats.

"If I can do it all," Drystan said as he climbed the stairs, "then I will."

I, in contrast, limped onto the stage, telling him that the powers had sent me to a storm without end, to a time long past, and it'd frightened me. I warned him that perhaps we were doing too much, and we didn't fully know what we risked. Drystan waved off my concerns.

My character quit both magic and his friendship, letting Drystan's tale and thirst for more power take center stage. Oli and I pushed a mechanism so that a sun set and a moon rose a few times in the background to show time passing as Drystan threw himself into his studies. By the end of it, I was panting.

On the other side of the stage, Cyan produced a little mechanical butterfly, and it fluttered over to Drystan to catch his attention. He ignored it, turning another page of the magical tome.

"Am I not enough?" she asked as the butterfly flew back to land on her hand.

He stayed silent, which was answer enough.

Cyan deflated at his lack of affection, causing the candles to extinguish and rekindle. So she, too, packed her bags and left.

It was only after the magician lost his lady that he realized how much he'd truly loved her. He tried to call her back, but she resisted him at every turn. A few minutes later, I came back and slid my arm around Cyan as she, with a great flourish, made a large engagement ring appear on her left hand.

She turned to leave, and Drystan grabbed her elbow. Cyan struck him, the theatrical slap not even touching his skin. Drystan yelled, hand rising to his cheek before he took out a false gun and fired at her, point blank. The prop gun sparked and glitter exploded. It was a similar trick to the Taliesin twins', but with a different, arguably darker context. Cyan paused, as if she'd been struck, and then she spat a bullet from her mouth, letting it skitter to the floor, while I fled.

Backstage, I threw the costume of a patched and ragged coat over my black clothes and stuck a pair of antlers on my head.

"I never want to see you again," Cyan said. She quit the stage, and, though I couldn't see them, I knew Oli had released a flurry of white dove feathers from the gridiron. They floated through the air, settling silently on the floorboards.

The lights dimmed. I crept to the wings. Drystan held his head in his hands.

"What have I done?" he asked the audience. He raised his chin, straightened his shoulders, and shook his head. "No matter. I don't need her. I don't need anyone. I can prove I'm the master of magic. I found a spell to raise the ghost of a Chimaera of the past. It's meant to be impossible. But I know I can do it."

That was my cue to head below stage.

This one was the Pepper's ghost illusion we'd only started practicing a month ago, and it was one of the more complicated illusions. Behind a drawn curtain, Oli had raised the clear plate glass, angling it toward the audience. Below the stage was a smaller level, like an extra orchestra pit. Down there, all was dark, with Oli swathed head-to-toe in black velvet. The only objects on the second area were a moving platform, angled so that a figure standing on it would tilt at the same angle as the mirror, and an oxyhydrogen spotlight that would illuminate the ghostly apparition.

I stood on a platform brandishing a curved prop sword. Oli made some last-minute adjustments before lighting the spotlight so my reflection showed above.

Drystan would have stepped back in shock, as if he hadn't expected his raised ghost to be so vicious.

I went through the rehearsed feints and stunts so that it looked like Drystan fought a Chimaera ghost. It was like a dance—jump forward, parry, slide back. Drystan moved fluidly, with increasing desperation. I twisted my face into a snarl and fought back just as viciously.

I hid a rueful smile. In the circus, I'd dressed as a girl for the pantomime after spending the first sixteen years of my life as one. Now, I played a Chimaera ghost, and none of the audience, save Doctor Pinecrest, knew that I was truly a Chimaera with a Phantom Damselfly hidden in my pocket.

Drystan gave a last swipe of the sword, which went straight through my reflected illusion. I cried out, as if in pain, and fell to the floor. Oli dimmed the light, and up on the stage, my echo slowly faded from view.

I sat up, took off the antlers and patched coat, and let out a tentative sigh of relief. We were almost done, and so far, all had gone according to plan. I went back to the wings to watch. Drystan declared he could create the love of his life. A perfect being who could never disappoint him.

"But can I do it?" he asked himself. "Is my magic strong enough?"

As in practice the other day, the gauze curtain behind him fluttered. Drystan pulled it away to reveal the automaton on the podium. The audience gasped and whispered. Cyan nudged me with her thoughts, and I glanced up at the box where Doctor Pinecrest sat with the Princess Royal. He leaned forward in his seat.

Drystan muttered and gestured as he began the "incantations" to bring the automaton to life.

—*Be careful*, Anisa said in my mind, startling me. *Something is happening.*

—*What do you mean?* I asked her.

—*There is a Chimaera here, and I believe he means you harm.* Her voice was faint and distorted.

—*Micah*, Cyan sent me. She was changing backstage, and I was certain she'd heard the Phantom Damselfly, too. *I think something's happened to Oli. I can't sense him. I can't feel him!*

—*What?*

—*Go check on him. I sensed . . . pain. Can't get much more . . . too many people. My ability is fluctuating. I can only reach you because I'm "shouting" as loud as I can.*

I sensed her straining, like when Anisa had tried to warn me that Shadow Elwood was following me on the beach promenade in Sicion.

—*I'll check*, I said, but I wasn't sure if Cyan heard me. Fear tingled my fingertips.

I went back below, searching for Oli. I heard footsteps, but from the tread, it wasn't Oli. My skin tightened with gooseflesh.

Biting my lip, I guessed I had ten minutes, at best, before I needed to be by the star trap. The Glamour buzzed beneath my shirt—it would need resetting soon, too. I sprinted behind the stage and then stopped. Oli lay sprawled across the floor, half-dragged behind a box of props. Next to him was Maske. Maske moaned, his head turning, and I saw a streak of blood at his forehead. I pressed my fingertips to Oli's temple. He was alive, but unconscious. Both needed medical attention—well did I know how dangerous head wounds could be.

I heard a rustle of movement behind me and crouched into a fighting stance.

Taliesin's bald and muscle-bound guard crept toward the stage, the bear tattoo peeking above his collar. He hadn't spotted me, but I took a step, and a floorboard creaked. He twisted, meeting my eyes. Distantly, I heard Cyan yelling in my mind. This was the man who had hurt Oli and Maske. A wave of anger crashed over me. Without thinking about the fact that this man was more than twice my size, I rushed at him.

He grabbed me and threw me as if I weighed nothing at all. I hit the wall, and the back of my head exploded with pain. With a grunt, I forced myself back to my feet and ran at him again, dancing out of his reach and landing a punch into his kidneys. His breath left in a *whoosh* of pain, but he stayed standing and reached for me.

I darted out of his grasp and grabbed a nearby skein of rope. But I was too slow—he grabbed me and threw me again, harder. I hit another wall and slid down it, my breath leaving my lungs. With a sickening lurch, I remembered Bil had thrown Aenea much the same way in the circus. This time, I'd hit my shoulder instead of my head, but I pretended to be unconscious. I stayed still until the bald guard turned away. I opened my eyes and saw him stalking back towards Maske. Fear spiked through me. Would he hurt the magician even worse?

With painful slowness, I sat up and reached out, desperate. My right hand found a spare belaying pin, a long, rounded metal spike used to secure ropes. I threw it at the guard with all my strength, hitting him square on the back of the head.

He roared and twisted, charging at me. Even though Anisa had warned me against it, I reached for that spark in my chest and used my powers to *push* him back. As I had the night we crossed Shadow Elwood on the streets, I felt the illusion of my Glamour fall.

"Ah," the guard said, and his voice deepened and roughened. "That's interesting. Looks like I don't even have to hide."

His eyes flashed gold as his lips pulled back from his teeth sharpening into points. Short, brown, bristling fur sprouted on his arms and face, thickening to a ruff at his throat. His clothing tore and fell to the floor in rags. The bear of a man became truly bear-like. I could only gape at him in surprise.

The guard was a Chimaera. Did Taliesin know that?

I hadn't had a chance of winning a physical fight against him when he was a man. What hope did I have against this bear? He swiped at me with a paw, and I barely jumped out of the way in time. His claws caught on my sleeve, ripping the fabric. I gripped my magic tighter, but I was so afraid and upset, I couldn't grab it.

—*Free me*, Anisa commanded.

I grabbed the Aleph from my pocket, flicked the switch, and dropped it. It rolled before coming to a stop, and the bear man looked at it, his eyes lighting in recognition—and a hint of fear.

Anisa rose like the avenging ghost she was. Without hesitation, she stepped into me, and I allowed her. My chest burned and my heart brightened as she took control of my magic.

With her help, I knew exactly what to do.

Cyan and Anisa had told me that Vestige helped enhance power. This theatre was full of it. A few nobles wearing Glamours to make themselves more beautiful. A child with an automaton clutched to her chest like a doll in the audience.

Anisa helped me draw power from those artefacts. Not enough to drain them, but enough to help make whatever I had in myself become . . . *more.* The bear-man paused, and I wondered if, for a moment, my eyes flashed blue. My whole body might glow with the power contained within me.

In the auditorium, the lights must have flickered, because I heard shocked gasps from the audience, and Drystan slightly flubbed his line.

I felt my lips curl into a smile as I threw the magic at him. Around me, time mercifully slowed down again.

The bear-man rose in mid-air, twisting, his muzzle opening in rage. Anisa and I raised him higher. I was drawing too deeply on whatever power I had or borrowed, but I couldn't let it go. The gas globes behind stage flickered, and that internal fire brightened until I felt I was illuminated with the power of a star, just as Anisa had described it. Blue shimmered at the ends of my fingers. The bear slammed into the stone wall at the back of the theatre. He fell with a thump.

I panted, glowing with magic and triumph.

—*Let it go now,* Anisa said. *Swallow it down. Extinguish the star.*

But I couldn't. The glow wanted to take power from every bit of Vestige in the theatre and the surrounding buildings.

I tried to stop it. So did Anisa. I felt her trying to take full control of my body, but my magic wouldn't let her. This power was growing and growing, building and building, threatening to explode.

—*Bring it back, little Kedi,* Anisa called to me, and her fear hit me in waves. *Please. Control your powers. You have to bring it back!*

As my power rose, a chilling thought came to me: What if I wasn't Dev . . . what if my powers were more like Ahti's?

I tried to push down my emotions. To banish the power, to smother the star.

But it wanted so badly to burn.

31

THE ROYAL HIPPODROME

"The Royal Hippodrome is the largest theatre in Elada. Nestled near the Royal Snakewood Palace in Imachara, it's a triumph of architecture. Grand murals of myth painted by Jon Snakewood, the younger brother of King Elliot Snakewood III, are depicted in the foyer and above the grand staircase. If you look closely, you'll see Chimaera carved into many of the bricks throughout the theatre, so subtle that they're easy to miss."

A HISTORY OF THE THEATRE,
PROFESSOR DARIAN BALSA, ROYAL SNAKEWOOD UNIVERSITY

Right as I felt on the verge of exploding, the power extinguished as if someone had kicked a pile of soot and dirt over a flame. The loss of it was like a ricochet, and I fell to my knees. I panted, staring down at my fingertips, amazed to find them whole when it felt like they'd burned down to cinders. Time was moving normally again. Distantly, I caught the sounds of Drystan saying his lines, building up to the final act.

I wanted to feel victorious, but I hadn't done it. Neither had Anisa, who had left me and returned to her Aleph.

Then how—?

A hunched figure came into view. Taliesin.

In his hand, he held an Eclipse. Of course. The artefact caused all other Vestige in the immediate vicinity to stop functioning. It seemed it'd switched me off just as effectively. How far did the radius go—was Drystan's Glamour still working?

I was still thrown, my muscles locked and stiff.

Taliesin must have come down here with me because he suspected that Maske *had* cheated—perhaps he thought that the automaton contained Vestige. Anisa might have helped, but the final result was nothing but clockwork. Taliesin stalked toward me. His pupils were blown from Lerium. How much had he seen?

The drug gave him more strength, and before I could blink, he'd pushed me to the ground and stalked straight past me. Without a pause, he slid his hands around Maske's neck.

Taliesin's breathing was harsh, features twisted with hatred, and I realized—like Bil, he was past the point of no return. He'd seen how well we performed. He'd realized he had a real chance of losing.

I needed to do something, but I couldn't move. I couldn't breathe, as if Taliesin's hands were around my neck instead of Maske's. The backstage of the theatre disappeared. I was back in that circus tent, the scent of whisky breath on my face. I was imagining the world ending in flame.

There was only fear.

Gritting my teeth, I forced my muscles past the inertia and knocked Taliesin to the floor. If I hadn't just been thrown across the room, and nearly undone by my own magic, it wouldn't have been a fair fight. I was young and lithe, far stronger than I had a right to be, and he was so fragile he might as well have been made of old bone and dry leaves. But I was hurt, cut off from my power, and he was high on Lerium.

Taliesin's lips pulled back from his broken teeth. I felt the snarl mirrored on my own features. Taliesin threw a glancing blow across my cheek, his fingernails scratching my skin. I pushed him away from me as hard as I could. He unbalanced and the Eclipse tumbled from his gnarled hands. I scrabbled for it.

With a last burst of Delerious strength, he punched me in the temple. For a moment, the world around me wobbled, and he tried to grab the Eclipse from my grasp. I recovered, wrestling him to the ground, using my entire body weight to keep him pinned.

"I won't let him win," Taliesin wheezed. "I'll do everything in my power to make him suffer. He ruined my life. He ruined me!"

"You were both stupid and tried to ruin each other," I said.

His hand fumbled and he grasped the Eclipse again.

"For the love of gods, let it go," I said, unsure whether I meant the Eclipse or his grudge. I plucked the Eclipse from his hands and switched it off.

My power flooded through me again, heady and strong. This time, though, I could control it. I wasn't afraid of Taliesin, and I was eerily calm. With a twist, I sent the spark of my magic somewhere else. I had no idea if time around us was beating at its usual pace or if it had slowed again. How long did we have?

I held Taliesin down. He couldn't fight back. Cyan's presence batted at the edges of my consciousness, so I let her in.

Taliesin glared at me with his yellowed eyes, his breath smelling of decay and the cloying spice of the drug. The leer subsided and he was only a pathetic man gasping for breath, his face purpling. I realized how easy it would be to kill him. To make sure he never tried to harm Maske or anyone else again.

Immediately, I skittered away from that thought, horror growing within me. Was that my own bloodlust, or was it Anisa's emotions feeding into mine? I could sense her from the depths of her Aleph, desperate for answers about Relean. If I let her, she'd take over my body again and she'd do what I couldn't or wouldn't.

With a shaking breath, I forced my fingers to loosen. Taliesin took great, shuddering gasps, his eyes rolling in his skull.

"Come on," Taliesin rasped, a last plea. "Let me just press the button long enough to take him down. I'll pay you for it."

With his henchman subdued and without the Eclipse, Taliesin was no threat. Not truly. "There's no price you could offer," I said. "If you leave now, I won't tell everyone out there"—I jerked my head toward the audience—"what you tried to do. And your grandsons won't need to learn you didn't think them talented enough to win on their own."

His eyes widened.

I let him go and stepped back, bending down to clutch the Eclipse, never taking my eyes off him.

"Go now, Taliesin," I said, my voice hard and sharp. Perhaps he saw a flash of warning blue in my eyes. He stumbled. The henchman had awoken and once again looked like a human.

"You go too, or I'll call the Policiers after the show," I bluffed. Cyan whispered his name in my mind. "I know your name, Jarek Lutier. I know where you live, and I know what you are. Trouble me again and you'll find out exactly how much you'll regret it."

Whatever he saw in my face frightened him. He fled, too, and I watched him go.

I checked in on Oli and Maske. Maske was already awake, sitting up, clutching his head, and Oli was coming to. Anisa answered my wordless question, assuring me they'd be all right.

"The performance . . ." Maske muttered.

—*Micah! Hurry!* Cyan called. Up above, I heard Drystan tell the audience he had finished his creation. Time was well and truly running out.

"I've got this," I said to Maske.

I heard Drystan say, "You shall become the love I never had . . ." as I raced toward the stage.

—Don't go up the star trap without me, Cyan, it's too dangerous! I yelled at her.

—Come on, Micah, or I might not have a choice. Her fear tangled with mine.

Cyan stood below the star trap, staring at it anxiously.

"Now, Micah!" she said.

I fiddled with the machinery. Just in time, the trap door opened, and the automaton slid down the star trap. I caught it, setting it down with effort. It was damned heavy.

"Come on, Cyan," I said. "Up you get."

She stepped onto the platform. Her face was painted with silver swirls, though at my request, she'd made them look less like Anisa's markings. She bent down and gave me a quick kiss on the cheek.

"Well done, Micah," she whispered.

I pulled the lever, and she rose up to the stage. She would unhook the sleeves next, and I heard the audience gasp as she revealed herself to them and I re-set my Glamour.

"My love!" Drystan spoke of the automaton's beauty and perfection. Cyan would be covering her face again, as if in shyness.

"But I am not yours, oh great magician," she said. "I am only my own."

Up above, Drystan would be reaching for her as the dress collapsed. I pulled the lever, Cyan came back down the star trap, and I helped her off the platform. To the audience, it was as if she'd disappeared completely. In reality, the dress was sucked into a tube, which Drystan covered with his leg. The tube and the dress dropped back down the star trap and landed on the mat.

Up above, Drystan cried out in surprise and dismay. He admitted the errors of his ways and vowed to repent to the Lord and Lady, throwing his magic books into a chest.

"Time for the grand finale," Cyan said as she hurried to the trap-door beneath the spirit cabinet and climbed the ladder. She emerged from the cabinet up above. I wasted no time, climbing up to the grid-iron above the stage and staring down at the tops of their heads.

"Is the real girl not better than a magical one?" she asked, teasingly.

Drystan fell to his knees. "Always, my sweet."

"Do you love me?" she asked.

"More than the moon loves the sun."

"Would you truly give up your magic for me?"

"In a heartbeat, even if it'd feel like tearing myself in two."

She reached down and tilted his head up at her. "Then I will not ask such a thing of you. But you must not forget who you are, and you must not turn towards darkness again. The light is always brighter."

As they embraced, I ran across the gridiron, releasing glitter and feathers. Cyan and Drystan bowed to thunderous applause before the curtains fell.

● ● ● ●

"So Taliesin nearly cost us everything," Maske said, holding a hand to his head. We were backstage.

We'd filled Drystan in on Taliesin's and the guard's meddling, though I left out a few key details. Oli was swaying slightly on his feet. Out in the foyer, the guests were congregating, nursing drinks and discussing the duel among themselves. In one of the back rooms of the Hippodrome, the Collective of Magic deliberated on our fate.

"You all did brilliantly, especially considering the unexpected challenges," Maske said. "No matter what happens, I want you to know that. You did my illusions justice."

My throat unexpectedly closed at his praise. Cyan's eyes were shining, too. Drystan bowed his head.

Maske exhaled. "And now we wait."

"You should both ice your injuries," I said. "You don't want them to swell."

Oli and Maske grimaced, but they didn't fight me. The bar in the foyer would have some, and they went off in search of it.

I wasted no time filling Drystan in on the rest of the details.

"He . . . what?" Drystan said, faintly, when I came to the part about Taliesin's guard turning into a bear.

"He's Chimaera."

"You fought a *bear*?" he exclaimed.

"More a bear-like man. But, uh, yes. And I won." I couldn't keep the pride from my voice. I took the Eclipse from my back pocket. "Taliesin had this, too."

Drystan whistled, and I tucked it into my suit pocket.

We huddled in the dressing room as the Collective of Magic deliberated. Maske and Oli returned. Maske downed a large gin, though I wasn't sure he should be drinking with a head wound. Oli had brought back an unopened bottle of champagne in a bucket, and we stared at it morosely, wondering if we'd crack it open to celebrate or drown our sorrows.

Drystan and I sat close together, holding hands so tightly it almost hurt. Oli and Maske held ice wrapped in napkins against their heads. Cyan leaned against Oli's shoulder, staring into the distance.

—*Can you listen to what the Collective are saying?* I asked.

—*No.* Cyan said. *They're too far away. I* am *listening to Taliesin and his grandsons. The twins have no idea what Taliesin tried to do. They're worried, though. Couldn't believe how well we performed.* Her mental voice was warm with triumph.

To be honest, neither could I.

• • • •

Half an hour later, the Collective called everyone back into the auditorium. The audience took what felt like a long time to settle back into
their seats. I fought the irrational urge to yell at them to hurry up.
Finally, everyone fell silent.

Professor David Delvin stood in the center of the stage, flanked by
some of the best magicians of the age—the leaders of the Collective of
Magic. There was a tall, thin man in a floor-length black cape with
long blonde hair. I didn't know his stage name, though I was sure that
Maske did. A shorter woman in a fine blue silk dress and bustle stood
next to him. She was easy: there was only one female magician who
had risen high enough in the Collective of Magic to be standing there:
the Mystical Marvel. I stifled a gasp when I recognized the last elderly
man's distinctive white sideburns and shorter, waist-length red cape.
It was none other than the Great Grimwood himself, the author of
The Secrets of Magic.

"Thank you everyone who came to witness such a momentous
event this evening," Professor Delvin said. "Let's welcome our rival
magicians to the stage."

Professor Delvin gestured to the left wing. Taliesin came out, limp-
ing with his cane. He tried to come across as triumphant, but I saw
how he favored his arm, and how he wouldn't look at me or Maske.

Sind, Jac, and Flora followed, straight-backed, smiling disarm-
ingly at the crowd. No bear-guard loomed in the wings. My stomach
felt as though it'd dropped to my knees. These twins had been born
on the stage and lived and breathed magic their entire lives. Their
show had far more money behind it, and, in many ways, their performance had been flashier. Drystan had hesitated on a few lines and had
to improvise a slight delay near the end. It was hard not to worry, even
if I had foiled Taliesin's plot.

Professor Delvin gestured to his right, and I released Drystan's hand as the four of us walked out. We blinked under the bright glass globes of the theatre. Maske flashed his magician's smile at the audience, playing the part of the showman, but his eyes showed his fear.

"This was not an easy decision to make," the Great Grimwood said. Part of me couldn't believe I was sharing the stage with the magician himself. "The Spectre's Shadows performed wonderfully, illustrating their supposed power over death."

"And the newcomers, Maske's Marionettes," the Mystical Marvel continued, "whom many proclaimed the underdogs, also gave a stunning performance, focusing their magic on showing the inherent dangers of letting it overwhelm you. Both acts stunned, delighted, and amazed, just as good magic should."

Professor Delvin tapped his lips. "We had a quandary, though. How to ever choose the victor?"

He paused, turning toward the other members of the Collective. Their blank magicians' smiles gave away no secrets. Had they found us worthy or wanting?

"After a long deliberation, with input from the Princess Royal Nicolette Snakewood of Elada herself, we have come to our decision."

He paused again, and I couldn't breathe. Maske, Cyan, and Drystan all linked hands. I tried to read Cyan's expression, but if she intuited anything, nothing showed. Taliesin glared past the Collective of Magic at us, his gaze resting on me the longest. Now that his fear was gone, there was only impotent rage. I glared right back at him, my throat tight with fear. What if he accused us of cheating, right here and now? I held my breath, but, thankfully, Taliesin's lips stayed shut.

"The winners of the duel between the scions of the great magicians the Taliesin Spectre and the Maske of Magic are . . ."

Another pause. The tension in the audience rose. Everyone in the theatre—and all the folk out in the parks on the cold night watching with the help of Vestige projectors and radios, I was sure—held their breaths. My entire body tingled, and I couldn't take my eyes from his face.

"Jasper Maske and his Marionettes!"

My knees shook in relief. My face hurt from smiling so widely. The sounds of the crowd filled the air up to the rafters.

My mouth fell open in astonishment. We'd done it. We'd actually done it.

When the applause quieted enough, Delvin continued. "As I said, it was very difficult—almost impossible—to choose between two teams of magicians of such obvious talent and skill. In the end, Maske's Marionettes won due to a slightly superior execution of tricks, a more cohesive storyline, and a truly spectacular finale. Well done to you all." He bowed to us, and we bowed back.

I couldn't believe it. Cyan wiped tears from her eyes, beaming from ear to ear, the grin echoed on Drystan's face. Maske stood straight and tall, a man come back to life.

Taliesin's expression darkened with rage. Sind and Jac, by contrast, were flabbergasted, their eyes wide and mouths open. Flora's nose wrinkled in disgust. Taliesin, his grandsons, and their assistant shuffled to the left of the stage. Their faces were slack in disappointment. One of the twins looked teary.

The curtains pulled back again. Our props had been cleared away and the scenery changed to a painted canvas of the sunset over Imachara Beach. My gaze rested on the spot where R.H. Ragona's Circus of Magic had camped last summer. I glanced away.

Murmurs rose in the audience as the Princess Royal herself entered the stage and walked toward Maske. She wore a pleasant and distant smile, but a missing front tooth made her look younger, and her eyes sparkled. She held a small box in her outstretched hands.

When she reached Maske, she craned her neck up at him. She barely came up to the bottom of his ribs.

She was followed by a man I'd only seen in portraits: her uncle, the Royal Steward of Elada. I'd never seen him up close. He had a full head of grey hair and deep pouches beneath his eyes that made him look sleepy, though his eyes were bright and keen as black buttons.

"Mister Jasper Maske and his Marionettes," the princess said. Her small, childish voice carried throughout the theatre. "I congratulate you on your victory tonight and offer you a small token of my gratitude for an evening of delightful entertainment." The words were rehearsed, but I could tell she had truly enjoyed the performance.

Maske took the box, bowing as low as he could.

"I thank you most sincerely, Your Highness." He opened the box, revealing four lapel pins set with diamonds and the emeralds of Elada. The young future queen asked us all to kneel, and she fastened the pins herself, the tip of her tongue sticking out from between her teeth as she concentrated. When she finished, she asked us to rise. We did, the pins sparkling at our breasts.

She inclined her head at us again. "I look forward to perhaps seeing you perform at the Royal Palace one day."

"It would be a singular pleasure, Your Highness," Maske said, his voice quivering with emotion.

She gave us a real, childish grin, revealing that missing front tooth, before making her way offstage, her uncle at her side. Professor Delvin and the other magicians gave short speeches about the merits of magic as entertainment and praising Maske for his performance, but I barely listened as I basked beneath the lights and the audience's approval. Out in the audience, Lily Verre had tears falling down her cheeks as she beamed up at us. I looked up at the private box, and Doctor Pinecrest inclined his head at me, raising his gloved hands to applaud in my direction.

When the last speech finished, the entire Royal Hippodrome gave us a standing ovation. Maske, Cyan, Drystan, and I linked hands, held them up, and bowed again. People threw flowers and coins onto the wooden floorboards. And then the curtains closed, obscuring them from sight.

I grinned in fierce triumph, letting it all sink in.

We'd won.

32

THE KYMRI THEATRE

"I did it. We did it. Somehow, these three came into my life, and now I have a world full of performance and magic again. It still doesn't seem possible, for all my repentance these last fifteen years. I don't feel as if I deserve it. But tonight, after much wine and dancing, all feels well."

JASPER MASKE'S PERSONAL DIARY

We rode in the carriage back to the theatre. The Eclipse was tucked into the pocket of my coat. Oli went straight to Cyan's bed to nurse the lump on his head, which had grown to the size of a clementine. At the warm kitchen table, I filled Maske in on everything that happened backstage.

Maske sighed when I'd finished. "Can't say I'm surprised he tried something like that. The twins had nothing to do with it?"

"No, they didn't. The loss of the Spectre Theatre means that they can't perform any longer, but neither do they wish to," Cyan said, with a certainty only she could possess.

"I wonder what they'll do next," I said.

Cyan shrugged. "I don't much care, myself."

Maske chuckled. "Seems I owe you both a life debt, now."

I waved the gesture away. "It was selfish enough. We rather like living here."

"Then here is your home as long as you want it," he promised. There, surrounded by the magician and his other marionettes, I'd realized exactly how much I'd gained since we'd shown up at his door.

● ● ● ●

The next day, we returned to the Collective of Magic's headquarters and gathered in the same room where we'd signed our names a few months ago. Taliesin and his grandsons had elected not to appear in person for it. Maske wore his crispest suit. Cyan had bought a new tunic, and Drystan and I wore the suits we'd worn to the duel. We still had our Glamours, though we mostly used it to change the color of our hair.

We all looked victorious. Christopher Aspall personally gave Maske the deed to the Spectre Theatre, and he took it with a bow, but, of course, it wasn't the prize he truly desired.

Aspall brought out a lacquered box painted with Kymri designs. With a flourish, he opened the lid to reveal an Aleph nestled on burgundy velvet. I leaned forward. It was indeed the spitting image of Anisa's Aleph, which was burning a hole in my pocket. Who was inside?

Maske clutched the metal in his hands before sliding it into his pocket. Anisa had helped him fix the automaton, but he was more than capable of creating grand illusions on his own without the need of any Aleph.

He picked up the deed to the theatre. The cut of our ticket sales had been deposited into Maske's account, and he'd already given us our share and started hiring out contractors to continue repairs to the Kymri. He'd sell the Spectre Theatre, which would make it easy to finish renovations and buy all the illusion props his heart desired from Twisting the Aces.

"Congratulations, Jasper Maske, Maske of Magic," Christopher Aspall said. "Enjoy your well-deserved win."

Maske shook his hand, and we left the Collective of Magic. We walked back to the theatre with elation in our steps. The future stretched wide before us.

• • • •

As soon as we entered the Kymri Theatre, Anisa's impatience was so overwhelming and desperate even Maske could feel it. He bowed his head.

In the main room of the theatre, I switched on Anisa's Aleph and set it down on the stage floor. She appeared, her hands clasped over her heart, her expression stricken with hope.

Maske reached out with trembling hands and switched on the other Aleph for the first time in fifteen years. We waited, expectant.

Nothing happened. The Aleph was empty. Slowly, we deflated.

Anisa let out a small cry, like a wounded bird. Cyan's hands rose to her mouth. Drystan's hand snaked around my waist as he pulled me towards him, and I leaned into his warmth.

"I don't understand," Maske muttered, turning the Aleph over in his hands. "It should have had plenty of power left."

Anisa's ghost walked up to him, reaching for the Vestige metal her transparent fingers couldn't touch. She bent down, her hair falling through the table as she read the markings on the Aleph.

—*It was him*, she said, her voice tight with pain. *It was my Relean. He was here.*

"But now . . . he's gone?" I asked, hesitantly.

—*He is gone.* She wrapped her arms tight around herself and, with a strangled sob, transformed back into mist and disappeared back into her Aleph.

Maske held the other disc in his hands. "I was so looking forward to seeing him again," he said, crestfallen.

I picked Anisa up gently, her grief radiating from the metal so strongly it risked overwhelming me. I dropped her into my pocket, shaking my fingertips as if I'd been shocked.

I couldn't imagine coming to terms with the sorrow across centuries and then having the chance of being reunited with the man one loved across a hundred lifetimes, only to lose him again.

It's hope, after all, that cuts deeper than despair.

●●●●

Three days later, Maske threw open the doors to the Kymri Theatre. Many of the people he held séances for, the Lord and Lady Elmbark among them, came to celebrate. Some of the friends he played cards with every now and again—for buttons instead of coins, as when he played with us—arrived, bringing spirits and hearty smiles.

In the Kymri Theatre, Maske was the cat with the cream. He'd tidied away his own grief at discovering Relean's empty Aleph. He couldn't stop smiling magnanimously at everyone. We held the party in the main theatre. The brass automaton watched over us from the stage. I had changed out of my stagehand gear into my stiff suit, but I kept tugging at my cravat.

Cyan came over to me. She tilted her chin toward the other end of the room, amused. "Look at Maske."

He was dancing with Lily Verre, the white of his smile visible from here. He looked twenty years younger.

"We saved him and ourselves," I said.

She nodded, and then hesitated. "Anisa showed me what she showed you. Those visions with Ahti and Dev."

"Ah."

"This isn't finished, is it?"

"Not even close." I tried to keep my voice light, but it fell flat. "Drystan knows, at least most of it. He wants to help."

Cyan looked over at him. Drystan was chatting comfortably with Lord Elmbark.

"You care for him a lot, don't you?" she asked.

When I'd first seen him in the circus, I had felt a spark. Now, I felt a flame. "Pretty sure I've fallen in love with him," I admitted.

"Have you told him that?"

"No. Not yet."

"You should."

I blinked. "Have you . . . ?" I tapped my temple.

She smiled. "I don't need to."

A rush of warmth flowed through me. I wouldn't believe her until I'd heard the words from his own lips, but the possibility was sweet as sugar all the same. We spoke to each other with the touch of our lips, our tongues, and our fingertips. When I lay my head against his chest and listened to the sound of his heart.

Across the room, Drystan threw back his head to laugh at something Lord Elmbark said. Tonight, at least, was a celebration.

"Have you told Maske your own secret yet?" I asked Cyan.

She bowed her head. "The right time hasn't appeared. He was always in his workshop, or with Lily, or . . ."

"Or excuses."

A corner of her mouth quirked. "Aye, excuses. What if he doesn't want to think of me as his daughter?"

"Cyan, he practically treats you as one already. Be brave, be bold," I echoed Anisa's words.

She chewed her lip. She went to tap Maske on the shoulder, and he nodded at whatever she said to him. Together, they made their way to the parlor.

Doctor Pinecrest came up to me, holding two glasses of wine. He passed me one with his clockwork hand. I accepted it and took a small sip. I didn't like him being here in the theatre, but he'd found a way to invite himself.

"I don't see your brother," he said.

"He returned to Sicion," I said. Cyril would be back in a few weeks to begin his schooling though, and I was looking forward to it. I hadn't spoken to my adopted parents, and I didn't plan to.

He inclined his head.

"And did you enjoy the performance, Doctor Pinecrest?" I asked.

"Very much so." He paused, delicately. "How are you feeling?"

"I'm in perfect health, I can assure you, Doctor."

"That's good to hear, Micah." He looked around the theatre. "This is an extraordinary building. Some parts of it mirror the Kymri temples I've been to."

"Maybe someday, we'll do a touring show around the Archipelago, and I can see them for myself."

"You should. Everyone should travel the world if they can. Open their eyes to different ways of life. I'm a changed man after my time abroad."

Changed for better or for worse? I wanted to ask.

Someone hailed Pinecrest from across the room, and he excused himself. I watched him go, wishing I had a better measure of the man.

When Cyan and Maske returned, they both beamed brighter than glass globes. Maske had his arm tight around his daughter.

—*It went well, then?* I ventured, looking over to Pinecrest. He didn't seem to notice how we spoke, or if he did, he gave no sign.

—*It's a little bizarre and awkward, but he's happy. I'm happy.*

She laughed in my mind.

I smiled.

33

THE WOMAN IN THE RED DRESS

"Take heed, Child of Man and Woman yet Neither. I see a woman in a wine-red dress. Her child is ill, eaten from the inside. I see figures on a stage, playing their parts, the audience applauding as magic surrounds them. Long ago, great feathers flap against the night sky. Another creature, with green, scaled skin, drips red blood onto a white floor. Here, now, Chimaera wait in the wings, and the one who would destroy them is gathering strength. I see a man, checking his pocket watch, counting down the time."

WORDS SPOKEN TO MICAH GREY AT THE SÉANCE

Séance requests flew in thick and fast, the Collective of Magic assigned us a manager, and we had plenty of magic show bookings in Imachara. My wardrobe was full of nice new clothing and shiny new boots. The Kymri Theatre was safely Maske's.

The peace, of course, did not last. A week later, Anisa woke me up far too early.

—*It is time,* she whispered in my mind.

"Time for what?" I asked aloud, still half-asleep.

—*I had a vision. You must go to that place where you last saw the woman with the ill child. It is beginning. It is time.*

I sighed, rolling out of bed. "All right, all right," I muttered, tugging on my shoes. Curiously, I wasn't afraid. Drystan's bed was empty. I rubbed my gritty eyes. My muscles hurt. I yawned.

—Hurry. You must hurry.

Her urgency gradually infected me. In her room, Cyan had likely already risen and was pulling on her clothes. Drystan returned from the washroom.

"Anisa says it's beginning," I said. "That we have to find the woman in the red dress."

Drystan's expression stiffened. "I say let's go back to bed instead."

"Tempting," I said, but Anisa's insistence tugged at me.

He sighed. "Lead the way, then."

Twenty minutes later, the three of us left the theatre as the sun rose.

I resented that we were drawn back into whatever Anisa wanted of us. We trudged through the city. The air promised spring. I was already so warm I barely needed my coat and left it unbuttoned.

"Who's this woman?" Drystan asked me as I walked.

"In my first vision at the séance, Maske—or, rather, the spirits or Anisa speaking through him—mentioned her. I suspect something about her and her child is important. I can feel it, but neither Anisa, Cyan, nor I know much more than that," I said.

"Time to find out, it seems." He looked resigned.

I nodded. Cyan drew her coat tighter around her shoulders. She'd barely said a word, and her face was pinched with worry. I recognized something of the owlish woman, Matla, in her expression, and I shivered in foreboding.

We reached the square near the medical school, but it was so early it wasn't yet open.

—Now what, Anisa?

—We wait. She will come.

We went to one of the nearby cafés and ordered a strong pot of coffee.

Anisa fell silent in my mind. I stirred sugar and milk into my drink, my hands shaking. Anisa's master plan was meant to be a vague event in the future. This was the first step, and I didn't know where it would lead.

"There she is," Cyan breathed.

A woman passed the square, red skirts peeking out from beneath her coat. She pushed the wicker wheelchair across the cobbles, her bonneted head hiding her face.

She paused in front of the café, telling the boy off for removing his scarf. She wrapped him up again and finally, I saw her face.

It was Lily Verre.

"Fuck," I swore under my breath. Quickly, I grabbed a newspaper on the empty table next to us and unfolded it. The three of us hid behind it, feeling ridiculously conspicuous.

"That's *Lily*," Drystan whispered to me. "What's going on? She never mentioned having a child."

I peeked around the newspaper. Lily had entered the café and was at the till. She kept glancing down at the boy in the wicker chair.

"One coffee, one hot chocolate, and two chocolate pastries," she said to the woman behind the till, and I reeled again. Gone were her flighty voice and rough mannerisms. She spoke with the smooth, educated voice of the nobility of Imachara.

"Oh, Lord and Lady," I breathed. "We've been had from the beginning."

Cyan's face slackened. "Her mind being so loud . . . that must have been by design. What all does she know?"

This woman had been waiting for us at Twisting the Aces. I searched my memory . . . and the first night we went to Maske's, there had been a woman walking down the street. I remember the sound of her heels echoing on the cobblestones. Had it been Lily? Who was she, and what did she want with us?

I went back through my memory, trying to see her ploy, as Lily waited for the drinks and pastries. Even earlier, I remembered a woman with a child in a wicker chair in the audience of one of the circus performances back in Sicion. My heart skipped a beat.

"I think she's a Shadow, or something like it," I said, my voice ringing with certainty as if the spirits themselves had told me. I sensed Anisa's confirmation. When I had that vision at Twisting the Aces, was Lily somehow to blame for that? If so, how?

Lily's drinks arrived. She perched on a table, drank her small cup of coffee with obvious relish, and helped her son with his hot chocolate. She kept the boy angled towards the wall, so we couldn't see him clearly.

"On the second visit to Twisting the Aces," I whispered. "She dropped something, and I caught it. Do you remember? A purple glass with the motley frame."

Cyan's mouth fell open as she realized what I was getting at.

"Yes," I said. "Take away the gaudy frame, wipe off a sheen of thin red paint, and it could have been a Mirror of Moirai. If so, easy enough to have an idea of where we are at all times, right?"

"Do you think she knows we're here just now, then?" Drystan's lips barely moved. Our every muscle was stiff. We couldn't leave without attracting attention, but equally, what if she noticed who was watching her?

"I have no idea," I said. I tugged at my collar, feeling warm. I wanted to scream.

After Lily and the child finished their drinks, she put the wrapped pastries on the small shelf below the wicker chair and pushed it back onto the street. She never once glanced in our direction. Was that by design, or did she truly not expect us to be following her this early? Were we being led into a trap?

As soon as she left, we threw our coins on the table and followed.

Lily disappeared around the corner.

"Let's follow her from above." I pointed towards a drainpipe, and we made our way up to the roof. As we climbed, I felt a little dizzy.

"Poor Maske," Cyan muttered. I'd been thinking the same. Was he only a pawn so she could be closer to us?

Lily made her way through the streets. She gave one of the pastries to the boy and we finally had a clearer view of the child in the wicker basket.

He must have been about eight. Despite the mild weather, he wore a coat, a hat, and a thick scarf that covered most of his face. He tugged down the scarf more than he had for the hot chocolate. I stared. The boy's face was peeling badly, and patches had fallen away. Beneath, the skin was dark green, like the back of a beetle. Under the hat, I caught two small protrusions.

Horns.

Like Ahti.

"Did I see what I think I saw?" Drystan asked.

"Yeah," I answered, faintly. "He's a Chimaera. A Theri Chimaera."

—*Of course,* Anisa breathed in my mind. *Once he finishes his transformation, he will look identical to Ahti. And I suspect he'll be just as powerful. I should have seen it. This is why the world is in danger. If someone hurts or frightens this little Chimaera, or if the blurred man finds him, then all is lost.*

Lily drew the scarf back again, surveying the street. Luckily, she didn't glance up. This time, she also didn't go to the medical school. We followed her as she made her way to the nicest part of town, close to the Palace. Luckily, the buildings were all clustered close together. She paused at the gates, and for a moment, I thought she would enter.

Instead, she gazed through the bars and continued onto Ruby Street, to press the buzzer for Doctor Samuel Pinecrest's apartments. The climbing had overheated me. I loosened my coat, sweating.

She was let in immediately.

Of course, I'd already seen them together when I had followed her to the medical school. But I still couldn't believe that the woman who had joked with and comforted us, who had supposedly fallen in love with Maske, was as much smoke and mirrors as any illusion. I shivered again, but it wasn't from cold. Drystan peered at me.

"Micah, are you all right? You're pale." He put his palm on my forehead. "Gods, you're burning up."

"Is this what a fever feels like?" I asked him, thickly. "It's terrible. I don't like it."

"Should we go to Pinecrest's?" Cyan asked. "He said to go back if you're ill."

"He's probably hired Lily Verre to spy on us from the beginning," I said. "Take me home. Hopefully the fever will break soon."

It was beyond difficult to climb back down the drainpipe and trudge home. I kept having to pause to catch my breath. My eyes felt like they were cooking in my skull.

"It's only a fever, Micah," Drystan reassured me. "You'll take a cool bath, get some soup and liquids, and you'll be fine in a day or two."

Cyan's lips tightened, but she didn't push it.

I stumbled into an alleyway and retched up my coffee. The bile burned my throat.

"Come on, Micah," Drystan urged. "We're almost home."

I opened my mouth to answer, but my eyes rolled up into my head. I had only enough time to be annoyed before I fainted once again.

34

THE DREAM, THE NIGHTMARE

"Magic may be too capricious for rules, but it still has its own twisted form of logic. If you listen, if you respect it, then it will show you the way."

TRANSLATED FRAGMENT OF ALDER TEXT

*P*art of me knew it was a fever dream. That didn't make it any less terrifying.

I was not me. Anisa was flying, or falling, through skies on fire. All was red, orange, black, and gold. I reached out my hands and they burned away to bone and ash.

I awoke in a body of clockwork and magic. No swirling silver markings of my family. No dragonfly wings rose from my back. I was clipped and earthbound. Even though I wanted this, I needed this, I still mourned the loss.

I skulked through the streets of this strange new city of Imachara, keeping to the shadows. I came to the market square before the Snakewood Palace, with a large stage set up in the middle, but no audience.

Storm clouds rumbled overhead, and the twin spires of the Celestial Cathedral were at my back.

The phantoms, the parts in this play to come, walked across the stage. The woman in the red dress whose son was shifting and changing until he looked so like my Ahti. The world might yet fall into place the way I thought—hoped—it would, but equally, the past might repeat itself once again.

The doctor with the clockwork hand appeared onstage, smiling a self-satisfied grin, though in many ways, he was as ignorant as all the rest. He did not even know what he truly wore against the stump of his arm. Other actors waited in the wings. The tarot reader, my little bird, her powers unfurling. The pale jester, who, despite his lack of power, could yet destroy everything. And my little Kedi, my newest charge— my last and greatest hope.

The lights extinguished, leaving the stage in the gloom. My lungs burned with the memory of smoke and soot.

A flash of bright blue and red light. A dull roar. A young girl, screaming. My little Kedi, the one meant to save everything, crying out. A flash of blinding red.

They were all dead and gone, the world dead and gone with them. I knew what I needed to do to stop the return of eternal darkness, even as the thought of it broke my heart.

But I would do anything to save the Chimaera and protect magic's place in the world.

Anything. Even what was to come.

● ● ● ●

"Micah."

I turned my head away from the noise.

"Micah." A cool cloth rested on my forehead.

I opened my eyes, but the brightness hurt. I closed them again.

A brush of lips against my cheek, and three whispered words in my ear. "Wake up, Micah."

Drystan. I opened my eyes, meeting his blue irises.

"Are you feeling any better?" he asked, his brow furrowed in worry.

I tried to sit up, but a swirl of nausea drove me back. My body racked with coughs. I hurt. Everything hurt.

"We need to go to Pinecrest," Drystan said.

"No," I managed. "Can't trust him."

"I don't see another option."

"Might not even be able to help. And if I die—"

"No," he cut me off. "Don't speak like that."

"Listen . . . I'm trying to tell you something important."

He paused, waiting for me to gather my breath.

"If I do die, I'd regret not telling you . . ."

"Telling me what?"

I closed my eyes again, not brave enough to tell him with my eyes open. "That I love you."

A sharp intake of breath. Silence. Horrible silence. *Say something, Drystan,* I wanted to say. *Say something while I can still hear it.* The dreams, the nightmares, crouched in the corner of my mind. My mouth was dry with fever and fear.

Drystan leaned close, pressed his palms against my warm cheeks. "I love you, too, Micah Grey. More than the sun loves the moon," he whispered, quoting the magic show.

I gave a half-laugh, half-sob. Drystan pressed his lips to mine.

My body began to jerk beneath the sweat-soaked sheets. The visions of the world ending pressed closer, their whispers filling my ears. I felt even warmer, as though I were a bit of tinder about to explode into flame.

"And now, my love," he said, "I'm going to save you."

ACKNOWLEDGEMENTS

Thank you to my friends and betas who provided such valuable critique the first time around: Shawn DeMille, Erica Bretall, Wesley Chu, Mike Kalar, Rob Haines, Molly Rabbitt, Vonny McKay, Megan Walker, Mike Stewart, Stephen Aryan, Anne Lyle, Amy McCulloch, Colin Sinclair, Joseph Morton, Lorna McKay, and Hannah Beresford. Thank you to the Inkbots and The Cabal. To Emma Maree Urquhart for the name "Alvis Tyndall." An especially huge thank you to Corinne Duyvis for help at the 11th hour.

Continued thanks to Aranya Jain for thoughtful editing and everyone at DAW, Astra, and Penguin Random House in the US and Hodderscape in the UK for giving Micah Grey a chance to find new readers on both sides of the pond. Likewise, my gratitude to Juliet Mushens and everyone at Mushens Entertainment.

This time around, thank you to Arcady Wolf, Emma Craib, Sasha Strangfeld, and CJ Henderson for thoughtful early reads. Thank you to Katie Cummins for continued social media assistance, and to all my friends I thanked in *Pantomime* for the cheerleading along the way.

My mother, Sally Baxter, continues to be one of my biggest supporters. This book is dedicated to her. Craig Lam, my partner in all things, is still there to catch me when I jump.

Last but not least, a gigantic thank you to the readers, new and old, who followed Micah Grey from the circus to the magician's stage.

A Conversation with L. R. Lam

What was it like writing a novel set in a theatre? Did it feel very different from writing a novel set in a circus?

It did and it didn't. The main difference is that the circus had quite a large cast of characters I had to balance as best I could. There are significantly fewer characters in the Kymri Theatre—just Micah, Drystan, Cyan, Maske, and a couple of new close friends, plus new and old antagonists. The atmosphere is a little darker and gloomier than the bright lights of the circus. I did a lot of new research into stage magic and illusion. I do like the contrast and the condensing of Micah's world in *Shadowplay*. He has to hide from what happened in *Pantomime* and learn enough to set the stage (ahem) for what's to come in *Masquerade*.

Without any spoilers, can you share how you felt about Micah's development in this novel?

In *Pantomime*, despite what he's been through, Micah is still fairly sheltered and naïve. What he experienced in the circus has a massive effect on him, particularly in the beginning of this volume. Throughout *Shadowplay*, he learns a lot more about himself, the world around him, and the secrets of the world long ago. Destiny is winding its way around him and tightening its grip, and there are multiple people after him. Micah matures a lot in this book—while he turned eighteen in *Pantomime*, this is where he grows up more and steps into his own.

What made you decide to add Cyan to the cast of characters?

I really like the dynamic of a core trio—I play with that in *Emberclaw*, too. It adds more potential for characters to bounce off each other or have shifting tensions and alliances while keeping the focus smaller than, say, the larger group I have in *Seven Devils* and *Seven Mercies*.

It's hard to say too many specifics of what she offers the narrative without spoilers, but Cyan widens the scope of the world in various ways. Because of her background, she experiences Elada a little differently to Drystan and Micah, who had similar, privileged upbringings to each other. She loves the performance of both the circus and the stage just as much as Micah and Drystan. They're both suspicious of her to begin with, understandably, and I enjoyed them getting to know her and vice versa as she unveils her own secrets.

How have you revised this book from its last edition?

I thought this one would have fewer changes than *Pantomime*, which I suppose it did, but not by much. First, I had to seed in the revelations of Book 1's changes. I made other edits as well: Cyan originally appeared on the page much later, and bringing her introduction forward offered more space for her character development. There was one subplot that I tugged, and I vividly remember the morning I was working in the café and realized the book had unspooled in my hands. I could immediately see how everything would fit back together. Unpicking and restitching everything took a long time and was exceedingly fiddly, but I'm glad I did it. The new order flows more logically and knits together various elements more elegantly, in my opinion.

What was your favorite scene to write?

There are a lot in this book! I love all the séance and stage magic scenes. The tender scenes between Micah and Drystan. Twisting the Aces and in general spending more time in the actual city of Imachara instead of the circus on the beach. A new scene I really enjoyed writing was when Micah asks to borrow some face paint from Cyan earlier in the narrative. Also, shout-out to Ricket the cat.

Reading Group Guide for *Shadowplay*

1. If the past year of your life were shown to you in a séance, which key images would you see? How might they make you feel?

2. Have you ever seen a magician perform? If so, what's the most impressive trick you've seen?

3. Do you have the "desire to spark wonder," like Micah? Why, or why not?

4. How do you think life in the theatre affects Micah and Drystan? How is it different from life in the circus?

5. Do you think stage magic is a metaphor for anything in Jasper Maske's life, or in Micah's, Cyan's, or Drystan's? If so, what?

6. What was your favorite chapter or scene?

7. How about some of your favorite quotes?

8. Which was your favorite instance of magic in this novel?

9. Micah, Drystan, Cyan, and Maske each have a past that's very different from the way they're currently living. What do you think this novel is trying to say about second chances?

10. What do you think will happen to Micah, Cyan, and Drystan next?

READ ON FOR AN EXCERPT FROM
MASQUERADE, THE THRILLING
CONCLUSION TO THE MICAH
GREY TRILOGY!

1

FEVER DREAM

"A fever may burn a man alive. Some of the wise men who called them-selves seers or mystics would deliberately kindle a temperature in the body. They said the fever dreams showed them their fate and the fate of those who followed them."

"MYSTICS AND SEERS," FROM A HISTORY OF
ELADA AND ITS FORMER COLONIES,
PROFESSOR CAED CEDAR, ROYAL SNAKEWOOD UNIVERSITY

When my eyes finally cracked open, echoes of the end of the world swirled in my mind.

The phantoms, the parts in this play to come, walked across the stage. The woman in the red dress whose son was eaten from the inside. The world might yet fall into place the way I thought—hoped—it would.

Anisa's voice echoed in my head as if I were still dreaming. I blinked the last of the sleep from my eyes. Drystan held my hand. Judging by the white silken wallpaper, we weren't at the Kymri Theatre.

"Where . . . ?" I managed, my voice a croak.

"Pinecrest's apartments," Drystan said. His blonde hair crowned his head in a messy halo. He had dark circles under his blue eyes. "You've been out for four days."

Four days. I let out a shaky breath, pushing myself onto my elbows.

The room was as pristine as a hospital room, but the walnut furniture was far too sumptuous. The floor was softened with rugs, but there were no paintings on the walls, making it feel impersonal. The bed's linen was so crisp it crinkled. I wore a plain tunic and felt a surge of panic.

"Where are my clothes?" I asked.

"They're here." Drystan nodded to a chair in the corner. "I've been coming every day, and he allowed me to be the one to change you."

My relief was palpable. I lowered my voice. "Where's the Aleph?" It'd been in my pocket when I'd fallen ill. Drystan took Anisa's disc from his coat. I held my hand out, and he dropped it into my palm. My fingers closed around the metal. Swirling Alder script was etched into the sides, the Vestige metal shining green, purple, and gold in the light. It thrummed in my hand, but Anisa was silent.

I'd found her in R.H. Ragona's Circus of Magic; or, rather, she'd found me. I had taken her from the ruins of the circus, and she had sent us visions of the past and her life. I'd learned about the Alder, the Chimaera they'd created, and the Vestige they'd left behind. She said she needed me for a plan to save the world. I never knew how much to believe.

On my arm, where the syringe had pinched me, was an already-fading bruise. I touched the scab of the needle mark and winced at the pain. What had Pinecrest given me?

"What happened after . . ." I trailed off. *After I said I loved you and you said you loved me?* I was almost afraid to say it aloud in case it had, too, been a fever dream.

"After you fainted, I took you straight to Pinecrest. I didn't want to, but I figured he was the only one who could help. He didn't seem particularly surprised to see you."

"He didn't?"

"No. It was like he'd been already expecting us at any moment."

His lips thinned, and he lapsed into silence. I felt stronger, but still not much better than a piece of meat that had been pummeled by a hammer. My head ached. Drystan drew me closer, resting his forehead against mine, grounding me.

"I had the strangest dream . . ." I said.

"What was it?"

I pulled back, my eyes darting to the door. "Not here," I mouthed, even though the details of the dream were already fading—Anisa at the end of the world, the threat of a bright light before darkness.

A knock sounded at the door. Without waiting for an answer, Doctor Pinecrest entered. The Royal Physician was cool, collected, and impeccably dressed, as usual. His clockwork hand caught the light, the brass Vestige within covered with translucent skin as if trapped in amber.

The doctor with the clockwork hand appeared onstage, smiling a self-satisfied grin, though he was as ignorant as all the rest. He did not even know what he truly wore against the stump of his arm.

"Micah," he said. "So good to see you awake." The slightest pause, the smallest look at Drystan. "There's a fresh pot of tea in the lounge, Drystan, if you'd like to help yourself." The use of his real name rather than his stage magician name, Amon, was deliberate.

I didn't want Drystan to go, but he reluctantly pulled the door shut behind him, Anisa's warning still whispering to me. *The pale jester, who, despite his lack of power, could yet destroy everything.*

I pulled my covers up to my neck.

"Micah," the doctor said. "It's good to see you awake. You gave us all quite a fright."

"What happened to me?" I asked, scrunching the coverlet so hard I feared tearing the fabric.

"Your body turned against you, I'm afraid. It's happened to some of the other Chimaera I've studied."

My mouth tightened.

"Your extrasensory abilities grew too quickly," he went on, pulling on a pair of white gloves. "A spike in your mind, if you will. A storming of your synapses. You're lucky you were able to see me straight away. Much longer and you might not have made it."

Gooseflesh pricked my arms. He was confirming I could have died. Growing up as the daughter of a noble family, I'd always been stronger and faster than my friends. I'd never grown ill. Even when I broke my arm the night Drystan and I fled the circus, it'd healed weeks faster than it should have. It felt strange to no longer be able to rely on this body. It was hard not to think of it as a betrayal.

"So, what? Have you cured me?" I asked.

A small shake of the head. "I've only alleviated the symptoms, for now." He opened a plain cabinet in the corner and brought out a metal tray, setting it on the bedside table. On it was a flask made of Vestige metal, glimmering in the light like oil mixed with water. The top was an uncut emerald polished to smoothness. Next to it was a filled syringe. He picked it up, and the dark green substance shone in the light from the window. I shivered. It looked a match to the liquid in the vials Drystan and I had discovered in Shadow Elwood's apartments. The lacquered box was hidden in the loft of the theatre beneath my bed.

I blanched, gripping Anisa's Aleph even tighter beneath the covers.

—*Be careful* . . . I heard the barest whisper.

So far, Pinecrest had claimed to have my best interests at heart. I still didn't trust him. After everything that had happened to me, I was understandably beyond wary of doctors and their cures.

"What's this?" I asked, gesturing to the vial and syringe with my chin.

"I dosed you with this tonic of my own making four days ago, but

I'll give you another dose before you head home. After this, you'll need weekly doses to keep the symptoms under control."

"So, there's the sting in the tail. I'm to be reliant on you."

"I'm afraid so."

"Side effects?" I asked.

"Vivid dreams. Possible increased manifestations of some of your emerging abilities, but without it attacking your body."

I sent him a tentative thought. *—Are you like me? A Chimaera?*

He smiled, but didn't answer.

—And if I decide I don't want to be reliant on your medication, and I run away to Linde or somewhere . . . My thoughts trailed off.

—Then you'd probably die within a month from a seizure brought on by a fever, he replied.

Well. Shit. My head fell back onto my pillow.

"I agree it's not ideal," he said aloud, "but it's the best option we have at the moment, Micah. In the meantime, I fear you must visit me once a week for your dosage. I'll continue my research, but this medicine is the first step, I'm sure of it."

He wiped a drop of sweat from his brow. My interest sharpened. I guessed it wasn't easy for him to speak mind to mind. I wondered why. My grip tightened on the Aleph beneath the covers.

Pinecrest gestured to the flask. "I discovered this in that jungle where I lost my hand, and I developed it while abroad in Byssia."

"What's in it?" I asked, not bothering to hide my suspicion.

"It's an Alder liquid, though no one knows the ingredients. There are some additives to make it more stable and last longer. It is not unduly dangerous, I assure you."

"Saying something is *not unduly dangerous* is not wholly comforting," I pointed out.

Doctor Pinecrest smiled ruefully as he set the flask aside and picked up the syringe. We both stared at it. "One ingredient is a form of opiate, partly derived from Lerium, but with other additives that suppress the spikes in power your body cannot handle. Another component is ground up Vestige crystals."

I blinked at him, shocked both by the answer and the fact he had given it.

"I understand this is a lot to take in," he said. "Ask your questions, and I will answer to the best of my ability."

A shiver of foreboding ran through me. I'd seen a few of the small blue crystals inside automatons, like ice-blue hearts. I'd drunk them? "You're telling me you injected me with a mysterious Vestige substance, actual Vestige, and an addictive opiate."

"It's not addictive at one dose a week."

I made a skeptical sound deep in my throat. "Am I to be a laboratory rat for this little experiment?"

"You're not the first I've dosed," he said.

I gaped at him.

"Initially," he continued, "I used it in desperation, when I had to either administer it to a dying child or let them perish. The risk paid off. There are now half a dozen in Byssia and Linde who have taken this medication weekly, for years, without issue. They are stable, and their powers are controllable and don't harm them."

I sputtered at him, but he only looked at me with that infuriating calmness. I had so many questions about these others across the sea, but I sensed he'd tell me nothing if I pressed the subject.

"What happens if you run out of this mysterious substance?" I demanded instead.

"I've more than enough to last years, never fear, and I expect to find a permanent cure long before then."

I didn't know whether to believe a word he said.

He picked up the syringe and tapped the glass lightly to break the bubbles. "Well," he said. "Are you ready?"

—*Can I refuse?* I asked Anisa.

—*I sense he is telling the truth,* she said, keeping her mental voice quiet as possible. *At least as he knows it. I have no idea if Alder-made elixirs can remain stable over centuries. There seems not to be a choice here, but that does not mean I like it.*

Neither did I, but I hung my head in defeat. I was trapped, and we all knew it. "Yes."

"It will be all right, Micah. I'll make sure of it."

With that, the doctor pulled up my sleeve and, with the prick of the syringe's needle, pushed the mysterious medicine into my veins.

RAISING READERS
Books Build Bright Futures

Dear Reader,

We'd love your attention for one more page to tell you about the crisis in children's reading, and what we can all do.

Studies have shown that reading for fun is the **single biggest predictor of a child's future life chances** – more than family circumstance, parents' educational background or income. It improves academic results, mental health, wealth, communication skills, ambition and happiness.[1]

The number of children reading for fun is in rapid decline. Young people have a lot of competition for their time. In 2024, 1 in 10 children and young people in the UK aged 5 to 18 did not own a single book at home.[2]

Hachette works extensively with schools, libraries and literacy charities, but here are some ways we can all raise more readers:

- Reading to children for just 10 minutes a day makes a difference
- Don't give up if children aren't regular readers – there will be books for them!
- Visit bookshops and libraries to get recommendations
- Encourage them to listen to audiobooks
- Support school libraries
- Give books as gifts

There's a lot more information about how to encourage children to read on our website: **www.RaisingReaders.co.uk**

Thank you for reading.

hachette UK

---

[1] OECD, '21st-Century Readers: Developing Literacy Skills in a Digital World', 2021, https://www.oecd.org/en/publications/21st-century-readers_a83d84cb-en.html

[2] National Literacy Trust, 'Book Ownership in 2024', November 2024, https://literacytrust.org.uk/research-services/research-reports/book-ownership-in-2024